# THE WINTER WAR

Otto wasn't sure where they were. Looking out the slit all he could see was whiteness and trees. It was difficult for him to determine their position from inside the tank. He could only hope they were going in the right direction: toward the Third Company sector of the defense line.

Suddenly Otto was lifted up and slammed down again and the tank jerked and shuddered to a stop. A land mine! he thought. Got to get out of here before they set us on fire.

"C'mon, Raimo," he said to his companion. "Raimo? Are you all right?" There was no answer. There was a large bloody bump on the Russian's forehead. Then Otto was relieved to see the big man move, though he was clearly dazed. The Russian moaned. "Raimo! We've got to get out of here!" he yelled as bullets zinged off the steel surface of the tank.

We will send you a free catalog on request. Any titles not in your local book store can be purchased by mail. Send the price of the book plus 50¢ shipping charge to Tower Books, P.O. Box 270, Norwalk, Connecticut 06852.

Titles currently in print are available for industrial and sales promotion at reduced rates. Address inquiries to Tower Publications, Inc., Two Park Avenue, New York, New York 10016, Attention: Premium Sales Department.

# MOLOTOV COCKTAIL

*John O. Virtanen*

TOWER BOOKS ▮ NEW YORK CITY

A TOWER BOOK

Published by

Tower Publications, Inc.
Two Park Avenue
New York, N.Y. 10016

# Chapter 1

The shattering sound of three rifle shots reverberated through the cool April dusky twilight, over ruddy fields to the village of Harkola, less than two kilometers away. That distant, ruffled warning fire bit into the villagers' ears with the burning sensation of gunpowder thrown upon an open flesh wound. Every workingman fled, in fear of death, to hide in the surrounding woods. It seemed that the shots echoed and re-echoed, high up to the hills, over the meadows, and sent tremors of fear racing through their workworn, quivering bodies. They all stared, wide-eyed, wondering who would be murdered next.

An innocent man, whose only crime was having been a workingman in civil-war-torn Finland, struggled desperately to avoid three bayonet-wielding attackers who kept murderously slashing at his exhausted body. Helpless now, though he still held his small, folding pocketknife in his hand, and overpowered by his attackers, he sank slowly to his knees. Grinding his teeth in agony, he grasped a small alder branch which quickly gave way under his weight. He fell flat on his back on the grassy forest floor, his eyes transfixed up at the sky in a dying stare. His grim-faced assailants, breathing hard from the efforts of their merciless mission, swore unintelligibly at their dying resister, whose blood was now turning a patch of the greenery into a dark, red pool.

Shaking from their barbarous exertions, and once more staring hatefully at the disheveled, work-besmudged farm laborer, the three armed soldiers swaggered to the road and resumed their vengeful hunt for other victims. With a joyful shout of conquest, they fired shots in the air and laughed raucously. They gave no thought to the fact that they had just murdered the hard-working father of seven children, but carefully wiped the blood off their bayonets before continuing their march toward the next village.

These three were one of many self-appointed execution squads of the White Guard army which had victoriously ended the five months of bloody, merciless civil war in Finland. The war had begun in 1918, provoked by the Bolshevik agitation there in conjunction with the revolution taking place in Russia. This Finnish conflict had been blamed on the rebels within the working class, and now that the Reds had been defeated, all those considered suspect were to be exterminated, whether they had participated in the fighting or not. That was the hue and cry of the White Guard victors!

The dead man now lying in the forest silence was the father of a baby boy, Otto Arola. The child, was stunned, and never to forgot the sight of his weeping mother pushing the wheelbarrow, carrying his father's body, to the yard of their small cabin. As he grew older, he heard, over and over again, how his father, who had been plowing in the field, was forced into service as a guide for the vicious trio. He had had nothing to do with the Reds—had not even fought in the war. He was just a simple farm hand!

Otto also learned that, because of his father's supposed involvement in the workingmen's revolt, his mother had been deprived of all her civil rights. Her social welfare and even her citizenship had been revoked—as though they and she never existed! He learned, too, that soon after this shocking tragedy in the forest, when there was no man available to work the tenant farm, she had been forced to leave her small, one-room cabin, and seek shelter elsewhere.

These atrocious acts of military revenge were re-enacted over and over again against the working class, during the aftermath of the war. For years afterwards, a sullen, unvoiced hatred welled deep in the suffering hearts of the Arolas, as it did in those of thousands of other similar victims of that terrible Civil War.

"Remember, son, if you ever serve in the army, you'l' become your father's murderer, too!" was the admonition indelibly planted into Otto's mind by his long suffering mother. For years, the family experienced unremitting discrimination because of an unproved accusation of Communist involvement, and, in consequence, they were forced to endure debilitating poverty and hunger.

It was for this reason that Otto Arola had no intentions of being a soldier.

As long as he could remember, from the time of his father's death surely, Otto felt slight loyalty to God or country. Life had taught him early that, somehow, he had no one to depend on but himself, that he, himself, was all that mattered in this life. What went on politically, was of little consequence to him, and would not be allowed to influence his actions.

By the time he was eight years old, Otto was hard at work, pulling weeds and digging ditches to help support the family. During the Depression years, when money was practically unobtainable, he was forced to work for just three meals as a day's wage. Finally, digusted with country life, he moved to Helsinki, hoping to find an easier way to earn a living. He especially wanted to get away from the village farmers, two of whom had been a part of the squad that killed his father.

By the age of nineteen, he was an apprentice at the Akrenius Electric Motor Factory and was studying violin in the evenings at the Helsinki Folk Conservatory. He had serious hopes of becoming a violin concert artist some day.

It was now the spring of 1938. Otto was rushing home with his paycheck in his pocket, ready to join his friends in celebrating the May Day Eve dance at the Alppila restaurant.

"Saatana-Perkele!" Otto invoked the devil and hell's wrath when he arrived home. His muscles tightened and his grease-blackened hands were moist after he finished reading the post card he had picked up from the entrance hall at his sister's apartment. He had been living with Sirkka since he

7

had arrived in the city.

Otto knew that he had passed the army's compulsory physical six months before, and he knew that he had to serve unless he was willing to leave the country, an option that kept entering his thoughts lately. Joining the Merchants Marine Service would have kept him out of the country, but his plans to become a concert artist had overcome his dread of army life.

Now Otto faced the dilemma of his life. He could join the army that had killed his father, or desert, leaving behind his country and family—forever.

Otto rushed into the living room, reading the order again, hoping the date was wrong.

No mistake. "Otto Arola, conscript: You are ordered to report for one year of Jaeger training on May 7, 1938. Order of the army of Finland."

"Damn the army," he muttered, "and the Jaeger units. They were my father's murderers." Now he had been ordered to learn to drill and take part in the Jaegers' fierce training program. He found himself writing an imaginary letter.

"You have no right to do this to me! I was born poor. I grew up as an orphan. You murdered my father, and gave no help to my mother to buy food . . ."

But he knew it was useless. He began to wonder how he could compete with well-fed farmers' sons who would have years of youth military training behind them. They would be strong and eager to fulfill patriotic assignments.

Otto went to the kitchen, climbed atop a stepstool, and retrieved a bottle from the top shelf. He shook his head and filled a green shotglass. Maybe this will soothe my nerves, he thought as he downed the liquor.

With the glass in one hand and a clear bottle of Karhuviina in the other, he walked over to the generous bay window which overlooked Porthanin Street from the sixth floor of Sirkka's apartment. He stepped over a copy of *Demari*, the morning newspaper, which had been left lying on the floor. Its black headlines told that a German, Adolph Hitler, had invaded and seized Austria. But this meant little to Otto as he watched the street. He didn't realize that war was breathing down his neck.

From the window, he could see all the way to Hakaniemi Square, four blocks away. He stared at the blue and yellow streetcars, bells ringing, and laden with workers going home to every part of Sorkka, the name of the labor section of Helsinki.

Why don't *you* have this army letter? Otto thought, looking out at the home-bound thousands. The liquor had eased him some. He thought about his favorite sister, Sirkka, a daring girl who had left the village to wait on tables in the city four years ago. She would be on her way home now. Sirkka—with her full, rich face, rose-kissed cheeks, and curly auburn hair. Men stared at her legs as she hurried between the tables at the Kolumbian Restaurant on Aleksanteri Street in the business district. Being around merchants had given her a sophisticated air and city manners.

The family had survived in extreme poverty in Harkola, a small village an hour from Helsinki. Now his sisters and older brother were scattered over Finland.

Otto had followed Sirkka to Helsinki a year after she'd left home, leaving his mother alone in the small one-room cabin that he had helped build. It was the first home his mother had ever owned. It had a log sauna now, a deep well in the yard, and a cowshed behind the wild apple trees next to their potato patch.

He had also left a girl behind—his first. She had taught him to dance, and how to handle her with tenderness. She had become a teen-age memory.

But now because of Sirkka, there was Anna. More than just a roommate to Sirkka, Anna had become her closest friend. Just the thought of her was enough to evoke a picture: her silky, blond hair cut short at the neck, a moon face with dimples at the cheeks when she smiled, blue eyes, white teeth, and a thin body with gentle curves. He thought of the Sundays they had planned to spend in spring and summer on the wide stretches of sandy beach around Helsinki, the picnics they had hoped to have on the islands close by, where they would be able to lie in each other's arms.

Anna! The thought of her stirred a delicious, pulsating wave inside him. Her wide lips curved like the petals of a rose. He had found them reluctant at first, but one night they had opened to his furious passion. They had spent

9

many nights together since then.

His loving thoughts were interrupted as he glanced at his orders. He thought again of its message. Only a week of freedom left. Then what? A boot camp full of men. No Anna with her tasty lips and silken skin, no Sirkka with her cooking and laughter. No Sundays at the Helsinki seashore. No apartment. No violin lessons. No life in the capital, with money in his pocket from the job at the Akrenius Electric Motor Factory.

Otto dried his palms on a wrinkled handkerchief. His breathing grew faster. He let his hand fall back as he emptied the glass and squeezed hard with his clammy fingers. He felt more distraught than ever.

And then, Sirkka and Anna were home. Sirkka grinned as she rushed past him to the kitchen with her shopping bag. Anna planted a wet kiss on his lips.

"Wait till you see what I bought for Sunday supper!" Sirkka exclaimed. "Delicious veal leg. I got it from our favorite butcher at Kauppatori's Farmer's Market," she said as she walked into the living room where Anna and Otto stood silently.

"What's the matter?" Sirkka asked, glancing at them and at the bottle. Otto's face was flushed. Anna had felt his cold, clammy hands as he touched her neck while trying to kiss her calmly.

The two girls followed Otto's walnut-brown eyes to the note that still lay crumpled on the floor. Anna picked it up and read it aloud.

"What can you do? You knew it would be coming. It'll make a man out of you like our brother Olavi," advised Sirkka.

"Or ruin my whole life!" Otto shouted, "The damn army!"

"Don't think of the Civil War. Things have changed since then. The White Guard is long gone . . ."

Otto cut Sirkka short. "Gone damn it! They are all army officers now, with their eyes set against alleged 'Reds' like me! How can I forget what they did to Father? They made us all suffer hunger and humiliation. How can you defend them?"

"I don't defend them! But you must be realistic."

10

Anna felt Sirkka and Otto's agony and realized how hard it would be for Otto to join the army. Sirkka had told Anna the story of her mother pushing the heavy, wooden wheelbarrow through the village to their hut. Inside the cart lay the butchered remnants of her husband Vaino. His death made it almost impossible for her to keep her family from starvation. Those hungry years had left their scars on Otto.

Instinctively Anna tried to direct the conversation away from those painful memories. "Remember what Professor Hursti at the Conservatory told you the other night about your violin lessons. He said you show great promise. Why don't you think ahead positively. In another two or three years you'll be able to join a string quartet. That could mean recitals, concerts, and who knows what else . . ."

Otto reached out for the bottle but checked himself.

"Hursti also told me that I should not let anything interfere with my study."

"It won't be so bad," Sirkka said firmly. "Remember what Olavi said when he got out? He said that you just have to do whatever they ask of you, pretend to be trying your very best, and you'll have no problems."

"Then why did they jail him? Why did they beat him? Should I pretend that I know nothing about the army's prejudice against the poor?" Otto sighed. "Well, I'll try to forget about it tonight. It's May Day Eve, time to celebrate the arrival of spring, and tonight we'll go dancing, army or no army."

"Good," Sirkka said. "I've reserved a table at the Alppila. It's opening night. Remember the fun we had last year?"

"I remember, but I didn't have to go into the army last year, either!" Otto shouted back. "I'm going to the sauna. I'll get Sauna-Mari to wash me real good. Might as well enjoy my last days!"

At eight o'clock Anna rose from her small dressing table, holding her hands in front of her. She hated the way her hands got so chafed and rough from handling the heavy sheets of metal which she fed into the drill press at the can factory. She had scrubbed them, soaked them in oil, and painted her fingernails. Now she waved them languidly in the air so that the bright-red polish would dry.

11

Otto stood in the doorway, watching her. He felt fresh and the scent of cologne filled the air as he approached her. He pulled her close to him, feeling her warmth through her thin dress. "Don't mess up my nail polish," she whispered into Otto's ear.

"You look beautiful. I like your new dress," he said, running his hands over her round, full breasts.

"I'm glad you like it because it will have to do for all summer," Anna laughed, while whirling around in front of Otto.

"You look just like a doll—beautiful. In fact, you look pretty inviting . . ."

"Not now," Anna told him, her dimples making her face charming and childlike. Her voice now was low and her eyes shone with a brightness that made Otto's heart pound. He could hardly wait to come back with her after the dance.

Otto was wearing his first and only suit. It was blue serge, shiny with years, but still unspotted despite the many meals he had eaten in it. He took scrupulous care of his clothes. It was single-breasted and a little tight-fitting, but Otto had no belly to break open the seams. His black shoes were worn, but new soles and fresh polish had them ready for the Vappu Festival.

From the living room came the sound of Sirkka's voice. "Come on! I'm waiting for you."

As Otto and Anna appeared in the doorway of the living room, Sirkka smiled at them. "You two look beautiful," she said, and then hurried them out to the waiting taxi.

The maitre d', husky as a wrestler in his evening clothes, bowed as he directed Otto's party to a table near the stage. The place was decorated with strings of crepe paper, balloons, and colored lightbulbs. Each table had a bouquet of Sinivuokko and Valkovuokko, the blue and white flowers which signalled the arrival of spring. On the stage at the rear of the dance floor, the Dallape band had already begun to play.

The evening passed like a dream. The large room was filled with laughter, dancing, and the swirl of brightly colored dresses. Jaloviina, wine, and akuavit flowed as freely as the dancers. It was late when they finally returned home.

Otto took Anna in his arms. She was the only one who

12

could keep him from thinking about the army. He undid the buttons on the back of her dress, carefully taking off the garments, one by one, until he felt her pulsating skin. He carried her to the bed, and kissed her lips, her neck, and her rigid nipples, until he felt her breathing in his ear, moaning with pleasure.

In the early afternoon of the following day Sirkka and Anna hired a horse-drawn carriage, and gave Otto a ride. They passed Hakaniemi Square and saw the student parade on Ullanlinna, with festive crowds everywhere on the streets. Children were holding balloons and blowing noise-makers. The carriage came to a halt at Elaintarha Park, where they joined thousands of workers listening to the May Day speeches.

When they arrived, Otto saw a woman speaking on the stage, who was known among the poor as the God-mother. She was a short, plump woman, and an extreme-leftist, political writer who had been an active, underground, member of the Communist party. Immediately after the Civil War, and then again in the thirties, she had served two prison terms for her outspokenness against the Finnish fascist movement. She had refused to flee to Russia after the Civil War as many of her comrades did. Instead, each time, she had emerged from prison undaunted.

". . . We can never forget the brutality of the butchers toward the working man," the Godmother was saying. "I saw with my own eyes how the White Guard, led by the blood-thirsty Mannerheim, murdered our comrades during the war, and how, in prison, men and women were cut to pieces or rotted to death. The Fascists will make this country a prison camp as it was after the Civil War if we allow . . ."

There was little response to her speech. It wasn't until the main speaker, Vaino Tanner, walked onto the podium that the crowd became alert. His leadership in the Social Democratic Party dated back to before the Civil War. Tanner had vehemently opposed the party rebels who organized the Red Guard forces and the striker's parades on the Helsinki streets, both of which had led to bloodshed. He had kept his head determinedly, stubbornly, and bravely against the rebels, and he had now gained the people's respect and the party's favor as a leader of workingmen. Thousands had

13

come to hear him. They cheered and stood up in response to his call for unity behind the Democratic Party leadership.

Otto's mind was restless. "Let's get out of here," he told Sirkka and Anna. They walked through the park, past Toolo Bay, to their apartment.

For the remainder of his free time before the date of conscription, Otto continued working by day and staying with Anna at night. He found that he had little enthusiasm for practicing his violin; lessons seemed so remote from what lay before him. Instead he could only find contentment in Anna's arms, trying to forget that in a few days he would be forced to face an uncertain future.

# Chapter 2

On May ninth, Otto was in formation, marching through the cobblestone streets of the frontier town of Terijoki. With him were one hundred and fifty other conscripts, many looking bedraggled and disgusted. They had just left the railroad station. The screeching whistle of the train sounded as it pulled out, after disgorging the men and their small mountain of baggage. Carrying his suitcase and violin case, he wondered about the twelve long months before he would be free and could enjoy a train ride home.

Terijoki, the location of the Jaeger-Battalion-One barracks, clung to the seashore of the Gulf of Finland. While well-to-do citizens saw it as a resort town, the military saw it as a location of the utmost strategic importance. It was on the Karelian Isthmus and was within thirty-five kilometers of Leningrad, and seven kilometers from Rajakoki, the winding river that was the border between Finland and Russia.

Otto dreaded the thought of basic training, and feared that his size would not make boot-camp life any easier for him. As the conscripts marched onto the compound's sandy training field, he realized that he was the smallest recruit.

They stood in three groups, in the center of a square compound, surrounded by four company barracks. Facing them was a tall, scrowling sergeant. All the shadowy misfortunes that Otto had worried about now began to take

15

shape and substance.

The sergeant eyed his charges with an expression of mock wonder.

"I've never seen such a bunch of dolts in my life," he brayed in a high tenor voice. "Who sent *you* here? If the army says you've got to become Jaegers, then Jaegers are what you'll become. Some of you may think you know what army life is. You're going to find you didn't have any idea! If you think you can follow me without getting lost I'll show you to the Third Company barracks."

Grouped with forty–nine others, Otto staggered into the army-gray barracks and down a long, narrow hallway to Room Eight, at the south end of the corridor. The rooms at the north end were for the veteran Jaegers who had been in the compound for six months. Conscripts started at the south end. Otto put his things on a top bunk and looked around. Eight other newcomers were stripping off their civilian clothes and putting on the ill-fitting winter uniforms that had been laid out on the bunks. The man next to Otto's bunk was tall, with bony hands and a rugged-looking face. He had an air of strength about him.

"I'm Jussi Hietala," he said, extending his hand. "From Sortavala. This place stinks," he added in a low tone. His hands were heavily calloused from logging in the forests around Sortavala, but he had a quick native intelligence.

"Damn right," said a smaller man, busy assembling his gear on the bunk below Hietala's. "My name is Elmer Aalto," the pink-faced man said, shaking hands with Otto and then Hietala. "I'm from Letku," he added. He had freckles on his cheeks, and narrow, staring eyes. His thin, reddish hair was combed back sleekly from his low forehead. The skin on his hands was dark and grimy from unwashable dirt and grease, the mark of his trade as a blacksmith's assistant. When Aalto ran his hand across his head, Hietala laughed and said "You'd better appreciate all that red hair while you still have it. The first they they'll do is shave our hair off. They won't even leave fuzz."

The three men looked around the room at the gray walls and ceiling, the cement floor, and the lone, low lightbulb hanging down in the center of the room.

"One year in this rotten hole is going to be a long time,"

said Otto, shaking his head. "It's too late to change our minds, but they'll have a hard time making a Jaeger out of me if it means I have to learn to love the army."

Hietala ran his hand through his thick, black hair. "I doubt if they could make me stand at attention if they kept me here for two years," he said.

The recruits milled around the room laughing at their heavy, wrinkled uniforms. The knee-high leather boots were dry, and as stiff as wood. They had to fit thick baggy pantcuffs inside the boot tops. Otto's uniform collar was tight, and he felt as if his head were in a bowl. The belt over the jacket had a large iron buckle. It and the iron buttons were embossed with a lion, the national Finnish emblem. They quickly learned that the lion's head in the buckle and on the buttons had to be upright. It was the first order to remember. The presence of a single, sloppy uniform within a squad resulted in severe, group punishment.

"This is spring. Why do we still have to wear these heavy winter uniforms?" Otto asked Hietala.

Hietala looked down. "I heard that the summer uniforms aren't given out until Midsummer's Day—and that's near the end of next month."

"That sounds like the army, all right."

Suddenly there was a petty officer standing in the doorway. He was Corporal Lottonen, of whom they had already been warned. He had come silently into the room and now shouted:

"Listen, idiots! When you see me standing at this door, you come to attention. When you see anyone who's not a wet-behind-the ears, soft, new recruit, you stand at attention! I smell sweaty socks in here already. Wash your feet or I'll paint tar over them!"

Otto swallowed to clear the lump in his throat. Were his feet the offenders?

"Pull in your stomachs," the corporal roared as he walked up and down the ragged line of men. "Straighten that back! You look like old men standing at a bar. You're in bad shape. We'll get you to work on that right now. Leave this room running. Run around the utility pole by the canteen on the far left corner and run back here. Now go!" he barked.

The men sprinted out of the room toward the pole, a kilometer away. They ran desperately over the soft sand, some still struggling to get their uniforms buttoned. Otto's lungs burned from the dust left behind by the other strong-legged men. He was running as fast as he could, but his short legs weren't equal to the task. He couldn't keep up with the others.

The conscripts returned to Room Eight and were about to flop down on their bunks when the corporal shouted, "Off those beds, conscripts! I didn't tell you to sit down. You never use these bunks except at night." He wheeled around and left the room.

The recruits muttered angrily. Then the fiery-eyed Corporal Holtto appeared.

"Attention!" he shouted, and then slowly wiped the top of the door with a white linen handkerchief. Although it did not appear dirty, he bellowed, "What is this! The dirt in here is as thick as horseshit in a barn! Every day, for as long as it takes you to learn how to do things, you'll run around that utility pole. You are serving in the Finnish Armed Forces now. Here only Jaegers, the best soldiers in the army, are manufactured. Don't you ever forget that! Now get out there and run for that pole!"

When they returned, one short, fat conscript staggered in and collapsed, vomiting on the floor. The corporal screamed shrilly, "If you ever puke again I'll make you eat it!"

That night, exhausted as he was, Otto couldn't sleep. He soon was listening to the snores from nine other bunks. He tried, unsuccessfully, not to think of his childhood, of his father's death, of his hatred for the army. Otto was well aware that Finland was now, for the first time in seven centuries, an independent nation, free from Russian or any other foreign domination. He realized the need for an army to protect this freedom and the need to conscript young men like himself. But he also knew that with that freedom had come a struggle that had between the working class and elite which had caused wounds, and that those wounds were still unhealed. The workers were not satisfied, and they didn't trust the government, or the army. To the working people, the government was still made up of the same butchers who had slaughtered hundreds of thousands during and after the Civil War. Otto couldn't forget those years of starvation. He finally fell asleep pursued by dreams of Corporal Lottonen sending him out into the training compound where he was ordered to stab his own father, again and again, with the bayonet on the end of his rifle.

# Chapter 3

Three weeks later, after a vigorous field drill, the rain-soaked conscripts entered the compound's lecture hall. They smelled of sweat and tobacco, and salted herring from the breakfast they had hurriedly eaten. Otto shook his head with disgust as he saw a young second lieutenant standing by a blackboard on the podium. The man was obviously one of those enthusiastic officers who looked forward to preaching to the recruits. He was eager to lead each and every man immediately into battle. For two hours he spewed forth facts, figures, and patriotism.

"I assume you all have a little familiarity with the geography of our nation," he said, glancing at the map on the wall behind him, and then back to the conscripts. "You will have noticed that Finland is prone to attack from the east. The city of Terijoki and our compound lie only seven kilometers from the river, which is our present but undesirable border with Russia." He pointed on the map to the Rajajoki, a river which emptied into the Gulf of Finland and washed the shores of the isle of Kronstadt.

"Of even greater importance is the fact that Leningrad lies only twenty-four kilometers to the east of this river. Needless to say, Leningrad, with all its naval bases and military installations at Kronstadt, is a great threat to our security." He stood silently for a moment.

"This will be along-winded lecture," Otto whispered to

Hietala.

"You're damn right. They're going to soak us in Finnish policy—past and present.

"Even during the Czars' time, the Russians dreamed of having free passage to the Atlantic, and for that reason they have wanted to conquer the Scandinavian countries. Our eastern border, from the gulf to the Polar Sea, is 1500 kilometers, and the areas are not densely populated. Thus, Russia always dangerously faces Finland.

"An example of this danger is the Aunus region, the heart of Eastern Karelia, which is north of Lake Laatokka. The Tarto Peace Treaty, on which current Russian and Finnish relations are based, granted autonomy to the people of the region, but the Russians have never honored that agreement. Instead, almost before the ink was dry, they started to Russify the entire area and eventually took control of it. Finns must be constantly alert and watchful that the same thing doesn't happen here, too."

He paused and pointed again. Otto looked at Hietala.

"The Karelian Isthmus is a narrow piece of land, only sixty-five kilometers wide at its broadest point. It has many bogs and marshy areas, making it easier for us to defend. The succession of lake after lake makes it very difficult for an enemy to cross this heavy wooded area. Even when the lakes freeze, it would take a brave enemy to cross such an open stretch of ice." He took a sip of water, then tightened his lips.

"But we can never rely on the assumption that the Russians pose no danger to us. We must keep planning for the day when we will reclaim all of our Karelian territory from Murmansk to the Gulf of Finland. We must secure our eastern border with the land Russia has taken from us, for a permanent defense line."

The lieutenant, like many officers, spoke vehemently of "Greater Finland," obviously hoping to impress the recruits with this concept. But many of the young men were from isolated logging and farming areas, sons of poor working men, and were completely unmoved by the territorial objectives to which the officers constantly referred.

"This military compound is here as a border guard, to defend our frontiers and be ready to attack when the time is right for such action. You will be trained to fight until your last drop of blood has been spilled, or until you haven't the strength left to pull a trigger. You will be taught never to surrender, and never to give up hope. Should we face hostilities from the Russians, you must never allow yourselves to be captured. They are barbarians who use the worst kind of torture to make soldiers talk. They will go to extremes. They will rip out your fingernails slowly and painfully. But Jaegers will never allow themselves to be captured, nor will they tell military secrets, even under the most severe torture.''

The lieutenant continued for another hour and a half before dismissing the men for lunch. Otto hardly heard a word. He was anxiously rubbing his fingertips across his fingernails, trying to recover from the shock of what the lieutenant had said.

"I need my fingernails," he thought, horrified. "Without them I could never play the violin again. All my dreams would be finished. I would tell them anything they wanted to know if they would leave my hands alone. What horrible torture!

Otto could hardly eat his lunch. He had been eating heartily every day and, despite his dislike of army life, he had to admit that he was being fed regularly. His body was developing and filling out. He had gained seven kilos in less than a month, and he was three centimeters taller. His back and shoulders had grown hard and muscular. Yet now he could do no more than pick at his noodle casserole.

Hietala, next to him, asked, "I wonder where the lieutenant gets all of his information about the Russians wanting to attack us. It sounds like crap to me."

"I don't know," answered Otto. "From what I've heard, the Russians provided work when they were in Finland before the Civil War. But we better watch what we say here."

After lunch, the lieutenant took out another map of Finland and started the afternoon session.

"We sure as hell must go through a lot of history before our service is over," Hietala whispered to Otto.

"They think they can make us into professional soldiers or something," Aalto whispered. "I'm going to sleep with my eyes open, rather than listen to all this."

The lieutenant started in again.

"Finland is shaped like a woman in an evening gown. Her hem spreads out to the south, almost touching Leningrad, and her outstretched left hand reaches into the Polar Sea, leaving her slim waist in the middle. This narrow portion of the land is where the Jaeger troops first proved their ability. The conflict began in Finland's early years, long before independence, when the Czars tried to Russify the Finns. In 1899 Nickolai II violated our constitution . . ."

The lieutenant spoke with quiet vehemence for over two hours, then paused, took a drink from a glass on the table beside him, and observed his audience with a quiet, yet probing look. There was absolute silence.

"Tomorrow morning you will be taken to the river at Rajajoki, where you will perform the most importtant task in your military service. You are dismissed," he concluded abruptly, and started gathering his materials into a briefcase.

They rushed to the corridor. Otto's stomach was beginning to growl with hunger. His face was solemn with thoughts of the lectures, but he had hopes of forgetting these agonies by the time he could see plates filled with steaming potatoes.

"Attention, conscripts. Room Eight, gather here!" shouted a voice at the end of the corridor. It was Corporal Lottonen's familiar angry growl.

"You, all of you, run to the stable! I'll be there in an hour, and you'd better have the place clean by then, or else. Run!"

Otto pulled the heavy smell of manure into his nostrils and his fingers tightened around the shovel as he lifted the dung into the wheelbarrow that Hietala would then wheel to the refuse pile at the end of the barn.

Otto cleared the sweat off his forehead and noted that Hietala's perspiring face was tight with anger. They finished working, and Aalto returned their cleaned shovels to the toolshed at the entrance of the stable just before Corporal Lottonen came to inspect the work. Silently, he stalked through the stable, then returned to the entrance.

"You don't deserve to eat tonight, but out of sheer goodness on my part, I'll take you to the mess hall," he said, motioning them to fall in behind him, single file. He would not admit that he was pleased.

The next morning, calisthenics lasted a dusty forty-five minutes. Conscripts puffed at each move, bending down, forward, backward, and running in place on the soft sand in the middle of the field.

At seven, the third company recruits stood before their barrack in full-dress uniform, next to their bicycles. Captain Pusa eyed them in silence.

"Face right—mount!" he ordered, and led the conscripts out of the compound and through the city, toward the border between Russia and Finland. On arrival at the river after a hard ride, the men assembled again before the captain.

"Every Finn knows the old saying that one Finn is worth ten Russians. Well, that's not good enough for the Jaegers! Each one of you must be superior to a hundred Russians," insisted the trim, athletic, enthusiastic Captain Pusa, as he paced along the bank of the Rajajoki. "First five conscripts, follow me," he ordered, and started to march down the sharp slope to the edge of the river.

Otto was among them. The men reached a small wooden platform built over the water on the well-concealed bay, where the clear, shallow water moved slowly toward the Gulf. Otto shuffled his feet on the unpainted, water-washed planks of the platform, and although he was amused by the seriousness with which the captain was behaving, he resisted the impulse to smile.

"I'm going to baptize you in this Soviet river water," Pusa told them. "This constitutes your military oath, your pledge to kill every Russian who illegally crosses this border. You'll fight for your country until your last drop of blood has been given." Then, motioning Otto to bend down, he sprinkled a cupped handful of water on his head.

The ceremony continued until all had been christened as Jaegers. The captain walked back to the top of the riverbank with the last group of conscripts.

"You'll be the most trusted men in the Finnish army now," Pusa said. "I want to congratulate you, and I trust that each one of you will prove your worth with every ounce of energy you devote to Finland.

"Well," said Hietala, after they had returned to their

24

barracks, "I'd hardly go so far as to say that it was one of the most important days in my life. It was a nice bike ride, and the river was beautiful. But ceremonies and baptisms are nonsense."

Otto agreed.

"Besides," Hietala continued, I couldn't see any difference between our side and the Russians. Their houses looked just as nice and neat as the ones on this side. I didn't see anything threatening, but the captain talked as if there were hordes of Russians ready to cross and slaughter Finns! I don't feel different, now that I've been baptized as a Jaeger. Do you, Arola?"

Otto laughed.

"No. Except that my legs are stiff from that ride and then having to stand around waiting for everyone to get their heads doused. I don't know why we couldn't sit down."

# Chapter 4

The conscripts never had time to sit down. Each day seemed worse than the last. The weeks that followed the baptismal ceremony were spent by Otto and his fellow conscripts in building up their physical stamina. They marched in formation for hours, did calisthenics, participated in long bike races and marches until they thought they would drop. Each day found some new form of physical torment for them to endure. Otto was amazed as each new exercise brought the discovery of a set of muscles which he had never known he had. Despite the stiffness and the aches and paines, he felt an athletic attraction to this sort of training, and worked hard at it. His body grew stronger, he gained more weight, and he filled out more in the shoulders. He was surprised to find himself becoming an ardent competitor. When he placed first in one of the platoon's fifty-kilometer bicycle races, he experienced a strong sense of gratification.

One Saturday morning in early June, the men were assembled in the center of the big training field. There Sergeant Mikkola briskly read a list of names of the fifteen men who had been chosen from the Third Company to enter Non-Commissioned Officers School. While Otto stood with the others and waited for the sergeant to finish his speech and get on with the business at hand, he thought, Well, here's one time I can be grateful for being the son of a man who was murdered by the army. No one with my background would ever be chosen for military officers' school. And it's a good thing, too. Who needs it? All it means is two more markkas a month in extra pay, but three more months that you have to stay in the army. Now there's an honor that I'll be glad to pass up—although I could use the raise.

When the sergeant read out "Otto Arola" Otto's mouth dropped open; he could scarcely believe his ears. He suddenly realized that he had been making a grave error by becoming so competitive. He had done much too well and had taken the training too seriously. He knew now that he should have been content to stay faceless among the other conscripts.

The platoon of fifteen men who had been chosen to attend the elite school stood in front of the company. They were to spend a month in special, intensive training, and would then move to the Non-Commissioned Reserve School which was also in Terijoki. Otto resented his selection, but he knew there was nothing he could do except resign himself to giving the army an additional three months.

At least when I'm done, he thought, brightening a bit, I won't have to put up with being humiliated by every corporal or sergeant who wants a promotion.

The remaining month of training at the compound was rigorous. They were put under the leadership of Sergeant Hannes Nikula, an athletic and patriotic Jaeger, who gave his orders in a clear, resounding voice. He drove his men hard, but he had the ability to assess each man's limits realistically, and he rarely asked more of anyone than he was able to give.

The men spent much of their time on the firing range, learning how to use their rifles and Suomi automatics, and how to assemble them blind-folded. With the Suomi's, they could fire seven hundred to a thousand forty-five-caliber rounds per minute. The weapon could be slung from the chest strap for rapid firing.

The night before Otto's departure, Hietala looked over at him. "We're going to celebrate once more before you go to join the rich." He took out his mouth organ, blew a few notes, and said, "Hey, Otto, you take yours, too, and we'll have a little chorus session."

"I'll take my violin, instead, okay fellows?" he responded, opening his violin case and starting to pluck the strings.

They had sung "Kulkurin Valssi" and "Sailor's Song" when Otto threw his violin on top of the bunk. "I got a letter today from my sister Sirkka, and guess what? She sent me five markkas. Let's go to Holopainen for coffee and doughnuts."

Hietala felt around in the bottom of his pockets. "I'll have enough for coffee, but not for doughnuts. You're lucky, Otto. Your pay will go up to thirty-two markkas a month when you go to school."

"I'll buy you a doughnut," Elmer Aalto said, after he examined his pockets and found enough money there. "We'll manage."

The conscripts took a shortcut through the woods and Otto's mind started wandering. His fingers were touching the photo in his pocket, the one his sister had sent with her letter.

"Look, Hietala," Otto finally said, "here's a picture of my girlfriend in Helsinki. Doesn't she put all the Terijoki girls to shame?"

"Ah!" Hietala said, as he took the photo from Otto to inspect it. "Look at her," he said, and handed the picture on to Aalto.

"She's something!" Aalto added and let his fingers run over Anna's lips.

"Hold it," Otto shouted. "Not with my girl!"

They all laughed loudly.

Otto Arola and the fourteen other chosen conscripts steered their bikes, in single file behind Sergeant Nikula, onto a large oak-lined, sandy yard on the east side of Terijoki. The brick building had once housed many Russian diplomats, and merchants who had visited the resort city, but now it was a training center for non-commissioned Jaeger officers.

Otto stood in front of his new home and surveyed the two-story brick building, admiring the decorative art and precision of detail that had gone into its construction. From the outside it reminded him of the Folk Conservatory in Helsinki, where he longed to give a violin recital one day.

The charm of the building disappeared, however, once he stepped inside. The interior was a typically bleak, military gray. As Otto waited in line to receive his instructions and room number, a feeling of hopeless resignation enveloped him. The duty officer, sitting behind the desk, handed Otto his papers and room assignment. The man told him, in a bored monotone, to report to his room and wait to be called to assembly in an hour.

Otto walked slowly down one of many long, identical hallways. He had his army-issue rucksack slung over his back and carried his violin case under his right arm. The room was small, but immaculately clean. There were two double bunks, two small tables, four stools, and two tiny closets. Despite its small size, it appeared to be a vast improvement over barrack life. Otto chose a top bunk.

Soon three young men entered the room, speaking quietly. They were Akseli Koskela, Aku Harma, and Santeri Helberg. Koskela had acquired the nickname "Superman" because of his patriotism and eagerness to do battle with anyone who he fancied was making a disparaging remark about Finland, her leaders, or her army. He was of medium height, and roundfaced, with fair skin and blond hair. He had studied medicine before entering the army, and he came from a well-to-do family in Helsinki. To Otto, his physique seemed to reflect the health that comes from an upbringing where there is always more than enough good food to go around.

Aku Harma was another medical student. He was a tall, thin fellow, with short-cropped dark hair, heavy eyebrows, and a serious manner. Harma was reserved, speaking only when spoken to, or when he had something germane to add to a discussion. He had no use for small talk. He preferred studying his medical textbooks to socializing. Otto decided that with his air of gravity and concentration, Harma someday would make an excellent doctor.

Otto's third roommate, Helberg, was the tallest of the three, slim, with a narrow face and a patrician's aquiline nose. He walked with a slight, perpetual stoop, as if all his life he had been ducking his great height under doorways. Helberg could hardly be serious about anything for more than five minutes. He had an endless repertoire of bad jokes which he considered to be riotously funny and which he would tell at the slightest provocation.

Although the school regimen was both mentally and physically exhausting, Otto found that he was, at last, treated with some degree of respect. He was no longer harassed by maniacal corporals, nor was he forced to perform absurd, degrading acts of punishment.

He began to like his three roommates more and more. Even Koskela was not a bad sort, in spite of his affected intellectuality and patriotic gibberish. In spite of their superior educations, all three respected Otto for his physical prowess on the training field, and for his willingness to help them whenever he could. They stuck together as a unit during meals and lectures, and excelled in both the academic and physical aspects of the training program.

On their two nights off, however, the social distinctions between Otto and his roommates became obvious. They, like the majority of officer trainees, were well supplied with money from home, and could afford to frequent the luxurious ocean-front Kasino Restaurant for drinks. Otto, however, patronized a nearby ballroom which provided music and dancing for the less fortunate Jaegers, and the factory girls of Terijoki. Otto loved to dance; it had been one of the things he had enjoyed doing most in Helsinki, and, while the girls in Terijoki were not so lovely as those in Helsinki, he rarely missed a chance to go dancing. He was also glad to be able to rendezvous with his friends Heilala and Aalto. Otto, as well as his friends, had been warned by the veteran Jaegers that they'd be better off to take it easy with the Terijoki girls. The civilian young men were a jealous bunch and disliked the army recruits. Otto brushed aside such warnings. Nothing would have kept him away from the dance hall.

The schooldays were spent in the classroom, on the firing range, or around the region rehearsing combat situations. One day Nikula took the trainees out and instructed them in the use of hand grenades. They were the size of large goose eggs, and they came both with and without wooden handles. Those with handles were designed for accuracy, while those without them were intended for long-range targets.

Later that same day, the trainees biked to a grassy knoll with a grove of pine trees. There Nikula set up the automatic, rapid-firing rifle. It fitted and fired twenty rounds from a curved clip beneath the chamber. The barrel was supported in front by two legs, thirty centimeters high, and the gunner lay on his belly behind it and fired from that position.

"Arola, come here and give us a demonstration."

Otto had already fired the gun many times while practicing with the Third Company. Although he had not yet mastered accuracy, he knew the procedure. He lay down the sighted over the barrel, toward the life-sized cardboard target four hundred meters away.

"Sergeant, I can't see the target, the sun is too bright. It's glaring off the front sight."

"I'll take care of that," the sergeant said, striking a match and smoking the sight on the barrel. "Now try it."

"Good," Otto replied, squeezing the trigger and rapid-firing four rounds at the target, two of which struck the head.

"Not too bad," the sergeant said, suddenly wheeling around in the direction of the frontier and staring up at the sky, as he and the others heard the distant drone of a low-flying airplane. "This weapon can also be used to bring down aircraft if their altitude is not too great," he mentioned, gazing up at the sky, trying to locate the source of the noise. "That's a Russian plane again, and I'd like to know what they think they're doing, continuously violating our borders," he added, with a troubled expression.

"Why are they flying over Karelia so often this summer?" asked Koskela, puzzled.

"Damned if I know," the sergeant muttered, keeping his eyes on the plane, which had now become visible.

Koskela rushed over to the automatic rifle while everyone else watched the plane. He started to pick it up, thinking to fire a few shots at the plane and teach the pilot a lesson. But as he put his right hand on the stock his forefinger brushed the trigger, and a burst of bullets arched through the air, just missing the trainess.

"What's going on?" Sergeant Nikula shouted, his face red and his lips tightening with anger.

31

"I was going to teach that pilot to pay some attention to the border," Koskela muttered defensively.

Any other trainee would have landed in jail for such an irresponsible action. But Kosekla had his reputation as a super-patriot. Since Nikula was filled with patriotic fervor himself and was a diehard Russian-hater, he never filed a complaint, letting the whole affair die, and telling his trainees, "We will never mention this to anyone. Is that understood?"

The platoon silently biked back to camp. They were shaken by the incident, but the mail that waited for them took their minds away from the potential accident that could have killed several of them. Otto joyously grabbed the letter he had received from Anna, and retired to his room to enjoy it in private.

# Chapter 5

Otto stretched out on top of the bunk and read Anna's letter. By the time he finished reading he felt homesick, but he was glad to know that they missed him.

Otto continued to mature physically while training in the Karelian countryside. He and the others witnessed many minor border incidents in the summer of 1938. The first time Otto realized that he faced some danger in the army, was while reading a letter from Sirkka. She mentioned some headlines in the daily paper about accidental explosions in trains and Army posts throughout Finland.

". . . I hope you do not get involved with dangerous weapons and explosives, where you might accidentally hurt yourself or damage your hands. Everyone is talking about these explosions at the coffee shop, but no one can understand why our men are so careless with what they do that such accidents happen."

I'm not so crazy about the military that I would touch anything unless I was ordered to, Otto thought, while reading of his sister's concern for his safety.

Otto's summer had ended, and autumn had come to Terijoki. The Gulf wind blew coldly across the resort city, now empty of vacationing sunbathers.

"It's quiet in here," Helberg said, as he ducked into the room, followed by Koskela, who spread out his package of delicacies from home.

"Here, have a piece of pulla," Koskela told Otto, first pouring a layer of honey over it.

"This is delicious. Your mother really knows how to bake coffeebread," Otto said, honey dripping all over his fingers. Koskela gave some of the honey-covered bread to his other roommates, along with some crisp cookies, and for a while it seemed as if it were Christmas Eve and Santa Claus had just visited the school.

After they finished their feast, they decided to go have a drink at the Kasino.

"I'm sure thirsty," Koskela said.

"I'll join you," Harma replied.

Helberg looked at Otto on the top bunk. "How about it?"

"I can't afford the Kasino. I'll go to the dance hall instead."

The men separated at the entrance to the Kasino, and Otto continued to the dance hall at the top of the hill where the music from a four-man band could be heard. He danced with Tanja as he had done for the past two weeks, and then walked her outside at intermission.

When Tanja went to the ladies' room, Hietala and Aalto walked toward Otto.

"I'd give my life for a girl like yours," Hietala whispered, his eyes gazing at the stairway where Tanja was already heading toward Otto.

He introduced his friends to her, then took her arm and guided her down to the edge of the hill. He held his arm around Tanja's waist, but before they had settled on top of a handy stump nearby, he suddenly came face to face with a husky civilian who loomed out from behind the bushes.

"You, Jaeger, don't you know you can't have my girl? You don't own the town and all the girls, you know! Let her go!"

Otto looked at Tanja. "Is he your friend?"

Tanja lifted her shoulders, looked at the man, and then said slowly and deliberately, "I dance with anyone I choose."

"You heard what the girl said. Beat it!"

"You're not giving the orders around here," the civilian said, puffing out his chest to impress Otto with his size.

34

"Beat it," Otto repeated. He barely had finished the words when he sensed heavy steps behind him. He couldn't turn around fast enough to see a long arm extending past his shoulder and an iron-fist land on the civilian's cheek with such power that the man rolled downhill for over a hundred meters.

"Thanks," Otto said to Hietala, who was standing beside him now. "I could have taken care of him myself."

"I know," nodded Hietala, "but I wanted that pleasure."

Otto's shirt was wet from perspiration as he walked down the hill later, holding Tanja's hand. He sensed that the man Hietala had felled earlier might return for revenge, so he was a bit wary as they walked slowly to the road. Soon Otto caught sight of a group of men standing by their bicycles near the road. He stopped, then ran to the side of the road and broke off a fence post about a meter long and the thickness of his wrist. At the end of it were some sharply pointed knots.

With his left arm around Tanja and the cane in his right hand, Otto glanced back and realized that Hietala and Aalto were following twenty meters behind. He counted six civilians standing on the roadside in the darkness, now only meters away.

"Let the girl go," the man said, but didn't step forward.

Otto took Tanja's right hand and walked closer to the men.

"Didn't you hear what the man told you?" asked another civilian.

Otto didn't reply. He stood still, observing their every movement.

The man with the bruised cheek suddenly let his bicycle fall to the ground. Otto pushed Tanja away to the side of the road and took hold of the stick with both hands.

"You'd be better off to stay where you are," Otto said in a low growl, his legs spread menacingly. Hietala and Aalto ran up and stopped.

Hietala stooped down and picked up a large fist-sized rock from the roadside near Tanja. He thrust it at Aalto, and said, "Otto, take your girl home. Let me have that stick!" Otto handed it to him. It rose in the air, and came down, aimed at the nearest man's head. The muddy sand

35

spattered, and fists flew, until the civilians took off on their bikes without looking back.

In the morning, when Otto's rommates awoke with hangovers, even the dedicated Harma grumbled and moaned as he stumbled out of bed.

"Well," said Otto, sitting on the edge of his bunk and looking at the few scratches on his hands, "you boys look like à train ran over you."

"Lay off, Otto," grumbled Koskela in his misery.

By the time the men were through with their morning field training they felt better, and Otto took Harma aside.

"Will you help me to fill out this application? I want to apply to the gunsmith school in Helsinki. They are sending a two-man team from the battalion this year and I want to be the second man, since the Machine-Gun Company gets the order to go as a 'regular.' While you go for four months of hard training at officer's school in Hamina, I'd like to be back in Helsinki for four months with Anna."

"Sure, Otto, I'll help you."

"Could we get started on it tonight?"

"Sure," Harma replied amiably.

It had actually been Harma who first noticed the announcement on the bulletin board, and pointed it out to Otto. "You're always saying how much you'd like to get back to Helsinki. Well, here's your chance. Someone from our group will be sent. Why not you?"

Otto and Harma sat in the conference room at a large table covered with papers. They had been up all night working on Otto's application. Otto leaned back and smiled at Harma.

"You've really got a way with words," he said in admiration, reading the final product of their night's labor. "You and I know what I think of the army, but this letter is great. You make me sound like the most devoted, hardworking Jaeger in the whole damn country."

"Well," Harma answered, smiling at the praise, "we both know what they want to hear. Your actual qualifications are only half of it. You've got to sound enthusiastic in order for these idiots to appreciate you. Guys like Koskela make it real big in the army. Know what I mean . . .?"

After a pause, Harma continued. "You and I don't give

a damn for the army. We have to fake it or we'll never get anywhere. And that's fine with me. I just want to become a civilian again and get through medical school. And you . . . well, you're a pretty smart country boy, Otto. Don't let the army use you—you use it. Get back to Helsinki and study the violin if that's what you want out of life. Don't let this half-assed army mess you up. Especially your hands. You'll need 'em to play the violin, just like I'll need mine for surgery. Now let's sneak out and get a beer to celebrate this great piece of creative writing.''

On a chilly November day, Otto was called into Sergeant Major Mattela's office. In his low voice, Mattela told him, ''Your application to gunsmith school has been considered and all your additional records have been supplied to me by your platoon leader, Sergeant Nikula. You are to report to Gunsmith and Weapons Training School in Helsinki at the end of your training here. It's not an easy assignment. All the other men there will have at least two years of college education, and you will have to work extremely hard to make it. Don't let us down.

''In addition to your educational opportunities,'' he continued, ''you have been promoted to the rank of corporal, and after you have completed your work in Helsinki, you will receive a further promotion to sergeant. You will take a train to Helsinki and report there. Any questions?''

''No, sir. Thank you, sir.''

''All right. You're dismissed. Congratulations and good luck!''

''Thanks again, sir,'' grinned Otto, and left to find his roommates and tell them the good news.

# *Chapter 6*

Otto arrived at the gunsmith school on a bitterly cold December day, when the streets of Helsinki were covered with ice and the trees were bare under the glowering skies. The old brick schoolbuilding still resembled the uninviting prison it had once been, with its small, square, barred windows, and gray exterior. With his first look at it, Otto felt a premonition that he had made a mistake.

When he saw the daily schedule that each man had to follow, he knew that he had no business being there. He realized that he would be lucky indeed to graduate, even if he spent twenty hours of every day studying. The curriculum was not easy, even for a man with college behind him. Otto had been forced to stop his schooling at the end of compulsory elementary school, when he was eleven years old, to give his mother a hand. He was completely ignorant of the intricacies of such things as physics, chemistry, calculus, and trigonometry.

For Otto, gunsmith school meant having to learn how to study and then doing so ceaselessly. He was able to keep abreast of the others only by working with his books all week-end, and even then he was lucky if he could get six hours of sleep a night. He was very much aware that his will was being sorely tested, and that his dreams of spending evenings at the Folk Conservatory taking lessons or attending concerts, and of long, leisurely nights in bed with

Anna, were not to become a reality.

His experience in the gunsmith school was beginning to leave its mark on Otto's character. He became a diligent scholar and began to master the voluminous textbooks. He gained self-confidence and consoled himself with the knowledge that, some day, all of this might help him after he was out of the army. Meanwhile, he still disliked the numerous lectures by patriotic officers, so full of praise for Germany and contempt for Russia, but he no longer paid them full attention.

He scarcely got to play his violin as the winter months passed. As far as Anna was concerned, he had to be satisfied with infrequent short visits, and by the time his graduation rolled around in March he had been able to make love with her only once. That had been such a hurried moment, squeezed into his impossible schedule, that they had agreed to postpone any amorous activities until school was over and they would have time to do more than just frustrate themselves with a small sample of pleasure.

The night before graduation, Otto and a classmate named Vieno had decided to spend an hour or so walking by the Katajanokka Harbor before the evening's roll call. As they walked along they noticed a number of vessels which looked, to the casual eye, like merchant ships, but after four months of studying weapons and ammunition both students instantly recognized the shapes of guns under the heavy tarpaulins on the decks of the light vessels. The names painted on the sides of the ships were German.

"What are German warships doing in our harbor?" Otto asked. "What do those bastards want? Who told the Nazis they were welcome to bring in gunboats?"

The traffic was light and they walked along near the docks discussing the unusual sight. Vieno knew something about the political situation and was giving Otto a long-winded explanation of the longstanding alliance between Germany and Finland, when suddenly two men rushed out of one of the vessels. They headed away from Otto and his companion, who immediately set out after them, aroused by their suspicious behavior and glad for any diversion. They gave up the chase after a block and a half, laughing and conjecturing that they must have been two German seamen sneaking off their ship for an unauthorized furlough. As they turned around to start back to the harbor a tremendous explosion knocked them down. Nearby buildings shook, windows broke, and debris flew everywhere. They realized that if they had not railed the two running men they would have been badly injured, perhaps even killed in the blast. •

"Did you see that tall, slim fellow running?" Otto asked Vieno in amazement. "He ran like a gazelle chased by hunters. He sure had long legs!"

"They were really in a hurry," Vieno agreed. "I'll bet they were Russians. Who else could they have been, Otto? It must have been some of the Russian sabotage that's been going on lately against the Germans."

"I don't believe it! Russia isn't at war with Germany, and neither are we—what the hell is going on here?" Otto fumed.

After they had returned to school and discussed it with their roommates, they dismissed it all as an unfortunate incident which they had been extremely lucky to survive. The unusually long legs of the man running from the ship, however, remained in the recesses of Otto's memory.

By the next afternoon the sun had come out from behind the clouds and the sky was bright blue. A clean, steady gust of wind blew across the heavy brick wall and into the training yard where the men were assembling. Rooms had been given a final cleaning, clothes had been packed, and now Headmaster Johan Kujala was passing out diplomas to the men. He told them that due to the exceptionally fine records they had accumulated over the past four months, he was giving all of them a three-day furlough.

Otto whopped for joy. He had no regrets as he left the school for the last time. He headed for his sister's, glad that he didn't have to report immediately back to Terijoki as he had feared he would.

He was proud of his accomplishments during the last four months. During, in fact, the almost five-year period since he had first arrived in Helsinki. He felt as if he had come a long way indeed.

## Chapter 7

The streetcar clanged to a stop at Porthan Street and Otto jumped off.

"Sergeant Arola, attention!" joked Anna as she opened the door for him and helped him remove his army overcoat.

"Tonight we're going to a concert," Otto said, trying to gear their thoughts away from his promotion. But before he could say any more Sirkka whispered to him:

"I don't give a hoot about the sergeant chevrons. But I do know that it required intensive study to graduate fifth, among the forty-five students, all with more years of schooling than you. I'm proud of you."

"Thank you, Sirkka. I appreciate that. But I know I could use even more education."

"Tonight I'm treating you both to the Conservatory concert," Anna joined in, hugging and kissing Otto.

The next two days belonged to Anna. She had taken time off from work at the metal factory and the lovers spent their time together, enjoying being alone.

On the evening before Otto was to leave, Sirkka had invited several friends over and the group departed to go dancing at the Workers Temple. Otto's joy at being home overwhelmed him as the evening wore on.

The next morning, Anna dressed in her best outfit, a soft beige jersey which outlined her lithe figure with exciting accuracy. Her blonde hair hung loose, and her eyes sparkled

41

with happiness. To Otto she appeared more lovely than he had ever seen her. When she brought him coffee in bed, he pulled her down to him and held her tightly.

"I want you . . ." Anna murmured. He drew her to him and kissed her. Hurriedly she undressed and crawled back into bed.

They spent most of the day in bed, until Anna got up and made him delicious dollar-sized pancakes with sugared lingonberries. After Sirkka returned from work they sat around the kitchen while Anna made his favorite dinner: meatballs with gravy, and mashed potatoes. Then they gorged themselves on Valio cheese and brown bread, washing it down with red wine. Finally Sirkka and Anna took a stuffed and contented Otto to the railroad station and put him on the night train for Terijoki.

## Chapter 8

Otto adjusted his overcoat collar over the two sewn on stripes that signified his promotion. It was hard to visualize how he would face his old buddies Hietala and Aalto, but he had assured himself that he would not require them to salute him, except when the rules demanded it.

The same train pulled into the Terijoki station that had brought him there ten months earlier. The huge and shining bright copper cupolas of the Russian orthodox church threw their shadows over the city.

Otto took a shortcut from the station to the Third Company barracks. He stepped over the mudholes created by spring thaw. The snow was almost gone now, and bicycles had been taken out to the troops.

Although the training field was a black and ugly sight to see after Helsinki, his mind was sharp and alert as he anticipated the praise he would receive from the sergeant major for having represented Third Company so well at school.

The sergeant major wasn't in the office when he arrived. The clerk directed him straight through the door to the Company Commander's office. Otto noticed that a new nameplate was on the desk, and behind it sat a rather strange-looking, baldheaded captain. He was slim and well-groomed, but his nose was flat, his ears stuck out from his shiny head like a dog's, and his eyes were cold and expressionless.

Otto came to attention in the strictest military manner. He proudly reported his return from the gunsmith school and then handed the captain his papers in a sealed envelope.

"Sergeant Arola," the captain said without looking at the envelope, "you are eleven hours late reporting to the company. What happened?"

"Sir . . ." Otto began hesitantly, "it has been customary for Jaegers to return on the morning train, sir . . ."

"I'm the company commander here, and no such privilege has been extended by me! You are an idiot to rely on such unauthorized practices. You have broken company rules. You'll report for fifteen days in the stockade and have the barber cut off your hair, down to the skin!"

Otto's knees began to wobble, but he stood at attention.

"Report to the stockade by three this afternoon, with your head shaved. This will give you time enough to get your belongings put away and in order. Put them in Room Ten. And you can rip off that sergeant's chevron, too. As of now, you're a corporal again."

Otto staggered, dazed, from the office. "It isn't possible, not possible . . ." he muttered. "This is it! I'm through with this lunacy. These bastards put me through eight months of hell to become a sergeant, and four days later they cut off all my hair and bust me down to corporal again. They're even throwing me in jail! I'll never do another thing for the army again, so help me God!"

Half an hour later he was sitting on a small stool in the Third Company's hallway, in front of the barber. He kept an angry, red-faced silence as the other Jaegers gathered around to watch the show and tease him.

"How are you doing now, conscript?" laughed one.

Otto glared sullenly at the jester.

"Hold still," said the barber.

"Come on, just put one extra plate under the cutter and leave a little stubble," Otto pleaded.

But the clippers had already begun to growl. "I'll have to use a razor blade. That's what the captain ordered."

The first person Otto saw when he stepped outside with his shaven head, partially concealed with his cap, was Hietala.

"My old buddy!" Hietala shouted. "Damn, it's good to see you, Arola! We've often wondered how you were getting along in Helsinki. We heard it was tough at the gunsmith school. I guess you didn't get to spend every night with your lovely girlfriend, huh? I hear that the captain caught you red-handed, coming back late."

"Damn that captain. I'd like to wring his neck."

"I've been waiting to see who his first victim would be," said Hietala, "but I'm damned sorry that it had to be you. I'd like to shoot the bastard myself. The anger on his face turned to dismay as he continued, "Your bad luck is spoiling my whole day. I was hoping we could get together for a few beers tonight, but now I'll have to watch you go off to jail. Well, it's lousy, that's for sure!"

Otto spent the next fifteen days planning elaborate schemes for revenge on the captain, most of which would leave the man mutilated, impotent, and in constant agony for a lifetime. His only other interest was watching his small but fearsome-looking roommate, a black spider, weave a delicate, complex web in one corner of the ceiling.

"If you expect a fly to survive in this hole, you're crazy," he advised the spider.

Otto swore to himself that when he got out he would spend the rest of his time in the army doing as little as possible. He knew that his shaved head would force him to spend nights in the compound because he would be too embarrassed to look up his old dancing partner, Tanja.

Otto's last four months in the Army as a demoted corporal were in great contrast to his first three. He was assigned to the ammunition warehouse, in keeping with his Helsinki schooling. It was a soft job, because the sergeant in charge was lazy and not inclined to creating any extra work. Otto showed up when he wanted to and often spent hours in the warehouse playing his violin. He could have gone into Terijoki every night if he had wished, but he remained at the compound. He took great care to avoid running into the Company Commander.

He went into town only twice. The first time was in May to put his friends Hietala and Aalto on the train when their year's service was over and they were discharged. The second time was to celebrate with his friends Koskela,

Helberg, and Harma when they returned from officer's school. They had all made the rank of second lieutenant, and although Otto enjoyed seeing them again, especially Harma, he felt strange being seen in town with three officers. Thereafter they would bring a bottle to the ammunition warehouse when they wanted to get together, and then sit around singing, drinking, and talking just like old times.

The remaining weeks passed slowly for Otto, but finally the day of his release arrived. It was a pleasantly hot day in July of 1939, and Otto thought it was the happiest day in his life. He said farewell to his three second-lieutenant friends; they had one more month to serve. He would miss them and his other friends in Terijoki, but all he could think about was getting out of the army. His step was light as he headed for the station.

# Chapter 9

Sunday morning—a warm, peaceful Sunday in Helsinki—began like a new era opening in Otto's life. Although his clothes were too tight, and his shoes pinched his feet, Otto didn't have a care in the world. Streetcars clanged merrily along on Helsinki streets, even though they were almost unoccupied. A few policemen patrolled the streets on foot, but most of the city folks had gone to their summer villas.

"Welcome back!" shouted Anna and Sirkka, who had waited eagerly at home for his arrival. "Look at you," Anna said admiringly.

"Tomorrow we're going out to get you new clothes," Sirkka insisted.

With their two signatures as collateral he bought a tailored suit, new shirts, a necktie, a hat, and an overcoat, all in harmonious blue. He couldn't stand the thought of wearing anything close color to that army gray.

By Saturday night he had settled happily back into his old routine at Sirkka's apartment, and they had decided that he should stay there until he had enough money to get his own place.

"Aren't you getting ready for the dance?" yelled Sirkka, knowing very well that Otto was just around the corner in the bathroom, already dressed in his new clothes.

They all started talking at once, none of them making

any sense or listening to one another.

"Listen, you girls, what's going on tonight? You're acting so silly . . ."

"We have a surprise for you!"

They were quiet for a second or two, and back and forth at each other in lighthearted conspiracy.

The doorbell rang. "That must be him!"

A tall, lean, and strongly built man stepped in the entrance hall. Otto recognized him as a man he had meet before in Harkola. He was four years older than Otto.

"Hi, Otto. Aren't you surprised to see me?"

Otto's eyes were fixed on the man, who extended his hand eagerly to Otto, his eyes shining.

"Hi, Hannes," Otto finally managed in response to the man's warm greeting. "You're a policeman, I see—I'm glad you're not on duty," he laughed. "Are you joining us tonight?"

"Sure. Sirkka and I have been going together for two months. She has kept it from you, sort of as a surprise," Hannes explained, taking Sirkka in his arms and giving her an affectionate kiss on the forehead.

They went to the Fennia Restaurant for an evening of beer and dancing. After they danced, it was time for the floor show. Although, to the people in the audience, the beautiful young dancer looked like an attractive entertainer from Estonia, she was actually an espionage agent from Leningrad. Her assignment was to flirt with Finnish army officers in the nightclubs of Helsinki, lure them to her apartment, and then use her feminine wiles to elicit as much military information from them as possible.

Within a few weeks this mysterious Estonian beauty was to be secretly apprehended and interrogated by Finnish counter-intelligence. She would eventually commit suicide to escape her punishment. Hannes, working at Helsinki Central Precinct, would learn all the details then. But tonight she was agile, graceful, and elegant.

Otto was enthralled by her charm too, but he was anxious to talk with Hannes and catch up on current events.

"What was the big fuss in the news about Rudolf Holsti resigning and begin replaced by Elijas Erkko as Foreign Minister? He's the publisher of the morning paper, isn't he?''

"Well, Holsti was a good man, of course," Hannes told him, "but not tough enough to be Foreign Minister now that Europe is in such turmoil. The Nazis are rushing in to gain control over as many small nations as they can. We have to have a strong, independent Foreign Minister to stand up to all the political pressures. Erkko is a patriotic, tough man when it comes to dealing with the Germans and the Russians. He is so self-disciplined as to be almost cold-blooded," Hannes said, making his face into an imitation of Erkko's stern countenance.

"The Russians don't want Finland. Why should they?" inquired Otto naively.

"It's the Russians who cause all our sabotage—all the explosions you've probably heard about," Hannes said.

Hannes knew about the political undercurrent that was being kept from the public. He told Otto later about the man who Stalin and Molotov had sent to Finland in early 1938, a month before Otto entered the Terijoki service.

His name was Boris Ivanich. He was a tall, slender, young man, with a broad forehead and a smooth chin. He conversed easily and had a pleasant manner, but his frequent laughter rarely spread as far as his sterm, piercing blue eyes. He had been given carte blanche to deal with the Finns, demanding that the Foreign Minister cede great portions of land in Karelia, and several islands in the Gulf of Finland to Moscow's control. They said it was for the defense of Leningrad against a possible German attack, something that they claimed was brewing in Hitler's mind.

Ivanich had a good knowledge of Finnish history, of the Civil War and its consequences. He knew about the political discrminations against the working class and especially against the outlawed Communists in the country. He secretly reactivated several Communist party groups who then carried his work underground against the Germans of Finland. They helped Ivanich in sabotage, and all the military destruction that Hannes was referring to was of their doing. His main work, however, had been his negotiations with the Foreign Minister. Yet he had been unable to persuade him to cede any portion of Finnish territory to the Russians.

"And what's more . . ." Hannes began, but stopped

abruptly as Anna and Sirkka sighed loudly. Otto and Hannes exchanged glances, and then pulled the girls' to their feet and led them to the dance floor. However much the boys tried though, the thoughts of political struggle were hard to put off.

Only a few weeks later, the morning paper headlines declared, HILTER-STALIN PACT—A Ten Year Non-Agression Treaty Between Germany and Russia!

The documents were signed in Moscow on August 23, 1939, with Molotov, the Russian Secretary of State, and Ribbentrop, the German Foreign Minister, which secretly granted Moscow a free hand to deal with Finland.

When Erkko had taken office as the new Foreign Minister, he did not consider Ivanich, the Second Secretary, qualified to negotiate with him.

"The Germans and Russians are friends now, so Leningrad can surely be in no danger from Germany," Erkko maintained, and Ivanich, trying to initiate negotiations for the purpose of gaining some of Finland's ancient landholdings for Russia, found him totally uncooperative. His refusal to deal with Ivanich necessitated further effort by the Russians: Moscow sent a new emissary, Ambassador Zetkin, to follow up on Ivanich's negotiations.

Erkko knew full well of the developments in Europe. Three hundred thousand Polish soldiers were dead, wounded, or taken prisoner, while the Russians had lost less than three thousand men during their brief but thorough conquest of Poland. He had not been deceived by the recent "liberation" of Estonia, Latvia, and Lithuania. He knew that the Russians had simply used this ruse to accomplish their goals without any bloodshed. The respective governments of these countries had been convinced, or allowed the world to assume they had been convinced, that Russia must occupy their lands in order to protect them from the threat of Nazism.

Zetkin had met several times with Erkko. Their negotiations had clearly defined the specifics for the establishment of Russian bases in Finland on the islands of Ahvenanmaa, on the Hanko Peninsula, and in the Karelian Isthmus. Erkko knew that while France and England had pledged protection to Poland, and had declared war against Germany after

Hitler had invaded Poland, still they had not provided any military assistance to the Poles. And they still had not declared war against Russia, although the Red army had conquered half of Poland. Where could the Finns look for help if the Russians decided to invade Finland? This was Erkko's primary concern, but he didn't yield to Zetkin's demands.

Of course, the Russians were not satisfied.

# Chapter 10

Following his release from the army, Otto repeatedly assured his friends that he would never want anything more to do with the military, nor would he be inclined to keep up with the political affairs of the government. Yet he often became angry with Sirkka's boyfriend. Hannes defended the Army and the government's position in the current political debate about Hitler's effort to gain control of all Europe. Despite his efforts not to show any anger toward his friend, Otto would blush, his breathing would become rapid whenever such discussions took place, and it would mar their evenings together.

Otto had gone back to Akrenius to find a new job in the drafting department. He considered himself fortunate to have landed a job in an office where he wouldn't have to work with presses or other dangerous machinery. The fear of having something happen to his hands had never left him. Otto was content now, wearing white overalls to work, his tools being a pencil and slide rule.

On the evening of September ninth, Otto left work tired from putting in two hours overtime, but pleased with the time-and-a-half rate for the extra work. The increased pay would help him to get back on his own feet and move into his own apartment soon. He even hoped to get a new and better violin.

He elbowed his way onto Streetcar Number Three, at

Eira, in the industrial section of Helsinki where he worked. The fall evening was already chilly, and a heavy gust of wind blew coldly on the Tehtaankatu directly from the ocean, whistling shrilly around Otto's ears until the conductor closed the door behind him. The streetcar clanged along the rails toward Sorkka, stopping at every other corner to add more commuters to the crowd already packed inside. The streets of Helsinki were laced with trolley tracks, where hundreds of coaches moved in a steady formation twenty-four hours a day.

Otto patted his pocket and felt his week's pay, thinking smugly that things were beginning to get back to normal.

He didn't notice the swaying, jostling crowd around him as he indulged in his reverie of the future. He could see it all clearly. When he had his own place he wouldn't have to practice in the bathroom anymore. He and Anna could spend whole weekends together, all alone, if they wished. Sirkka had been unfailingly kind to him, and he appreciated it. But the girls might enjoy their privacy again.

Tonight he would take both Anna and Sirkka out and show them a good time. Where could they go? Dancing at Osakunta Hall or at the Worker's Temple? His violin teacher had insisted that he got to hear a violin concert being performed at the Sibelius Conservatory. He wished they could do both and make a real night of it, but it would cost too much.

The streetcar rolled past the Atteneum. Across the street was the railroad station, filled with people milling about. Finally they reached Otto's stop, Hakaniemi Square. When he alighted there was a feeling of imminent rain in the air, but rather than catch another trolley, he decided to run the five blocks to Sirkka's apartment. He enjoyed the cool wind in his face.

I don't get enough exercise anymore, he thought, chuckling. These days I only run when I want to!

He was puffing when he entered his sister's door, but he had just managed to beat the rain. He stopped inside the entrance to hang up his coat, and Sirkka called out to him from the kitchen.

"Hello! Anna's not home yet—she's working overtime, but she should be here any minute. I just got home from

53

work myself. There was quite a crowd at the restaurant today. I made some good tips. Is it raining yet? Oh, Otto, your mail is on the table in front of the mirror."

Otto idly reached for the white card on the little table.

Suddenly he shouted, "Goddamn it, no! No! I won't go! If they think I'm going back, they've got another thing coming!"

Sirkka ran in from the tiny kitchen, rubbing her hands nervously on her apron.

"Otto what is it? What's wrong?"

"This card! It says I have to report Monday for three weeks of 'general maneuvers' at Viipuri. They can go whistle up their sleeves if they think I'm going back in the army. If they couldn't teach me what they wanted to in fifteen months, three weeks isn't going to do a damned thing for me. I'm not going, and that's that."

"Oh, calm down, Otto. Calm down. You've developed such a temper, and the army didn't do it any good at all, either. It's a shame, though. Just when you were starting to get used to being in Helsinki again . . . But why would they call you back?"

"Who knows what the bastards want! First, just three weeks, then, a month . . . then who knows . . . I'm just not going. I've got my own goddamned life to live, without having to worry if there's going to be a notice from those damn butchers every time I come home. To hell with them! They'll have to come and drag me, kicking and screaming, to Viipuri, because that's the only way I'll go!"

Sirkka listened silently. She knew that her words would not cool Otto's temper until he had let off some steam. He must be calmed down with understanding.

"Maybe . . . maybe it's for a good reason . . ." she started carefully.

"How would you know? You've never been near the compound!" Otto's temple throbbed and his palms were wet. He drew in each breath as if he had just run a ten-kilometer race. His eyes were flaming, and his fist punched repeated blows on the soft couch where he sat.

Sirkka, always good-natured, felt sad as she looked at Otto's rage.

"Three weeks won't be that bad . . ." she began, but

stopped short as she saw her brother's eyes glowing like coals. She would have to appeal to him on behalf of their mother.

"Otto, imagine the shame it would bring in Harkola to our dear mother. The folks there would say, 'His father must have been a communist, since the son is a deserter.' Think of Mother, even if it means making a sacrifice. Think what the gossip would do to her . . . if her son were hunted as a fugitive from the army. They would think of you as the son of a Red who was justly murdered. So, please, pull yourself together, Otto, my dear, dear brother . . . for all our sakes."

In a few minutes Anna arrived home, and seeing her helped calm Otto. After they had eaten, Sirkka's policeman arrived, and they set out to spend the evening dancing, even though Otto's depression darkened their mood perceptibly.

Otto couldn't stop thinking about the train all during that evening, the train that would pull out of the station the next night, carrying him to Viipuri. Long after Sirkka and Anna had gone to bed, he sat alone on the chair in the semi-darkened living room with a bottle of Karhuviina, trying to drink enough so that he could get to sleep and forget his worries. He still felt depressingly sober by the time he had finished what was left of the bottle.

Finally Anna tiptoed in. She looked tousled, but beautiful.

"Otto," she whispered, "this is our last night together for three weeks. Please come to bed. I can't sleep if you're in here all alone. I want you beside me, where you belong."

He allowed himself to be led into the bedroom. Anna made him stretch out on the bed. She undressed him and began massaging him all over, relaxing his tight muscles. When the tension had begun to flow out of his body, Otto began to become aroused, and reached up for her.

"Not yet, darling. Lie still, now."

She stood up and slipped the negligee over her head. He marveled again at her smooth belly, her tiny waist, her round breasts with their brown, pointed nipples. Then, she lay beside him and reached for him.

"Now. Take me now," she whispered.

It was to be a long time before Otto would get to spend

another such satisfying night in Helsinki. As he watched the train platform receding and the waving figures of Anna and Sirkka, he put his head out the window to wave at them. He only prayed that the three weeks would pass soon so that he might return to the life he loved.

# Chapter 11

The train was filled with men who had been called to maneuvers. The noisy protest was overwhelmingly loud from those young men who had been released from the regular compulsory service only a month or two ago.

The men drank, sang songs, and told dirty jokes. In the corner of the coach where Otto sat, a group of a dozen men gathered to sing the protest songs created during the Civil War.

Otto was disgusted with it all and wasn't in the mood to join in the chorus of songs, or to share in the bottle that someone passed around. He sat quietly by the window and watched the rain pelt the pane in the darkness.

Unnoticed by Otto as he sat slumped in his seat was a civilian, two rows behind him, who wasn't going to the reserves. His presence in the train wasn't accidental, but a well-coordinated act of Russian intelligence work. Kalle Kaira, the long-legged runner Otto had seen running at Katajanokka Harbor, was on his way home to the Karelian border. He had been at the Godmother's estate for a meeting with twenty-two other agents and Ivanich. Kaira had been given specific instructions for sabotage among the troops.

Kaira had already been to the Godmother's country home twice before, some twenty-five kilometers north of Helsinki. He had run the twenty steps up to the white colonial frame house, passing the two large bronze elks that guarded the entrance and admiring the fancy ironwork rail on the second floor balcony. The house was an inheritance; the Godmother used it, as well as her income from writing, to help Ivanich reactivate the communist cells after years of operating underground. They were mostly old men whose scars were severe from sufferings during the Civil War. An exception was Kaira, who had lived on the border all of his life and had only heard from others about the Whites' brutality.

Kaira hadn't at first been keen about communism. He had grown to be proud knowing a ''diplomat'' whom he had met at Helsinki's railroad station restaurant while visiting the capital city. Now he had Ivanich's money in his pocket and a brown carton under his seat filled with equipment. He kept his eyes on the men on either side of the aisle and his ears open to hear the mood of the reserves, which was not very militaristic. He was delighted to see reluctant men like Otto about whom he could report to Ivanich.

In their secret, basement meetings, Kaira had learned to remain tight-mouthed. He thought of the meeting from which he was now returning, where he had been schooled in radio operation and bomb making.

Ivanich had been especially pleased with Kaira's enthusiasm, and had given him specific orders.

''On the military side you'll be expected to report with regard to corps, divisions, and brigades, including the names of commanding officers and accurate locations of the Finnish army units. From time to time you'll be given requests for pieces of information that will be vitally important. There may be some drastic actions needed as well, similar to what you did at Katajanokka. You'll do a good job, I'm sure.''

While Otto dozed in his seat and the rest of the men had fallen silent from hours of travel, Kaira remained alert and had made mental notes of the reluctance of the men to enter the reserves. As the reserves disembarked at Viipuri, Kaira stayed on alone, traveling to the border of the Karelian Isthmus.

# *Chapter 12*

A cool September sun greeted the reserves in Viipuri. The barracks were depressingly similar to those Otto had so happily left behind in Terijoki. All the reserves shared the bleak knowledge of what would fill their lives for the next three weeks: dull food, ill-fitting uniforms, and interminable waiting in lines. The only point in their favor was that discipline in the reserves was not so severe as that of the regular army.

A sergeant major was on duty to receive each man's records for the Central Reporting Office. The men lined up in front of his desk at the end of the long hallway. Otto found himself behind a small, husky man.

"Your name, soldier," the man was asked.

"Pentti Joonas Tuoppi, but my mother calls me Pena."

"The army isn't interested in what your mother calls you," barked the sergeant major. "Born?"

"Yes, sir. That's correct," Tuoppi replied.

"I *know* you were born, I'm asking the date of your birth! Don't try to get smart with me, Tuoppi," he cautioned in a stern voice.

"No, sir, I'm not very smart at all. In fact, my mother calls me a dummy."

"What was the date of your birth?"

"I believe it was January thirtieth," he answered timidly.

"What year?" asked the sergeant major.

"I'm just not sure. My mother tells me it was 1917, but my father claims it was 1916."

"Let me have your military passport."

"But sir, I have no papers or passport."

"What happened to your military passport? You were ordered to bring it along with you," the sergeant major lectured.

"I know that, but I had to leave it at home."

"What do you mean you had to leave it at home? Didn't you read the instructions on the card which directed you to report here?" demanded the officer with increasing irritation.

"Yes, sir, I read that, but my mother wasn't home when I left and she had the key to the drawer where we keep our valuable papers. Then I had to leave before she returned because of the train schedule to Viipuri."

"But don't you remember the date of your birthday? Everyone knows that much about themselves," insisted the exasperated sergeant major.

"I am quite sure it must have been 1916," Tuoppi confided, with a little more assurance in his voice than before.

"Okay, I'll write in 1916, but remember to get your papers here right away. If there are any discrepancies, you must bring them to my attention."

"Yes, sir, I'll do that."

"Very well. Now let's get on with it, or we'll be here all day. Are you married, Tuoppi?" Unfortunately for poor Tuoppi, the words in Finnish for "married" may also be used to mean "made love." Tuoppi was visibly confused. There was a long moment of silence. "I asked you a question, Tuoppi. Didn't you hear me?"

Tuoppi looked around shamefacedly, as if for help from someone. "Well, you see, I live way out in the woods where there are no girls . . ."

"Look, Tuoppi, I'm not asking you where or how you live. I'm asking the simplest of questions about your life. You can answer can't you?"

Tuoppi leaned forward and whispered, "If you are asking whether I've ever . . . that is, if I ever . . . that is, made love, you know . . . to a woman . . . well, no, I never have."

The impatient officer stared silently at the man in front of him. Then he marked the space on the form for "single" and glanced at the line of men behind Tuoppi extending far down the hallway.

"It's probably going to take a long time for you to answer, Tuoppi, but what is your profession?"

The man stood silently for a moment. "I work on the farm in the summertime and in the forest, logging, in the winter."

"I didn't ask what your activities are in the summer or winter. I'm simply asking what your profession is. Are you a farmer or not?" he demanded in desperation.

"Oh, no, I'm not a farmer. I work for Mr. Taavis, who owns the ranch. I mainly dig and clean ditches," he explained, after giving it some serious thought.

"Okay, fine. Ditch digger."

After he had finished recording this on the form, the sergeant major looked up. "One more question, Tuoppi, if you can manage it. What are the names of your mother and father?"

"My mother has a different name than I do. You see, she has lived with my father for years and years . . ."

Otto was standing silently, next in line, shaking with repressed laughter. He whispered to the man behind him who was also enjoying the dialogue, "Maybe if we all behave like this clown, they'll send us home."

"Next, please," ordered the sergeant major, waving Tuoppi off to get his supplies. "Your name, soldier?"

"Otto Arno Arola, born October 24, 1916. Here is my military passport. You'll find all the information there up-to-date. The ink hasn't even dried yet on my discharge."

Ignoring the jibe, the sergeant major looked through the pages, recorded the information, and kept the passport. "Corporal Arola, your equipment is in your room, Number 202, Bed Number Eight."

Otto noted that it was the usual barracks, with sixteen bunk beds per room. He made his bed, arranged his gear, and then stretched out. But he couldn't relax. As he observed the activity in the room, where the other men were occupied making their beds and putting things away, he saw the same man who had given the sergeant major such a hard time.

"Is this Room 202?" Tuoppi asked.

"Yes," one of the men answered.

"Where is Bed Number Ten?" he asked shyly.

"There by the window," someone pointed out.

Tuoppi went and sat on the bunk a long time, staring down at his interlocked hands, before he started to make up his bed. Otto heard him murmuring to himself, "The questions that sergeant was asking . . . Imagine . . . me . . . making love to a woman . . ."

# Chapter 13

Otto was resting on his bunk before going into the mess hall, when he heard a voice boom out from the doorway, "Otto, Otto Arola!" and looking up, he saw an old friend towering over him.

"Jussi! Old Jussi Hietala," Otto exclaimed happily, jumping up to pump the big man's hand.

"Yes, sir, it's me! I just had to come on out here and see how you were doing. It's high time we met again!" Hietala laughed, his mirth edged with a slight tone of irony.

"Well, you picked a lousy place for it. I can tell from your sour face that you're as mad as I am about being dragged back here."

"Mad as hell! How do we get out?"

"I don't know. Haven't figured it out yet. I guess we're in for three weeks of maneuvers."

"I hope we don't have to tear this barracks down board by board to get back home," Hietala said threateningly.

Hietala found his bunk near Otto's and started to put his things away. Otto stood by and watched him make his bed, glad to have a friend whom he could vent his anger.

"It's crazy to call us back just to learn some new trick they think they can teach us," Otto complained, his voice low, and rumbling like a bull's.

"I get mixed up with all this talk of Russians and Germans. Did you read in the paper that they signed some sort of treaty last month?'' Hietala asked.

"You mean that ten-year nonagression treaty? Yes, I heard about it. In Helsinki, everyone seemed to think that it would settle things for good. But who can trust the politicians?''

"Our hometown newspaper in Sortavala called it 'pulling the wool over the people's eyes'—whatever that means. Maybe just a lot of talk. But who knows? Hitler and Stalin could have anything in mind, they're so power hungry,'' Hietala mused fretfully.

You don't think there's some connection between that treaty and our being called back in, do you? Hietala, I can't see it! Neither of those two countries needs any help from our reserves.''

"Whatever they did or didn't do, and whatever the reason, all the maneuvers will be good for is shooting off a lot of blanks. A lot of fun that will be in this cold, rainy weather. I'd rather be fishing in Saimaa or Paijanne, and getting ready to go out to the logging camps,'' Hietala said. "Something worthwhile.''

Otto's eyes lit on Tuoppi, who was still making his bed on the other side of the room.

"Tuoppi,'' Otto called, "you don't have to worry about how your bed looks. There are no inspections in the reserves. Just lie down and get used to a hard bunk again.''

"Call me Pena,'' the stubby little man replied. "That's my name. Pena is what my mother calls me . . . I don't feel much at home here, myself. I never did feel at home in the army, anyway.''

"You mean you don't like the army?'' Otto feigned amazement. "But we all love it! We adore the uniform and everything that goes with it. Don't we, Hietala?''

"Hell, yes,'' agreed Hietala, joining in the game. "I can't begin to tell you how much fun it's going to be. Just look at these handsome tailored uniforms they made for us! The girls will go wild over you—don't you think so, Tuoppi?'' he asked in mock seriousness, jumping around to model his wrinkled uniform.

"You don't like me, huh?'' Tuoppi asked, crestfallen as a puppy that has just been disciplined. Otto and Hietala realized that the man wasn't used to being teased.

"I hardly know you," said Hietala. "I wasn't making fun of you. I was saying that the girls are going to go mad over us all, just you wait and see. Speaking of which, why don't we go into town tonight. I'm curious about life in Viipuri," he said, striding to the door. He turned and waited for Otto and Tuoppi.

By the end of their second day there had still been no word about passes or furloughs. The men had nothing to do, and soon every room in the barracks had two or three continuous poker games going on. The second evening, Otto looked up from his cards and spied another Jaeger Compound alumnus peering in the door of Room 202. It was Elmer Aalto, the young blacksmith with the grease-blackened hands.

"Hey, Elmer, is that you?" Otto shouted.

"Hi, Corporal. So they got to you too? I'm glad to see that civilian life wasn't too much for you. And there's old Hietala. Damn, the whole Terijoki gang is here. What's going on? How come we're all here at once?"

"Maneuvers, Elmer. You know, 'left, right, present arms' up and down the field and all," Otto laughed sarcastically. "As if we didn't know how to hide behind a stump when someone's shooting at us!"

"Well," Aalto laughed, "I can see they've got you guys working on some tough maneuvers right now. Mind if I take this seat and try my luck?" He gestured at an empty seat at the table.

"No, not at all," Otto said, waving him to the chair. "Make yourself at home."

Hietala came in and greeted Aalto. "Elmer, my boy, I'm glad you heard we were having a reunion. Arola, did you see the new bulletin? We're free to come and go outside of the barracks as long as we make it back within an hour after they blow the whistle for maneuvers. Let's get out of here."

"Let me try one more game," Otto shouted. His thought was to bluff, and he did.

"I'll raise the pot by twenty markkas."

Silence followed the announcement of such a raise.

"I'll double that," said the man facing Otto.

"Raise it fifty," Otto said, and realized that he was the

only one betting against the man. He remained calm, and prepared himself for the loss, but suddenly the man threw his cards on the table and Otto scooped up the money. "Let's go!" he said to Hietala. The two started toward the door.

Just before they walked out, they noticed Tuoppi sitting forlornly on his bunk.

"How about a good-looking broad, Pena?" Hietala asked him, not knowing that Tuoppi had confessed to never having been with a girl.

"My mother warned me about the city girls. She said they're not healthy," Tuoppi answered.

"Don't ask your mother, damn it. We're in Viipuri and might as well live it up!" Hietala told him.

The three took off, leaving thoughts of the army behind them. Despite the beauty of the town, the Viipuri Castle, and the Fisherman's Wharf, the three men weren't in the mood to take advantage of cultural opportunities. They headed straight for the Round Tower Restaurant, which was brightly lit and emitted loud music and raucous laughter. Inside, it was packed with reservists who had arrived before them. Finally, a pretty, dark-haired waitress led them to a table on the far side of the large room.

"Gentlemen," she said, once they were seated, "what can I bring you?"

"Beer for all of us," Otto said. As the waitress turned to go, he leaned over toward Hietala. "She's something!"

"When you're in the army every girl looks inviting," Hietala commented sagely, watching the waitress walk away. She glided effortlessly in her tight blouse and skirt, with smooth wave-like motions of her hips, oblivious to the appreciative looks that followed her every move.

"Here are your beers," she said upon returning. She had a light, lilting quality in her voice and twinkling eyes. Otto was so charmed that he couldn't resist lightly touching her wrist and asking her name.

"Johanna," she replied quickly and smiled at him.

"You have a pretty name," Otto said, trying to ignore the pounding of his heart and hoping that his voice sounded casual.

She smiled again, and then moved to the next table.

The sound of soldiers' voice heightened and became almost a roar. Every table in the place had four or five men crowded around it, but there were only a few girls in the entire place. Soon every stool and chair were pressed into service for the big crowd. The few waitresses rushed back and forth from the bar to bring more drinks. Soon the revellers burst out in boisterous songs, accompanied by much drunken laughter.

As Otto and his friends started their fifth round of beers, Otto noticed that Tuoppi was beginning to look glassy-eyed.

"You'd better make this one your last, Tuoppi. Beer can be very deceiving—can knock your feet right out from under you if you aren't used to drinking much of it," Otto advised.

"I'll be all—hic—right. But I can tell that I'd better slow down. This stuff is longer . . . er, stronger than the brew that my ma makes back . . . home."

Otto's eyes lazily followed Johanna around the room as she waited on the various tables. His reverie was interrupted when he saw three officers who looked familiar to him standing at the entrance. He made out their features through the haze of smoke, then stood up and walked over to get a closer look, just to be sure. His pace quickened as he recognized old friends.

"Hello, boys!" he sang out.

"Arola, you old bastard," laughed Aku Harma, grabbing Otto's shoulders and shaking him gleefully. Helberg and Koskela were equally happy to see him, and the four men stood in the entranceway, laughing and joking. A waitress soon asked them to move out of the doorway, so Otto led them to his table. Hietala and Tuoppi looked startled to see the second lieutenants approaching them, and Hietala started to get up.

"Hey, you don't have to stand up for us." Helberg stopped him. "We're reserves just like you. We're not in Terijoki any more, thank God!"

Otto introduced them all. Then he voiced his curiosity about recent happenings.

"What's really going on around here? Are we here to spy on the Germans, or to fight the Russians, or for no reason at all?"

"That's nonsense!" Koskela chastised him, as patriotic as ever. "You're never wasting your time if it's spent in the service of our country."

"You're a little overwrought, as usual, Koskela. You'd better have a great big mug of beer to soothe those frazzled nerves," Otto laughed, and the men began catching up on what each of them had been doing in the interim since leaving Terijoki.

Hietala remained ill-at-ease in the present of the officers and spoke little, while Tuoppi, his eyes nearly closed and his chin dropping intermittently onto his chest, apparently felt nothing at all.

"I'd better get Tuoppi back to the barracks," Hietala said, glad for any excuse to get out of the awkward situation. "I'll see you in the morning, Arola." He nodded to the three officers as they told him goodnight and then half-walked, half-dragged his drunken companion out of the restaurant.

"I get the feeling," Koskela said, nodding toward the departing Hietala, "that your friend felt uncomfortable being around us."

"You're right," Otto replied with a shrug of his shoulders. "He did, and I can't blame him either. He doesn't like the army or its officers any more than I do. He thinks that all officers are equally responsible for dragging us back into the reserves."

"We're just as angry as you are, Otto!" Helberg insisted. "We only had five weeks off before they called us back. At least you have a couple of months. They haven't told us any more than they've told you. 'Maneuvers' is all they'll say. Why did they bother to let us out at all?"

"That's right, Otto," Harma agreed. "All we hear are rumors. Just the regular line of nonsense."

"Wait a minute—you don't have to explain anything to me!" Otto said. "I made the mistake of trying too hard once, thinking I could use the army instead of the other way around, but they just screwed me every time they got the chance. So that's it. I'm just going to ride this one out nice and easy."

"I don't blame you," Harma said seriously. "In fact, when I got my call-up card in the mail, I wondered if you'd gotten one, too. I really didn't think you'd report for duty, not after what they did to you the last time."

"Well, after fifteen days in that cesspool they call a jail, I figure this is a hell of a lot better."

Koskela quietly listened to the others, but gave no comment.

The men drank a few more rounds and, as closing time approached, Harma suggested that they all be on their way. Otto declined, saying that he'd like to drink one more beer. He wished his friends goodnight.

He had decided to ask Johanna if he could walk her home. She was on the far side of the room, and Otto waited patiently, slumped in his chair. When he saw her glance in his direction, he waved his empty mug in the air at her. She came over.

"Another beer, Corporal?" she asked attentively, still smiling, but her voice showing signs of fatigue.

"Johanna . . ." he said slowly, trying to appear sober, "I was wondering if I could walk you home after work . . ."

"I'll get you another beer," she said and walked off toward the bar, then returned with the order.

"What's your name?" she asked, setting his beer in front of him.

"Otto."

"Well, Otto, you can walk me home, I guess, but that's it, okay? Just to my door, and then you're on your way. You look like you could use a good night's sleep, anyway."

"When do you get off?"

"In about half an hour. Can you wait that long?"

"Sure."

When Johanna got off work they ambled along the street, and the cold wind blowing in from Viipuri Bay helped to clear Otto's head. He gave her a brief summary of his army life. She spoke very little. In about fifteen minutes they were standing in front of a modest brick apartment building.

"This is where I live, Otto. Thank you very much for escorting me home," she said, extending her hand toward him, which he accepted, pulling her toward him.

"I said you could walk me home, but that's all. I should have told you before—I'm married."

"That's okay. I'm not the jealous type," he said, trying

69

to kiss her.

She pushed him back gently. "Really? Well, he is. Very jealous."

"Then how come I'm walking you home if he's so damned jealous?"

"He's in the reserves too. He was shipped to Andrea six days ago."

"Well, that's life, I guess," Otto said, still holding Johanna's hand and drawing her closer and closer to him, until he finally got his arms around her.

"I told you not to do that," she said quietly.

"I'm sorry, I must not have heard you," Otto said, and gently brushed her warm, full lips with his. "Look at this building. It's too dark. I can't let you walk into the darkness all alone," he said, leading her through the entrance to the hallway inside.

"Otto, you promised . . ." she started to say, but he muffled her words with his lips.

Hours later, Otto walked through the empty streets back toward the barracks. He felt overjoyed with his new acquaintance. "Maybe Viipuri won't be so bad, after all," he was thinking. He felt a little twinge of guilt over Anna, but then he thought of his unfortunate fate—first landing in the army, and now the reserves. Otto brushed aside his guilty feelings. Surely he deserved some fun!

# Chapter 14

Otto enjoyed Viipuri because of Johanna. Yet he was becoming more and more restless with the passing days, as were the other reserves. Days turned into weeks, and the weeks began to pile up. The men waited impatiently for the "general maneuvers" that never began. Helberg, Harma, and Koskela had been shipped out to supervise the digging of trenches for some expected military exercises beyond the Andrea region, but most of the men, including Otto, Hietala, Tuoppi, and Aalto, remained at Viipuri. They avoided boredom by playing poker incessantly. Occasionally, when he had lost all his money at the card tables, Otto was too broke to go into town and nurse a beer at the Round Tower, but most nights found him sitting at a little table, waiting patiently, winking or smiling at Johanna as she hustled past him, carrying trays loaded with beer.

One day, with only fifty markkas left, Otto decided to take his chances once again at the card table. He knew that if he lost his little remaining money, he wouldn't be able to go and wait at the restaurant for Joanna to finish work. But playing cards was habit-forming, and it grew on him just as it did on the rest of the reserves.

He borrowed a little money from Hietala and sat down at a table with four recent arrivals, taking the place of a disgruntled private who had just dropped his last two hundred markkas to a sergeant named Kosti Pelto in a game of five-card draw.

The cards were handed to Otto to deal, and he called five-card draw again. It was a good game to break into action with, and to get some idea of how the other players handled their cards. Otto dealt and waited for the man on his left to bet or pass. He bet one hundred markkas, as did the others. Otto gave them each the number of cards they wanted to replace in their hands. He kept two kings and drew three cards for himself: a seven, a ten, and another king. The man to his left bet again, as did the others. Otto called him and raised the amount of the bet to double.

Only Sergeant Pelto stayed in the game. He looked at his cards and took a long look at Otto's face, trying to discern whether he was bluffing. He called Otto's raise and raised again. Otto called and put his three kings on the table. The sergeant had only two pair, jacks and fives. Otto raked in the money with both hands, unable to restrain a smile of satisfaction.

"Let's try the same game again," said the man to Otto's left as he shuffled the cards to deal.

Otto spoke only when someone spoke to him, and listened to the sporadic chatter around the table without comment. He wasn't surprised that the conversation seemed to center around the general discontent among the men, the boredom they felt during their extended stay at Viipuri, and various schemes that some had employed, successfully and unsuccessfully, to try to get out of the reserves.

"One lieutenant got discharged just the other day," Sergeant Pelto was saying, "because he was the sole support of his parents. He applied for the discharge about two weeks ago, and by now he is long gone. I'd try the same thing myself but I've got three older brothers, all civilians, and all well off," he laughed. "Just my luck!"

Although Otto remained silent, he became highly agitated at hearing about this kind of discharge, and bright red spots brightened his cheeks as his excitement grew. The sergeant seemed to know what he was talking about, so Otto decided to speak with him after the game.

Perhaps the adrenalin caused by his excitement gave his poker playing the impetus it needed; at any rate, Otto was three hundred and fifty markkas richer by the time the game ended a couple of hours later. He offered to buy Pelto a cup of coffee. The sergeant accepted readily and the two men introduced themselves as they walked over to the canteen.

Pelto was also from Helsinki, and was just three years older than Otto. He was a large, heavyset, handsome man with a great walrus moustache. He had a ready smile, and a voice that boomed when he laughed or raised it to emphasize his meaning. They had a good time sitting in the canteen, discussing their life back in the neighborhood, their jobs, and their girls. It turned out that Pelto's home was just two blocks from the Hakaniemi Square and that he knew Porthan street, where Sirkka lived. Inevitably, however, the conversation turned to the army and what was in store for them.

"Hey, how much do you know about this discharge business?" Otto asked. "You know, the one you can get if you are supporting a dependent. How do you go about applying for it?"

"Arola, all I know is what I already told you about the lieutenant. Why? Are you eligible? I guess you just have to go and apply at the sergeant major's office, that's all."

Otto told Sergeant Pelto of his unpleasant experience in the regular army, and how anxious he was to get back to Helsinki. He told him that he had a widowed mother.

The sergeant said, "Hell, it sounds like you could get it easy. It sure won't do you any harm to apply. Maybe you'll be out for good in a couple of weeks."

Otto stood up and shook Pelto's hand warmly. "It was good meeting you and thanks a lot for the information."

"Don't mention it. I hope it works," Pelto replied. "Maybe sometime I'll drop by your sister's apartment and see how things turn out for you. Good luck!"

Otto was in good spirits after filling out the application and winning so much at the poker table. The only thing that dampened his hopes of receiving a discharge was the fact that his mother's civil rights had been revoked because of her husband's alleged participation in the Civil War. He wasn't sure whether this might prevent him from succeeding, so he was careful not to get his hopes up too much. He went to find Hietala and Tuoppi to see if they wanted to go to the Round Tower with him that night.

During the following week Otto's money dwindled away as if he had a hole in his pocket. He had sent fifty markkas to his mother, bought his friends beer, given Johanna a gift, and lost the rest again playing poker. He was sitting in the canteen complaining about it to Hietala, when a young lieutenant approached their table.

"Corporal Arola?" he inquired in a brisk, military voice.

"I'm Arola," Otto answered without saluting. The lieutenant looked a little frustrated, but he did not try to intimidate the two men. He knew it would be useless.

"The quartermaster major wants to see you immediately," he said sharply.

Otto looked at the officer with a question mark written across his face. "Thanks very much, officer." Then he remembered his application.

"You know, Hietala, it just might be that my discharge has come through! I think I'll run over there and find out. Wish me luck!"

The quartermaster's office was filled with men, some milling about and others waiting in line to receive papers. Most were grumbling and cursing.

He felt a chill as he realized that they were being shipped out! Then a set of papers was shoved at him and he learned, to his dismay, that he too was being shipped to Kuuritsan-suo, way off in Karelia. He'd never even heard of it before. He walked back to his barracks, dazed and disappointed. Now there was no chance of an early discharge.

"Shipped out," he kept mumbling through clenched teeth, unwilling to accept the reality of it.

He felt like a robot, mechanically packing his belongings. Hietala kept firing questions at him, but Otto didn't hear them. His mind buzzed with rage and a feeling of helplessness. Finally, after he had crammed all of his gear into the rucksack, he sat down on the bunk and tried to collect his thoughts. Hietala had become silent, waiting for Otto to speak.

"Hietala, do me one last favor, will you? Say goodbye to Johanna for me."

"I'll do it this evening."

"Well, where the hell is Tuoppi? Say goodbye to him

74

for me, too, will you? And Aalto.''

"Don't worry. I'll take care of it.''

"Okay,'' Otto said solemnly, shaking his friend's hand as if he didn't want to let go of it again. "Take care of yourself. I'll see you around, I hope.''

He threw the rucksack over his shoulder and went back to the quartermaster's office, where he was to board an army bus. It had not arrived and they were told by an officer that the bus would be four hours late.

"Be here at eleven o'clock sharp,'' he warned the men.

Otto rushed to a bus stop and headed into Viipuri. He knew that Johanna had the night off and went directly to her apartment. He knocked and waited. His face broke into a happy grin of relief when she opened the door.

"Otto,'' she smiled, and they embraced before she had even closed the door. He kissed her, almost with desperation.

"I've come with some bad news, Johanna. I'm being shipped out tonight, God knows where.''

"Oh Otto, I'm so sorry to hear that! We've had so much fun together—you know I'll miss you. Let me get a bottle, and we'll have a farewell toast, anyway.''

He watched her with an aching heart as she went into the kitchen. In a moment she returned with a bottle of Jaloviina.

"To your safe and quick return,'' she said.

"I'll really miss you Johanna, I enjoy being with you so much. I'll think of you often, you know.'' He put his arm around her shoulder and pulled her to him.

His lips found hers. Her tongue was in his mouth and his excitement grew. He unbuttoned her blouse, and felt her nipples harden under the light touch of his fingertips. His left hand traveled slowly down her stomach, slowly down her smooth skin. Her small panties slid off easily. Suddenly her hips thrust up against him and he was on top of her. They both gasped with excitement, then satisfaction.

Later, they sat together sipping brandy and coffee.

"Are you hungry? I can make you a couple of sandwiches before you go.''

"No, that's all right. Don't move. Just let me hold you for a moment longer,'' Otto said, sadly and quietly.

75

"You've been very kind to let me spend my last hours here. It has meant so much to me."

He got up suddenly, knowing that he must leave now or he might never go back at all.

"You might think I'm crazy, Johanna, but I must tell you how much I like you—how much . . ."

She stood up, too, and kissed him.

"You're young, Otto, and you have a bright future ahead of you. I've enjoyed knowing you, too, but now we must go on without each other. Take care of youself and be brave."

"Goodbye, darling Johanna. I must go back or they'll turn Viipuri upside down looking for me. I'll miss you."

Otto made the bus with only minutes to spare. As it pulled out of the camp, he watched the lights of the city disappear, his mind revolving around Johanna.

# Chapter 15

Shortly before dawn, Otto was gazing out the bus window as it headed directly eastward. They had passed Kyyrola hours before. He had counted fifteen buses coming from the opposite direction, and out of curiosity he asked the driver where they were going.

"They're going back to Viipuri for another load," was the reply. Then the driver added, "I wouldn't be surprised if the whole center was shipped out. I'm afraid that something more than just the maneuvers is going to happen . . . and soon."

Otto sat back uneasily, pondering the driver's ominous words. Damn it, this whole thing couldn't be for real. Probably they'd have maneuvers here, that's all. Otto hoped that this was all he was facing. He wanted to go home.

He leaned his head against the window, trying to ignore the chatter of the man next to him. The roads were bumpy and winding, and the suspension system of the bus was old and stiff. Otto's head kept knocking against the window every time he started to doze off, making it impossible for him to get any sleep.

The bus reached Valkjarvi about seven o'clock in the morning, and deposited everyone except Otto.

"You must be the ordnance officer," guessed the driver.

"I guess that's what I'm supposed to be," answered Otto, somewhat uncertainly.

"Well, I'll have you there in an hour if this old bus makes it," he swore. "One hour for twenty-two kilometers—typical army efficiency!"

When the bus pulled into Kuuritsansuo, Otto stumbled stiffly from the bus into the cold darkness, his rucksack over his shoulder.

Apparently the driver thought some degree of kindness was in order for this single passenger, so he called out in a fatherly tone, "Good luck, boy!"

Otto stood by the road until the bus had disappeared. Then there was silence, punctuated by the bark of a dog in the still morning air, followed by another dog barking, then another. The heavy line of timber that edged the sky cast its shadow on the west. The stars were low, almost touching the trees, it seemed. On the east, toward the border, was a shallow marshland where nothing but dwarfed pines grew. Everything was misty with morning fog, and Otto felt uneasy. A rooster joined in with the dogs, crowing his wake-up song. One light appeared, then far away, another, then a third, then four lights were visible, the only signs of life in the desolate landscape. Otto walked toward the nearest light in a small cabin, about fifty meters from the road. He knocked, then entered with uncertain steps.

Three half-dressed soldiers were sitting around a wood-burning brick stove, drinking coffee.

"I'm Corporal Arola. Where am I supposed to report?"

One of the men turned his head slightly, looking over his shoulder unconcernedly.

"Over at the lieutenant's office." His face, yellowish from the light of the kerosense lamp, was dull and expressionless. "Headquarters is half a kilometer down the road, in a large farmhouse. You can't miss it," he directed impassively.

Otto walked back into the darkness and stumbled along through deep mudholes made by wagon wheels. The only automobiles that had ever come into the area were army vehicles. He found a footpath and followed it. Finally he stopped in the middle of a large farmyard. It was quiet, but he could see lights in the house. There was a barn with a stable. He knocked at the house and entered without waiting for a response. The large room was only partially lit, but he could see four soldiers sitting around a large table, drinking coffee.

Otto again introduced himself and inquired where the office was.

"Across the yard . . . but I wouldn't worry about it this early in the morning, if I were you," one of the men said. "You look worn out. Have a cup of coffee, and catch your breath. We have an extra bunk here that you're welcome to use. We heard that you'd probably arrive this morning."

"Thanks," he said, feeling a bit better now that he had found someone who at least expected him. He threw his gear on the empty bunk in the corner of the living room.

"Have a cup of coffee, Corporal," the same fellow repeated.

"I could use some." He took the coffee and excused himself. He felt like stretching his legs after being cooped up for such a long time on the bus. He walked out onto the porch and leaned against a support post as he sipped the steaming coffee. He could see a few more lights from adjacent farms, five hundred meters down the road, and the outline of what appeared to be tents scattered throughout the barnyard. From the barn, directly across the yard from where he was, the sound of many voices could be heard. There was yelling, laughter, an occasional lull, and then more of the same. He couldn't judge exactly where all the noise came from, but he guessed that they were gathered in the tents around the heating stoves.

He finished his coffee, and as he put down his cup he spotted a rickety chair behind him. He pulled it up closer to the front railing of the porch and sat down, propping his feet up on the railing. He was tired of lamenting his situation; he just wanted to relax and enjoy the crisp October dawn. As he lowered his eyes from the sky, he saw an extremely tall, lanky figure emerge from a small shack next to the barn.

The man was dressed in civilian clothes. He walked toward Otto with such long, loping strides that Otto found it difficult to suppress his laughter. The man had a craggy face that looked as if it had been roughly hewn from stone.

As the man stepped up on the porch, Otto leaned forward in his chair.

"Hello," he said, offering his hand, "I'm Corporal Arola. I just pulled in about half an hour ago from Viipuri. Do you work on the farm?"

The civilian stared down at Otto, ignoring his outstretched hand.

"I'm the Kairas' son," he said in a deep voice.

Otto finally lowered his hand and looked self-consciously down at his feet.

"This is a nice place you've got here," he said, awkwardly, "but I . . . uh—I'd rather be home in Helsinki, of course, but . . ."

"You'd rather be home in Helsinki? Well, I wish you were, too! All of you. We didn't ask you to come here and take over our farm, so if you want to go back where you came from, go right ahead!" The man glared at Otto for a moment, then opened the front door of the house, ducking his head as he went inside.

Otto stood stunned, on the porch. That's one of the strangest men I've ever come across, he thought. I wonder if all the locals are this friendly!

He sat back down in the chair. He couldn't really blame these people for resenting the army. It was true that their farms had been taken over by soldiers, and he was only one more soldier in their eyes. He felt like going in and telling him: "Look, I don't want to be here at all. I hate the army as much as you do, even more! But if I don't do what they say, they'll put me in jail."

He remained outside long enough to see Kaira leave the house and return to his shack. Neither man spoke. Otto finally got up and went into the house, ate some bread and cheese, and lay down to sleep.

Late in the afternoon, Otto reported to the company commander's office and was greeted by the company clerk, Kauko Talvi, a soft, roly-poly man with a jovial personality.

"The lieutenant wants to talk to you, Corporal," he said. "He'll see you as soon as he's through with some of the day's mail and reports."

He waited for a few minutes, then the inner door opened, and Otto heard his name being called. The lieutenant's name was Viljo Salmi. As he walked into the office, Otto saluted rather haphazardly.

"I called you in to give you your assignment," the lieutenant said. "I want you to help my men sight their rifles. Start by taking one squad at a time out to the range. Some have really lousy guns. You can start tomorrow, Corporal."

"Yes, sir, I'll take care of it," Otto said, saluting sloppily again before leaving the lieutenant's office.

Otto walked back into the clerk's office and watched Kauko Talvi waddle around the office, filing papers and straightening up. The clerk talked constantly, but Otto paid little attention to what he was saying. Then he heard Talvi mention "that long-legged guy."

"You mean Kaira's son?" Otto asked. "He's one of the weirdest guys I've ever seen, and he sure didn't go to any effort to make me feel welcome here."

"Oh, you noticed?" Talvi said with a laugh. "He's a strange one, all right. He keeps pretty much to himself, though, and doesn't bother anyone unless he's spoken to."

"How old is he, anyway?"

"Oh, I don't know for sure. Twenty-two or three, I would guess."

"How did he manage to stay out of the army?"

"That's a good story," chuckled Talvi. "The lieutenant says that he got out because he claimed his parents needed him to help run the farm. His father is actually in pretty bad health. But in all the time I've been here, I have yet to see him lift a finger to help his old man. He usually stays in his shack or takes off and stays away for days."

"My mother is a widow and they won't let me out to take care of her," Otto said.

"The army's funny about a lot of things," Talvi philosophized.

"Funny as hell!" snorted Otto.

He walked out the door, but immediately stuck his head back in.

"Where are all the platoons located?"

"Platoon number three are the guys in the tent out behind the hay barn. The first platoon has their quarters at the farm building a couple of hundred meters down the road. The second platoon is by the meadow, and the fourth platoon is the place you first stopped this morning. The kitchen crew is cooking at the neighboring farm, a kilometer down the road,'' Talvi answered with authority.

"Are all the platoons full-sized—four squads in each platoon?"

"Not yet, but more men are expected. I really wouldn't worry about the size of the company unless we end up having a maneuver soon."

"Right. See you tomorrow."

Early the next morning Otto walked out behind the hay barn to see what kind of men he would be working with. They turned out to be his kind of people. One was a rather tall, muscular man whose entire life had been spent at hard labor, logging in the woods or plowing fields. He was Erik Stromberg, and who now become "brew master" for his platoon, producing pontikka in the Kairas' old, abandoned dugout sauna.

"Have a drink, Corporal," Stromberg said sociably, handing Otto a glass of clear brew, which had been blended with sugar water to cut the bite.

"Humm, that's good. I haven't tasted pontikka since I left Harkola, years ago. What are your ingredients, and where do you get them?"

Stromberg looked at the other men, somewhat puzzled by the question.

"Is he on the level?"

"I won't arrest you for making moonshine!" Otto exclaimed, before anyone could say anything.

"Okay, you're in," Stromberg replied, resuming his easy manner. "Have another taste and see if you can guess."

Otto took a sip, rolled it over his tongue and swished it around in his mouth, allowing the aroma to enter his sinuses.

"I have no idea what it's made from, but it's pure. This stuff is good."

"It's made of pure malt and sugar. The finest there is," Stromberg replied proudly, with a lift of his chin. He passed the cup around until it was empty, grinning with pleasure.

"Listen, fellows," Otto interrupted the kind tipplers. He told the men about the lieutenant's orders, saying that he would take them out to the range as soon as possible.

In the First Squad tent Otto joined one of the poker games in progress. "Five card draw," he said, when the cards were passed to him for his deal. He was pleased to discover that the men of the First Squad were terrible players. He tripled his remaining twenty-five markkas in less than two hours. Then he toured the camp and went on to locate the ammunition shed in the backyard, behind the stable.

The next day he took the First Squad to the rifle range at the bottom of a hill, half a kilometer from the farmhouse, to practice marksmanship. The rifles which had been distributed among them were old, Russian-made weapons which the army had confiscated from the Red Guard troops after the Civil War. They were so inaccurate that Otto had to fire several shots before he was able to hit even a large target. No wonder the Reds lost the war, he thought.

"Here," he said at last, "it's pretty nearly zeroed in now. Balance the sight to your own eyes," he said, passing the rifle to one of the men, "and remember to move the front sight toward the last bullet hole, to zero it down."

He repeated the same procedure with each rifle and didn't find a single one in good shape. Some had bent barrels and had to be sighted very carefully before they would fire where they were aimed.

For the next hour the men fired repeatedly, adjusting their sights until they were consistently able to hit the target, which was the size and shape of a man, from two hundred meters away. Otto remembered his own first experience at the Terijoki firing range, and he was pleased. He knew well how hard it was to hit the target with any degree of accuracy.

After the squad had returned to the camp, Otto wandered around aimlessly. When he passed the lieutenant's quarters, he saw Kalle Kaira fiddling at the door.

"Hey you, what are you doing? Is the lieutenant in?"

The tall man jerked his head up, crammed some papers into his pocket and loped away. Maybe he finally got orders to join the reserves, Otto thought, and didn't pursue the matter.

There was something familiar about Kaira, but Otto couldn't pinpoint where he had seen him before. "Well, this is his farm and we don't really have any business being here . . ." He let it go without further thought.

# Chapter 16

Otto didn't like Kalle Kaira, but it never occurred to him that Kaira was spying on all the military activities in the area. Even when Kaira was gone for days, no one thought anything about it.

Kalle Kaira had been discreetly watching the small-scale maneuvers that were in fact being staged at Karelia, near Viipuri, in the latter part of September and first part of October, although Otto and his friends were never ordered to participate. Kaira was relating all the detailed information to Ivanich in Helsinki. The maneuvers revealed the weakness of the Finnish army, there were no cannons or heavy, military hardware. Men wore ill-fitting uniforms and participated rather lazily in the maneuvers.

Otto continued to sight the rifles each day with the squad of men. The men in this remote village were kept in isolation, without radio, newspapers, or news of the other troops. Their only sources of information were newcomers drifting in, and letters from home.

"I have delightful news for you," Sirkka wrote to Otto from Helsinki. "Hannes and I are still going steady, and we are getting quite serious. Hannes has been promoted! Instead of patrolling the streets, he is now assigned to the Intelligence Department. Perhaps we can marry soon!"

Although Sirkka didn't at this point provide any details about Hannes' work, she did so a few months later. Hannes had trailed Ivanich in Helsinki, including his visits to the Foreign Ministry. When he followed Zetkin to Erkko's office, he had heard parts of an important confrontation between the two men while hidden in an adjoining room. He reconstructed the whole thing later for Sirkka.

Zetkin had been disturbed by Erkko's apparent unwillingness to travel to Moscow in order to complete the negotiations that seemed to have bogged down in Helsinki.

"You are deliberately delaying any resolution of these problems," Zetkin had said in accusatory tones.

"We will inform Moscow the minute this matter has been considered through our normal diplomatic processes," Erkko assured him.

"Finland is certainly considering the matter in an entirely different fashion than Estonia did," Zetkin remarked dryly.

"I have absolutely no knowledge of the way in which Estonia handles its foreign policy."

"None of our previous requests to you have met with satisfactory replies," Zetkin complained. "Why don't you travel to Moscow and straighten this all out?"

"We shall send a delegation which will have exactly the same level of authority as I would," Erkko replied evenly.

"We require a quick reply and a delegation with full authority to complete these negotiations. The seriousness of the European situation demands it."

"Our delegation cannot, under the laws of our constitution, sign any documents without governmental authority and the Finnish Parliament's approval."

"Our Baltic region is being seriously threatened by the Germans and we must have an immediate reply," Zetkin repeated.

"Finland wants to live in peace. We have joined the Nordic nations' mutual neutrality agreement. We are a neutral nation and cannot agree to any nation's demands if it would endanger our sovereignty. Russia must realize this. We are ready to negotiate with you, but only under conditions that will not, under any circumstances, pose a danger to our neutrality or to our independence," Erkko responded.

"The Soviet Union has no intention of endangering your neutrality or independence. We have, with our words and actions, demonstrated and defended peaceful coexistence.

We are completely serious in all our efforts to maintain peace. Are you sending your best men to continue negotiations in Moscow?''

''We have selected three men who are qualified and experienced. Two of them took part in the Tartu Treaty negotiations, where our existing treaty with Russia was signed. They are all men who are knowledgeable concerning our constitutional limitations.''

''Estonia is a good example of how peaceful negotiations can be quickly handled,'' Zetkin mused.

''It is impossible to think that Finland would agree to the same arrangements that you seem to have made with Estonia,'' Erkko stated firmly.

''When will your delegates leave for Moscow?''

''As soon as possible. On October ninth, let's say.''

The long letters from Anna and Sirkka cheered Otto, but they also made him homesick, and he was growing more and more disgusted with wasting his time in the reserves.

While Otto continued to read all of their letters several times, the news in Sirkka's recent letters failed to ease his mind—it only confused him. Her last letter said:

''Hannes and I went to the railroad station last night. First there were rumors, then the rumors were confirmed by the radio newscast. Our government is sending delegates to Moscow to negotiate with Molotov about some security matters, although it's not clear just what these matters are.

''At the station there were thousands gathered to see what was going on. Hannes pointed out a man—the same man who always comes into the coffee shop. He said his name is Ivanich. He was sitting at the shoeshine booth and watching the crowd, just as we were. The place was jammed by the time those delegates arrived. Vaino Tanner—you remember him, I'm sure—and Juho Paasikivi, and a third member (Hannes didn't know his name), stepped into the night train for Leningrad.

''The men walked up on the open platform of the last coach. They took off their hats and bowed genteelly in greeting to the gathered thousands. They waved but did not attempt to speak over the noise of the crowd. Then there was a dead silence. Everyone took off their hats and began singing the words to the Finnish National Anthem! Every voice joined in: 'Our country Finland, the fatherland . . .'

"The song exploded from the crowd, while the honored delegates stood bareheaded on the platform. It resounded through the station as a message from the people of Finland to Stalin and Molotov in the Kremlin. As we learned later, it was sung in every Finnish city, town, and hamlet that the train passed through that night, and we heard that a huge crowd assembled to wait for the train at Viipuri, where a similar demonstration took place.

"Hannes believes that the trouble that seems to have flared up between Russia and Finland will soon be settled, and that you will be sent back home. I'm looking forward to the day that you'll be here again. Your loving sister, Sirkka."

Otto laid Sirkka's letter on top of his chest as he stretched out on his bunk, still fully clothed.

Home. I'll be home soon, you wait and see. I'll do it on my own, he assured himself. Then he took Anna's letter from the same envelope, drew the scent of perfume into his nostrils, closed his eyes and thought how of delightful it would be to embrace her right then.

The letters, the thoughts they evoked, the actions that filled his fantasies . . . all these made Otto almost frantic in his desire to return to Helsinki. I must work on getting out of here, he thought determinedly, and went outside.

# Chapter 17

Otto walked aimlessly around the farmyard, and then stopped at the First Platoon camp where he discovered that the men there had created a new enterprise. They were brewing "kilju," a strong homemade beer that they fermented with malt and sugar. Some of the men managed to stay continuously drunk on it; most got a hangover if they drank too much of it. Erik Stromberg of Platoon Number Three always managed to find flour and sugar enough to distill moonshine, so the camp was well supplied with spirits. Otto spent time with one squad after another, playing poker, or sipping kilju or pontikka.

Early one morning in October, a chilly Monday, Otto was delighted to see his sour-faced old friends Jussi Hietala, Pena Tuoppi, and Elmber Aalto, among fifty other crestfallen faces arriving from Viipuri's Reserve Distribution Center.

Otto arranged with the Kairas to find room for Tuoppi and Hietala in the main farmhouse, and he managed to obtain two ragged old mattresses from a neighboring farm. He filled these with straw for his friends. Elmer had to settle in the First Platoon camp.

Otto continued his work at the rifle range, taking one squad there at a time, sighting their rifles for them, and giving them tips on marksmanship. Other days, however, he and his friends went hiking and hunting, enjoying the beautiful fall weather in the Karelian countryside.

One morning Otto took Hietala and Tuoppi out to the rifle range. Hietala examined his rifle when they got there, and he was disgusted by the rusty old Russian-made gun.

"Our fathers lost the Civil War with these damned things, and now they give them to us! Are we going to be losers, too?"

"Don't complain to me," Otto laughed. "Try it anyway—maybe it works."

Tuoppi was examining the rifle in his hands curiously, when Hietala suddenly fired his first shot. Tuoppi jumped back, startled.

"I have never fired a rifle," he confessed to Otto. "Never in my life."

"I thought you'd served your year in the army," Otto said, squinting in puzzlement.

"I served twelve months in the mess hall, washing dishes and peeling millions of potatoes! They never gave me a rifle."

"Great! I'll show you how to use it."

Tuoppi listened to Otto's instructions and then fired his first shot. His whole body jerked backwards several inches.

"This thing kicked me worse than a horse. Damn, it hurts!" he hollered, rubbing his right shoulder.

"I know. You have to learn to hold it very tightly against your shoulder."

"Well, all right," Tuoppi said, resuming his position behind the log.

Otto walked over to Hietala, who had learned to shoot in Terijoki but had never become a good shot.

"What's your problem?" he asked his friend helpfully.

"Look at this damned thing. It's crooked as a dog's hind leg," Hietala replied.

Otto examined the rifle, adjusted the sight, and gave it back to Hietala. Eventually, the big man was able to hit the target consistently.

It was late afternoon when the trio returned to camp.

One morning, before the rest of the camp had managed to leave their warm beds, Otto got up feeling particularly restless. He put up some coffee and woke his two friends. Hietala grunted irritably and rolled over on his stomach, but Tuoppi was more cheerful.

"Good morning, Arola," he mumbled, yawning widely. "What are you doing up so early?"

"I couldn't sleep. Let's have some breakfast and head out to the woods. We can grab some ammo at the hut, and maybe even a few grenades."

Tuoppi got up quickly, dressed, joined Otto at the wood stove, and drank some coffee. Then they grabbed their old rifles, and headed for the hut.

The morning was crisp and cold. The sun had not yet risen over the wooded hills to the east. Otto enjoyed being up at this hour and walking around the deserted farm before there was any activity to show that it was an army post. The only sounds this morning were the barking of a dog and a few bleats from the adjoining pasture where sheep and horses were grazing. The Kairas' old husky came up to them, crouching low and wagging his tail, looking up pitifully for a little attention, and Tuoppi obliged him and spent a few minutes scratching his belly, until Otto pulled him away.

The ammunition shack was a rickety, old, wooden rectangle with a roof thrown over it. The lieutenant had ordered it boarded up and a heavy padlock had been put on the windowless door. The shack was on the far side of the horses' stable, and as Otto and Tuoppi approached it, they were surprised to see Kalle Kaira.

He was adjusting the boards which covered the window. Otto yelled at him and Kaira jumped back, staring stupidly before he turned to run away. Otto ran and tackled him from behind, turned him over, and punched him twice, hard, in the face.

"What the hell do you think you're doing, Kaira?"

Kaira was kneeling, wiping blood from his nose and mouth on his shirt sleeve.

"I was just trying to fix up the loose boards on that window, you bastard!" he yelled, scowling at Otto.

"You just happened to be walking by this early in the day, huh?"

"I was going to do some work on the stable this morning, before you came along and loosened my teeth!" Kaira spit blood and wiggled a front tooth to show Otto the damage.

Otto looked at the gangly man and felt contempt. "I don't know what you're up to, but this is the second time I've caught you messing around where you don't belong and . . ."

"Where I don't belong?" boomed Kaira. "I live here, you fascist! This is my home. You're the ones who don't belong here!" He glared at the two men standing over him.

Again, Otto was astounded by Kaira's outburst.

"I don't really give a damn what you were doing messing around the lieutenant's office. That's his problem. But this ammo shack is my responsibility. So keep the hell away from here, Kaira. I'm going to keep my eye on you, and if I catch you messing around with army property, I'm going to take care of you myself. I don't like you, Kaira. I can understand how you feel about our being here, but that doesn't make me dislike you any less. So just keep away from me. And don't let me catch you around here again!"

"You said it already, *Corporal*." Kaira then walked away, holding his head tilted back to slow the flow of blood from his nose.

Tuoppi was staring at Otto. "Jesus, Arola," he exclaimed, "that was some show! I never knew you had such a temper."

"Well, Tuoppi, it surprised me as much as it did you. That just goes to show what the army can do to you, doesn't it? All that frustration had to come out somehow, I guess. Kaira just happened to give me the excuse."

Tuoppi nodded his head, eyes still wide, not understanding a word of Otto's explanation.

Otto unlocked the door to the shack and found that everything seemed to be in order. Tuoppi stood watching as Otto prowled around the shack.

"Well," Otto finally said, "if Kaira has been in here he was careful about it, because everything looks fine to me."

"Looks fine to me, too," Tuoppi added, anxious to get going.

"Listen, Tuoppi, take some ammo, go ahead out to the range, and get some practice in. Kaira has ruined the morning for me. I'm just going to hang around, play some cards, and probably go back to bed."

That afternoon Otto was lying half awake on his bunk. Random thoughts were running through his head while he twisted and turned, trying to find the most comfortable position. He was listening, in his mind, to a beautiful violin concerto by Sibelius, and behind his closed eyes he watched himself nimbly fingering the strings and drawing the bow fluidly back and forth across them. His luxurious semi-consciousness was abruptly shattered by a harsh voice, and the music ceased.

"Arola, wake up." It was Hietala. "Sorry to wake you, but Talvi just told me that the lieutenant wants to see you."

Otto stretched languorously and propped himself up on his elbow.

"Damn it," he laughed good-naturedly, "I was back in Helsinki playing a beautiful Sibelius concerto on the violin for a crowd of beautiful women, and you had to wake me up Hietala."

He pulled on his boots and walked over to the lieutenant's office. Talvi was sitting in the outer room with his feet up on the tiny desk.

"Hello, Talvi. Does the lieutenant want to see me?"

"Go right in."

He knocked lightly on the door and walked in.

"Hello, Arola. Have a chair."

Otto sat down in front of the officer's desk and pulled out his pipe. Lieutenant Salmi was smoking a cigarette, and as Otto searched his pocket for matches, the lieutenant passed him a lighter.

"You wanted to see me?" Otto asked.

"Yes. Tomorrow a team of demolition experts are finally coming from Viipuri to demonstrate the use of our land mines. I'd like you to open up the ammo shack about an hour after lunch and help them set up their demonstration."

"Sure, I'll be around. I may go out with Tuoppi for target practice in the morning, but we can easily be back here by two."

"Good, good. I hope we never have to use any of those damned mines, but it should be interesting to see what they can do. Have you ever had an experience with them, Arola?"

"No. I've never even seen one explode, but I hear they're

pretty vicious.''

"Yes. Well, we'll find out tomorrow. That's all.''

Otto saluted, and walked out the door.

## Chapter 18

The next morning Tuoppi woke Otto at eight o'clock, handing him a cup of coffee. "How do you feel?" he inquired sympathetically. "You had quite a time last night."

"Last night?" Otto asked, wincing at the throbbing in his head. He could barely remember the kilju he had drunk. "Oh, God, my head is killing me."

"Here, drink some of this. It'll make you feel better," Tuoppi predicted solicitously, putting a steaming cup of strong black coffee under his nose.

Otto grunted, sat up, took the coffee, and began sipping it slowly. "What did I do last night?"

"Besides drinking, you won almost seventy markkas in the poker game. You had to borrow a hundred and fifty to do it, but you wiped out two guys who thought you were too drunk to know what you were doing."

Otto moaned, but he was relieved to know that the night had been profitable.

"Can you eat something?" Tuoppi asked. "There's some hot cereal."

"Just a piece of hardtack, Tuoppi. Thanks."

Tuoppi finally got him on his feet and they headed over to the ammunition shack to pick up some cartridges for the morning's target practice. The crisp morning air began to revive Otto, but he felt sluggish, and knew it would be three or four hours before he really began to feel human.

94

Tuoppi was enthusiastic and cheerful, and Otto couldn't help being infected by his good spirits as they trudged on toward the firing range. Hietala called Tuoppi "the happiest son of a bitch alive," and Otto wondered how this simple man held so firmly to his good nature.

The hike to the meadow was hard on Otto at first, but after a kilometer or two, he began to warm up and feel better. He knew that the exercise and the oxygen were helping to clear his head. Still, what he really wanted was some more sleep. As they plodded up the last hill overlooking the meadow, Otto stumbled and fell, laughing at his own exhaustion and clumsiness. He lay at the bottom of the hill, his rifle by his side.

"You're on your own, again, today, Tuoppi," he said, sitting up and pulling an army blanket from his rucksack. "Take a couple of targets and some shells and have at it. Take your time and don't get discouraged."

"What are you going to do?" asked Tuoppi.

"My friend, I am going back to sleep. Wake me up at noon, please."

Tuoppi blasted away for almost two hours at the fixed targets he had set up about a hundred meters away, taking careful aim, firing, and then looking through Otto's binoculars to see how well he had done. He wasn't doing very well, but he could see a definite improvement since he had begun this regular practice. At eleven–thirty he took a break for lunch, deciding to let Otto sleep a little longer. The sun was shining warmly on the hillside. He huddled nest to a tree and munched on buttered hardtack. Then, propped against the tree, he too fell asleep.

Otto woke up at one–thirty. He jumped up, trying to remember where he was. He also remembered that he was supposed to be back at camp before two o'clock, and realized that there was no hope of making it on time. He spied Tuoppi, curled up at the base of the pine tree and he woke him up.

"You clown!" Otto chided, "you were supposed to wake me up at noon."

"I'm sorry, Otto! I guess I just fell asleep myself."

"Don't worry about it. Talvi has a key to the ammo shack. He can open it up and hand over the mines for the demolition men.''

"What are you going to tell Lieutenant Salmi?''

"The truth. But I guess we'd better get going. You don't want to miss seeing those land mines go off, do you, Tuoppi?''

"No, no. I sure don't,'' he replied seriously.

Otto was refreshed from his nap, and the pair made good time walking back to the Kairas' farm. As they started down the last hill, Otto glanced at his watch. It was two–fifteen. Suddenly, two tremendous explosions erupted from the farmland below, echoing through the pastures and rebounding off the surrounding hills.

When Otto reached the bottom of the hill he could see a crowd of men standing in a clearing, two hundred meters in back of the barn. He reached the crowd, and as he elbowed his way through, he heard the words ''land mines'' and ''Talvi'' spoken by someone.

His stomach turned over and his face paled when he saw the scattered bits of gore on the ground. Two legs lay ten meters away from what appeared to be the trunk of a human body, the chest cavity blown open. Another leg lay a few meters from the smoldering earth, and an arm had been blown fifteen meters away from that. Still further separated from the other members were a leg and another arm. He felt sick, with an agonizing knot in his stomach. His eyes stared; he walked a few steps, swayed slightly, then regained his senses and went on to examine the scene. There was nothing but pulp and blood, covering a radius of twenty meters from the center of the blast.

Several men were vomiting, and Otto, too, fell to his knees, his stomach heaving. Tuoppi put a hand under his arm and helped him back up. Lieutenant Salmi was standing in front of him.

"When you didn't show up,'' he said pointedly, "I sent Talvi to help the two demolition men set up the mines, as they were in a hurry to get to Viipuri. Ten minutes later they were all blown to bits.''

The lieutenant looked pale and stricken. He ordered several very unlucky men to form a clean-up detail and told the rest of the men to return to their quarters. He asked Otto to come to his office in an hour. Otto nodded and returned to the farmhouse.

As Otto lay there in his bunk, the full impact of his part in the tragedy descended on him. He shuddered as he visualized the death scene. His lips quivered uncontrollably with a terrible feeling of shame, as he realized that he was grateful . . . yes, even glad that it had been Talvi and not himself who had died. He knew the others would blame him for Talvi's death. But it had not been his fault, after all. Besides, those men were demolition experts, and they should have known what they were doing.

He continued to rationalize away his guilt and seek comfort in these half-truths, but it didn't erase the reality of it all. He kept thinking of the explosion, and then, for an instant, his mind turned to that other blast . . . the one he had heard at Katajanokka Harbor in Helsinki. In his mind's eye he saw the German ship and the two men running from the scene. One of them had been so tall and long of limb that he was almost comical to watch as he fled. In a flash, Otto realized that the tall, gangly man had been Kalle Kaira. There was no mistake.

Otto bolted out of the farmhouse and across the yard to Kaira's room. He kicked open the door and burst into the shack, ready to drag the man outside and beat him into submission, to drag him back and make him sniff the smell of burned human flesh—to make him admit that he had tampered with the mines used in the demonstration and caused the tragic explosion. But Kaira wasn't there, and Otto hadn't seen him in the crowd that had been around the disaster scene.

Otto sprinted over to the lieutenant's office. The door was open and Otto saw the lieutenant sitting at his desk gazing out of the window. There was a bottle of vodka on the desk and he was holding a cup full of the clear liquid. His eyes were staring straight ahead of him without seeing anything.

"Lieutenant," gasped Otto, out of breath, "I've got to talk to you! I think I know how this thing happened. Kaira . . . Kaira did something to those mines! He set it up somehow, rigged them to go off."

Salmi turned toward Otto, his eyes puffy and red. He had been weeping.

97

"What the hell are you raving about, Arola? What is this about Kaira?"

Otto sat down, and told Salmi about the explosion in Helsinki and the long-legged man he had seen running away. He told him about Kaira's suspicious behavior around the ammunition shack, and about his sneaking around the office where they were sitting.

"I knew I'd seen him someplace, but I just couldn't remember where it was until this afternoon. Those legs of his are hard to mistake. I'm sure it was him that I saw in Helsinki."

"Why didn't you say something to me when you saw him tampering here?" Salmi wanted to know. "I had some papers missing, but I thought . . ."

"I don't know," Otto admitted reluctantly. "I guess I just thought he was some dim-witted clown who was harmless. I just didn't put two and two together."

"Come on, Arola. Let's go. I want you to tear his room apart and I want to see anything you find, that looks suspicious. And I mean anything! I'll go talk to his parents."

"I think that there's a quicker way to make sure that this was his doing, Lieutenant. Let's go over to the ammo shack and take a look at those remaining mines. I'm no expert, but I know how to tell if they've been tampered with."

"Do you know enough to keep from blowing us both up?"

"I think so, because I'm assuming that they *are* booby trapped, and Talvi and those other two guys weren't working under that assumption."

"All right. Let's take a look," Salmi said.

Otto unlocked the door to the shack and entered, very slowly, followed by Salmi. There were only eight mines left, and Otto opened the top box in the stack, carefully lifting out the bomb without distrubing the other cartons.

"Arola, for the love of Christ, take it easy! If you want to blow us up, you could at least do it outside the ammunition dump. No sense in wasting all this stuff," the lieutenant said, sounding as if he were feeling the effects of the vodka.

Otto was glad it was himself and not the lieutenant handling the mines.

"Don't worry, Lieutenant, I think I've spotted the problem already."

He took his knife and slipped the point between the head of a screw and a metal shield which covered the detonator. The screw had been sawed off at its base; only the head and three millimeters of its shaft remained. This loosened the metal shield and made it wobble, so that it could easily press the sensitive plunger and detonate the mine.

"Look at this, Lieutenant! That's all he had to do—just saw off those screws, and as soon as somebody pressed this shield . . ."

"Yes, I see what you mean! I don't want you to take any chances with those damned things. Take them out in the field and blow them up with your rifle. We could probably get some more safety screws, but I'm just not going to take a chance."

"I'll get rid of them right now. You'd better pass the word that they're going to be some more explosions."

"I'll do that. Then I'll go have that word with Kaira's parents. I'd sure love to find that bastard!"

Otto gently set down the mine he was holding, and left the shed, locking the door behind him. He went to find Tuoppi and Hietala. He would need their help if he was going to destroy the mines before it got dark.

To Otto's relief, he found that only three of the remaining mines had been "fixed," and he and his friends cautiously carried them well outside the boundaries of the farm and fired their rifles until the last one had exploded.

When they returned to the farmhouse, Otto was totally exhausted and depressed. He told his companions that he needed to be left alone, and they assured him that his privacy would be respected. Tuoppi reached behind his bunk and pulled out a canteen, tossing it onto Otto's bunk.

"You could probably use this," he said, and left.

Otto sat down on the bunk, opened the canteen and smelled its contents.

"Pontikka. Bless you, Tuoppi."

He lay on his back, with the canteen on his stomach, and tried to organize his feelings and thoughts. But there was no order to them. He felt hatred, grief, guilt, and loneliness. He took a long pull from the canteen and greeted another emotion: self-pity. But he couldn't lose his guilt, nor his hatred, no matter what other feelings swept over his senses.

He continued to bolster his deflated ego with swigs of the pontikka, and soon he began seriously considering various ways he could get out of the army. Desertion seemed the only foolproof way, since his application for a discharge had been denied. Desertion, however, wasn't a very practical solution for one who happened to be billeted in an isolated border village.

I have to get to Helsinki and then make plans. From there I'll have access to transportation, and Anna will help me. Anna will surely hide me, perhaps she'll even come with me when I leave the country. I'll have to leave, if I desert. It'll be the end of my life in Finland.

Through the fog which was slowly enveloping him from the drink, Otto vaguely remembered something he had heard about furloughs. Men who were going to get married got special furloughs. He couldn't remember who had told him about this, but he jogged his memory until he could remember that the furlough was for five days.

Five days isn't much, but it's enough time for me to get to Helsinki, make some plans, and get along. I'm going to do it! Anna will help me. I'll marry her. I'm going to ask the lieutenant for that furlough tomorrow. I can't stay here after today. Not after all that's happened, he thought, taking another long drink from the canteen.

Otto continued to sip pontikka while his mind wavered between his plan to leave the army and his vivid memory of Talvi's death. Within an hour he had worked his way through two-thirds of the canteen, and fell asleep.

# Chapter 19

Otto woke up early the next morning, before anyone else
stirred. He roamed between the tents and buildings, listening to the shuffling sounds of the cows in the barn. He
heard the birds; strangely, they were singing despite the
cold November wind which was whistling through the treetops. His thoughts were in such a turmoil that Otto shook
his head, trying to clear his mind. He tried to reason with
himself, but he could think only that he must see the lieutenant as soon as possible.

Rumors flew through the camp: the Finnish government
was on the verge of reaching an agreement with the Russians . . . the reserves would be discharged soon to go
home. But Otto had a feeling that none of them were true,
that no one would be discharged. He walked back and forth,
trying to calm himself and reach a decision.

Lieutenant Salmi was the most reasonable and least demanding officer that Otto had ever encountered. It seemed
unfair that it was this humane man Otto would have to lie
to—the man he had learned to most respect. He walked
past the door to the lieutenant's office for the third time,
then finally turned and opened the door. He instinctively
glanced around, expecting to see the company clerk, but
remembered that Talvi was dead. Blown to pieces! His
throat tightened.

"It wasn't my fault . . . it wasn't my fault . . ." he

sighed.

Lieutenant Salmi smiled mechanically. "What's the matter? Are you still feeling sick?" he asked.

"Good morning, Lieutenant. I was just . . . ah . . . just going to ask . . ." Otto was having a hard time finding the words. It was hard for him to lie.

He lowered his eyes, unwilling to meet the clear-eyed gaze of the lieutenant. "I was just going to ask if I could go home." His lips quivered nervously but he managed to continue. "You see, I . . . ah . . . I want to get married and . . . well . . . I need a furlough."

Salmi's face faded to a look of wonder.

"You never mentioned that you were engaged, Arola."

"Well, Lieutenant, we only recently . . . ah . . . made up our minds to go through with it. I . . . well, you know, we've been writing each other a lot, and you know how girls are . . . ah, well, anyhow we finally decided to get married."

"Well, congratulations, Corporal."

"Thank you, sir."

"I can give you five days off, but no more. That's the rule. Do you think you'll be able to make it back in five days?" The lieutenant's eyes met Otto's in a curious way. Otto found it hard to look into them directly. He looked past the lieutenant's face instead, thinking about the world that was waiting for him outside of Kuuritsansuo. A new life. His own life again.

"I'm sure I can make it back," he lied.

"You sound a bit doubtful. I'll tell you what I'll do. I'll grant you a five-day furlough, but if you're not back in five days," Salmi said with a straight face, "and it takes you six days, why, still, I won't have you shot."

"Shot!" Then Otto realized the lieutenant was joking with him. Otto managed a feeble laugh that came out mostly air. "Everything has been arranged, sir. I . . . ah . . . I'll be back in five days." He wanted so much to tell this kindly lieutenant what was really on his mind, but he knew that he mustn't.

"Good, good. I'll find out when you can catch a bus out of here and I'll let you know."

Otto left the office, relieved.

Just before the evening meal, Salmi walked over to the farmhouse and found Otto lying on his bunk. "Good news, Arola. There's a truck coming from Viipuri some time tomorrow. You can ride back on it and catch the train to Helsinki."

"That is good news. Thanks a lot, Lieutenant."

"Sure. Well, good luck to you and your bride. What's her name? And congratulations, again. Here are your orders," he said before Otto had time to answer his questions.

The truck pulled in at nine the next morning and headed back to Viipuri at nine–thirty, after the driver had had a bite to eat and the provisions had been unloaded. Tuoppi, Hietala, and Stromberg waved to Otto as the truck creaked and groaned away.

"See you in five days," Tuoppi yelled after them.

Otto looked back and waved feebly. He sat up by the driver and stared blankly through the windshield as the truck jolted along the dirt road.

Less than half an hour into the journey a group of about twenty people—men, women, and children, too—blocked the road. With them was a menagerie of goats, sheep, cattle, dogs, pigs, and horse-drawn wagons. They appeared to have with them all of their worldly possessions. They moved slowly and with difficulty to the side of the road, some of the adults acknowledging the driver's insistent honking with raised fists and angry curses.

"What is this all about?" Otto asked the driver increduously.

"They're being evacuated from the border," he told Otto. "Where they expect to go, I don't know, but I guess they don't plan to get caught in the middle if the Russians make an advance."

Otto looked back at the refugees. This is for real, he thought. I'm getting out of here just in time. God know what's going to happen now.

Before they had even gone another two kilometers they passed another group of families, heading toward the west, too. They must know something I don't, Otto thought. The whole damned border population is running for cover, and the soldiers don't even know what the hell is going on.

The truck didn't pull into the city until mid-afternoon.

Otto was hungry and he went into a small shop where he bought some beef sausage and bagels to eat on the train. He walked to the station for the four–thirty train to Helsinki, and sat waiting to board it. The station was bustling with people as always.

The train started to pull out for Helsinki right on time; but shouting from outside stopped the train. Two military policemen jumped on and roamed from one coach to another. Outside they had left a five-member guard. A stern-faced MP was checking everyone's papers and luggage. Suddenly Otto happened to think, did I or did I not leave the army pistol at Kuuritsansuo?

No, it was in his rucksack. He had forgotten to return it to the ammunition shack, since he had been using it every day for target practice. They will say I stole it, he fretted. The MP was already in the other end of Otto's coach. They were orderly, but they were talking in loud voices. A pair of army boots was found in one man's rucksack. He was put off the train and sent to the line behind the guards.

Then one of the MP's entered Otto's end of the coach. "Have you been checked?" he asked unsuspectingly.

"Yes," Arola lied with a straight face.

There was complete silence, or so it seemed to Otto. He could hear and feel his heart beating through his heavy clothing—it must have pumped two hundred times in that one minute. Suddenly there was yelling from outside and a shot was fired.

"All MP's out!" The order was given suddenly in a loud voice from outside the train. The MP's rushed through the crowd, heading to the platform. Otto stood up; he saw from his window the five guards rushing into the station, leaving the men they had been guarding to stand there alone on the platform.

"All on board!" the red-capped train conductor shouted. The train whistled again and started chugging down the track.

Otto's eyes watched every movement the other soldiers on the train made; he had suddenly been made very alert by the thought of becoming a fugitive from the army, hunted by the MP's. What path of escape should he take? The Finnish wilderness is the first answer, he thought. Then I'll cross the border and travel to some friendly foreign country, maybe even the United States—that's the greatest country of them all. But how? He would have to find a way.

The closer the train came to Helsinki, the more confident Otto felt. He and Anna would decide together. She's a bright girl, he thought. She sees things clearly, and she's independent, too.

He gazed out the window into the darkness, wondering why he saw no lights from the many farms he knew were there along the tracks. When he arrived in Helsinki, shortly after one o'clock in the morning, he learned why.

The entire city was blacked out. He boarded the darkened streetcar for Anna and Sirkka's apartment. As the trolley hummed along the silent streets with its curtains drawn, the only signs of life Otto was able to see as the door opened were faint lights coming from behind black curtains in a few windows. Then he saw that the bars were still going strong. It was a relief to see the doors of one tavern swing open to expel a drunk.

Otto took the stairs to the apartment two at a time. But as he reached the top he paused, nervous at the thought of seeing Anna again. This, combined with his drastic plan to marry her and desert from the army, made his stomach draw up into a knot. His palms felt moist and clammy as he rang the doorbell. It's too late to back out now, he thought.

Soft tiptoeing footsteps made a sandy sound on the hardwood floor as they approached the door from the other side. The door slowly opened, and Anna stood staring into Otto's face in complete surprise. Her eyes were puffy with sleep and a light pink nightgown covered her down to her ankles, although the neckline was open partially, exposing her generous breasts. Her eyes widened in recognition.

"It's Otto, Sirkka! Sirkka!" With that she threw herself into Otto's arms. He didn't bother to remove the rucksack from his back, he just picked up Anna and carried her into the living room. He kissed her and hugged her and didn't let her go until Sirkka pulled them apart.

Sirkka hugged her brother with warm affection. They laughed happily, Otto with his arms around Anna's waist, Sirkka holding onto his right hand.

"Welcome home," she said. She felt warm tears rolling down her cheeks. "We're so happy to see you, and Mother will be so glad, too!"

Otto felt warm and welcome.

"You must be thirsty. I'll go get you something to drink," Sirkka said and departed to the kitchen. She returned shortly with three glasses and a bottle of Karhuviina.

"How long has Helsinki been blacked out? And why? What's going on?" Otto began firing questions at the girls as Anna poured the drinks.

"It's been like this over a week now," Sirkka replied. "Announcements came over the radio. Posters went up everywhere, telling us that we should blacken every window in every room. They say Russian reconnaissance planes are flying over the border areas . . . they say we'll be bombed if the negotiations don't satisfy the Russians. So far our government has refused to give the Russians anything."

"Damn it all," said Otto, frustrated. "We've been out there for two months and we haven't received a scrap of honest news. More and more troops keep pouring in from Viipuri, but none of them seem to have any news about what's going on, either." He shook his head, as if to put away such thoughts. "Well, let's no talk about it any more for now," Otto said decisively. "I want to hear all about the two of you. And how's Mama? How's everything in Harkola?"

Otto sat and listened as the two took turns relating their news to him. Sirkka did most of the talking, Otto noticed, and Anna spoke only when she was asked a direct question. She seemed ill-at-ease.

Several times during their conversation he thought he caught the two girls exchanging glances not meant for him to see. At first he thought it was only his imagination, but when he returned from a trip to the bathroom they instantly stopped a whispered conversation and Sirkka stammered something inane in a transparent effort to appear nonchalant.

"What are you whispering about?" he asked, trying to mask the irritation he felt.

"Otto, I guess I'd better be going to bed," Sirkka said quietly. "It's late. How long are you going to be in town?"

"For a while."

"Oh, that's wonderful! I'll see you in the morning, then, okay? Goodnight." She kissed him and disappeared quickly behind the closed door of her bedroom before Otto could react to her nasty departure.

He stood looking at the closed door. "Anna, what's going on? Why did she leave like that?"

"She just thought she'd better leave us alone," Anna said, looking up at Otto and smiling tentatively.

Otto sat on the couch and put his arm around her. "Anna, my dear Anna," he said, "I want to marry you . . . right away. I'm not going back to Kuuritsansuo. I want you to come with me. We'll go to some wilderness area—then out of the country. I can't stand the army any more. I can't stand being away from you. I need you with me. Anna . . . Anna?"

Anna had turned her face away from him so he couldn't see her tears.

"Anna," he plunged on, "I've thought about this for a long time, and I know that we can make a good life for ourselves. This country is going to hell, and I don't want us to be a part of that. I thought we might stay in your uncle's cabin in the woods until we could arrange to cross the border at Haaparanta . . . into Sweden . . . and then . . ."

"Stop it, Otto!" she cried. "You don't know what you're saying. You don't know what you're doing to me!"

"What are you talking about, Anna? I know this is sudden, but I thought you wanted to . . ."

"Otto, please!" He sat back and waited nervously for her to regain her composure. Her crying finally subsided and she looked at Otto with reddened eyes. Otto had never seen her like this before. She stared sadly at him, and her lips quivered briefly before she was able to master them. There was a slowly growing paralysis, it seemed, and Otto could no more continue than Anna.

"This is the most agonizing moment in my life, Otto," she began, finally. "I have a sick feeling inside even before I tell you . . ." She cried again, took Otto's handkerchief and blew her nose. Then she dried her eyes. Her will seemed to ebb back and forth; she wanted to tell Otto something, but she couldn't bring herself to do it.

"You can tell me anything! I love you. I want to marry you . . ." Otto tried to comfort her, but she pushed him aside. Otto felt how cold Anna's hands were, and moist, like ice.

"Is Sergeant Pelto your friend?" she blurted.

"Sergeant Pelto? Who is Sergeant Pelto? What are you talking about?"

"Well, he came here one night—oh, weeks ago! He was returning to Viipuri and he wanted to know if we wanted to send you a package, or something . . ." Anna sobbed quietly. "He talked about you, your winning manners, your . . . and I was alone in the apartment . . ." Anna could not continue.

"Go on," Otto encouraged her, but he sensed that something was terribly wrong.

"Pelto turned off the lights, and I felt, I thought . . . he was you . . . you only . . . and I couldn't control . . ."

"Did you let him into bed with you?" Otto asked trying to remain calm.

Anna nodded, her tears still running down her cheeks, her hands covering her face and trying to wipe them away.

"Have you got any more surprises for me?" Otto asked coldly.

Anna looked at him again in total dismay. This time Otto's thoughts were racing ahead of Anna's replies. "You're not pregnant, are you, Anna? . . . Oh, God . . ."

Anna turned away from him, unable to meet his gaze. Silence fell like a curtain between them. Otto looked at her first in dismay; then his expression gradually changed to one of bitterness and rancor. He jumped up, pointing an accusing finger at her. "You *are* pregnant!"

"Yes! Why do you think I told you all this?"

Otto turned, facing her, both his hands holding his forehead.

"Oh, God, do I have to believe this? What's happening to me? All this . . . and what for? He began to pace furiously back and forth.

"Where is he now, this fine sergeant? What happened, did the gold on his officer's uniform blind you? Where is he now?"

Anna followed Otto's change in mood, and now his bitterness scared her. She stammered, "I don't know . . . he never wrote me . . . never said where he was going . . . except that he was going to return to Viipuri."

"Is he going to pay for an abortion? Is he? Well, is he? Answer me!"

Anna remained silent. Her eyes grew enormous with fright.

"My God!" Otto said, turning on his heels, facing Anna and bending forward to shout at her, but somehow he controlled his temper.

Anna cowered. She threw herself on the bed, pressing her mouth into the pillow, which muffled her crying to a dull sobbing sound. She buried her face tighter in the pillow, almost suffocating herself. Her entire body shook, and she could feel the impending disaster in her every nerve. Her cries grew louder, then subsided. She moaned again and writhed like a child in pain. Finally Anna raised her head slightly, pleading, "Forgive me! Forgive me, please . . . Otto? Please . . . why don't you say something?"

Otto stood silently, looking at her coldly. There was absolute silence. Anna stared up toward his face. "If you can't forgive me, what will I do? Oh God!" Anna covered her face with both hands, pressing them hard against her face.

"If you had married me, you would have promised to share my joy and my agony, to carry every burden with me . . ." Anna's words grew almost inaudible.

"That was before," Otto replied quietly. "I didn't know, I never expected . . . I wasn't prepared to play father to some sergeant's child. You . . . you . . . you were different then . . ."

Otto tried vainly to tell her of his feelings, his disillusionment and despair, but the more he saw Anna's agony, the more he thought of how she had caused it all herself . . . how she was carrying a child that wasn't his. He felt numb.

"Hold me in your arms, close to you . . . just once more, please, please hold me once more . . . Otto . . ." Anna's last words were muffled by the soft pillow that she drew over her face.

Otto didn't say a word. He slowly drew his hands over his face, and shook his head. Things could never be the same between them . . . never. He turned, picked up his rucksack, and stormed out the door into the darkness.

# Chapter 20

Sirkka hurried toward the back entrance of the Kolumbia Restaurant early that Sunday morning. She was pale and tired from the stress of the night before, but felt strong enough to deal with anything that might come along today. Anna hadn't fared so well, though, and she was still at home in her apartment sleeping when Sirkka left. Anna's eyes were so red and her face so swollen from crying that she had decided against going out that day. Sirkka was very concerned about the two lovers, and she kept hoping that Otto would come to see her at the restaurant to talk about his quarrel with Anna.

The restaurant opened at seven o'clock, and by the time Sirkka arrived a few minutes later there were already two customers waiting. A third and fourth arrived shortly thereafter. The third one was Alexei Ivanich, a regular customer in recent months. Sirkka's boyfriend Hannes stopped to see her this morning and greeted Sirkka warmly. He guessed immediately that something was bothering her, but she didn't have time to explain.

Ivanich was still in Helsinki although the Finns were no closer to agreement with the Russians—despite the fact that they had offered to buy the Finnish land that they desired. The Russians offered twice as much land for trade farther north in Eastern Karelia, but Erkko had replied that Finn's could not and would not lease, cede, or sell the ancient land within her borders to be used for military bases.

Ivanich drank strong coffee and munched a crisp, buttered roll while Hannes kept his eye on him.

Ivanich knew that three Russian soldiers, dressed in Finnish army uniforms, had been sent out to the vicinity of the Finnish border and directed to fire toward the city of Mainila, where Russian troops were stationed. They fired seven shells aimed carefully at their comrades, sleeping in camp, and killed and wounded many soldiers.

A Finnish watchtower sentry reported the explosion as "grenade blasts" to his superiors. The news went out that the Finns had shot up the camp and killed four Russians, and wounded nine others.

"We can only assume that the Finns are using this means to emphasize their refusal to cooperate with us!" the Molotov broadcaster said of the incident. His voice chilled the hearts of the Finns. "A detestable action," he called it. "A loathsome, nauseating provocation. A cowardly and disgusting attack against a neighboring country."

That morning, while Ivanich read his report and the policeman kept his eye on him, the crowd at the Kolumbia kept Sirkka busy and unable to converse with Hannes. While the radio related the news to the world, Kolumbia Restaurant had not tuned in, and all the fury went unnoticed by them.

Sirkka was busy carrying food to the tables, but her mind was filled with anxiety. Otto was still not in sight.

Otto hadn't been near a radio and had heard nothing of the Mainila shelling either. Nor would he have understood its significance if he had learned about it. He was too confused, as he staggered into the third class restaurant at Helsinki's train terminal early that morning, even while Sirkka was watching for him. He was thirsty, hungry, and wanted a bottle of pontikka like the one Erik was probably distilling right now back at Kuuritsansuo. But, of course, no restaurant in Finland would serve spirits of any kind until noon. He had to settle for coffee and a doughnut.

Nobody in the place knew Otto, and he was glad. He watched as men, women, soldiers, officers, and children rushed past the entrance of the restaurant, heading toward the platform for departing trains. His thoughts seemed

112

vague, shapeless, and void of any identifiable content. His face spelled out his hopelessness and misery. He felt hurt inside, as if a sharp knife had cut through his heart. Random thoughts passed through his chaotic mind. Where would he go . . . to Haaparanta, to cross the border to Sweden . . . from there to the United States?

"I ought to see Sirkka before I go," he said aloud, but he didn't feel up to talking to anyone now, not even her. He couldn't stand the thought of spending another minute in Helsinki, where memories of Anna would continue forever to assault him. But which train should he take?

As he let his gaze roam around the nearly empty restaurant, he saw a spider spinning a web in a shady corner of the tall window curtain. It reminded him of the black spider that had kept him company for fifteen days in the military jail at Terijoki. He shuddered at the thought of the penalty for desertion during peacetime—ten years in prison, or maybe even fifteen!

No question about it, he thought sadly, if I take that train north to Sweden, I'll never be able to return to Finland, not even when I'm an old man. Never is a long time. It means living the rest of my life—and even dying—without seeing Helsinki, Sirkka, or Mama and the rest of the family.

Otto thought of Kauko Talvi, and a surge of guilt washed over him like a red tide. Oh, God, he thought, I don't want to go back to Kuuritsansuo . . . I can't! But I don't know if I want to go to Sweden, either. And I can't stay here now. What am I going to do?

By eight–thirty he still hadn't made up his mind. For the past hour he had been sitting in a semi-stupor, while the coffee in front of him grew cold. Then he heard an announcement over the loudspeakers in the station. The train to Tornio, Haaparanta, and Stockholm was loading passengers. He struggled into his overcoat and grabbed his things. Shifting his bundles from one arm to the other, he dug out the change to pay for his coffee and then stumbled out of the restaurant and made his way to the ticket window. Standing in line to buy the ticket, his thoughts became clearer.

To hell with it. I'll just disappear. I'll give it all up and start over again. Why not? I've lost everything in the world.

My freedom, my fiancee . . . Now I might as well get lost. I'll start with a different name, a different country a different . . . "Pardon me?"

The man behind the ticket window was looking at him curiously.

"I said you're next, Corporal. Where are you going?"

"Oh—give me a ticket to Tornio and Stockholm, please."

"All right, that's eighty-two markkas. Boarding right now on Platform Four. But why are you paying for your ticket? You're a soldier, don't you have travel orders, or free travel vouchers? And by the way, you'll need to have your foreign-travel passport and your military passport handy. The MP's are checking everything. There have been some arrests, you know, of phony soldiers. You know what I mean. You've heard the Mainilla newscast . . ."

"I don't know what you're talking about," Otto said, elevating his eyebrows in surprise as he looked at the ticket seller.

"Haven't you been listing to the news on the radio—about Mainila?"

"I've been up—on the street—traveling all night," Otto began to tell the ticket seller but was interrupted by another traveler.

"Pardon me, Corporal, I must catch the train to Tornio. Please, may I get ahead of you?" said a thin man standing behind Otto, who then placed his hand rather suddenly, and a bit heavily, on Otto's shoulder.

Otto reacted in fright. He thought the man behind him was trying to grab him. He whirled around and planted his fist firmly in the man's stomach. The man was caught completely by surprise, moaned, and then quivered violently, falling to his knees and crumpling onto the floor.

"Hey, what's going on?" the ticket seller demanded, but Otto had panicked. He scooped up his things and dashed wildly out the terminal's side door, rushing toward the nearest train, any train, in order to get away from the police who were sure to search the place as soon as the ticket seller gave the alarm.

Otto managed to grab the iron bar of a departing train before it pulled out of the terminal, and threw his things on board with a surprising force, born of sheer panic. He stayed crouched like a hunted animal until the train was out of sight of the station. Then he stood up. He took a deep breath and felt the cold November air on his face.

The door opened, and a tall woman stepped out on the passageway. He carefully avoided looking at her.

"Cigarette, Corporal?" the woman asked, raising her black eyebrows and extending the package of cigarettes toward Otto.

"Thanks," he finally answered, after a long silence. His voice was almost quivering with fear.

Otto had difficulty lighting the cigarette in the strong wind, but he finally succeeded. A mild pink color spread over his face as he inhaled the smoke and looked directly at the woman for the first time.

"Where are you going, Corporal?" she asked in an even voice, not out of eagerness, but merely in order to have something to say.

Otto didn't reply. He didn't want to say he didn't know where he was going.

"Returning to the reserves," he finally lied to her, relieved that he was safe at last from that question. "What's your destination?" Otto asked her politely, trying to learn where the train was headed, or at least in what direction he was going.

The lady pulled in the heavy smoke and blew it out again, inhaling only every third or fourth pull. Otto stood still like a window mannequin before her. Finally she took the cigarette from her lips.

"I'm returning home, too—we might have to evacuate the city. Who knows what'll happen after last night's incident. Viipuri is going to be a dangerous place to stay, I'm afraid."

Otto didn't know enough about the Mainila incident to venture an opinion. He turned his back toward her, unwilling to let her see the surprised expression on his face.

Viipuri—damn it! I didn't . . . I wasn't going to . . . He fingered the button on his overcoat. He couldn't find anything appropriate to say.

"The army is going to need every man, old and young, and all of the women who've joined up, too. I know—I'm

115

a Lotta myself, although I didn't wear my uniform for this trip.''

The door opened again. Two soldiers with military-police armbands walked onto the platform.

''Your papers, please, Corporal,'' the taller man said to Otto. Otto was confused. What could he tell them? He felt in one pocket, then another, but couldn't find his papers.

''Look in the rucksack,'' the shorter man prompted him. The blood surged into Otto's face. He felt hot in the cold breeze. He was sure he hadn't left his papers at Sirkka's apartment. He tried every pocket, then the rucksack. Finally, he opened a small outside pocket ont he rucksack, retrieved a large envelope, and turned the entire bundle over to the waiting MP.

Silently the man looked over the papers. ''You should have had these stamped at Helsinki . . . Hmmm, as a matter of fact, you have four days left of your furlough. I must compliment you, Corporal, for returning to duty right after the news of Mainila, although no one compelled you to do so.'' Both soldiers then saluted Otto, who stood dumfounded.

''Well, you surely are to be complimented for your patriotism Corporal. Few soldiers would be willing to cut short their furloughs to return to duty.''

Otto stared blankly at the woman. Her eyes were warm and shining. They spoke more about Mainila and then she went back inside the compartment. He began to feel different from the way he had felt when he ran from the station. His fear that the MP's were after him was beginning to fade away. He was feeling more self-possessed, but he still wasn't sure what he really should do. He debated within himself. He suddenly realized that he could take a train from Kouvola, or from Lappeenranta just as well, to Tornio and Haaparanta for Sweden . . .

Otto was getting a little cold. The November breeze forced its chilling way through his heavy army overcoat and finally forced him inside the coach. Only one seat was vacant, next to the Lotta whom he had already met. She was busily chatting with another Lotta, this one in uniform, seated beyond her.

''May I?'' Otto asked politely, pointing with his finger

to the vacant seat.

"Why, most certainly," she said. Her face beamed with a wide smile, as she told her companion about Otto's patriotism.

"Shut up!" Otto wanted to yell at them. His mind was occupied by thoughts of escape from the army . . . from the country, even.

The tall cigarette-puffing lady smoked one cigarette after another. She smiled at Otto occasionally. Suddenly she asked the other Lotta, "How is your father, the colonel?"

"He's fine. He's still in Helsinki, at the chief-of-staff's headquarters. That place has been like a madhouse ever since Mainila. They just issued an all-points bulletin to shoot all deserters, even all suspects. I think it's a disastrous situation."

Otto's face turned scarlet. He was visibly shaken, and he was sure that they could hear his heart pounding wildly. The train sped along the tracks, clacking an even rhythm, the hard wooden seats bouncing up and down evenly. He gazed fearfully at the two Lottas, but they were facing each other and didn't see Otto's frightened look.

"Shot . . . killed . . . without question . . ."

Kouvola, Lappeenranta, then Viipuri. The train pulled into the station at Viipuri with Otto as a reluctant passenger—this was the last place he would have chosen for his destination. He tried vainly to muster a weak smile to cover his dismay and confusion. He thanked the Lotta for cigarettes and politely wished them well. The words came out mechanically.

Well, at least I have four days left of the furlough. Maybe I can decide what to do and get going while I still have time, he thought to himself, boosting his morale. He began to think of Johanna. Four days left on the furlough, and Johanna would be at the Round Tower Restaurant.

Otto arrived at the Round Tower and looked around, trying to find Johanna. The restaurant was as crowded as ever, and it took some time before he decided that she wasn't there. He asked the pert young blond who brought him his second beer, and she told him that Johanna had three days off. He sat there and emptied the mug. Time passed and he finished another beer. His indecision became

117

almost unbearable.

There will be a train toward the North, through the Kuopio, he thought. But how am I going to get there on pure luck? Maybe by clever lies? Otto knew he wasn't very good at lying. My mother raised me to be honest, he remembered, tears welling up in his eyes. I've been her favorite out of all seven children she raised, and if I desert and get shot, she would be left . . .

This self-torture continued until he started thinking of Johanna again. He had a momentary vision of her as she was a month ago when he had left her, when she was so loving and tender with him.

Surely I can visit Johanna. She knows me, she cares for me, Otto thought. He paid for the beers and headed out toward Johanna's apartment.

When she sees I'm back, she'll open her arms to welcome me, he thought confidently.

Without a moment's hesitation Otto rang the bell, as he had always done before. Sometimes looks are more important than actions, he thought, as he straightened his posture to look impressive, happy, and eager. I'll have to impress her with a happy smile before I can tell her the truth.

Seconds later Otto's face showed nothing but anguish, because the door was opened not by Johanna but by her husband, whom he recognized from a photo he had seen. Shock and amazement almost paralyzed Otto as he stood there trying to think of something to say that might enable him to come out of this alive.

"Who is it, dear?" he heard Johanna's lilting voice from the kitchen. The man at the door was tall and handsome. His well-proportioned features and oval face made him a perfect match for Johanna's beauty.

"I'm sorry . . . I must have made some mistake . . . but I-I was sure that this is where the Vaatanens lived . . .?"

The man was watching him with keen, sharp eyes, and it took all of Otto's effort to keep looking calm and innocent, yet surprised, as though he had actually made a mistake.

"I'm sorry, Corporal, but you've come to the wrong apartment," the man told him matter-of-factly. "If you want to find the Vaatanens, you could go to the City's

118

Registration Office—that's only five blocks down the street—and find your friends' address there.''

Otto stared at the man, then turned around silently and left.

Disappointed and shaken, Otto started back toward the train terminal, scarcely knowing what to do. He found himself looking at the schedules on the timetable at the station. Soon a train would depart to Sortavala, and from there to Tornio.

Seeing the names in black and white somehow impressed him with the reality of what he was planning, and he began to think more seriously of the consequences of desertion. He thought especially of his mother.

Almost mechanically, without a sense of conscious choice, Otto found himself back at the old barracks in Viipuri, where he ate at the mess hall, hardly seeing the food he put into his mouth. Before midnight he had written a post card to Sirkka and was on the bus back to Kuuritsansuo. ''The only choice . . . the only choice'' he assured himself. He was exhausted, both in mind and body. As the old army bus bounced eastward along the familiar road toward the frontier, he fell in and out of sleep.

The bus turned in at the Kairas' farm, and Otto trod wearily back to the old farmhouse. He accidentally let the door slam shut and it disturbed the sleeping men in the house.

''What are you doing back so soon? What happened? Hey, Hietala, wake up! Look who's back already!''

His friends welcomed him with a canteen of kilju and questioned him in whispers, so as not to disturb the others. He told them about the conditions in Helsinki, how the city was blacked out and seemed to be preparing for the worst, and about the border villages evacuating. Of his marriage he told them merely that he and Anna had ''reconsidered'' and that he didn't want to discuss it. Finally their curiosity was satisfied, and they went back to sleep.

Otto stretched out on his bunk, feeling strangely relieved to be back.

# Chapter 21

Otto hated to tell the lieutenant that the marriage had not taken place, and was worried about how to handle the situation. He was glad that he had not revealed his desertion plans even to his closest friends.

"I hope he won't chew me out," he muttered to himself as he paced back and forth near the entrance, hesitating to go in.

The thought of Talvi and that bastard Kalle instantly reminded him of his reason for going to Helsinki in the first place. When he noticed that the lieutenant's door was ajar, he stepped inside.

"Good morning, Arola. You got back early, I see. Don't you remember I told you that I wouldn't have you shot?" Salmi lighted his cigarette, grinning slightly. "How does it feel to be a married man?"

Otto's hand was fumbling in his pocket, pulling out his pipe. He concentrated all his attention on trying, with some difficulty, to light it. He tried to smile, but found to his discomfort that he wouldn't manage it.

"You see, sir . . . ah . . . we decided against it . . . sir."

He put some more tobacco in his pipe, then tamped it cautiously, his hands not entirely under control. He was still standing in front of the lieutenant's table.

"Sit down, Arola," the lieutenant said, pointing to the chair by his table.

"Thank you, sir. When I saw . . . you know, the situation in Helsinki . . . all blacked out, you know, it made me think, you know . . . I figured it wasn't the right thing to do . . . that we might as well wait until this is all over."

The lieutenant nodded vaguely.

His mind isn't on me, Otto thought with relief.

The distracted Salmi thumbed through papers on his desk. "I received details this morning of the border incident in Mainila. But my field telephone connection to the battalion commander was bad. I couldn't make it out. I want you to take . . . now where have I . . . ?" he interrupted himself, trying to locate a specific piece of paper on his desk. "Here, bring your chair, I'll show you the map."

Lieutenant Salmi spread the map over the papers on his desk.

"Here's the place. You and five other men are going to a cabin here on the border."

He reviewed the map with Otto, detailing the route and discussing with him what kind of provisions and weapons the men would need.

"Can I select my own men?" Otto asked.

The lieutenant looked seriously at Otto. He flicked an ash from his cigarette.

"Okay, select your own people. Post two of the men near the river, in shifts, for patrol, starting upon your arrival."

"I'll take Hietala, Aalto, Tuoppi, Erik Stromberg, and Harru Taisto."

"Have them ready as quickly as you can," Salmi advised, nodding his approval of the choices.

"Yes, sir, thank you," Arola said. Before he left the room, he turned around at the doorway and asked, "Has anybody seen Kalle Kaira around here since the explosions? I was thinking about him while I was in Helsinki."

"No, nobody has seen or heard from the bastard! Not even his parents. I think perhaps you were right about him. I searched his cabin again myself, but nothing turned up. I'll bet he's on the other side of the border by now," Salmi said, pausing thoughtfully for a moment. "I don't want you to feel responsible for Talvi. You know Kaira could have fooled anyone. It wasn't your fault."

"I've been trying to convince myself of that, Lieutenant, but it's not easy," Otto said, turning to leave.

"Report back here in half an hour."

"Yes, sir. I'll be here."

In half an hour, the five men were ready and waiting outside.

"What do you have in the paper bag?" Otto inquired of Aalto, who carried a small brown package under this arm.

"Flour. We could fry pancakes. I have some butter, too, in my rucksack," Aalto replied. His face held the shadow of a smile.

"I'll be damned."

"We'll get a fire going as soon as we get there," Hietala said. "We'll have a regular feast!"

For a moment the seriousness of being sent to guard the border had disappeared from their minds.

"What are we going to do at the border?" Tuoppi asked, bringing their minds back to the assignment at hand.

Otto answered obliquely. "All I can tell you is that there have been frequent sightings of Russian troops at various points along the border. Our job is to cover a part of the area until the frontier army increases their border patrol. There's a cabin on the river for us to stay in."

Kuuritsansuo was a two-kilometer strip of swampland that lay between the Rajajoki and the Kaira's farm. Several narrow paths cut around the marshy areas, but a light snowfall had made the paths almost indistinguishable. As a result, travel by foot was slow. The six men conversed freely during the hike, and Otto noted that one of the new men, the husky Stromberg, seemed particularly intelligent and likable. He was as tall as Hietala. He held his back straight and his seriousness made him appear trustworthy. His uniform fit well on his muscular frame, and he had taken the time to shine his boots.

"Who knocked half your ear off?" Otto asked curiously as he happened to notice from his vantage point behind the big man that the lobe of his ear was missing.

"Damn lousy fight," he said, but added no explanation.

Shortly after one o'clock they had set up their camp in the cabin.

"Let's get the fire going. We'll have pancakes in no

time," Aalto promised, and began to mix the batter while Tuoppi went looking for firewood.

Hietala went with Stromberg to take the first patrol.

Clouds covered the Karelian border area, and darkness soon fell over the region. Several light flurries of snow left a thin blanket on the ground as the night wore on. Inside the cabin, however, Otto and the other three men were snug and warm.

Every few hours the two men on patrol would return to the cabin and be replaced by two others. The fresh men would take their position at the river, where the shallow water moved sluggishly toward the Gulf of Finland. They were only twenty kilometers north of Terijoki. Mainila, where the shelling incident had occurred, was about twelve kilometers south of the cabin and only five or six kilometers from the border toward the Gulf, but on the Russian side.

The following morning Aalto was up at dawn, and eagerly made another batch of pancakes from the remaining flour. From then on they ate army rations of canned meat and hardtack, and played cards. Hietala had brought his mouth organ and began to play some tunes while the others sang along. Otto walked into the cabin from his turn at watch.

"Don't be so loud, you guys. You can be heard all the way to the river," he scolded the men.

"The Russians won't mind," Hietala predicted. "And if they should, we'll have plenty of time to get out."

"Shut up! Who said anything about the Russians coming?" Otto said, nearly yelling at his friend.

"To tell the truth, if the Russians knew that we, the real working-class people were here, they'd never bother us anyway," laughed Hietala. "Who really thinks they'd come here? And what for?"

"The lieutenant said something about the Russians wanting Finnish army troops to be pulled back from the border for twenty-five kilometers. As far as I'm concerned, they can pull back as far as a hundred kilometers! The farther, the better," Otto said.

He climbed up and sat down on the big box by the brick stove that was used for storing firewood, and kicked his feet rhythmically against the side of the box while Hietala played and Aalto mimed with him.

"Where is your harmonica?" Aalto asked Otto.

"I don't feel like playing, really. If I had my violin with me, I would reconsider."

The music was only a temporary relief. The wilderness area around them was neither inviting nor pleasant. It was unnerving to patrol the river during the daytime, and terrifying at night. They heard the grinding sounds of motorized equipment, but otherwise there was a strange silence.

"Does anyone really think Russia will rob us of our own land?" Hietala said, starting up the same conversation again. "Do you really believe they'd send a group of bandits, like outlaws, to rob our homes? I don't believe any of the news or rumors that we hear, but if they should come for some reason, we'd be dead. They'd kill us just like that!" Hietala said, drawing his hand across his throat meaningfully.

Otto spoke more quietly than the others, but more seriously, too.

"For all we know—what we've learned from our families—the Russians have always helped the Finnish working people. I don't know what to believe."

When Tuoppi and Otto walked back to the cabin at two o'clock on the third night, they were elated at the knowledge that the next day was to be their last on this assignment. Their tension had diminished somewhat, and the other side of the river seemed quiet. They had detected nothing alarming, not even visible action.

Otto and his men continued their watch. The November weather was turning cold, and the nights were freezing. Small windows on the east and west sides of the cabin had paper-thin glass panes, and the wind blew through cracks in the caulking. The stars appeared to be falling, whenever they peeked out from behind the clouds, and the darkness seemed to increase the coldness of the night.

"How about a few more hours of sleep?" Otto suggested, as he and Tuoppi entered the cabin. "We'll soon be back in the camp, so we might just as well rest here as much as we can."

Hietala laughed. "At least we're not here to conquer Russia and build that 'greater Finland' our fanatic army officers are so obsessed with. Keep your heads warm under the old army gray, lads," he chuckled, and burrowed deep into the covers on the cold wooden floor.

Suddenly their snoring was interrupted by a series of tremendous explosions. The windowpanes of the cabin were blown inside, shattering all over the room and covering the blanketed men with splinters.

"Get out of here, fast!" Otto ordered, knowing full well that they had to dress before they could get out.

"My rifle, my pants, boots—where the hell . . .? Does anyone have a match?" Tuoppi asked.

"Don't strike a match, get out . . . try to find your things . . ." Otto was as confused as the others.

Three large craters were smoldering in the ground around the cabin. Suddenly another shell screamed its high-pitched warning and landed just five meters from the cabin. Then another shell exploded in the forest behind the men.

Despite the roaring, the men looked at each other incredulously. "Can the Russians be attacking?" they asked with their eyes. They could hardly believe what was happening.

The early morning moon shone on them, illuminating their frightened faces. Despite the cold, fear caused them to perspire profusely. Otto had slung his overcoat over his shoulder, his rifle ready to fire. They moved together like a single shadow, without a word, sharing each other's agony nonetheless. The shelling continued.

Why was this happening? The question kept flashing in Otto's mind. He remained speechless, however, despite the furor in his mind. They moved silently.

"It's out turn to fight for the earth of Finland!" Otto said to the others at last, but his voice was so thick with emotion that no one heard his words. He didn't have to say it out loud anyway. They all knew. Hietala, Tuoppi, Stromberg—their calloused hands testified to their years of heavy labor. The strong muscles in their arms, backs, and legs had developed from toiling in the woods, felling trees, tilling the soil.

Otto tried again to speak to the others, but his eyes blinked as he looked at them and he said nothing. Their eyes reflected the same fears and the same thoughts as his.

Tuoppi walked a few steps behind him, visibly frightened.

Arola shook his muddy arm; a shell had spilled black earth all over it.

"Stromberg, you go and get Taisto and Aalto back from the river and . . ." Before Otto had finished his sentence, Stromberg motioned him to hit the ground. In a flash Otto followed Stromberg into the shell crater, his eyes watching the forest, where movement could be seen.

"It's not Aalto and Elmer," Otto whispered to Stromberg. He sighted over his rifle barrel, and fired at the moving target behind the trees.

Otto heard the stumbling sound of a man falling, and saw another shadow behind the trees.

"Fire!" Otto shouted, and the squad emptied their chambers. They heard a moaning sound and a faint cry.

Shells roared over them. Otto raised his head, signalled his men to follow, and ran downhill, taking cover on the slope from the advancing Russians.

They stumbled through the forest and swamp toward camp, as fast as they could.

It was seven in the morning, November 30, 1939, when the Russians had fired their salvo. The Winter War between Russia and Finland had begun.

# Chapter 22

In less than an hour Arola's squad arrived at the camp. The night chill had frosted the earth, and a thin white blanket of snow covered everything. It was slippery and icy but they had managed to avoid slipping into the swamp's bottomless pits, where a man could fall without leaving a trace. Otto looked back, fearing that the Russians were following, and roaring shells flew over them.

Otto shook his head as he saw the panic-stricken reserves, some drunk, some with such bad hangovers that they were confused and rushing around madly, gathering up what belongings they could, often stumbling into each other.

Otto's hands felt clumsy and unable to function. His eyes watched the border area keenly, where Russians could fire from any moment.

One person was calm. The well-organized Lieutenant Salmi had arrived in the yard to quiet his nearly-hysterical men. He shouted to his platoon leaders to bring them under control immediately.

"Pack everything you can carry with you and throw the rest in the house or barn. When you've got all your stuff packed, set fire to everything and kill all the livestock."

"Lieutenant . . ." Otto tried to catch the officer's attention, but his words got stuck in his throat.

"Christ!" the lieutenant exclaimed. "I thought you guys were finished. We have three sleighs. Load them with ammunition, but keep those land mines handy—we'll need them to cover our retreat. Move, it, Arola!'' Salmi's stern manner shook Otto. He was still troubled by his own fears and confusion. He set out running for the bunkhouse to get help.

"Tuoppi, Hietala!" he called them. "Hurry up, I need help. Go get the horses and sleighs and meet me at the shack."

Hietala ran to get Stromberg, and Tuoppi took off after the horses. The shelling was moving closer in range. As Otto ran to the munitions shacks, an explosion knocked him down and he felt something smash into his right foot. He lay still for a moment. He felt no pain, but when he summoned the nerve to look down, he saw a fragment of jagged shrapnel imbedded in the heel of his boot. He jumped up immediately and within seconds had the shack door open.

"Where are those damned horses?" he cursed, but then he saw Stromberg leading the frightened animals out. By the time all three sleighs were loaded, most of the livestock had been slaughtered and the buildings set aflame. Otto hated to leave so much ammunition behind, but there was no sense packing any more of it than the horses could pull.

The Third Company headed north of the farm to an area called Kekrola, three kilometers away. Otto set fire to the munitions shack and skied hard to catch up with the rest of the company before the remaining ammunition exploded. The skis had arrived at camp during Otto's border patrol, and there was just enough new snow on the ground to use them.

Lieutenant Salmi met him at the rear of the disorganized group of men.

"Get those mines planted on the road!" he yelled, struggling to make himself heard over the roar of the bursting shells, and ordered three men to dig the shallow holes. Otto planted five mines along the road.

The Russian artillery was shelling at full capacity, but the men of the Third Company quickly learned to judge the distance of the shells by the shrill screaming noise they made in the air. Now they ignored the aimless shells falling twenty to thirty meters away that had terrified them only moments before.

They trudged up the road to set up a defense against the Russian troops who would surely follow the artillery salvo. Otto was at the end of the procession, trying to calm the frightened sleigh horses. He himself was no less frightened than the horses when he thought of a shell making a direct hit. He had packed enough grenades and ammunition on the sleighs to blow himself and the animals to bits if they were hit by a shell.

Out of the corner of his left eye Otto spotted something white, bobbing along at ground level. As he turned, he saw a lamb running rapidly along at his side. She apparently had escaped the slaughter at the farmhouse. The orphaned animal bleated pathetically in terror and confusion, but Otto couldn't afford to waste any time on her. He knew that it would be better to kill the animal, but he didn't have the heart.

"You had better get into those woods if you want to stay alive much longer," he advised her.

Kekrola lay adjacent to the same swamp as Kuuritsansuo, and it was Lieutenant Salmi's hope that he could draw the approaching enemy into the swamp by establishing his line of defense directly behind it. A narrow logging road, built by farmers years before, led through the swamp and toward the village. Here Salmi formed his first line.

Three squads of men had fallen back to delay the enemy's advance. They fired from the forest at the Russians, who were marching in formation and seemed unable to detect where the gunfire was coming from. A burst of rifle and Suomi discharges would erupt, and instantly several Russians would fall. The Finnish squads would disappear into the thicket. All the while, however, they were drawing the Russians closer to the swamp and the main body of the Third Company.

Lieutenant Salmi positioned three automatic machine guns at the end of the logging road, in the swamp. The main body of men took their places on the side of a hill, looking down into the bog. There they waited for the rear guard squads to come across the road, with the Russians on their tails. Otto distributed additional ammunition among the men. Several squad leaders were circulating through the ranks, quieting the young, inexperienced men with words

129

of encouragement. Otto grabbed his rifle and joined his friends at the firing line. His mouth was as dry as cotton, and he did not speak as they waited and watched the road.

Within minutes, the three squads of Finnish soldiers appeared at the edge of the swamp. They skied across the logging road and up the hill to join the main body of men. Otto listened as the squad leader reported to the lieutenant. Five tanks had been immobilized, four by land mines, and one by a well-placed grenade. Fifty to sixty Russian soldiers had fallen and their ranks were disorganized and confused. The squad leader was excited and jubilant over their first success in disrupting the Russian advance.

"Four tanks," Otto said to Hietala, scarcely able to believe it. "I got four tanks with those land mines."

The shelling was now directed far beyond their defense line and a tank could be heard somewhere in the distance, although it did not appear. Russian soldiers, however, did appear, their rifles over their shoulders as if they were unaware that enemy snipers had already picked off sixty of their comrades.

The Russians followed the road and headed directly toward the hidden machine guns which were waiting for them on the other side of the swamp. When they were halfway across the bog, Lieutenant Salmi fired a burst from his Suomi. The entire Third Company opened up on the Russians. Bullets ripped into the mass of soldiers in their quilted overcoats, driving them off the road and into the swamp. They sank to their knees—easy targets. Some turned back, only to be cut down by the Finns or enveloped in the deep holes dotting the treacherous muck.

Despite their losses, more and more Russiand emerged from the forest. They trampled over their own dead and wounded, struggling to cross the swamp. They, too, were slaughtered by the Finnish guns.

A tank came clanking and crashing through the woods. Then it hesitated and lumbered off the road and into the swamp, where it slowly began to disappear. The driver raced the engine, but the treads were mired too deep in the watery mush of decaying vegetation and mud. Its crew scrambled out. Two of them died immeidately under fire. The third man fell back into the tank.

Otto fired steadily, coolly focusing on each target. Seeing hordes of enemy fall below drove him into a sort of frenzy, and he continued shooting until the lieutenant ordered them to cease firing. Piles of dead and wounded lay on the road.

Now the Russians poured out again—out of the woods to cross the swamp. Again and again they were cut down by the Third Company. The fighting continued through the day and into the night with only momentary breaks in the firing, when the Russians paused to regroup. The night was clear and bright with a lot of moonlight, so the Russians found no shelter during the evening and early morning hours.

The fighting at Kekrola lasted a total of three days and three nights. At least six hundred Russians were left dead and wounded. The Third Company had not lost a single man since the first shelling, but they were hungry, and in need of rest.

The first heavy snowfall of the winter finally came, on the third day of the fighting. Soon the marshes and lakes scattered throughout eastern Finland would freeze and be covered with snow. This would allow the Russians to advance with less difficulty, but the heavy snowfall would also help to camouflage the Finnish troups. They were now equipped with white parkas and trousers, and thus were almost invisible, both on the ground and from the air.

The greatest advantage provided by the snow was that the Finns could now fully utilize their skis, traveling through the woods and avoiding the roads. A foot soldier would be slowed down by heavy snow, but a man on skis could strike, disappear, and strike again, with great speed. Every Finn had learned to ski as a child; now it would prove to be an invaluable asset.

During one of the brief breaks on the third day of fighting, a young private approached Otto and told him that the lieutenant wished to speak with him.

"We're going to fall back to a village, four and a half kilometers north of here, called Vehmainen," the lieutenant told him. "I want you and your squad to take the ammunition sleighs to a farm just north of the village. We'll hold the Russians for another hour or two—you should be able to make it by then. The men need rest, and the Second

131

Company will cover our retreat between here and Vehmainen.''

"Anything else?" Otto asked.

"When you get there, tell the kitchen crew to find anything to eat, to ransack the stores before they are burned,
and to get extra provisions."

"Damn it," Otto muttered as he skied back to the sleighs.
"No Finnish artillery to support us, and no airplanes. This
must be the most insane war the Finns have ever fought."

Otto gathered his five squad members and they hitched
the horses to the sleighs, leaving the Third Company with
several crates of ammunition. The idea of traveling with
only five other men frightened him, but he was careful not
to display his fears to the others. They were frightened
enough already.

Otto looked at the sky which had been clearing. There
was a patch of blue to the north. The clouds might break
up and leave them as easy mark for aerially directed artillery.

Otto instructed Tuoppi, Aalto, and Taisto to lead the
horses, while he and the other two watched closely for any
enemy activity in the forest. As they scanned the woods for
movement, Otto saw something behind him. Barely visible
in the newly fallen snow was the white lamb that had followed him from the Kairas' farm.

"Hey, Hietala, look at this!" he called out over the noise
of the shells.

"Well, I'll be damned!" Hietala shouted back. "It must
think you know your way out of this mess."

"Well, it can't do much harm, I guess," Otto said, glancing again at the sky.

As Otto had feared, the cloud cover had broken up and
a Russian observation plane appeared.

"Get the horses into the woods!" Otto screamed, grabbing a pair of reins from Taisto.

Before they could find cover the shells rained down
around them, pounding behind them at the remains of buildings. The horses bolted and ran from the men.

"Let them go!" Otto yelled. "Find a crater and stay
still."

Otto dived into a deep ditch by the road and the lamb

132

joined him. Then the animal suddenly raised her head, jumped out, and rushed across the road to an even deeper ditch.

Without knowing why, Otto followed the lamb. He stumbled headlong into the meter-deep crater. A shell exploded in the spot that he and the lamb had just abandoned four meters away. He was afraid to move.

"Surely my body is full of holes!" he thought in anguish. He cautiously elevated his arms, then legs, without feeling any pain. He looked at the smoking crater from which he had escaped, not knowing why he had followed the lamb to safety.

"Nobody's going to eat *you*," he told the lamb as he curled up in the ditch beside her to watch the bombardment. "Nobody!" he repeated emphatically.

The shelling inched toward the direction of the forest on his left. Otto called to everyone to lie still, in case the reconnaissance plane returned, but it was gone. He jumped back up to the road. They rounded up the horses and sleighs from the side of the road, and took refuge in a farmhouse one kilometer north of the village.

The main body of the Third Company straggled through the devastated village four hours after Otto's squad. They had not lost a single man.

The men slept in shifts. Aching in every joint, Otto stretched out on a narrow, wooden bench, closed his eyes, and fell into a long, deep sleep.

# *Chapter 23*

Otto was shaken awake by Sergeant Lars Ekstrom, a husky, good-looking man with deep-set blue eyes, high cheekbones, and a mustache. Ekstrom had learned the art of war when he volunteered, at the age of sixteen, for the White Guard troops. His daring efforts had gained him a reputation. He handled his men with respect and he demanded that each give back all he could in return.

With Ekstrom was Sergeant Jorma Hakli, a twenty-eight-year-old farmer. His eyes were set wide apart under bushy brows. He had trimmed his mustache in a style that resembled Hitler's. The men teased him, knowing that Hakli was as friendly as a puppy. During his regular army service he had qualified for the highest medal of honor in every sharpshooting competition. He had a short neck and a round face, which gave him a strong, reliable appearance.

"C'mon, Corporal," Ekstrom growled. "The Russians are back on our tails again. Lieutenant Salmi wants to see you."

Otto brushed at his hand across his forehead, as if to clear the thoughts in his mind. He followed Ekstrom and Hakli to the farmhouse, where the lieutenant was going over a map with three platoon leaders. A stack of rifles, ammunition belts, and felt boots lay on the porch of the house. Upon inspection, Otto found them to be Russian-made. After pushing the Russians back, the Third Company had taken booty from the Russian dead on their way from Kek-rola. Otto glanced around the farmyard and noted that this time the men were calm and orderly in the face of attack.

We're learning fast, he thought as, he entered the farm-house.

"We've got about two hundred and fifty Russians head-ing this way, with six tanks," Lieutenant Salmi was saying. "I'm sending men out to hold them. Arola, you and your men are to take the ammo back to Siiranmaki and wait there," he said, pointing to another small village on the map, about two and a half kilometers to the west.

Salmi paused, folded the map back up, and replaced it in its case. "Give those rifles and ammunition belts to our men. They're in excellent shape and are the same caliber as ours."

"Okay, Lieutenant," Otto said. "We can sure use better rifles."

On this way out, Otto draped six belts over his shoulder and loaded himself up with an equal number of rifles. Then he headed for the barn. Stromberg met him on the way and relieved him of the rifles. Soon all the squad was there. They hitched up the horses, loaded their rifles onto the sleighs, and set out for Siiranmaki.

The main road to Vehmainen cut through state forest, which was so dense that the Russian tanks had to stay on the road, followed by their ground troops. Lieutenant Salmi directed forty men to hide in the woods, twenty to each side of the road, until the tanks rolled past them, and then to catch the Russians in cross-fire. In their white uniforms, the Finns were almost impossible to spot. They were ready to take care of the soldiers, and then deal with the tanks.

They waited patiently. The lieutenant had estimated cor-rectly that the huge Russian tanks could not turn around in the narrow road. They cut down the ground troops before half of them were able to retreat, and stuck well-placed grenades into the tank treads, mobilizing two. One daring Finn waited and then climbed on top of the tank, knocked on the hatch door, and when it opened dropped a grenade inside.

"You are not to kill yourself with such actions," the lieutenant said, almost scolding the man for his bravery.

Camouflaged Finns pursued the Russians as they panicked and tried heading back. The Finns still had not lost a single man.

The forty men joined the rest of the company heading back, after Arola's squad, toward Siiranmaki.

Unexpectedly, Otto and his men had found that the village of Siiranmaki had been put to the torch by the last of its inhabitants as they evacuated. The narrow road through the village was impassable because of the tremendous heat. Otto knew that he must reach some point on the western side of the village, and his only option was to lead the sleighs off the road and through the dense forest. To remain on the road would be suicide, should the clouds break as they had done the day before.

Otto and Stromberg led the first horse, while the four other men pushed the sleigh. It soon became jammed between two tree trunks. The men had to force it through the narrow space, only to have it jam again. They pushed it back and tried an alternate route with the second sleigh, but it too became hopelessly caught on a hidden stump.

"Let's get the last one into the woods," Otto instructed his men. They quickly moved the remaining sleigh into the forest, then decided to wait, and covered all three with branches from the surrounding spruce trees.

They lay in the snow for over an hour, until the procession of white-cloaked soldiers came skiing gracefully into view, led by Lieutenant Salmi. Otto stepped out into the road.

"We ran into a little trouble, Lieutenant. The sleighs are stuck in the forest. The heat from the burning village is so bad that we couldn't even get near it on the road."

"What about the horses, Arola?"

"They're camouflaged in the woods."

"Get the horses. I'll put some men to work on those sleighs."

Stromberg and Hietala brought the horses back, and it took thirty men more than four hours to move the sleighs through the forest to the farmhouse.

As Otto watched the lieutenant in action, he wondered how this man had transformed a mob of undisciplined loafers, overnight, into a company of veterans. Otto thought about how he had reacted under enemy fire. His initial actions had been motivated entirely by self-preservation. His fear of death and imprisonment was so strong that he would kill unhesitatingly to protect himself. Was that all there was to it? Were the men merely trying to stay alive? That must be it, Otto decided. Lieutenant Salmi had made his mark on every man. Each of them was convinced that the best chance for his own survival lay in following him.

The Third Company made camp late that afternoon. Lieutenant Salmi told them that he hoped they could rest a full night, and congratulated them on their performance during the past five days.

His men knew that sleep and food would be luxuries from that point on. Many of them fell asleep in their tents while still eating their ration of stew.

The following morning, fresh snow was falling.

Salmi had been in contact with headquarters and that hundreds and thousands of troops with tanks had crossed over the border in the past five days. The Finns had only about thirteen thousand men on the border-defense line, with neither artillery nor tanks. Their job was to prevent the Russians from reaching the main defense line before it was completed. Salmi knew it was an enormous task. But he was confident.

"Arola, we are to fall back to Ahijarvi for at least two days, and then to Parkkila and Oinala for a period of time which will be decided by the Battalion Command. From there we'll go to Kyyrola, where our main force is preparing to drive the Russians back. We're going to stay there as long as possible or until our permanent defense line—what the Russians are now calling the Mannerheim Line—is constructed."

Salmi looked at the meandering red line on the map, which ran from Taipale on the shore of Lake Laatokka in the north, to Kyroniemi on the Gulf of Finland to the south.

"Lieutenant, hurry," cried a man rushing into the tent, and speaking breathlessly. "Russians, a whole platoon!"

"Arola, get moving to Ahijarvi. It's about ten kilometers up the road to the inland. Set up camp there. We'll follow soon!"

Once again Otto gathered his squad, camouflaged his load and horses with white tarpaulins, and set off. The lamb

137

again following behind them quietly, as if it had adopted the squad.

# Chapter 24

Otto's men hurried westward to Ahijarvi. The drivers, pulling at the reigns, cursed the horses to go faster. Snow-covered branches interlaced their icy fingers against the sky, but what would once have been seen as winter wonderland, now seemed like a nightmare labyrinth. Shells burst regularly to the left and right. Otto and his men listened to the steady scrape of their horses' hooves in the snow, drawing from the regular beat a kind of stability in the midst of chaos.

Ahijarvi was intact when Arola's squad arrived. To the delight of the men, the general store had not been completely looted by the departing villagers. They broke into the store, stuffing their packs full of delicacies and sweets. They made camp in a farmhouse west of the village. Otto's squad then unloaded the sleighs for inventory, adding one stolen sack of flour, one of sugar, and a box of dynamite to their existing supplies.

Three hours later the lieutenant brought the company to Ahijarvi, but before they set their camp, shells flew overhead, and a total bombardment of the village began.

"Get the horses to the woods!" Otto yelled to his squad.

The men rushed to any shelter they could find. It was clear now there was no end to the Russians' ammunition. Otto inched his way toward the lieutenant's crater, watching the barns being burned and the ground turning black.

Sergeant Hakli and Ekstrom were nearby and also inched closer to the lieutenant.

"Before this shelling I was in contact with the Battalion command. We have orders to return and strike at Siiranmaki, where the entire Soviet battalion is moving northward on the Kekrola road." He stopped as the sound of an explosion muffled his voice.

"Get your men ready after the shelling. We'll have no time to eat. We must cover the south side of the road, while other Finnish troops take care of the north."

"But the men are hungry and ready to collapse," Hakli protested. Ekstorm was looking at the lieutenant as if he were mad to drive the men so hard.

"Damn it! The Russians don't care if we're hungry—and we have no choice." The lieutenant's face was stern, but one could detect his concern for the men. "We must delay the Russians. And Arola, you'd better have your sleighs ready to move if we fail to stop them."

"Yes, sir. I'll have my men ready."

It dawned on Otto that he and the others who had doubted their capacity to fight had fought anyway, without realizing quite why. But now the reason was apparent. If they didn't stop the enemy they could be taken prisoners, suffering the tortures they had heard of at Terijoki.

The shelling grew more sporadic and Otto was able to get to the sleighs, where he found Tuoppi, who was dutifully counting boxes. Stromberg arrived, and then Hietala.

"We have one hundred and twenty hand grenades," Tuoppi announced to Otto. "Plus a few Russian grenades that we don't know how to ignite."

"Forget the Russian grenades," Otto said, but then suddenly he had a thought. Why not reinforce the small grenades to make them more powerful against the tanks?

Otto rushed back to the lieutenant, who was standing near the road.

"I just thought of something, perhaps worth considering," he said, his eyes gleaming for the first time with some eagerness.

"Let's hear it," the lieutenant said.

"Why couldn't we wrap some dynamite to one of the grenades that has a handle? It would be heavier to throw,

140

but with the handle it should be fairly accurate—and more powerful. With one well-placed explosion, one man could do the damage of three, in a third of the time. I found some sticks of dynamite in the general store and a ball of strong string. We could wrap them on with burlap.''

The other three looked at Otto and considered the suggestion.

''I don't see why it wouldn't work, if we make sure they are solidly wrapped together,'' Sergeant Hakli said, his mustache jumping under his nose in excitement.

''Go ahead, Arola,'' the lieutenant ordered. ''I want you to bring Hietala and Stromberg back with you in an hour. We'll need them tonight.''

Otto walked back to the sleighs. When he got there he found all five of his squad members huddled around a brown hardwood box. Hietala was holding it, trying to pry it open with his knife.

''What are you doing?'' Otto asked.

''Tuoppi packed this thing onto the sleigh at Kaira's farm,'' Hietala answered.

''I found it in the barn, Otto,'' Tuoppi assured him proudly. ''It looked like it was worth saving, but I forgot to tell you about it. I thought maybe Kalle left if behind.''

''Forget about it!'' Otto snapped, not thinking of Kalle or any of the incidents that had happened at the farm. ''There's a lot of work to do and not much time for doing it.''

He showed them what he wanted done with the grenades, and the men started fastening the dynamite to the grenades and wrapping them in burlap. The brown box was forgotten.

Late that afternoon, Stromberg and Hietala passed out the satchel charges to the men, and issued extra rounds of ammunition to them all. The temperature had dropped to nine degrees and Otto reminded the riflemen to take the precaution of keeping their weapons at a constant temperature. If the rifles, and particularly the Suomis, were exposed to the open air and not kept in motion after being in a warm room or tent, the automatic mechanisms could freeze up. The fear of having a weapon freeze while facing the enemy was so great that even the laziest of men worked meticulously on their weapons to prevent any malfunction.

They hoped the weather wouldn't get colder that night.

At midnight, the platoon assembled in the farmyard and headed back east. The entire forest, from ground to treetops, was covered with a thick blanket of fresh snow. Each man, dressed completely in white, cast his own ghostly shadow in the night, weaving through the trees in almost total silence. For protection against the cold, each man had been supplied with one of the white, woolen masks that the women of Finland had knitted for the army. No one spoke, for fear that the Russian patrols might be lurking nearby in the woods.

Otto thought about the coming battle. He had been trained to fight at Terijoki, but he had never thought he would actually find himself in battle. Now, however, he appreciated what he had learned. Those exhausting drills had made the recruits into tougher, stronger, more confident men. The were soldiers now, waiting for their orders.

The lieutenant brought the platoon to a halt and waited for the men to gather around. He whispered for two men to go on ahead and locate the Russian camp. The platoon rested, awaiting the return of the scouts.

Otto felt his nervousness return. Maybe the intelligence reports are wrong, he hoped. Maybe the Russians haven't made it as far as Siiranmaki yet.

He began to think of the countless, horrible ways he could be killed, mutilated, or taken prisoner. He recalled the bloody aftermath of Talvi's death, and then he thought of the hundreds of Russians he had seen bleeding to death in the snow, staring at the sky with glassy eyes. He looked up to see if anyone was watching him, if anyone had noticed his fear.

Only when he noticed that the men were huddled around the lieutenant did he realize that the two scouts had gotten back safely. He strained to hear what they were saying.

". . . forty-eight tanks lined up single file in the road," one of the scouts was saying. "It couldn't be an easier setup," he added confidently.

"How many guards?" the lieutenant asked. "Where are they located?"

"We could see ten guards that around the tanks," the scout replied. "There are probably more around the tents, but we couldn't see them through all the snow, and we didn't dare to get any closer."

The platoon regrouped and made its way toward the Russian camp. They moved slowly and deliberately, making little sound, and blending in with the white forest. The two scouts led the platoon. They raised their arms and signaled the troops to stop. Silently, the lieutenant began motioning the men into position, dividing the platoon into two, combined groups of men with Suomis and grenade throwers, one to be placed at each end of the line of tanks. It was three–thirty in the morning. The men settled down for a fifteen-minute wait. The temperature had dropped to ten degrees below zero and, for the first time, Otto was aware of the bitter cold.

He had heard of cases of frostbite, of men who had lost their toes and feet. He tried to distract himself by watching the tanks, not sixty meters away, and the guards marching around them. The Russians were dressed in quilted wool coats with tremendous fur hoods. The sight served to help him forget the cold. He felt his heart pound as he planned his actions, step by step, over and over again. He and Hietala were to throw their grenades at the tank second from the end. Each man had two triple-strength grenades. For the attack to be successful, at least one grenade from each man would have to find its mark.

Twenty minutes later, Sergeant Hakli signalled to the men, alerting them to get ready to move up to within ten meters of the tanks. An explosion erupted from the other side of the village, and Lieutenant Salmi opened up with his Suomi to signal the other men to commence firing.

The distance between the Finnish riflemen and their targets was less than ten meters. Otto saw four Russian guards fall immediately. Several others returned the fire from behind the tanks, however.

Sergeant Hakli lobbed a triple grenade directly into the tread of the last tank. He dropped behind a tree as the explosion flashed in the night. Otto and Hietala threw two grenades simultaneously and ducked. Suomi shots and grenades were erupting in unison. Within three minutes, the supply of grenades was exhausted. Before the Finns could fall back, though, more Russians poured out of their tents and fired blindly into the forest. One of the turrets on an undamaged tank swung around and its gun began firing, ripping through the trees to Otto's left.

Something heavy fell across his leg. Terrified, he saw one of the men, with his mask bloodied, lying across him. He struggled to free himself, then emptied his Suomi clip into the Russians.

"Fall back!" Hakli screamed above the popping of gunfire.

Otto looked down the line to his left and saw the lieutenant behind the brush, signaling retreat. They moved back forty or fifty meters and ceased firing.

The Russians continued firing, but didn't follow them into the woods. Tank engines were heard, but the machines didn't move. The lieutenant held fast, listening for the distinctive sound of treads rolling across the snow. It did not come. Satisfied that the tanks at both ends of the line had been immobilized, Salmi gave the order to move back. The men slung the Suomi machine guns in front of them and followed him.

Otto was about to head back toward Ahijarvi, but someone grabbed him from behind. He panicked and began to struggle violently.

"Arola, Arola—it's me," Hakli growled. "Help me get this guy out of here," he said, directing Otto's attention back to the wounded man who had fallen on him.

Rifle fire continued to rip through the woods. In his terror, Otto had neglected the wounded man—he had forgotten about him completely! The sergeant took off his overcoat and stretched it over the wounded man's skis, while Otto knelt by a tree, his Suomi ready.

"Arola, give me a hand!" Hakli snapped.

Otto picked up one end of the impromptu stretcher while the sergeant held the other, and they slowly hauled the wounded man back to where Lieutenant Salmi was supervising care of the casualties.

Otto and Sergeant Hakli lowered their man to the snow and the sergeant knelt to inspect his wound. It was dark and Otto couldn't see any blood, except on the mask, but the man had been moaning horribly while they were carrying him. He had not uttered a sound as they had lowered him to the ground. Hakli searched for a pulse and found none. The man had been hit in the chest by two bullets and another had apparently grazed his head.

Otto felt weak as he turned away from the dead man and leaned against a tree while the medic hurried among the six others. Otto heard skis skimming over the snow and soon the remainder of the platoon appeared.

"How are they?" Salmi inquired of the medic.

"Three dead. The others will make it back to the farm, but I can't say much more than that."

"Do what you can here," Salmi said. "We're not being pursued yet. But hurry it up!"

The platoon arrived back at Ahijarvi at seven–thirty. The temperature had fallen during the early morning hours to eleven degrees below zero. Otto headed for his tent and reached in his pocket for his pipe. He needed a good smoke before sleep, but he found that during the retreat he had lost his pipe. He searched the kitchen sleigh, found a large potato and carved it into a bowl, fitted it with the mouthpiece of an old, wooden, cigarette tip, and enjoyed a smoke.

Otto crawled over to the lamb, curled up in the corner. He realized again that she had saved his life by a matter of seconds. He patted her white thick wool. She had totally adopted the company's ordnance squad as her new home. She ate with the horses, walked behind the sleigh, and made no effort to run away. Otto marveled how one tiny mistake or move in the wrong direction in battle could cost a man's life. He emptied his potato-bowl pipe, dug into the tent while the roar of shells still filled the air, and fell into a deep sleep.

# Chapter 25

Lieutenant Salmi informed the Battalion commander that the raid had been a success. A total of seventeen tanks had been immobilized. He was confident that the Russian ground troops wouldn't advance until the roads were clear.

Salmi checked his supplies of ammunition and food. He studied the detailed maps until his eyes could no longer focus. Then, staggering as if drunk, he fell onto the bench by his table and was snoring almost before his head hit the folded coat he was using for a pillow.

Although Lieutenant Salmi was only twenty-eight years old, his forehead was furrowed, and dark patches had appeared under his eyes. The skin on his face was drawn and wrinkled, and with his matted, dirty brown hair, he now looked ten years older.

Otto came to the farmhouse after a few hours of rest, but the sight of the lieutenant shocked him. Even in his sleep he looked pathetically wasted. He realized that the lieutenant was sleeping for the first time in two days, so he tiptoed back out.

On the way back to his tent Tuoppi rushed toward him, breathless.

"What's up?" Otto asked.

Tuoppi was struggling to say something, but his way of speaking often seemed like the heaviest of labors. He coughed. "Ai, ah, . . ."

"Take your time," Otto said, amused by Tuoppi's seriousness.

"I found it—the tank—it's burning . . ." Tuoppi searched for the words to explain, but every effort failed.

"Did you let him escape?" Otto laughed. "You had your rifle?"

Tuoppi pointed toward the woods.

"Tank . . . the entire tank is burning . . ." He could hardly continue. "It was driving on, toward me," he said, beginning to catch his breath. "The Russian tank was in the woods . . ."

"Tuoppi, let's start over at the beginning, slowly and carefully," Otto calmed the excited man.

"Hakli posted me as sentry on the edge of that open field—about a kilometer from here—with a soldier from the First Platoon. We discovered an old dugout sauna and took our post inside. The door faced east, where the enemy was supposed to come from. My partner—Helge—then closed the door for a while to prevent the wind from blowing into the sauna. There was an old lantern, smoky and rusted, but it had kerosene in it. He lighted it so we could warm our hands. Then there was this noise, the sound of a motor, heavy like an airplane. Helge went out to look—and that was the end of him! They shot him!"

"Who shot him?" Otto asked patiently.

"There was this tank—a huge monster-like machine! I was holding the lantern in my hand and I went after Helge to help him, but that tank kept coming on me. I forgot my rifle in the sauna . . ."

"That's your first mistake in war—never walk one step without your rifle. You remember the training? What happened then?"

"I got mad. Really mad!"

Knowing Tuoppi's way of thinking and acting, Otto knew it took a lot of provocation to get Tuoppi mad. "You saw the tank and you had forgotten your rifle. But where did you get that blood on your cloak?" Otto asked with concern.

"I ran toward that tank . . . I said . . . 'You damned Russians killed my partner,' and I threw the lantern at the tank. It broke, and kerosene went all over the tank, and the whole thing caught on fire."

147

"Just like that!" Otto said, staring in disbelief. Yet he knew that the man had never lied to him.

"It burned. The grease all over the tank ignited! The man climbed out of the tank—jumped down to the snow and ran toward me—his hands up like he was going to attack me or something. He mumbled something in Russian, but I didn't know what he said. I took out my knife, jumped on his back and cut his throat . . ."

"Then that's Russian blood, not yours?" Otto asked, pointing his finger at Tuoppi's chest.

"I didn't get hurt. I'm all right."

"Wasn't there more than one man in the tank?" Otto wanted to know.

"If there was, he didn't come out. With all that smoke and fire, he must be dead!"

Could you take me there? Where is it?"

Tuoppi and Otto returned to camp in less than an hour. Otto rushed straight to the lieutenant's office to report. The commander was seated on his cot. He looked up brightly when Otto entered and smiled.

"Hello, Arola, I want to talk to you. There are several tanks spotted at twenty kilometers south of here. How many explosives do you have left?"

"Lieutenant, we might have a new weapon, an antitank weapon! I came to explain it to you!" Otto spoke quickly, his face flushed with excitement.

Salmi looked at him rather sharply.

Otto told the lieutenant what Tuoppi had done, then added, "I went to examine the wreckage of that tank. It had burned. It's useless. The factory grease evidently was still fresh enough and, with a little kerosene over it, it burned right through the cracks, burned inside too, and suffocated the crew. We could get bottles and fill them with kerosene like the lantern Tuoppi used, couldn't we?"

"Damn it, Arola, go find bottles and kerosene! Fill up those bombs—move!"

And so the new weapon was invented. The Third Company began manufacturing the new antitank weapon, unaware that such a bottle bomb was being used and tested in other units as well.

Otto and his men collected bottles and kerosene from

148

every farmhouse, and the men were instructed how to use the weapon to greatest effect. Despite Salmi's enthusiasm for the "gas bombs" the men were at first hesitant and frightened of using them.

By dawn, the main body of the Third Company skied through the densely wooded countryside toward the road leading to Kivennapa.

Each man now carried with him, in addition to his regular supply of ammunition and grenades, two bottles filled almost to the top with kerosene. The bottles were tightly corked to prevent spillage, but through the cork a scrap of cloth protruded. It reached down into the liquid and was saturated with enough kerosene to act as a fuse when lit.

The Third Company had assembled along the road on the outskirts of Kivennapa. Salmi stepped out of the forest onto the snow-covered road to meet his scouts.

"How far behind are they?" he asked.

"More than a kilometer and a half away," the soldier replied.

Rifle and machine-gun fire broke out in the distance, and the big cannons started firing. Salmi kept his two platoons positioned tightly along both sides of the road, so he could direct them when he was ready. He spread his men out in a long line, with machine guns mounted at both ends, to box in the Russians and their tanks.

The Russian soldiers, up to this point, had proven to be poorly led and easily confused. They were hesitant, almost terrified, to enter the forest to fight, and the Finns took full advantage of this weakness. They remained in the cover of the woods, unseen and deadly. Sharpshooters climbed the thick-branched spruces and fired accurately from above.

The Finns still had fear and respect for the tanks, however. Those awesome monsters didn't turn and flee as did the panic-stricken Soviet troops. It took a tremendous amount of courage to get close enough to a moving tank to place a grenade in its treads.

Salmi skied up and down the line of men for one last check and then dropped to the powdery snow in the center of the line. In addition to the sound of shelling, a roar came from the approaching tanks as they wound around the bend. There were ten of them, followed by troops.

149

The troops walked slowly behind the massive tanks, in four lines of at least one hundred men each, followed by more tanks. When about a hundred men had entered the target area, Salmi opened fire. The heavy machine guns, Suomis, and rifles cut into the Russian ranks, driving a quarter of them back toward the second formation of tanks. The first tank of the second formation opened fire with its own heavy gun, firing aimlessly while Russian troops were being mowed down by Finnish gunfire. A Finn skied behind the trees which were parallel to the road and tossed a triple-strength grenade into the treads of the lead tank, crippling it.

Otto and Lieutenant Salmi lay only thirty meters from the road, directly facing the first formation of tanks. Grenades showered the armored vehicles as the three cannons fired wildly into the forest, but not one kerosene bomb was thrown in the first three minutes of fighting. Salmi motioned Otto to follow him; he realized that the men needed encouragement to use the new weapon. Even Salmi had his doubts, but he didn't let on to Otto.

The two men took cover among the trees. They advanced nearer to the tanks, then settled behind a wide spruce about four meters high and over three meters wide. It was weighed down by heavy layers of snow—it made perfect cover.

Otto's hands were shaking. It was cold, and striking a match with clumsy, cold-numbed hands in this freezing weather was not easy. I'd better do this right, he thought—just one blast from that tank could finish us both.

There was an awkward silence suddenly, just as if the Russian artillery suspected that something new and strange was going on, and the shelling stopped for a minute. Salmi showed Otto that he was holding the bottle in his left hand with the matches in his right. He's a left-handed thrower, Otto thought and took the bottle in his right, the matches in his left hand. Suddenly Otto heard a voice from the Russian side shouting so loudly that he almost dropped the bottle.

"Okay—one, two, *three!*" Salmi's bottle flew in the air leaving behind a thin trail of smoke. Otto repeated Salmi's action, and both bombs landed on the turrets. The bottles splintered on the icy metal, spilling their contents. Both tanks burst into flames, and smoke billowed high into the air. Flames licked the tanks' surfaces and curled their way into the interiors via cracks. One turret lid opened and a fur-capped Russian started climbing out. Before he could climb free, Suomi fire caught him and he fell forward over the edge, blood oozing from his head. Another Russian came forward, coughing and gagging, and then he, too, was shot, and propelled back into the burning tank.

The effectiveness of the kerosene bomb had been proven. In the space of just one minute, bombs whirled through the air and six Russian tanks were burning in the cold winter night. Stromberg placed his right on target, then Hietala repeated what Stromberg had already done, and Tuoppi wasn't far behind. In each instance, when a Russian soldier in his heavy quilted jacket and thick fur cap emerged from his tank, he was cut down by the Suomis.

A young Russian captain was barking orders, trying to organize some kind of defense. The captain was about the same age as Salmi, and he was behaving bravely. His face betrayed no fear, only defiance and anger at what was happening to his men. Otto squeezed his trigger and sent bullets deep into the chest of the officer. The officer's knees gave out under him. He reached vainly for support from a small tree, leaned against it briefly, but his legs wouldn't hold his weight. His head fell back and he stared toward the sky.

Is he dead, Otto wondered, letting another burst of bullets pierce through the officer. The Russian's body jerked two or three times, then remained motionless.

The fighting last about an hour. Tanks burned on the road, some of them lying tilted, at awkward angles. Russian soldiers lay dead on the bloody snow. The rest of the formation that had advanced intrepidly toward the Finnish territory had panicked and retreated to their own lines.

The Finns did not chase the Russians, and so did not take prisoners. A few were lucky enough to get felt boots off some dead soldier who had come through the Finnish line.

Lieutenant Salmi breathed a sigh of relief, and led his company back to Ahijarvi.

151

# Chapter 26

Ahijarvi was only four kilometers to the west, and the Third Company arrived there without mishap.

The kerosene bomb was an effective weapon that gave the men confidence when facing the Russian troops which endlessly rolled on across the border. Otto thought of Tuoppi at the Kaira farm, and of how determined he had been to learn to fire a rifle accurately. He had succeeded, and gone even farther, he had now taught his fellow-soldiers a new way of fighting.

Otto had told Salmi about Tuoppi and followed the lieutenant's instructions. He had gathered his own squad and four others to this sheltered spot at the barn.

Otto watched the soldiers enter the barn. He did not hurry them, even though shells were falling in the woods nearby. His excitement seemed stronger to him now than the fear of shells had ever been—a thrilling knot in his chest that came from the feeling of gratitude for another's heroism.

Arola looked closely at the soldier's faces, trying to see what they expressed. He saw suffering, fear, confidence, and even eagerness.

It was time to carry on with the business at hand. Lieutenant Salmi hadn't arrived yet, but Otto wanted to get on with the impromptu ceremony before Russian shelling rained directly over the area. He stood before the men.

"Never in my life have I had any enthusiasm for the

army, nor for killing people, and I don't want you to consider my actions now any more than respectful duty to my fellow soldier—to a man I have learned to trust with my life.''

Arola looked at Tuoppi, who was standing in front of the assembly. He still had on a dirty, white cloak, smeared with Russian blood. As he continued looking at Tuoppi, he saw the square features of his face, almost as if for the first time: his dark-circled eyes, his prominent mouth, and the dirty, weather-tanned skin of his face, bare beneath the fur cap. Otto said in an even voice, as the lieutenant entered the barn, ''I feel that my squad member Tuoppi is a simple reservist who does his duty, whatever it is, without any complaints. He has never made any unreasonable demands or requests to get out of any assignment given to him. He has succeeded in developing an antitank weapon which has already helped us destroy more of the Russian tanks than our satchel charges ever could. He has called it just a lucky break but he deserves great recognition.''

The stubble on Tuopp's square chin had become almost black, and this beard made him look thin and emaciated. He was distressed while Arola talked about him. He looked continually down at this hands, kneading his interlocked fingers in anxiety, and didn't once raise his eyes to see what reaction the other men had to the honor he was receiving.

Arola continued, ''This man has peeled more potatoes in the army than any of us ever knew existed, but he has never once complained because of the boredom. He may have been small in accomplishment, but he stands high in reliability, and he is an obedient soldier. He does not like to kill, yet he does his duty in the army, just as we all must. Now he has given us a weapon that will save many Finnish lives. I am grateful to Tuoppi, and proud to call him my friend.''

Otto stepped back and there was a slight murmur of approval, although no applause. After a moment Lieutenant Salmi stepped forward. His face was almost hidden by a thick black beard, but his eyes shone with vitality and eagerness. He began to speak.

''One of the notable features of the military group of which we are a part, is that each man here is an individually

153

solid and inventive source for the survival of all of us—inventive in using weapons so primitive and even strange, in modern warfare, that it is miraculous that we have been able to beat the enemy with such poor weapons in these few days of action. The latest invention is the kerosene bomb which Tuoppi discovered.'' Salmi fell silent. He had found out that similar kerosene bombs had been used in other units with good results, but he didn't want the men to think that Tuoppi had only rediscovered a bomb that had already been invented. ''For giving us the kerosene bomb, I feel he deserves the army's recognition. Will you please step forward, Tuoppi?''

Rather reluctantly, Tuoppi approached the lieutenant at the front of the group. It was almost unbearable to him to be the center of attention.

''Here I decorate you with the Mannerheim Medal of Bravery,'' said Salmi, pinning the bronze medal on Tuoppi's blood-stained parka.

Tuoppi's frightened voice was difficult to hear. He was very slow and hesitant in delivering his words.

''Thank you . . . ah, sir.'' He looked at Otto, who was staring at him, remembering his first experience with Tuoppi's hesitant speech. Tuoppi had had so much difficulty answering the sergeant major's questions at Viipuri. Now he was having just as much difficulty.

''You have been an excellent example to others,'' Lieutenant Salmi said in conclusion.

The men were ready to leave the barn when the whistle of a shell was heard, and another exploded only two meters away from the barn wall. The men fell on the hay-covered floor of the barn, waiting for a repeat of the shell. When no other shells came, the lieutenant shouted:

''Disperse! Disperse! Not in groups.''

The congratulations to Tuoppi would have to wait. The new Mannerheim hero quickly removed his medal while he was still flat on the ground. Otto raised his head and yelled over to him when he saw Tuoppi on his way outside.

''Mannerheim hero!''

A slow grin spread over Tuoppi's bland face. Weeks ago he had stood by silently while other reservists played cards and joked—but he was the one now classified as a hero!

Arola and Tuoppi hid under a thickly-branched spruce. Otto noticed that Tuoppi was still coughing and choking in nervousness.

While they were waiting for the shelling to stop, Hietala crawled over to extend his hand in congratulations. "You have given us a weapon, a sort of cocktail that will be an antidote to Molotov—that's it—a Molotov Cocktail!"

The men made their way back to the camp. As they walked toward the sleighs, Otto noticed that the sky had cleared, and he gazed fretfully at the few scattered clouds.

"They'll send planes out after us again soon," Otto speculated to Tuoppi.

"Take a look!" Tuoppi said, gesturing upward at a single-engine plane flying just below the departing clouds.

"I see him, I see him," Otto said. "Everybody stay put! They only look for movement. They won't see us if we stay still."

The men at the camp looked up at the one thing they feared even more than tanks. A single plane, simply by directing the artillery fire, could be more deadly than ten tanks. The plane continued to circle over the forested area. It was still overhead when the whistle of a shell flew over them again. Then another and another.

"Arola, come up here," Salmi called, and Otto inched over to the lieutenant. "Take Stromberg, Hietala, and Tuoppi, and try to get back to your sleigh. When it's safe, move your sleigh into the woods about a kilometer from here and wait for us."

Otto nodded, and with the other three men skied cautiously away, glancing at the sky and listening fearfully to the sound of shells. The plane continued to circle menacingly over the area.

Aalto and Taisto had maintained watch over the ammunition and provision sleighs. They had spotted the plane and immediately hitched up the horses and covered the sleighs with white tarps, laying long white bedsheets over the animals as well. When the plane swooped momentarily out of sight, the two soldiers shuffled the sleighs quickly into the forest and remained hidden there, waiting for Lieutenant Salmi. When Otto arrived, he found the men huddled around the sleighs, their rifles unslung and ready to fire.

Otto knew that he need not have any further doubts as to their reliability and alertness.

The shelling continued, its target the Ahijarvi road. In minutes, the farmhouse and barn were demolished. The forest was bombarded as well, and as Otto surveyed the shelling from the slight slope to which they had retreated, he was amazed at the number of unexploded "duds" that came crashing down from the sky. About a forth of them failed to detonate. Through the trees he spotted movement and recognized the lamb.

"Well, I'll be damned," he yelled to Tuoppi. "My little friend survived."

Otto made his way to where the lamb was scurrying through the woods, panicked by the shelling. He returned, holding her tightly and scratching her woolly head. She nuzzled up to him and wriggled happily.

"I don't know how you've made it this far," he said, pleased by the miracle.

The Russian surveillance plane reappeared in the distance as the Third Company was making its way up the road, but Salmi had chosen to take the chance of exposure. If he remained pinned down, the Russians at Kivennapa could easily roll up to Ahijarvi and surround the Third Company. They had no choice but to fall back and hope for a snowstorm.

At nightfall the three ammunition sleighs emerged from the forest. The six men had been in the woods, but now Aalto, Taisto, and Tuoppi drove the horses while Hietala, Stromberg, and Otto skied along parallel to the road, the lamb following behind the last sleigh. Salmi had received orders to retreat all the way to Oinola, some twenty kilometers west, to form a defense line. A huge Russian contingent, the size of a division, and with hundreds of tanks, was reported to be advancing from the south.

The regathered Third Company followed about a kilometer behind the ammunition and provisions sleighs. The men skied swiftly, streaking through the forest where shells interrupted the silence. The moon complicated their movement by providing bright visibility.

It was cold, and the soldiers had pulled up their knitted wollen masks to prevent frostbite. They skied along in

156

stooped positions, avoiding low branches. The lieutenant led his men forward, watching closely for the feared enemy scout. Each man kept a vigil, looking left, right, and back over his shoulder.

The horses hooves scraped the crusted snow in a regular rhythm. These long-haired, strong-muscled work horses struggled through the narrow passages between the trees, steam rising from their overheated bodies. They were pulling the sleighs as if they knew, somehow, that they were on a do-or-die mission.

The hours of travel to Oinala began to be tedious and Otto's thoughts turned inward. He thought of Anna and began to feel guilty about his behavior in Helsinki. Suppose he never saw Anna again, was never able to apologize to her and tell her that he forgave her? But had he really forgiven her? I am sorry for my actions, he thought, but could it ever be the same again?

Otto thought of home, a hot sauna, the comfort of having Sirkka in the kitchen baking bread, and Anna waiting for him in her warm bed.

I wish the mail would catch up with us soon! News from home would relieve my mind, he thought.

# *Chapter 27*

Lieutenant Salmi had been worried when the company had not received their mail. He knew that it would be a morale builder if the soldiers had news from home, a package to share, word from loved ones.

After Talvi was killed, Salmi had appointed another company clerk. He was Vilho Porvari, a slim, tiny man who was fast on his skis. He was shy, but efficient.

Porvari had taken off quietly from Ahijarvi, heading off alone toward Battalion headquarters. He met the Third Company on their way to Oinola.

Oinola lay east of Lake Muolaa, a small village that was still intact when they arrived.

Porvari had a rucksack full of mail when he caught up with the company. He had skied hard for several kilometers to fetch the mail, and now his army gear, the mail, and four packages hung from his belt. He hadn't left anything behind. He too, knew the meaning of mail.

Otto stood anxiously waiting to see if he had gotten a letter. He felt a surge of blood rising from the bottom of his heart to the top of his head when a thick letter was thrust in his hands. He turned his face up to the sky where the moon shone brightly, as it had, during each of the long, battle-plagued evenings. It gave enough light for him to read his letter, and he was grateful for that, but at the same time, he would rather have seen clouds gathering to give them better cover.

He thought of Johanna in Viipuri, but knew he would never hear from her. Not as long as she had her handsome husband. Otto sighed. Johanna had been such a source of comfort. He wished he could talk to her now, could kiss her, and share her warmth and goodness.

He turned back to the letter, and looked at the handwriting on it. He was glad to see that it was from Sirkka and not from Anna.

He was happy and comforted by the first page of Sirkka's letter, until he started reading about Anna. "You have tortured her unjustly and ignored her suffering. the bombing here in Helsinki is so severe that it might take our lives any day, and you would never see Anna or me again. But sometimes happiness requires suffering. I hope this war renders some sense into your soul to forgive her. It hurts me to see her suffering. I know you still love her, and I'm sure you'll have regrets if you don't forgive her . . ."

He had to look away for a moment, but soon continued reading.

"Anna had worked long hours, guiding metal through the punch press, despite bombing all the time. It's all war material for the army. You might even have machinery that has passed through her hands. She works sixteen hours a day—and in her condition . . ."

Otto stopped. "Why does she preach at me, damn it!" he muttered through clenched teeth.

"Through six days of bombing, Helsinki's streets have remained still clear of rubble. Everything is cleaned up instantly, as soon as the bombing stops.

"We knit hours on end, while we sit crowded in those tiny bomb shelters waiting for the raids to stop. Every woman is knitting masks and mittens for the soldiers at the front: to keep their faces and hands protected against the cruel weather.

"Last night we came out of the shelter about four–thirty in the morning and walked on top of the roofs in the dawn air. Entire workers' sections of Helsinki's Vallila, behind Sorkka, were in flames. It was a horrible sight.

"Hannes has been assigned to guard the Foreign Minister, Vaino Tanner, who replaced Erkko at the beginning of this war. Tanner is trusted by the working people, and by the entire country, really, because he is a man with iron nerves and has the capacity to weigh matters carefully. Hannes said that the President of the United States, Franklin Roosevelt, has offered his assistance as an intermediary in negotiations with Molotov to stop the war. Tanner had gratefully accepted, but Molotov turned down Roosevelt's offer.

"Hungary had been asked to find some way of reaching Moscow, but their efforts failed, too. Sweden tried using their friendly relations with the Soviets to persuade Molotov to change his course of action, but they have all met with firm negative replies.

"Hannes also learned the other day how Russian spies are working in the Finnish army. He said that one cold December morning Colonel Havila, his friend, was spending his last day of furlough at home in Toolo before returning to the front. The colonel's nine-year-old son Immo had been dressing up in his father's uniform. He had been very much impressed by the figures of lions which are embossed on the metal buttons. The colonel had explained that this was the symbol of Finland, and represented the nation's strength. An hour later, Immo was standing in line to buy a quart of milk at the dairy store, when he saw that the officer behind him had no lions on the buttons of his uniform. He went right home and told his father. Within just a short time the man was arrested and unmasked as a Soviet agent!

"We have all been warned to keep an eye on each uniformed soldier, to be sure that he isn't some Russian spy."

Otto paused, thinking of Kalle Kaira.

Otto read on. He learned something of the city of Terijoki, where he had spent his year of compulsory service in the army. He knew every building and every street in the whole vicinity, now held by the Russians. It made him sick with anger to read what Sirkka had written to him about the war there:

"Molotov has named the city of Terijoki to be the capital of 'The People's Republic of Karelia,' where the new government is stationed that will take over our present government at the end of the war if we lose. Otto Kuusinen, the Finnish communist who fled the country after the Civil War, has been named Prime Minister of the phony government. He's Stalin's and Molotov's closest adviser in Finnish affairs. He is waiting at Terijoki to come to Helsinki for a victory parade with his puppet government. Molotov has said that Kuusinen's government is the only one he'll negotiate with for peace.''

Otto's fists clenched. It wasn't enough that they had to fight at the front line! Back home there was another war going on—a propaganda war.

Otto placed the letter back in the envelope and sat silently for a long time. He looked at the other men who had also read letters from home; he wondered if they, too, had read the same kinds of news. Otto's conscience began to bother him about the way he had treated Anna, but he was still not ready to write to her.

He felt sad about Terijoki, but he knew that losing cities was all part of the course of war; once they drove the Russians out, Terijoki would be safe again. The newspaper reports Sirkka had told him about were the most confusing and bothersome part of her letter. He had heard before that all kinds of rumors were flying about the Finns, who were still undefeated, after all—but being on the front line, he knew all too well what the situation really was.

His delicate face looked downward in contemplation, but then he heard Salmi call the men to continue. As they skied off, there was not the flicker of a smile on anyone's face.

# Chapter 28

Otto lingered silently behind the sleigh as the company reached Oinola. His face was hollowed and anxious, and he longed to talk to someone about Anna, Helsinki, and Terijoki—about everything he had read in Sirkka's letter. But to whom could he tell his troubles? To whom could he talk about his heartache over Helsinki, since everyone felt the cruelty of war?

He kept the letter in his hip pocket. It would be safe there, and available for reading again, whenever there was time. For now he had to direct his squad in setting up camp. Suddenly he remembered Lieutenant Salmi's orders before the Third Company moved away from Ahijarvi:

"Check once again in the store for any explosives. There's bound to be some dynamite somewhere," he had told Otto. "Leave the farmhouse and the village as it is. Don't burn it. I want you to booby trap everything possible—doors, windows, and cupboards. Wrap enough dynamite around the grenades so that when they go off they'll blow up a house. Use your imagination—and do it fast!"

Otto had found Ekstrom to be devillishly creative at booby trapping. In the cellar of the village store they had found a case of dynamite. They rigged cans of food, bottles, and even spoons to set off blasts when pulled from their shelves. The process was a simple one. A can of food would be tied with fishing line to the sensitive pin of a grenade.

Around the grenade were six sticks of dynamite hidden behind the shelf. When a hungry Russian soldier grabbed the can, the grenade would trigger the dynamite. They repeated the process, using clothes, weapons, and tins of tobacco as bait. Then they carefully exited through the village, avoiding their own traps, and taking the rest of the dynamite with them. Later, Otto heard the explosions and knew that their traps had worked.

The defense line at Oinola lay on the eastern shore of the frozen Muolaa lake. It stretched three kilometers southwest of the village. Barbed-wired barricades had been strung along the line, and heavy boulders had been positioned to deter thanks. Dugouts were set up near the trenches that had been dug before the company arrived there. The unloaded sleighs were covered by tarpaulins. Huge cauldrons of hot beef stew and coffee were served to the men—their first good hot meal in days.

The Third Company set up camp at a preassigned position. They were on the slope of a hill which looked down onto a broad, clear swamp area, frozen hard and covered with a pure white pelt of knee-high snow. The village had been almost totally destroyed. The men couldn't see what had happened, but smoke from behind the hill told them the story.

The land was pockmarked with craters and dotted with unexploded shells. Whole forest areas were sheared away, but this had now become a commonplace sight.

Victories over the Russians had inspired the men's confidence, and many were disgruntled at having given way to the Soviets at a point when it appeared that they could so easily have been defeated. Rumors began to circulate about the strategy of the Finnish Commander-in-Chief, Marshal Mannerheim. The most popular theory was that they were taunting the Russians, in order to draw them deeper and deeper into Finland, where they would eventually encounter an impenetrable defense line and be ambushed. This defense line, according to various sources, was already under construction and soon would be completed. The entire front line would then fall back and join forces with Mannerheim's fresh divisions.

The morning following the Third Company's arrival at

Oinola was cold. No fire could be built to make food or to warm the dugouts or tents, since the smoke would rise like an Indian smoke signal. The men were hungry, tired, and uneasy. They had no way of knowing how soon fighting would resume in the trenches. Some of the troops stood alertly on guard.

Sergeant Hakli had managed to trim his mustache, and it looked even more like the Fuehrer's as he stood in front of the several squads of men who waited for the provisions sleigh to arrive. Hakli was as alert as ever. He held his head up as if he were at review. He had been among an elite group, selected to represent the army in special state parades and national holiday marches.

"I'll shown you some warm-up tricks," Hakli said, noting the uneasiness among the men. He tossed his rifle into the air, where it did several somersaults and returned to his hands. Holding the rifle barrel between two fingers of his right hand, he gave it a kick. It twirled in a circle in front of him, and suddenly he was holding it in perfect position to fire.

The men stood watching for several minutes until Sergeant Ekstrom arrived. "If you had music with that act, I'd think it was a show," he said, and laughed along with the men.

The men tensed for a minute at a sudden eruption of machine-gun fire from the front line. Then they heard the Finnish rifles responding to the Russian shots and there was quiet again.

"The Russians are back on our tails," Hakli said, putting his rifle on his shoulder just as the mess kettle arrived.

The provisions officer, who was a stumbled along across the soft snow on the heels of the kitchen crew. He began mincing up and down the line of hungry, waiting men, snapping orders to those dishing up the inevitable stew and hardtack.

"You men, hurry up, I haven't got all day to spend here," he muttered, although everyone was moving as fast as possible.

Thin smoke and steam rose in the air as the soldiers stood patiently with their pails, each of which had at least a centimeter of old food frozen inside.

"Where did they dig up that clown?" Hietala asked, watching the major. "He even has a riding crop!"

"I'm surprised he doesn't wear a monocle," Stromberg put in, shaking his head and laughing.

Otto chuckled with the others. It was comical to see such a pompous, strutting fool taking charge of the meal, as if he were some great general bolstering his men to do battle against overwhelming odds.

"Now this is what I'd call your 'typical' officer. If I weren't so hungry, I'd move to the end of the line just to take in the show again," Otto said to Stromberg.

"We ought to get Lietuenant Salmi out here. He could learn a thing or two from him," Hietala said, looking down the line for him. "Where is he now?"

"Back in his tent," Ekstrom volunteered. "Going over his orders to form a solid line of defense for us."

As they moved forward, artillery fire began. It was coming from a single cannon, behind the hill. The Finnish artillery was in the field at last. Some of the men cheered, for this was the first Finnish artillery fire they had heard. Ekstrom and Otto knew, however, that within minutes Russian artillery would come down to wipe out the brave artillery men. And that would leave them directly in the line of fire.

"Third Company," Ekstrom shouted, "disperse to any safe place you can find. We're going to get shelled any second."

"Stay where you are," shouted the provisions major. "Nobody goes anywhere until I say so!"

The men looked toward Ekstrom, who pushed his way up to the mess kettle.

"Major," he yelled over the roar from the Finnish cannonade, "the Russians are going to open up in about half a minute to wipe out that cannon, and if we stay here they'll wipe us out, too. They'll start with short shots and work their way in until they reach the target.

"I'm in command here, and you'll do as I say," the officer snapped.

Ekstrom stomped back to Otto and the others. "Arola, go get Lieutenant Salmi, fast!"

Before Otto got ten meters away a shell burst behind

him. Then another and another. The third landed less than two meters from where Otto had hit the snow. The explosion threw dirt and snow all over him. His feet fell into the newly-created crater and he felt numb. He could hardly hear a thing. He curled up in the bottom of the crater and stayed there while the shelling continued. He moved his arms and legs and found gratefully that he was unhurt. Earth had been scattered over the provisions sleigh, bringing an end to their first hot meal in two days. The major had flattened out on the snow, covering his head with his arms.

Hietala joined Otto in the crater.

"What an idiot!" Otto said. "I hope we doin't have to put up with him for long."

"I doubt that the major will stay alive much longer," Hietala predicted cheerfully. "If he survives the shelling, somebody is bound to shoot him."

Stromberg inched over to them.

"Somebody ought to get on the field telephone and tell that cannon crew to stop firing," he said. "Want me to go find the lieutenant, Arola?"

"Stay put. Salmi is taking care of it. If the field telephone is working, that is."

The Finnish cannon fire didn't stop. The Russian guns lobbed hundreds of rounds into the Third Company camp. This wasn't the random shelling that they had experience in the past. This time their own artillery had given away their position as accurately as if the Russian had the exact coordinates on a map.

When a crater burst open in the earth only a few meters from Otto he automatically hopped into it, comforted by the assurance that two shells wouldn't land in the same spot, one after the other.

As suddenly as it had begun, the shelling from the Finnish side ceased. After ten more minutes the Russians directed their shelling to the right, away from the Third Company camp. Heads popped out of trenches and craters, looking all around, ready to drop back down at the whistle of a shell. The men cautiously got to their feet, hobbling painfully on stiff joints that had been tightly bent in the freezing cold during the five hours of shelling.

Now the screams of the two wounded men became sickeningly audible. Toivo Viiro, the young medic, rushed about tending them. Otto sat on the edge of a crater, his short legs dangling in the hole, his elbows resting on his thighs, chin in his hands. He looked up and surveyed the scene around him. Tuoppi, Stromberg, Hietala, Taisto, and Aalto. The squad was still complete. He heard Ekstrom asking, "Arola, are you all right?"

"I'm all right," Otto said.

"Stromberg and Hietala, get the others and meet me at the supply trench," Otto called out to them. He picked his way gingerly through the debris and noted the great amount of damage that had been done.

Only two of the horses had survived the shelling, and they had fled frantically out toward the lake shore. The bloody remains of the other beasts seemed to be scattered all over the camp. One horse lay on its side, unmarked except for a hole in its throat from which only a little blood had drained before clotting from the cold. Its eyes were open, and frozen in an expression of terror so awful that Otto turned from the sight. This was a bad one, he thought dismally. God help us if they keep it up!

Many rifles had been left uncovered in the ammunition trench, and dirt and mud had to be cleaned from the barrels and breeches. Otto, Tuoppi, and Stromberg would be kept hard at work.

# Chapter 29

"Arola, come over here a minute, will you?" Ekstrom called. "I just got a message from the front line. They've got a man with a bad case of shell shock. Crazy, you know. He thinks everybody is trying to kill him. I want you to take a sleigh, go pick him up, and bring him back here. We can't spare a medic for this."

"You want me to go now?" Otto asked, incredulous. "We haven't even found the horses yet."

"No, no. Go during the night. You have to face that moonlight, but that's the best we can do. I'll show you where to go," he said, pulling out a map and indicating the place where Otto was to pick up the sick man.

"Where's Lieutenant Salmi? Does he know about this?" Otto asked.

"I haven't seen him since this morning. He said something about going up to the front, maybe he sat out the shelling there. He may still be there when you get there. All I know is that he puts me in command whenever he isn't around and I know it's our responsibility to shuttle the sick back from the front line. I wouldn't ask you to do this if I could help it, Arola."

"I know you wouldn't. I was just wondering where Salmi is, Sergeant. I wasn't questioning you," Otto explained.

"Let me know when you're ready to go—and try to find those horses. Take someone else along with you, in case

168

your man gets violent.''

Aalto and Taisto returned to camp before dark, leading the horses. Otto, looking serious and edgy, took Stromberg aside.

''Erik, you and I are going up to the front about eleven tonight. We've got to pick up a man and bring him back here.''

The two men found a horse and led it to the road which led to the frontline trenches. The sleigh moved around the bend. The moon cast a ghostly shadow over the trees and shimmered through the gloom. Otto felt a strange foreboding. He was sad and scared at the same time—sad for the poor man who had lost his mind, but afraid that the Russian scouts might cut them down at any minute from behind the trees.

The squeak of the sleigh runners as they crunched over the dry snow seemed ten times louder during the night than it had during the day. The woods were alive with imaginary shapes—snipers running from tree to tree, waiting for the right moment to attack. Stromberg twisted and jumped as the apparitions flashed momentarily into view and then vanished. Otto held the reins and silently cursed the horse, as if it were responsible for the noise of the sleigh. His nerves were frayed and he cursed the sick man, Ekstrom, and Lieutenant Salmi too.

''What right do they have to send us out here?'' he grumbled.

The road turned to the right and the moon was suddenly directly above them. Under its full illumination, every specter in the woods cast a terrifying image upon the whiteness.

''Otto, Otto,'' Erik whispered, ''did you see that?'' Over there!'' Otto stared into the shadows, grabbing frantically for his Suomi while trying to hold onto the reins. But there was nothing there.

For the first time, the possibility of capture seemed very real. Thumbscrews, castration, fingernails, being ripped out with pliers—these and other similarly excruciating thoughts cascaded through Otto's mind.

What he feared most was that there had been a mistake and that the Finns in the front line had withdrawn or been overrun. He and Erik would then run right into the Russians

169

and surely be captured before they had a chance to destroy either themselves or the Russians.

A white apparition suddenly appeared, this time in the road, and he held a rifle.

"Hold it right there," the ghost said, "Are you from the Third?"

Otto gratefully realized that the ghost was a Finn.

"We're from the Third," he answered.

"Come on then," the soldier motioned. "Follow me."

He led the horse a hundred meters up the road, pointing to a dugout.

Otto thanked the man and lowered himself into the dugout. The shelter was completely black and he could see nothing. He wanted to light a match because he could only dimly make out the two figures by the far wall. But the flash of a match might bring instant fire from the enemy.

"I'm from the Third Company," he spoke into the darkness, hoping he wouldn't have to offer any further explanation.

A voice in the darkness said, "All right, Arvo. You get to go home."

"I'm not going home," another voice said accusingly. "You're taking me to the Russians."

Otto could hear the man breathing hard. Then he spoke in Otto's direction. "This other guy is the one you want, not me! He and the others want you to think I'm crazy because I found out who they really are."

Goddamn it, thought Otto, he's really gone. He'll probably fight us all the way back to camp. No wonder they want to get him out of here.

Otto's eyes finally focused in the darkness, but all he could see where two men holding tightly to each other—one claiming that he wasn't crazy while the other claimed he was. Otto was nonplussed.

What to do? Which man would it be? How can I tell which one is crazy, Otto thought.

Seizing on a solution, he told his partner, "Erik, give me a hand. We have to gag this man before we can take him out of here."

Otto thought he, too, might lose his mind if another shell

hit as close as had the one back at the camp a few hours before.

"Raise him up to stand," Arola ordered, hoping that the right one would respond.

"And don't raise your voices," he whispered.

At that instant both men stood up, each holding onto the other.

"Shoot the Russians!" Otto said, and one man let go to reach for his rifle. He must be the crazy one, Otto thought. Otto felt himself to be in charge again. "Hold him, Stromberg. I'll gag him."

Stromberg put a hand over the fellow's mouth and forced his hands behind his back.

"Gag him," he told Otto, keeping a grip on the struggling man.

"Ready!" Otto said, covering the man's mouth with his handkerchief, which he then knotted at the back of the man's neck. "Take him out," he said above the murmur of the struggling man who was trying to shout through the tight cloth, and was doing everything in his power to avoid being dragged outside.

Otto looked back at the other man who was sitting quietly on a bench. The man suddenly ran into the corner, reaching for a rifle that leaned against the earthen wall.

"You Russian, I'll shoot you," the man said, pointing the rifle toward Otto. He tried desperately to load the gun, but his hands were too cold and clumsy. "I'll kill all you Russians. You're devils, beasts—you murdered my sister!" Then he burst into tears.

Otto saw his mistake. He jumped at the man and forced the rifle from his grasp. He threw the gun to the floor and put his glove over the man's mouth. Looking at the man in the darkness, he saw a square, honest face, a short nose, and large nostrils. His eyes would have gleamed if there had been light to see them. Otto felt a surge of embarrassment at having gagged the wrong man.

"Stromberg!" he whispered, "we almost took the wrong man!" Otto shifted Arvo to his right and forced him to walk to the entrance, while Stromberg let the gagged man speak.

The wrong man stood silent for a minute, calming his

171

anger. He realized the mistake. They loaded Arvo on the sleigh and then secured him with ropes. His friend wrapped an extra blanket around him.

"Don't worry," Otto tried to reassure Arvo's guard, "we'll get him back to a hospital. He'll be all right."

The horse's shadow moved over the icy snow as they headed back. If it weren't for the squeak of the runners and the sound of the horses hooves, the stillness would have been unbearable.

Otto held onto the reins tightly, looking over his shoulder at the gagged man. Stromberg kept his eyes open for any movement in the woods.

It was past midnight when Otto and Stromberg returned to camp with their charge. They deposited Arvo at the medic's tent. Stromberg went to take care of the horse and sleigh while Otto went to report to Sergeant Ekstrom.

Otto heard a muffled voice from inside Ekstrom's tent and hesitated before requesting permission to enter. Sergeant Hakli was sitting crosslegged on the tent floor and Ekstrom sat opposite him.

"Any problems, Arola?" Ekstrom asked, motioning Otto to sit down.

"No, we got him back and delivered him to the medic. I wouldn't say it has been a real pleasure seeing that poor guy, though. He was really gone."

"Arola, did Viiro say anything to you about the lieutenant?" Ekstrom asked, rather shakily, looking down at his pipe and scraping the bowl with his knife. He handed Otto his pouch to fill his own pipe.

Otto looked at Ekstrom, then at Hakli. He felt a familiar hot tingling sensation spread across his face.

"What about him? Is he hurt? Viiro didn't say anything about him."

"Otto, he's dead. Got it today in the shelling. It was a direct hit."

There was an uneasy silence in the tent. Otto could neither light his pipe nor speak. Neither of the sergeants said anything more.

Otto swallowed, trying to utter a word, any word. He tried again and again, but he could only make short, choking sounds. He wept then and shook silently, rocking on his

172

haunches. The shelling, the lunatic Arvo . . . and now this! The impact exploded somewhere inside him and drained out through his sad eyes. Ekstrom reached out and put a hand on his shoulder, but Otto didn't feel it. He took a deep, jerky breath, trying to regain his composure. When he exhaled he broke down into sobs again. Finally he caught a breath and held it, then exhaled slowly, regaining control with great effort. Wiping his eyes and nose on his sleeve, he sat quietly until he was sure he could succeed in producing words.

"What happens now?" he croaked.

"We wait here until they send us another officer," Ekstrom answered, "and hope to God it's not some idiot like that fool of a major. I was sorry it wasn't him who got it today, instead of Salmi, but I guess it doesn't work that way."

"Ekstrom, you ought to run the company," Otto said sincerely. "You and Hakli know as much as any officer, and the men respect you more than they will some new man."

"I am in charge now, for as long as it takes for them to get a commander out here."

"What about the rest of the men? Do they know about Salmi?" Otto wanted to know.

"Most everybody knows. As far as we could tell, he was in his dugout when he got it."

Otto focused carefully on the words "as far as we could tell," and knew that meant that little had remained of Salmi's body. His death must have been instantaneous.

The men stayed close to their foxholes at Oinola in the following days. The shelling and Salmi's death and demoralized them.

Otto could see a veil of sadness over the men's eyes. He felt the change in all of them. He himself was too numb to communicate with anyone.

On the second day of waiting the new commander and five young replacements made it into camp.

The new company commander was Lieutenant Aimo Klami, from the reserve compound at Viipuri. Although he was twenty-six years old, he had a boyish face and could have passed for eighteen. The trip from Viipuri had been a long, arduous one. Their truck had been forced to leave the road repeatedly in order to avoid the shells, and several times they had had to dig the vehicle out of snow banks.

Ekstrom introduced himself and literally had to drag the six men into his tent. They were dazed and numb from their experience of being under fire. Otto brought them their ammunition and they headed for their designated platoons under his supervision. Sergeant Ekstrom began to explain the Third Company's situation to Klami, who appeared to be recovering his composure.

"I'm quite aware of the situation here," he suddenly interrupted. "I've been thoroughly briefed as to what Lieutenant Salmi had accomplished and, quite frankly, I'm not impressed."

Sergeant Ekstrom sat in shocked silence. He realized that he had a drawing-board general on his hands, and that only experience would change his attitude. Words would be useless.

"I don't know what kind of leadership you men expect," Klami continued, "but I must tell you that I have been trained as an officer and I expect therefore to be treated as one. Don't let my age deceive you, Sergeant."

"Yes, sir," Ekstrom replied, expressionless.

"I want you to call the company platoon leaders in here. We are moving out to Kyyrola in the morning, and I think we should get a few things straight. I want to see your ordnance and provisions officers as well."

Ekstrom left the tent and immediately went searching for Hakli and Arola. He wanted to warn them of what they would be up against before they attended the meeting, and perhaps the three of them, working together, would be able to save the company from the disaster that this new man's leadership seemed destined to create.

# Chapter 30

The Third Company men were to get no rest after the boyish-looking Lieutenant Klami took charge of the company. His order was to fire, fire, fire—at their own shadows or anything.

"They came to take our land from us, and we must show them our strength!" Klami shouted.

"He is a vile officer," Otto declared at the ammunition depot, reluctantly giving out rounds from a dwindling supply. "He'll destroy us," Otto predicted. "What will happen to the company when the men are left without any rounds to fire?"

Tuoppi silently looked toward the men dragging one foot in front of the other over the snow, famished and weak from long hours without sleep. He spat on the snow, but would have spat deliberately in Klami's face if he could have.

Arola sat on the sleigh in despair, looking at Tuoppi, Hietala, and Stromberg. He rose slowly and mechanically to his feet.

"What kind of a beast did we get?" he whispered through lips that were dry and white from the cold.

Early at dawn the lieutenant ordered the cessation of the empty, futile firing that had killed no one, but used up a critical amount of ammunication.

"We're moving three kilometers north of here, to the outskirts of Kyyrola. We'll wipe out the enemy there,"

Klami had told them.

After all their supplies and ammunition had been packed, the company skied arriving at Kyyrola by noon.

Arola's squad led the two horses. His mouth was as dry as cotton and he moved his lips back painfully. He was almost in tears. How on earth would he be able to supply the men with ammunition if that idiot Klami kept ordering them to fire blindly toward no man's land? But if he protested Klami could have him shot for disobeying orders.

They settled down at the south edge of the village in a wooded area, well protected by a dense growth of timber and underbrush.

"We start digging our dugouts here," Klami ordered in his high voice, eyes bright with the joy of command, as if he were still in boot camp.

Otto looked solemnly at Ekstrom and returned his gaze to Klami. After a moment of silence he said, "I'm going to find a place for my own shelters."

The Third Company worked through the afternoon and night, and into the next morning, hacking at the frozen ground. The dugouts were nearly two meters deep and five meters square. The men chopped down trees to provide support timbers for the ceilings. The tents were stored under heavy spruce trees.

The new dugouts were ready by early dawn. They had been completely covered by timber and earth. The men shoveled clean white snow over them to provide camouflage. The entrances were well concealed with snow-covered branches. The chimneys from the wood-burning stoves were directed under the thick spruce trees, so that the boughs would dissipate the smoke and prevent it from rising in a direct, easily observable column.

Otto had hated Klami instantly. His speech to the platoon leaders at Oinola marked him to be everything that Otto had learned to despise about the military. When he first arrived at Kyyrola, though, he was too busy to pay much attention to Klami. While looking for a safe place to store the ammunition he had come upon a huge crater in a slope. The hole was far too large to have been made by a shell, so Otto guessed that it had been made by a bomb from one of the Russian bombers returning from Viipuri or Helsinki.

When their dugout was finished Otto gathered his squad and they set to work on the crater. First they widened it and leveled the floor. Then they covered it, first with timbers for support, then with branches and earth, and, finally, with snow for camouflage. The dirt floor was covered with spruce and pine boughs. They made the structure large enough to store all of their ammunition, or to shelter twenty men if necessary, and there was even room for a horse if the animals had to be brought in during a shelling. Hietala, who was not usually quick-witted referred to the shelter as the Molotov Crater, and the name stuck.

The work was exhausting, but there was little time for rest. Reconnaissance patrols returned with news of many tanks, and staggering numbers of Russians troops camped ten to twelve kilometers to the east. The bunkers had to be finished before daylight in order prevent observation by aircraft.

The only man who didn't work was Lieutenant Klami; although it was his privilege as company commander, he certainly gained no respect from the men by remaining entirely in the role of supervisor.

After the men had been working ceaselessly for hours on the Molotov Crater, Klami walked over Otto. "You don't need all these men working here anymore," he said in an arrogant voice, making a show of inspecting the crater.

"I need my men!" Otto shouted back. "In time we might even need more men."

"I gave an order to have all the dugouts ready by now. Is yours done?" the lieutenant asked, his boyish eyes staring at Otto.

"I heard your order, Lieutenenat. I think this place is now serviceable," Otto answered in a firm voice, suppressing his rage.

"Now one more thing, Corporal Arola. Keep a full supply of ammunition on hand. We will need plenty at the front to defend our position. Don't let the supplies diminish," said Klami, raising his tenor voice and pushing his cap up from his forehead, as if to get a better look at Otto.

"You tell the Battalion Command to send us ammunition. Look at the ammo here. That's all we have since almost half of it was wasted at Oinola. You don't know a damn thing about war!'' Otto's voice was trembling, and his fists were ready inside his gloves.

Tuoppi had just stepped inside the crater and heard the lieutenant. He remained at the entrance, legs spread, and then Hietala stepped in.

"If you so much as raise your voice once more, let alone order the men around as if they were a bunch of sheep, you'll find yourself hanging from your testicals on the highest branch of a tree in the middle of camp,'' Hietala growled.

Klami touched his pistol on his belt.

"Before you could fire it, you'd be dead. Try it.''

Klami dropped his hand to his side. "You will all be courtmartialed.''

Hietala hit him in the stomach, and Klami rolled on the floor, crying in pain.

"Not one word of this anywhere, or you'll be calling death's name. You are hated by each man in this company.''

The lieutenant left just as Sergeant Ekstrom walked over.

"He looked like a whipped dog, what happened?''

Otto looked at his men, and then Ekstrom, but he didn't know if he could be trusted, so he said; "He came to inspect the place and asked about the ammunition supply. I told him the truth, and he was surprised that nothing had come yet to replace the stock.''

Ekstrom smiled, showing his smoke-stained teeth. "I'll talk to the lieutenant about supplies too, so take it easy, Arola.''

Ekstrom left, suspecting that there had been at least a hot exchange of words between the men and the lieutenant. He was hoping that time would perhaps cure the young officer's enthusiasm for war. But none of the men could be sure. They could only wait and see how things would develop.

# Chapter 31

The first night at the front line, Lieutenant Klami repeated his Oinola mistake and ordered the men to continue firing, regardless of their limited visibility. But to Otto's surprise, he had not said a word about the incident at the Molotov Crater. While Ekstrom had suspected a hot exchange of words, he had decided against asking Klami about it.

Russian patrols soon ventured to the garrison the Finnish defense lines. They had apparently become even more fearful of the woods where they had suffered such tremendous losses. They tried to advance in the open, searching for a weak spot in the Finnish defense, but were unsuccessful.

The temperature had dropped to twenty-five degrees below, and there was constant fear that the weapons would freeze, especially the automatic weapons that had proven so effective during warmer weather.

Otto worked hard on the frozen weapons, eagerly employing all the skills he had learned so painfully at gunsmith school. Timing mechanisms had to be thawed out and reassembled. Cartridge clips had to be emptied, cleaned of frozen oil, and reloaded. Excess grease had to be wiped off in order to prevent freezing but, even so, the weapons occasionally froze at critical moments.

The feeling of futility, of utter fear and frustration, was described by one man just back from the trenches. He told how he had been firing his Suomi in short sporadic bursts at a Russian patrol when two of the enemy came charging across the snow to his right. The Finn twisted around and pulled the trigger frantically as he swept his weapon from left to right, hoping to hit both of the approaching men—but nothing happened! He jerked violently at the breech bolt in an attempt to clear the chamber, but it was frozen at 25° below zero. He was defenseless. Luckily, another soldier to his left had seen the two approaching Russians and was able to drop both of them with his rifle. The incident wasn't an isolated one, however, and the men in the Third Company began to take even greater care of their weapons, pampering them, as it were.

Otto's fears about Klami were realized: the officer repeated the order to fire endlessly night and day. "It's a hopeless case," Otto raved to Ekstrom, and both men and Hakli too, went to see the lieutenant at his command post to tell him that only if he could guarantee that an endless supply of ammunition would arrive daily, could they afford to keep up the incessant firing. Otherwise, the platoon leaders would have to ignore his order, since it was their responsibility to the men to have ammunition for them when they needed it.

The lieutenant looked at the men silently for a moment, almost perceptibly expanding his chest with air, like a bantam rooster.

"I've issued my orders and they must be followed. The first man refusing to do so will be shot. That's front-line military discipline."

Ekstrom, Otto, and Hakli silently left the lieutenant's quarters and headed for the Molotov Crater. Ekstrom promised Otto that he would tell the men to take it easy with the firing.

Four days went by with the horrible fear that the Russians might make an effort to break through and that they would not have rounds enough to stay put. The tension at Molotov Crater was almost unbearable. The squad leaders felt as if it were their sacred duty to keep the men well-supplied, but they were also fearful of a disciplinary disasters.

Bright sunny days continued, and so did the sub-zero temperatures. Only a few cases of ammo had arrived.

While Otto was counting out the rounds on hand, he

came upon a bundle wrapped in a horse blanket. It was lying on the corner of the crater and had escaped his attention thus far.

"Look Tuoppi, here's the box you rescued from Kaira's farm."

"Yes, I saw it there the other day, but didn't want to bother you at the time. Be careful, there's something else in that pile of hay."

Otto rummaged around in the hay, and discovered a violin case hidden away.

"Where did you get this?"

"At one of the houses in Ahijarvi. I thought you might like to have it. Does it look okay?"

"It sure does. It even has all it's strings!" Otto said, after opening the case. "But it's too cold to play the violin. It loses its sound if its played in weather like this." He wrapped it safely in the blanket again, and placed it on top of the ammo cases.

"Thanks, Tuoppi."

"What are we going to do with the brown box?" Tuoppi wanted to know, trying to shift the conversation away from himself.

Otto picked up the box. It was a forty centimeter cube, made of stained, polished birch, with a small brass lock securing the hinged top.

Otto set to work trying to pry open the box with a knife blade. The cover would not open. Ekstrom arrived in the crater, and Otto told him of his suspicion that the box might have been left purposely for them to find.

"Well," Ekstrom cautioned, "if we're going to open it, let's get out of this place. I hate to think what would happen if it blew up in here!"

"Good point," Otto agreed. "Where shall we take it?"

They moved over to the sergeant's bunker, which was empty at that moment, and Otto resumed his efforts but with considerably greater caution. When he was finally able to force the bolt, it came open slowly, breaking the lock. He looked anxiously toward Ekstrom, keeping one hand on the top of the box.

"I'll do it," Ekstrom said quietly. "You two get over in the corner just to be safe. No point in all of us risking it."

Ekstrom pulled his knife from his belt and knelt down so that the box was at eye level. Cautiously he slipped the blade horizontally through the crack at the hinged top. He lifted up the handle of the knife, peering through the slight opening. Seeing nothing, he opened the lid completely and let it fall backward on the table.

"A radio! It's a radio," he exclaimed.

Otto and Tuoppi were already looking over his shoulder in amazement at the compact panel, the earphones, and the microphone. On top of the radio lay a small booklet. Ekstrom opened it. The page contained a list of locations in Karelia and a corresponding list of unrelated words.

"This is an instruction booklet!" Ekstrom shouted, flipping through it, reading the translations for a number of Russian phrases.

"Look at this," Otto said, examining a broken wire dangling from the inside of the box lid. Ekstrom put the booklet aside and leaned down to look. The wire was corroded at one end. A small pile of corrosive material had gathered on the panel top, as if it had bubbled up from within the box. The three men stared silently at each other.

"I think we are very, very lucky" the sergeant said, taking a calming deep breath. He used his knife to unscrew the four screws which fastened the panel to the box. The panel was stuck with the corrosive substance, but Ekstrom delicately pried it up with his knife. He whistled softly as he stared down at the four sticks of dynamite tied together and wired to two badly corroded batteries. The "guts" of the radio took up only half the space of the box, and the dynamite and batteries occupied the remainder.

The three of them were dumfounded. They knew full well who had left the box for them. Had it not been for the leaky batteries and the broken wire, they wouldn't be alive to curse Kalle for his misdeeds.

"I should have known right away that he was up to something when I saw him sneaking around the lieutenant's office," Otto said in retrospect.

"And the supply shack! Remember the supply shack? I knew this thing had something to do with Kaira," Tuoppi said, obviously proud of the fact that he had helped to expose a traitor, even though it was too late to catch up with him.

"You know what really bothers me more than his being a traitor?" Otto asked rhetorically. "He gave the Russians our exact position, knowing it would be shelled, and then he left his parents there to be blown away with the rest of us! A man like that surely can't be normal."

"That is really unbelievable," Ekstrom growled, pulling the dynamite out of the box and ripping off the detonator. "I wonder what they could have offered him, to make him do something so outrageous to his family. Here are four extra sticks of dynamite that we can put to good use. We'll blow up one of their tanks with their own dynamite!" he chuckled, delighted by the irony of it.

"Ekstrom, do you know anything about radios?" Otto asked.

"Not a damned thing, but there's a kid in Hakli's platoon who is supposed to be good with them. Let's give it to him."

On December twentieth, the men got a treat which raised their spirits: the mail sleigh pulled in among the dugouts. Despite the shelling, men from every shelter crawled out of their holes, like tunnel-dwelling rodents escaping a flood, to wait hopefully for their names to be called. The corporal who had brought the sleigh wasn't brave enough—or fool-hardy enough—to stand out in the open while shells rained down all around him, so he was quickly ushered to Ek-strom's dugout. There the platoon leaders who were off duty quickly organized the mail and delivered it to their respective platoons.

Otto was sitting on the pile of ammunition boxes. His mind went to Helsinki, and he remembered again the night when he had run away from Anna in anger because of what she had done. He had thought that their love would have lasted for years, or for a lifetime, but now he wondered. He had not yet written her a letter. He couldn't just jump back in and restore his relationship with her, despite his sister Sirkka's blunt appeals to him to do so.

Now the mail clerk handed him a sweet-scented letter. He suddenly realized, when he saw the date on the letter, that it was almost Christmas time. How can I maintain this coldness toward Anna, he wondered, as his nostrils inhaled a feminine fragrance that went right to his head and stimulated all of his senses.

He longed for another Christmas at home, where he would be able to sit by the fire with his sister, his mother, and perhaps . . . Anna, too. Why was it that his world that had been turned upside down?

"Merry Christmas, dear brother! This will be a Christmas we look forward to with sadness, not expecting to see you gathered with us around the dinner table. We might have to do what we have done every night for so long—stay in the basement shelter of our apartment building. I hope it's not the night that a bomb decides to fall on our building. Bombs have already destroyed so many buildings, even as tall as this one. With the good Lord willing, maybe we can at least have a quiet meal in peace. Wherever we are, you can be sure we will be thinking of you, Otto, dear.

"Every day as I walk past the National Theater, I read the sign left on top of the entrance about Thornton Wilder's play *Our Town*. It makes me wonder if Helsinki is still our town, and for how long. We pray to God you boys at the front can keep on fighting until some reasonable change comes to our rescue.

"I have been serving an endless stream of foreign correspondents who have come to Helsinki to report to the world about the war. But most of the time, they drink at Kamp Bar, where they evidently do most of their interviewing, and I wonder what kind of reporting can be done about the war from bars.

"Hannes and I are together as much as he has time to spare. Since he has become a guard at Foreign Minister Vaino Tanner's office, he has at least a better knowledge of what happens in the government, and how the war is going.

"Tanner is determined to end the war with a negotiated peace. He is trying to get to Molotov one way or the other, without giving up our rights as an independent nation. He is iron-willed in his determination and we all wish him success in ending the war.

"Now for the sad family news. Your brother Olavi has been wounded in action. He was shot in the right foot and is in the hospital somewhere in Lahti. Our brother-in-law, Helvi's husband, was killed in action, and Helvi had to be hospitalized in a state of shock. She is still being kept under sedation. There is also a rumor that Helena's husband has been wounded, but we have received no official information about him yet.

"I must also write to you about Anna's love for you. She has not gone out once since you left her. She trusts that you'll come to her by the time the war ends. Please Otto, write to her, even if you have not yet forgiven her."

The letter continued with other, less depressing news. Otto read and reread the long letter.

How could this sad state of affairs suddenly have come upon them? Where were they going? What was happening in their lives? He felt very frightened by these unanswered and unanswerable questions.

He looked at Tuoppi and Stromberg who sat nearby reading their own letters from home, and he wished they could help him. But, of course, they couldn't. They had problems of their own—maybe even worse ones.

Finally Otto folded the letter neatly and tucked it into his coat pocket. He would have to write to both girls soon.

What right do I have to condemn Anna, he asked himself, and vowed that he must try to get over some of his bitterness toward her. I was doing the same thing in Terijoki and Viipuri! But . . . do I really love her? If I loved her, would this matter so much? Otto sighed, feeling confused and lonely.

The others in the bunker had all received letters and packages from home too. They sat around shuffling pages, opening up boxes, and munching homemade cookies. Although it wasn't Christmas yet, it seemed like it in the Third Company. The shelling had subsided for a while, and Otto leaned back against the dirt wall, closed his eyes, conjured up an image of the accoutrements of past Christmases: a hot sauna, a good ham with all the trimmings and casseroles that would accompany it, a fruit soup, rice pudding, and a good glass of wine. What luxury! He wondered if he would live long enough to ever be so fortunate again.

The joy of receiving news—even tragic news, with so many messages about loved ones being hurt and killed—brought about a change in the Third Company's morale. The lieutenant hadn't carried out his foolhardy idea of doubling the amount of firing on the line, and this provided another much-needed boost to sagging spirits. They began to feel a little of the Christmas spirit and decided that, for this one day at least, they would do their best to have a joyful celebration.

"Hey, Otto," Hietala called to him, "how about making this day merry with a song or two?" He looked at Otto with a broad grin.

"Wait a minute before you start," Tuoppi said, unwrapping a bundle of three candles, lighting them on the top of ammunition boxes, and then placing pine boughs around them. "I hope this lifts our spirits."

In a few minutes Otto and Hietala sat on top of the ammunition boxes where several men had gathered. The lamb curled up near the haystack, as if she were in her old barn. Both of the players were running their harmonicas between their lips to tune them.

"What do you want to hear?" Hietala asked.

"Kaksipa Poikaa Kurikasta," said a voice behind Otto.

"Okay, 'Two Boys from Kurikka' it is. Let's go—one, two, three," he counted. Every voice in the dugout joined in as Arola and Hietala played the fast rhythmic polka, then another, and then yet another song, until it seemed as if they all had forgotten where they actually were.

Their songfest was rudely interrupted by a shell exploding only twenty meters away from the dugout. The ground shook violently.

Silence followed and there was no followup to the first shell. Hietala and Otto began playing again, but this time more quietly. The sober-faced men listened silently, some reading their over again and some munching cookies. Soon the peacefulness would end and the expedition to Kyyrola would being.

# Chapter 32

In the early morning, Otto cautiously led his ordnance squad north, toward Kyyrola village. He had developed a fear of meeting a Russian patrol that might manage to break through the Finnish front line. In addition there was the fear that everything in the village might have been booby-trapped by the Finns as they left, against the possibility of a Russian advancement.

Kyyrola hadn't been set to the torch, fortunately, and this uniquely Karelian village seemed a very quaint, interesting place, with many traces of the Karelian customs left behind. Evidence of their art was in every yard, where piles of terracotta bowls, pots, and vases of every size and style provided abundant testimony to the skill of the evacuated dwellers.

Otto needed some special springs to use in making timed-satchel charges for the soldiers to use against the Russian tanks. Throwing the strengthened, dynamite-grenade charges and Molotov Cocktails was not enough. The men couldn't always get close enough to the tanks to destroy them on the first try, and the instant explosion limited any possible second attempt. They had only the capacity to destroy one tank at a time. Otto wanted to do better than that.

Hardware wasn't the only thing that Otto and his squad needed. They were always on the lookout for any kind of food, to break the awful monotony of Army rations. They headed straight to the general store. Hardtack and canned rations, with an occasional helping of stew would sustain a man, but the craving for something good to eat was always with them.

The store had been pilfered earlier, but a variety of foods remained scattered on the shelves and floor, and around the storage area. Otto warned his squad not to touch anything until they made a careful study of the things that had attracted their hungry attention and ascertained that nothing had been bobby trapped.

But soon he forgot the danger and yelled, "Hey, look at this, look at this!" smashing in the top of a pickle barrel with his rifle butt. He grabbed a big dill pickle out of the brine, removed his mask, and stuffed a third of it into his mouth at one bite, snapping it off and munching in ecstasy. He leaned back against the wall as the others rushed over and indulged themselves in one of the most exquisite meals they had ever eaten.

They laughed at the ridiculous spectacle they made, stuffing the juicy pickles into their mouths as if each one were afraid that another would get more to eat than he.

Hietala looked around and realized that he was leaning against a fifty-pound sack of flour.

"Pancakes!" he yelled gleefully, patting the bag. "Let's see if we can find some sugar now," he said, running around excitedly looking on the shelves.

"Over here," Stromberg called out from the storage room. "Do you think a hundred kilos will do for now?" he asked, gently kicking the four twenty-five kilo bags.

"Sugar and coffee!" Hietala said. "Can you imagine it? Sugar and coffee!"

They continued to rummage through the store. Most of the smaller items had been taken, but there were several tins of tobacco and a carton of raisins. Otto took Stromberg with him and went out to search for a hardware store or a gun shop while the others stayed to load up the sleigh with their booty.

There was no gun shop, but there was a hardware store which had some used weapons and accessories. Otto found what he needed most, small springs which could replace those from the firing mechanisms that had snapped due to the cold, and which could also be worked into explosives as part of a detonating device. They loaded everything that could be of any possible use into their packs.

"Look what I found," Stromberg called out, rolling a large drum of kerosene toward the front door. "This ought to come in handy, don't you think!"

"Damned right it will," Otto agreed enthusiastically. "Go get the sleigh and we'll lead it up here. We've really done all right for ourselves."

Otto skied back to the general store to hurry the others along. He took a pickle from his pocket and ate it as he went, savoring the crispness of it, and the sharp, sour juice. He felt good. He had enough springs and steel wire now from the hardware store, and the food would raise the men's spirits.

"Pancakes for Christmas!" he announced as he walked into the general store and grabbed two cast-iron frying pans.

A dense cloud covered the sun, providing some protection on their way back to camp. Aalto and Taisto, each of whom had accepted the role of sleighman, sat on top of the pickle barrel, guiding and prodding the horse. The other four skied ahead, rifles slung over their shoulders, constantly watching for any sign of the enemy. They were all feeling good.

The fighting at the front line was going strong by the time they got back to the Molotov Crater. Both Klami and Ekstrom were at the front. Otto had the men store the food in the bunker, and went immediately to the crater, where he started repairing weapons as fast as he could. Stromberg helped him, but the cold made it difficult for them to work with the tiny screws and springs of the firing mechanisms. They couldn't do the work with gloves on, and their hands became numb in a matter of seconds as they fumbled with screwdrivers and the icy metal parts.

They worked long into the night by the light of a lantern at low flame. This was against regulations, but Otto made a "tent" within the crater to keep warm and to block the light from escaping. He could hear gunfire from the trenches and he knew that the fighting was heavy.

Around eight o'clock that night Ekstrom, totally exhausted, stumbled into the crater to get some more ammunition.

"I'm glad you're back, Arola," he exclaimed, collapsing against the wall. "They're thousands of those Russians out there and they're starting to get pushy."

"How's the ammunition holding out?" Otto wanted to know.

"How do you think it's holding out?" Ekstrom replied sarcastically. "Klami has wasted half of it, the stupid bastard!" The sergeant was obviously wrought up, so Otto and Stromberg kept quiet, waiting for him to calm down. After a long minute of silence he asked, "How did you do in the village this morning? Find anything useful?"

"We found springs, screws, and even a whole barrel of kerosene," Otto said, waiting for a word of approval from Ekstrom, but the sergeant remained silent and glum.

"We also brought back some flour and sugar for Christmas pancakes," Stromberg added. "And Karelian pickles."

"Pickles? You found some real Kyyrola pickles?" Ekstrom's mood brightened. "You got any left?" he asked, with new energy.

"We've got plenty! Want me to get you some? I'm kind of hungry myself."

Stromberg crawled out of the crater, leaving the two men sitting in the dimly lit shelter. Otto tinkered with the rifle in his lap and kept silent, hoping that Ekstrom would be the first to speak. He was upset—that much was obvious and Otto knew he was worried about what he had seen that day.

"If the Russians are really pushing in again, be sure that all the men keep their rifles out in the cold awhile before they fire, or they'll freeze in the change of temperature," Otto advised Ekstrom.

"I'll do that. You and your squad stay here and get these rifles ready. We'll see a lot of action in the coming days, I promise you that," Ekstrom predicted dourly.

"The only kind of action I want to see is everybody going home," Otto replied.

"I sure wish we could, but you know we can't . . . Now if Klami doesn't give me any trouble, every squad to the man is going to start making night raids. And that includes your squad, Arola."

Otto admired Ekstrom and felt him to be as competent

and trustworthy as Salmi had been. He wondered what he would have thought about Ekstrom if he had met him back in basic training in Terijoki. It was hard to imagine him as one of those petty, sadistic sergeants, but he knew that Ekstrom had fought in the Civil War with the White Guard. He must have been very young at the time—the Civil War had been over twenty years ago. Otto thought about how much a man can change in twenty years.

Stromberg ducked into the crater and passed some pickles to Ekstrom and Otto.

"That's good!" Ekstrom said appreciatively, swallowing half of the pickle to make room in his mouth for the other end. "That's good," he repeated. "Got another one?"

The men felt that they were having a celebration, but their joy was momentary. The sound of machine-gun and Suomi fire soon increased.

"Damn it, Arola," muttered the sergeant, "they're going to come hard at us. A lot of tanks and a lot of men. I lost two guys today trying to get at those tanks—Kivisto and Paarma." He fumbled with his pipe and Otto tossed him a tin of tobacco.

"I'm telling you, the only way we can stop them, with the number of men we have, is to go behind their lines and hit them hard at night. We've got to get those tanks before they come straight at the trenches!"

"Do you think we could do that?" Otto asked.

"We *have* to destroy them and discourage them from coming at us way back behind the lines."

"What about Klami? What does he think about the idea of night raids?"

"I don't care what he thinks anymore. Besides, after today I think maybe he'll listen to a little advice, if only to save his own ass. You should've seen him today when they got within firing range. He was pathetic!"

"What did he do?" Otto asked, eager to hear anything derogatory about Klami.

"He started screaming at everybody to keep firing, just like always, but this time he really panicked." The sergeant fell silent, his eyes staring in hatred. Then he changed the subject. "How are we doing for Molotov Cocktails?"

"Good. We've got a stockpile of them, and more coming

in with that kerosene we found today. We found a lot of empty bottles too.''

"It's my guess that they're going to make a big move either sometime tomorrow or early Christmas morning. I'm going out tonight. Hakli and his men are coming with me.'' He ate one more pickle, then licked his lips in satisfaction. He pulled out a dirty handkerchief from his side pocket and wiped his face with it. "I'll be here in about an hour with five of my men to get supplies for the raid tonight. We need Suomis for each man. Satchels and Cocktails, too, okay?''

Otto grasped the meaning of his last words after the sergeant had left the crater. Night raids behind the enemy lines! It will sure take guts to go out there and survive. He began to check to see that he had all the guns and ammunition ready.

# Chapter 33

Otto had equipped Ekstrom's squad with special supplies for their first night raid behind the enemy's lines, but he had continued working in the Molotov Crater all night. Exhausted, he finally fell asleep on top of the ammunition boxes. The explosion of a nearby shell woke him up. He didn't even think of it then, but it was Christmas Eve, 1939. He patted the lamb which had curled up by him and helped to keep him warm. He was thankful for his friends, who had covered him with several army horse blankets before going to the front and distributing ammunition during the Russians' bold attempt to break through the lines.

While Otto was lighting an improvised kerosene stove, his squad returned from the front. He thanked the men for letting him sleep for a few hours and then asked another favor.

"Tuoppi, would you bring in some snow? I'll warm some water to get my circulation going again." The stove produced enough heat to melt the snow but it wasn't enough to fry pancakes. The clear sky outside made it too dangerous to build fire in the wood stove.

"It's Christmas Eve and we can't even have pancakes," Stromberg complained, standing by the stove, watching the snow slowly melt.

"I know it should be a day to rest, but here we are in Karelia fighting," Hietala added. "But at least we could sing 'Silent Night,' " he suggested, looking around to see the other men's reactions. "Will you join in if Arola and I play our harmonicas?"

"That sounds like a nice break from the madness of war," Stromberg said agreeably. Otto and Hietala took out there small harmonicas, first warming up quietly. Then, they played the song softly, while Stromberg hummed along and Tuoppi, Aalto, and Taisto sat listening to the old, familiar music.

The harmonicas were almost drowned out by a sudden burst of shelling. Hietala gulped, choked, coughed, cleared his throat, and then began to play a more spirited song. In the cold air the instruments sounded like cats crying in a tunnel, and the only real beauty of it was in the effort made by the men to take shake off the fear that engulfed them all. The little bit of music relaxed them.

Aalto, who had been working tirelessly, came out of his thoughts and fears long enough to enjoy the music. "Listening to that reminds me of being back home," he said to Taisto, who was sadly looking on. Then he added a word of encouragement to him: "Do try to be a little more light-hearted—it's the day before Christmas!"

As their enthusiasm was just beginning to gain momentum, two men peeked into the crater and demanded a supply of ammunition. They said that the Russians had started pouring a lot of men and fire power into the no man's land, and that the fighting was already heavy. As soon as the music had stopped, the man's news was verified by the endless sound of machine-gun fire.

Otto stepped toward the open ammunition boxes and stopped for a moment to calm down the lamb, who had been excited by the music. "I think that lamb's in love!" Aalto said teasingly.

Otto laughed at Aalto's rare attempt at humor. "This lamb *is* good luck, so let's not ever hear any talk about lambchops."

Heavy shelling continued. The Ordnance Squad spent the day in the Molotov Crater. The Russians, according to a private named Helle, were concentrating their strength along the southwest shore of the Yskjarvi. Ekstrom and Hakli, with their squads, had destroyed eight tanks so far

194

during their first night's raid.

"When do they push us out on one of those raids?" Stromberg wondered out loud, to no one in particular.

"They'll get us out there, Stromberg," Otto answered, "don't you worry about that!" He didn't mention Ekstrom's unofficial takeover of command and left his certainty about the raids unexplained.

Lieutenant Klami remained in his dugout during the day's fighting, with a map in front of him. This wasn't the way he had imagined his first command would be. The men were cold toward him, and insolent. His training in officer's school hadn't prepared him for this reaction.

There was no celebration on Christmas Eve, except for the songs that had cheered the morning. Each man's silent thanksgiving that he had survived another day marked the extent of his celebration. The sky remained clear and the temperature was twenty-two degrees below zero, which meant that there still could be no fires and no pancakes. The men had to satisfy their hunger on this holiday the same as on other days, with cold stew and hardtack. The word was passed that the Russians would make the "big push" on Christmas morning. Taking no rest and only a little food, the sergeant organized another raid for that night, in order to discourage the Russians and to take some of the punch out of their tank assault.

Otto gave every land mine in the crater to Corporal Peltonen, whose squad slipped through the barbed wire at night to plant more mines in the open field between the forest and the trenches. The frozen field was littered with the grotesque frozen bodies of Russian soldiers who had been caught by some of the mines.

Almost the entire company spent Christmas Eve in the front-line trenches. Ekstrom ordered Stromberg, Hietala, and Tuoppi up to the front, leaving Otto with only Aalto and Taisto to man the camp. The little lamb stayed curled up in the corner. Otto was grateful for her company.

At five-thirty on Christmas morning, the Russian artillery increased its shelling twofold. Otto knew that a big attack would follow this.

"Let's get the last of these ammunition crates opened," he told the other two. "They're going to need all they can get, and they won't want to wait for it."

By eight-thirty, the cannons on the tanks had opened up. Otto could easily distinguish them from the howitzer reports. There was another type of explosion, too, more muffled in tone. That was sound of the land mines. Rifle and machine-gun fire barked and chattered, adding a brass section to this symphony, as if some grand, diabolical conductor were directing a bizarre piece of music.

Otto let Aalto and Taisto rest, but made them stay in the crater in case of an emergency. He continued checking and rechecking the weapons that had been repaired, and then stepped out of the crater to replace the weapon supply outside. He noticed two men wandering around the camp. Both were dressed in Finnish uniforms, but Otto didn't recognize either of them. He grabbed his own rifle, drew back the bolt to make sure there was a shell in the chamber, and approached the two men.

"Identify yourselves," he yelled to them over the roar of the explosions.

The taller of the two men turned to him first. "Kovapanos," he said, which was the camp password, and then asked, "Where is everybody? My name is Eero Koivisto, and I work for the Finnish Broadcasting Company."

Otto recognized the name. The man was a radio newscaster from Helsinki. He lowered the rifle. "Let's go inside," he said, leading the men into the crater. He hoped this might mean he would get some news about Helsinki.

Koivisto was a tall, blond man, thirty-five or forty years old. The other man was older, in his fifties, and Otto deduced from his black collar and the black band on his arm that he was a chaplain. The two men looked around the shelter, and Koivisto began.

"How's it going, Corporal . . . ?"

"Arola, Corporal Otto Arola," Otto said, looking at the chaplain.

"I'm Chaplain Vehtonen," the man said, extending his hand warmly.

"How's it going?" Otto said, repeating Koivisto's question rhetorically. "Gentlemen, you both have ears. I think you can hear how it's going." The lantern was at full flame and he could see both men clearly.

196

"I didn't mean to be trite," Koivisto apologized.

"What are you doing here?" Otto asked, ignoring the apology.

"We're making rounds all along the front line," the chaplain explained. Sergeant Koivisto is gathering first-hand information for his news broadcast and I'm here because it's my duty to be here, just as it's yours."

"Well, you got here at the wrong time, I'm afraid. The Russians have been pouring it on heavily for the last three days and this morning they're making their big push. Everybody is at the front except a few guards and us ordnance men. And our illustrious company commander, Lieutenant Klami. He's in his dugout as usual. If you want a story, you should go talk to him. He is scared to death."

"Corporal, do I need remind you that I am an officer, too?" the Chaplain interrupted firmly.

"Of course, Chaplain. Well, excuse me, but why don't you two let me get back to my work? If you want a story," he said, looking at Koivisto, "it's right out there. Just follow your eyes and ears and you'll get all the story you need. Or better yet, I'll give you the whole story, and I'll make it real short. This company has been fighting every day and night since the whole thing began. We rarely sleep, we eat little, and it's mostly cold food when we get the time. We wear dirty clothes, we all have lice, and we don't have enough weapons or ammunition. On top of that, we're outnumbered by about a million to one, and we're out here freezing to death!"

Otto stopped to wait for a rebuke. But none was offered, so he continued.

"That noise you hear is about one hundred men taking on at least that many tanks and a hundred times that many infantrymen. And here's what we kill tanks with," he said, wagging a Molotov Cocktail in front of their noses. "Other than that, why, everything is going great!

"Now, why don't you write all that down, and tell Mannerheim and the big man back in Helsinki to send us weapons, ammo, food, clean clothing, tanks, some air support, and replacements so that we can get some sleep!" Taisto and Aalto were awake by now and fascinated by Otto's oration, but neither of them joined in.

Koivisto said, "Okay, Corporal, I know our being here may seem incongrous to you, but you might be interested to know that my station is broadcasting the news to try and help clarify just what is needed, and to try and get all those things you mentioned from other countries. My job is to find out just how bad things are out here and to go back and tell the rest of the world about it. So you can get off you high horse, Corporal," he said, anxious to get in the last lick, "because this isn't the first front-line camp we've visited, and there are many companies worse off than yours."

Otto was quiet for a few minutes.

"I think you should go and visit our commanding officer, Lieutenant Klami. He could use some moral support. Aalto, would you please show these gentlemen to the Lieutenant's dugout," he said, turning his back on them.

The two men got up, said goodbye, and left.

"That Koivisto has a lot of gall," he mumbled to Toisto, who gave him no answer.

An hour later, while filling and fusing bottles with kerosene, Koivisto and the chaplain returned to the crater. Otto turned and watched them crawl clumsily through the canvas entrance.

"How long has that man been your commanding officer?" Koivisto asked incredulously.

Otto smiled to himself. "Oh, about two weeks or so, I guess. I'm not exactly sure."

"What happened to him? He's no more capable of commanding a fighting unit that that lamb there!" he declared, pointing emphatically to the peaceful animal.

"You're absolutely right," Otto said. "I was hoping you would notice, because that man could make a lot of trouble for us."

"Go on, Corporal."

"Well, when this war started we were at Kuuritsansuo, and it was a real circus! We didn't do much of anything except get drunk and gripe about being back in the army. Our company commander there, Lieutenant Salmi, could have brought the whip down on us, but he was too smart, too good a leader for that. When the war started Lieutenant Salmi showed us the value of life and freedom, that we had

198

something special to defend now. It took him only a couple of days to do it, and the transformation was incredible."

Koivisto was scratching notes in a small notebook. Otto continued, "The way I see it is that he showed us what was important, what we could do, and how we could do it. He didn't give us any speeches, but in his own way he instilled a spirit in us that gave us the strength to face everything the Russians have thrown against us. It's not exactly patriotism . . . it's hard to explain. I . . ."

"Take your time, Corporal. This is worth setting down straight."

Otto looked at Koivisto coldly and went on. "It's more like the personal courage and tenacity of many men, that has been molded into a single force. I mean, we've had it pretty rough, but whenever there's a chance to fight back I'm amazed at the way these men seem to take it!"

Suddenly a shell exploded at the entrance of the crater. In pure reflex the men fell flat on the floor of the crater. Then there was another, and another, landing further and further away.

Finally it subsided and the men stood up, shaken and frightened. It was difficult to continue with the story.

"Perhaps an example I can give you is myself. I never thought I would fight in the army. I had learned to hate every officer, and everything military made me sick, until I met Salmi . . ." Otto fell silent.

"What happened to Lieutenant Salmi?" the chaplain asked sympathetically.

"He's dead. Got it back at Oinola," Otto replied sadly, not going into any of the details.

There was a pause, then Otto continued: "This Lieutenant Klami came here all blustery and military. He believed what he had soaked up in officer's school—that the common man is nothing and that the bourgeois, Finnish fascists are the salvation of mankind. But when he faced the problem of staying alive, faced Russian bullets instead of hot-worded propaganda, none of that blind patriotism did him a damned bit of good. We're different. We believe in *ourselves*, and it was Salmi who taught us to do that. And because we do believe in ourselves, and not in these lousy weapons, I think we may just hold out here as long as it takes them to finish the Mannerheim Line. Then somebody else can do the fighting while we rest. Of course, that doesn't mean we couldn't use all those supplies and replacmnts I asked you for!'' Otto added, trying to lighten his tone and smiling lightly.

"Thanks, Corporal Arola. You've given me a good story," Koivisto said. He filled Otto in on news of Helsinki, and then the two men left.

The battle lasted for three days, until the Russians finally gave up the attempt to overrun the trenches. Almost nine hundred Russians were killed or left to freeze in the open field, and thirty-seven tanks lay transformed into broken caskets for their asphyxiated crews. These tanks had rolled over the mines in the first minutes of the attack, blocking the others that followed behind them, forcing them to knock down trees and pull around the stranded vehicles, only to encounter other mines. The Third Company had swarmed over the closest tanks, setting them ablaze with Molotov Cocktails, and then fallen to the trenches. The Russian military plodded into the Suomi and rifle fire and were pushed back toward their own lines, only to be forced forward again by machine-gun fire from their own comrades.

"We couldn't believe it," Hietala said after the battle, "but they shot down their own men to keep them going. Poor bastards!"

The Third Company didn't escape losing some men. Weapons froze and three men were shot down because they couldn't work their rifles.

Will they ever come to rescue us, Otto asked himself as the fighting continued. Will anyone listen to those complaints I made to the newscaster? And if someone does hear them, will they do anything to help us?

# Chapter 34

The radio was on at Sirkka's home where she, Anna, and Hannes listened to broadcasts reporting continued cold weather, and fierce, sunny days with the temperatures of twenty-one degrees below zero. "A clear day for another bombing," the broadcaster said gloomly. After his voice faded, another voice came on. It was a reporter's voice from the front line, Koivisto making his daily report to the Finnish people. "Corporal Arola . . .," the voice said, and all three leaned forward in surprise and eagerness to hear what the man said. The content of his message was secondary—it was the joyful news that Otto was alive and well that made their hearts leap.

Sirkka wanted to write to Otto immediately and tell him of the diplomatic problems Finland was encountering. Hannes, however, cautioned her against it.

"Is it really wise to tell Otto that Tanner has failed to reach Molotov through every diplomatic channel? I don't think he should know that the effort through the League of Nations has failed, too, or that even the King of Sweden, who had promised the President to help Finland last fall, failed to honor his commitment."

"I hate those damn Swedes—what false friends they turned out to be!" Sirkka said, raising her voice. "Here they have been ruling and taxing this country for over six hundred years, and now when we need military help they won't lift a finger to assist us.''

"Well, you have to remember that war means profits for them,'' Hannes explained. ''Sweden supplies Germany with iron ore, and they are getting rich from the war. If the Allied countries would come to help us, Sweden would have to get involved with the transportation of the military forces, and they are not going to risk war to do it. But, hell, the French and English did nothing to help Poland or the Czechs. Their word is no damn good! That's what Tanner said the other day.'' And Hannes fell silent, thinking of Tanner's diplomatic plans.

"I don't understand a thing you've been talking about!'' Anna said, laughing. ''I'm going to write to Otto of nothing but love, and that's what you should do, too,'' she said, looking at Sirkka. ''Don't burden his mind with rumors about peace—just tell him how much we love him, that's all.''

The trio stood silently, each thinking of Otto. Finally Hannes said, ''I agree with Anna. Let's not tell Otto any more than the government tells the troops. Nobody believes Tiltu's daily broadcasts anyhow, any more here than the men at the front. Tanner is a brilliant man, and if there's a way to find peace, he'll do it.''

"You're probably right,'' Sirkka agreed, and when the door closed behind Hannes as he left for work, she and Anna were composing their letters to Otto. The main worry in their minds was how long Otto and the others could stand it in those frozen trenches.

The men of the Third Company had become impatient and frustrated almost beyond endurance, as they waited for any sign of movement to the Mannerheim Line.

"Where are those foreign troops and their heavy armor?'' Otto kept asking Tuoppi, Hietala, and Stromberg.

The men didn't sit by idly, however, waiting for the move. New gadgets were always being tried to destroy tanks, and the Finns' fearsome, deadly night raids had demoralized the Russian camps before they had a chance to attack or cross into no-man's land.

Otto had feared that his squad would be ordered on one of those dreaded moonlit nights to enter the enemy's territory. Although he had faith in Sergeant Ekstrom's ability to instruct them, he knew that once they crossed the line they would be on their own.

Now that night had come. Planning ahead, Otto had saved some newly-washed, white cloaks that had arrived a week ago, which he handed out to his squad members an hour before they were to depart on their mission.

They gathered at the front of the Molotov Crater and Sergeant Ekstrom briefed the men carefully with every possible detail, instructing them to do as much damage as possible and to save themselves from death.

Otto stood before the squad with the sergeant. They were both on skis, each wearing Russian, felt boots that slipped into the leather strap on the skis for easy removal when a man had to dive for the protection of the snow. Otto touched Tuoppi's Suomi, which hung in front of his bulky chest. A long-bladed, sheathed knife hung on Tuoppi's belt. It was the same knife he had used before to gash a Russian's throat. Two Molotov Cocktails, two satchel charges, and two heavy round chambers with one hundred bullets in each for the Suomis were also hanging around his middle. In the rucksack were two day's rations of food and satchel charges.

The woolen masks worn by the men served a purpose beyond providing protection from the cold. Breathing inside the masks allowed the moisture from their breaths to dissipate slowly. Thus, the all-too-visible halo of their breaths, which would have endangered them in the bright moonlight, was eliminated. The temperature was $-28°$ below.

When Ekstrom finished with the details, he talked a bit longer, not loudly, not aggressively or forcefully, but quietly, and with assurance. He walked along in front of the men, touching each one's equipment as if it were a tender child he was caring for. He smiled at them as he said, "Remember, we've already made several raids before, and we haven't lost a man during our visits behind the lines. Stay in the woods with your Suomi by your side, because the Russians are afraid to come into the woods and they aren't on skis. You have a tremendous advantage over them. The snow in places is at least knee high, and the Russians won't be able to run easily in that much snow.

"Your success in this attack depends on the element of surprise," Ekstrom added. He paused and stared into the men's eyes. "I can't emphasize strongly enough how important it is to surprise them, then do as much damage as quickly as possible, and get the hell out. Don't wait around to engage the troops—*they* would have the advantage then. Get out fast as soon as the Russians swarm out of their tents. Make a dash for the woods and head home!"

"What if one of us gets killed? Do we have to carry back the body?" Stromberg asked, a little embarrassed to ask such a question. "Or how about the wounded? Wouldn't it slow our retreat?"

"Arola will have to use his best judgment on that. He's your leader tonight the same as always. We can't plan everything in advance. Things still have to be decided on the spot. Let's hope you don't get into any trouble, though. Remember what good luck we've had so far." Ekstrom's words were slow and confident.

"You'd better be prepared for anything," Otto said, taking over leadership of the squad. "Does anyone else have a question?" he asked, leaning on his ski poles to steady himself, and to avoid displaying the fear that was gripping him. He knew he must never show his own fright, or others might panic. "Tuoppi, are you ready?"

Tuoppi didn't reply at once. He raised his head, straightened the Suomi across his chest, and tested to see if he could get his trigger-finger quickly out of the hole in his glove. Everything seemed to be working to his satisfaction. "I'm ready," Tuoppi finally said in his slow, even voice. What a rock he is, thought Otto in admiration.

"Stromberg?" Otto asked.

"Been waiting for this for a long time," he replied with apparent enthusiasm. He was the only one who had wanted to volunteer for a night raid.

"Hietala, how about you?"

Jussi hesitated, looking from side to side at the others. "I'm scared if you want to know the truth!" he blurted out from trembling lips. In fact, he was trembling all over.

"Are you really scared?" Otto asked quietly. "Do you want to stay here?"

"I'll come," Hietala said in a slightly firmer voice. Otto's kind attitude had relaxed him a little. "Don't worry about me, I'll be okay."

"Aalto?"

The man nodded without saying anything, and Otto knew that he was scared, but willing.

"Taisto?"

"Ready," came the crisp reply.

Ekstrom had been standing by while Otto made his roll call.

"Do you have anything more to add, Sergeant Ekstrom?"

"Remember that there will be guards around the tanks," Ekstrom said, reiterating his earlier remarks. "Usually anywhere from six to ten, depending on the number of tanks. Remain calm when you get there. Watch the guards. Notice the patterns in their behavior. If you have to get rid of some of them, use your knives—at least until you have planted the explosives. After that, you can use the Suomis. But don't start shooting until you've destroyed the tanks and are ready to get out."

The men nodded automatically. Their target was at least a two-hour ski away.

At midnight they turned into ghostly figures. They crawled through the barbed wire in the designated spot that had been cut earlier. They headed through the forest in single file, skiing in each other's tracks to make less sound as they skimmed through the grooves in the snow.

The shadows were silent, but Otto again recognized the same feeling of fear he had experienced when he took the sleigh from Oinala to the front line to pick up that soldier with battle fatigue. It was intense. He couldn't seem to keep his skis from crunching noisily through the woods, and the shadows of the trees stimulated his imagination to the point where he expected gunfire to mow him down in the snow at any second. His fingers automatically sought the pistol on his belt, his personal security against being taken alive by the enemy.

He thought of the dead and wounded he had seen hauled back from the trenches, and he thought of Lieutenant Salmi, blown apart beyond recognition. Perhaps tonight the six of us will wind up frozen or torn into fragments. Worse yet, we might be taken prisoner . . . stop it Arola, he warned himself. Sergeant Ekstrom would never allow himself to have thoughts like these. I must stop it. If the others can stand it, so can I.

Suddenly a voice cut through the night air, and all six men dropped like stones to the snow. They had barely covered three hundred meters since slipping through their own barbed wire! Then Otto remembered that the Russians had put loudspeakers high up in the trees to broadcast their advice of surrender to the Finns. He signalled the men to stay down anyway. The speaker croaked and crackled. Otto guessed that it was forty or fifty meters away.

The men rose slowly and continued south, toward a reported concentration of Soviet tanks somewhere to the east, along the frozen shores of Yskjarvi. Behind them the speakers blared something about giving up weapons and joining the Red army. The men chuckled over the fright they had received at the sound of the harsh voice that spoke in Finnish. Otto hoped their reflexes would be that fast when real trouble presented itself.

After skiing for more than an hour and a half, Otto brought the squad to a halt. He thought he had heard something, but the noise of the skis on the snow and the sound of the Russian cannons made it difficult to be sure. They knelt and listened.

"You hear that?" Otto whispered.

There was something. They remained where they were, but the sound seemed to grow neither louder nor weaker. Just the drone of engines somewhere to the south.

"What do you think, Arola?" Stromberg whispered after a minute.

"I think we had better take a look."

Three-quarters of a kilometer farther, directed by the sounds of the engines they'd heard, they came upon their quarry. The Russian camp lay in a clearing, two hundred meters down a gentle slope. The Ordnance Squad spotted it from their hiding place among the trees. The moon was bright and the visibility was good. Otto saw a formation of about thirty tanks. The engines they had heard were those of the last two tanks, positioning themselves at the end of the formation. Within ten minutes those engines, too, had ceased. The voices of the tank crews could be heard as they scrambled out of their huge vehicles and headed for the warmth of the tents.

They never learn, Otto thought. He had seen the Russian tanks lined up in similar fashion before the massive raid at Siiranmaki. The Finns had swarmed down on them and had easily caused great destruction. This time there were only six men against what looked to be an entire battalion. It was a frightening feeling to be in the midst of an enemy so huge and savage.

They knelt behind the trees and watched the guards walk up and down the rows of tanks. As the last lights in the camp disappeared the guards huddled together to pass the time. They seemed sure that they were in no danger.

There is no hurry, Otto reminded himself. The longer we wait, the better our chance of surprising them. But I don't know how long we can stay here in this miserable cold, he thought. Still, they remained kneeling in the snow, watching the guards. The moon shone directly overhead. It was serving their purpose, for once, instead of endangering their lives.

Otto began formulating his plan of attack.

"Stromberg, Taisto, and Aalto—You take all the satchel charges and give us your cocktails. Tuoppi, Hietala, and I will go after the tanks at this end. You three have got to take out those guards first while they're still grouped together," Otto whispered, handing his charges to Aalto, who gave him two Molotov Cocktails.

"Stay on your skis. If we do this right, we won't have to use these damned knives!" he continued. "Stromberg, go down there and get as close as you can before you throw. As soon as we hear the first blast we'll hit as many as we can, and then everybody gets the hell out! If anybody gets separated, follow the tracks we made coming in and ski as if you were in a race."

They nodded in agreement. Tuoppi and Hietala crawled on either side of Otto, and Stromberg checked his equipment once more, making sure that Aalto and Taisto did the same.

"Let's go," he said and they skied off toward the tanks.

Otto, Hietala, and Tuoppi remained crouched behind the row of trees, waiting for the first explosion. Otto knew that Stromberg would get as close as anyone could. He glanced at Tuoppi and Hietala, but they were completely occupied, fastening the Molotov Cocktails to their belts and checking the positions of the tanks they were about to attack. Tuoppi had been unusually quiet, even hours before they had left camp, and Otto was concerned about him. "He's never let us down yet," he reassured himself.

Stromberg, Taisto, and Aalto had vanished, and there was no way of knowing how fast they would be in position. Otto tapped the others on the shoulder and motioned for them to be ready. He hoped that Stromberg would make the first move. His stomach was in knots and his chin rattled from cold and nervousness. His fingers were cold and he worried about how he could light a match.

The eight guards were still in a cluster, like sitting ducks, flapping their arms and stamping their feet trying to keep warm, when the first satchel charge blew them to bits. Otto pushed hard on his ski poles and took off down the slope toward the lead tank. He swept up not ten meters away from it, lit the two wooden matches tied to the side of the bottle, and hurled it against the side of the tank. It went into flames. He skied on, and repeated the process three more times. In all the excitement, Tuoppi and Hietala ran into each other, and Otto saw them helping each other up. He raced over, grabbed a Cocktail from Tuoppi and threw it at a tank.

"Come on, come on!" he screamed while explosions of satchels thundered through the air.

Rifle fire was crackling now, but Otto didn't look around to see where it was coming from as he pushed up the slope among the protective trees. Tuoppi was directly behind him, but Hietala was still down by the burning tanks. Otto stopped halfway up the hill and began firing short bursts from his Suomi to provide some cover for Hietala. Several Russians were firing at him from the end of the tank formation, but the flames and heat prevented them from firing accurately. Tuoppi turned to cover Hietala too.

"Take off, Tuoppi!" Otto yelled at him. "I'll wait for Hietala."

One more satchel charge went off. Otto looked down the line and saw Stromberg scrambling up the hill, turning to fire as he retreated. Then he stopped and struggled with something in the snow. Two of the guards who hadn't been killed by the original blast were firing rapidly at Stromberg from behind a smoldering tank, but they didn't see Hietala skiing toward them, crouching low behind the line of un-damaged tanks. He reached the tank the Russians were behind, crept around it, and emptied a clip into the two men.

Otto watched, amazed by Hietala's daring. Stromberg was struggling up the hill with a body slung over his shoulder. It was Taisto! Hietala backed away slowly from the tanks to cover Stromberg's retreat and was joined by Aalto. Otto glanced back at the burning machines on his end of the line and saw five more Russians plodding through the snow toward Aalto and Hietala. They didn't see Otto above them, and he cut three of them down before the other two realized where the shots were coming from.

He moved slowly toward his retreating comrades, to give them more cover, but as he did so, one of the undamaged tanks in the middle of the formation opened up on them with the gun mounted atop its turret. He moved behind a tree and fired a long burst at the turret; he heard the whining of the slugs as they bounced harmlessly off the thick metal armor. The machine-gunner swiveled his weapon and fired toward Otto, hitting the trees instead. Hietala and Aalto both concentrated their fire as the tank gunner and, as the Russian swiveled to return their fire, Otto directed another long burst at the turret. The gun fell silent at last.

Stromberg was now in the woods and Otto skied to help him. Taisto was unconscious, and there was no way of telling how badly he was hurt.

"Stromberg, you and Hietala stay here and cover Aalto and me. I'll take Taisto and meet you by the path. Draw their fire this way as long as you can. Then meet us back up the trail. Let's go, Aalto!"

Arola hoisted Taisto over his shoulder and skied off through the woods. The wounded man wasn't small, and Otto wasn't nearly so strong as Stromberg. By the time he reached the path, he was exhausted and had to stop. Tuoppi emerged from behind a tree.

"Here. I'll take him," he offered.

"All right . . . good," gasped Otto. "You two take him about a kilometer up the path. I'll wait here for Stromberg and Hietala, and we'll meet you as soon as we can catch up. Tuoppi, give me your clips." Tuoppi handed Otto two

209

full clips and then hoisted Taisto over his shoulder.

"Go ahead, Tuoppi," Aalto said, with some authority, "I'll follow behind."

Come on, you guys, Otto pleaded silently, as he heard Stromberg and Hietala still firing. Russian riflemen were returning the fire, but the two Finns were well hidden in the trees. Otto held his fire, not wanting to give away the direction of their escape, but he cursed harshly under his breath, wishing Hietala and Stromberg would make good their retreat. He waited for three more minutes and was about to go after them, when they came into view. He called to them and directed them to the path. As they escaped, the Russians continued firing into the woods.

They overtook Tuoppi and Aalto shortly, and Taisto was shifted to Hietala's massive shoulder.

"What happened to Taisto?" Otto asked Stromberg, after a few minutes of skiing.

"I don't know. I didn't see him get it. Must have been right after he dumped his satchels and was going up the hill. He did a good job though, Arola. Got right up to that tank and rolled his charges right next to those guards. A damned good job!"

"Yeah," said Otto grimly.

"Don't count him out yet. Arola. We haven't even taken a look at him yet."

"But he's unconscious."

"That doesn't mean a thing," Stromberg said. "Take it easy, he'll be all right."

Tuoppi hadn't yet spoken, and Otto knew that he was ashamed of having run into Hietala when they attacked. Having his gun freeze hadn't helped him either. Otto clapped him on the shoulder. "You did fine, Tuoppi." Tuoppi wasn't to be consoled, though, and maintained his silence.

They waited quietly among the trees until they were sure that they weren't being pursued. Then they stretched Taisto out on the snow. He was conscious now and Aalto was bent over him, examining a wound in his side.

"The force of the bullet broke a rib, I think," Aalto said, "but he's not losing too much blood."

None of them had anything to ease Taisto's pain, and he

groaned softly as they stared down at him. Otto knelt down and put his gloved hand on Taisto's shoulder.

"Take it easy. We're in the clear now. Just hold on and we'll get you back to camp." Taisto nodded, wincing in pain, but he didn't try to say anything.

"I'll take him for awhile," Otto said. "Let's get moving." They helped Taisto to his feet. Otto bent low and started to hoist him onto his shoulder, but an awful gurgling cry came from deep in Taisto's throat. The pain was obviously extreme.

"We can't take him like this any farther," Otto said. "Lay him down again and let's make a stretcher." He unbuttoned Taisto's white cloak and took it off him. Aalto had picked up Taisto's ski poles during the retreat and brought them along. They quickly buttoned the cloak around the poles and placed Taisto on it.

"Erik, you and I will take him first," Otto said. "We'll switch off in fifteen minutes or so." They moved slowly off through the forest.

Otto was exhausted. Just as he was beginning to relish the satisfaction that accompanied his relief, he felt a surge of fear run through him like a cold chill. It was the aftershock—the realization of what he had just been through and how close he had come to death. He wondered if the others shared this feeling as well.

The moon was still high up on the horizon, and it was just as cold as ever when they crossed no-man's land and returned to the encampment. Once Taisto had been safely deposited in the medic's dugout, the other five collapsed in their own shelter. The report to Ekstrom could wait, Otto decided, until the next day.

# Chapter 35

The night raids had a morale and physical effect on the Russians, and for the first time there was a lull in the front-line action. Only sporadic gunfire continued, and occasional shelling. The report was that that the Russians were re-grouping before they renewed an all out effort to push the Finns back.

One morning it seemed to Otto that the weather was about to turn in their favor. There were clouds in the sky and a chill bite to the wind that had been missing for the last two weeks. He thought that snow might even fall later in the day. Tuoppi and Hietala were the only men in the dugout. Stromberg and Aalto were fighting in the trenches and Taisto had been sent to the rear to the hospital.

The wind made Otto shiver as he stood outside. He watched a lonely squirrel on the bough of a spruce tree as it dropped bits of the seeds it was frantically nibbling from a cone. The little animal made a pretty sight on the branch, but Otto's enjoyment of the scene was limited somewhat by the roar of shells. He wondered why the animal had not been scared away by the shelling.

He went back into the dugout and found Hietala leaning back against one of the supports, quietly playing his mouth organ. Otto took out his violin but it was out of tune. He got out his harmonica and joined Hietala. Tuoppi applauded enthusiastically. They played for another ten minutes, then

Otto put the harmonica in his pocket.

In his pocket was a worn newspaper clipping that Sirkka had mailed to him. It was an article by a music critic about his teacher Sulo Hursti's last concert before the war started. "His taste is impeccable, his technique sovereign, his command of the repertory masterful. His playing, which combines the best elements of spontaneity and control, has the resources of temperament, power, and fluency. He guides his audience gently, with his persuasive musical rhetoric. It was a stunning performance . . ." He thought of Helsinki and the violin concerts he had heard there.

Otto put away the clipping for another time. He hoped that some day he would read a similar review of himself that was half as glowing as one about his teacher. He wanted to be that kind of deeply moving musician, and he was determined to do the hard work he knew was needed to achieve his goal. He longed for the war to be over. It was impossible to practice at all—and he feared that his hands might have lost their touch. It would certainly take him months of dedication to regain the control and feeling for his instrument that he had once had.

"Hey, Arola," Hietala said, interrupting his thoughts. "Let's play another number." Otto joined him in playing a Karelian polka.

As they played, shells seemed to land closer and closer. Otto heard the sound of a dud dropping behind the dugout. Suddenly a man whose face was totally blackened and badly burned tumbled into the dugout.

"Help us, help us!" he babbled. "Post Six has been shelled—they're all buried! Help us!"

"Tuoppi, take care of him," Otto ordered, scrambling out of the dugout. Hietala was right behind him. Two hundred meters away they saw the smoldering wreckage of the Post Six dugout, and they ran stumbling through the snow to the edge of a giant shell crater. Otto and Hietala tore furiously at the rubble and debris as men from other dugouts rushed over too. Ekstrom was beside them now, and twenty other pairs of hands were digging through the dirt and shattered timbers to uncover any survivors.

Hietala grabbed a partially buried man by his belt and tugged hard to pull him out from the loose dirt and mud, but the belt tore clear through the mangled pulp, and suddenly he held only dirt and bloody leather. He looked diffidently at the others, as if waiting for them to tell him that it wasn't real. He pressed his nostrils shut to avoid smelling the stench of burned flesh, then dropped the belt and crawled frantically out of the crater to vomit in the snow.

The others continued to dig desperately, but they soon realized that there could be no survivors. The hole and the snow around it were strewn with bits and pieces of men.

"Give it up, men," Ekstrom shouted. "Throw some dirt over them and go back to your dugouts. That's the best we can do for them." Five men had died in the direct hit.

The Post Six disaster depressed the men of the Third Company for the next two days. On the afternoon of the second day, Sergeant Hakli walked into the Molotov Crater. With him was the radio man whom Ekstrom had mentioned to Otto when they had opened up the box. He was carrying the boobytrapped radio that Tuoppi had found at Kuuritsansuo.

"Corporal Arola, this is Private Osku Raimo," Hakli said. "He's been working on this radio of yours."

"Have you had any luck getting the thing to work?" Otto asked.

"Yes, I did, after a little improvising. I found some batteries in the village that just barely work, but they're strong enough to pick up some of the Russian signals. Can't transmit, though. The transmitter is shot."

"Well, that's interesting, Raimo," Otto said, smiling. He could tell from Hakli's behavior and his ironic smile that there was something more to the story. "Tell me about it, gentlemen!"

"Raimo is from Kivennapa and speaks pretty good Russian," Hakli said proudly. "We figure that he could listen to some of the Russians' messages—troop movement and that sort of thing might come through."

"Of course, that's providing that they use words I can understand," interjected Raimo. "An entirely different system may be used now. It's hard to tell. The only way to find out is to keep tuned in."

"What do you mean?" Otto asked.

"Assuming that they are still sending messages, we may

be able to learn when and where their movements occur. Then if our patrols could penetrate deeply enough behind their lines, we could be waiting for them! The effect would be very demoralizing. You follow me?'' Raimo's pleasant manner and cherubic face were at variance with his blood thirsty plans for the Russians.

"I follow you, soldier," Otto said. "Only how do we know that they are still using the same words? In any event, I'm beginning to think we may have underestimated our friend Kalle Kaira," he said, smiling sardonically at Tuoppi and Hietala.

"He was a very practical, efficient agent, by the looks of what he did. We can only determine the validity of their messages by sending out patrols to check the Russians' movements in the areas mentioned. Risky, I admit, but the results could prove well worth the risk.''

"That's sure interesting," Otto said, "but why tell me about it? Hakli and Ekstrom make the decisions around here, not me.''

"We figured that your squad should be entitled to the first shot at testing it out. Raimo would go along, too, of course.'' Hakli spoke looking directly at Otto.

"So you figure to put us on night raid again. I tell you, we aren't volunteering to get killed—you'll have to order us to go.'' Otto was firm.

"I just completed the work on this baby today," Raimo said, patting the radio with mock affection. "It may be some time before we can pick up any orders of importance. But I'll keep listening.''

Otto looked around at his men. They sat quietly on top of the ammunition boxes with impassive faces, absorbing the fear that the idea of another raid had produced.

"Well, Sergeant, if you think we have to go once more, you'd better give us time to prepare for it.'' Otto looked at Hakli, whose Hitleresque moustache was overgrown and not well trimmed. "It's like entering the slaughterhouse.''

After they gave him a few more details, Hakli and Raimo departed and Otto and his squad began to talk apprehensively about the prospective raid. He soon realized it was doing their morale no good and changed the subject back to recalling the pickles they had enjoyed just before Christ-

215

mas.

"We haven't had any civilian food for a long time," he said nostalgically. "How about another raid to Kyyrola before we do anything else?"

"That sounds like a great idea," Hietala said in unison with Stromberg. "We need a break don't we?" he said, to an enthusiastic nodding of heads.

"We sure do need a break, all right," Otto agreed.

On their detour to Kyyrola, Stromberg spotted a farm-house perhaps half a kilometer southwest of the village. He wanted to explore it.

"I don't know, Erik," Otto said thoughtfully. "That's just asking for trouble. It's too close to the front."

"That's just the point, Arola! Maybe nobody else has had the nerve to pilfer it. We might even bring back some smoked pork! Who knows what might have been left there. Let's take a look."

"All right. Let's approach from behind the trees. And don't pick anything up before we are sure the whole damned place hasn't been booby trapped by our own men."

"Don't worry, Corporal. I'll go first, alone," Stromberg volunteered.

The farm was deserted. It had been thoroughly sacked of everything edible except for a pile of frozen, moldy potatoes left in the cellar. "I'll check the barn," Stromberg said. "Might be some chickens or eggs frozen in there."

There were neither chickens nor eggs in the barn, and when he came outside again Stromberg grabbed a log and smashed it up against the rickety barn door in disgust. It made a loud cracking noise as the door splintered.

"That wasn't very bright, Stromberg," Otto chastised him. "Not very bright at all! Let's get out of here."

They skied off toward Kyyrola and were less than a hundred meters away when the first shell exploded next to the barn.

"Son of a bitch!" Hietala yelled, and another shell blew the side of the barn away. Then there was another and another. They skied quickly back into the woods while the Russian artillery peppered the entire area with shells. It was nothing new to any of them, but the fact that a single sound of a log slamming against a door had alerted the Soviets

lead back the same number of men as I take with me." He briefed Raimo on what would be expected of him while the other men filed in. They all prepared themselves for the next night.

Ekstrom slipped into the crater, followed by a lanky blond in a woolen mask.

"This is Eino Leppo," the sergeant told Arola.

Leppo nodded politely to Otto. Ekstrom introduced him to the rest of the men and let Otto continue his briefing. Leppo, unlike Raimo, had been on two previous night raids with Ekstrom, and had gained a reputation as a ruthless fighter, despite his quiet manner and good nature. Otto was glad to have him along. He knew that a man like that could make the difference between a successful mission and a disaster. Otto questioned him about the geography around Vuolaa. He was obviously very familiar with the area, giving concise, useful answers. Otto went outside once, when his fears grew so intense that he had to leave in order not to expose them to the others.

"Those damned Russians!" Otto stared out into the woods fixedly, until finally the cold numbed his face and nose, and he had to go back into the crater.

# Chapter 36

Late the next night, after a full meal of lukewarm beef stew, Otto stood at the front of the crater before his masked squad. There were no more details to take care of after the completion of his close, careful inspection. Each man was now equipped with enough rations and other supplies to last three days behind the enemy lines should he get lost or be unable to follow the others back.

The tops of the trees sagged under the thick layer of snow. Otto led his men carefully toward the hidden entrance to Tunnel Number Five under no-man's land. The tunnel had been made by the Battalion Pioneer Squads. It was cut deep into the snow underneath the barbed wire barrier.

Otto directed each man to lie on his stomach, over his skies, and thus form an improvised sleigh. He tied a toboggan rope to his belt, dragging his lood of equipment behind him as he pushed himself forward with his arms, and reached the other end of the tunnel on the Russian side. He waited, lying on the snow, until each man done the same, and had quietly put their skis back on. Otto, Stromberg, and Hietala pulled toboggans behind them, loaded with enough explosives to destroy several tanks. He lifted his hand, signalling them to move on, deeper into enemy territory.

They moved with extreme caution in the bright moonlight. They were headed for Yskjarvi. Suddenly a sharp sound burst out behind them directly above their heads. They dropped down, burying themselves in the powdery snow beneath the trees.

They lay breathless for a moment, each man suspecting that the Soviets had adopted the Finnish tactic of putting sharpshooters in the trees. To their surprise and embarrassment, but also to their great relief, they realized that they had been frightened again by a loudspeaker in a nearby tree. The familiar monotone of the Finnish voice filled the air with propaganda suggesting that the Finns should surrender their primitive weapons and give up the hopeless fight.

"I wish I could have the pleasure of killing that bastard," Stromberg cursed viciously.

They continued slowly, pulling the toboggans. Otto gave his toboggan to Aalto and went skiing ahead with Leppo. After an hour of zigzagging through the forest Leppo thrust his left arm across Otto's chest, his signal to stop. He pointed his hand toward the strange shadow of a figure that seemed to be hanging from a tree about ten meters away. The other men came up from behind, reaching for their Suomis when they saw it.

"Looks like a body," Stromberg whispered.

Leppo and Tuoppi will check it out," Otto decided. "We'll wait here. If it's a decoy and if there's any shooting, head back to camp," Otto instructed them firmly.

The moon cast a slow-moving shadow behind Tuoppi and Leppo as they approached the figure in the tree. When they got a little closer they could distinguish the bloody white cloak on the corpse. Coming still closer, Leppo was able to identify the body of Corporal Mauno Pyoli, who had failed to return from a night raid three days ago. His body dangled from an iron hook stuck through his back. His hands were tied behind him and he had a bullet hole in his forehead.

Leppo took down the body and Tuoppi turned it over to look at the frozen hands behind the man's back. The left had was covered with a stiff leather glove, but, to Tuoppi's horror, all the fingernails were missing from the frozen right hand. Tuoppi, wanting to spare the others that gruesome sight, covered the body with snow. Later he dutifully whis-

221

pered the details to Otto.

Otto managed to remain standing when Tuoppi told him about the torture. But his knees felt as if they would give way, sinking down into the snow under him, and burying him forever.

Otto tried to escape from the inner turmoil produced by this evidence that supported all his fears. Inside his fur-lined gloves his fingertips felt as if they were frozen stiff, numb and without any sensation in them. He curved his fingers tightly around the ski poles and with some effort pulled forward.

"Let's get going."

"We've got to get to the other side of this field," Leppo said, indicating the large, open area. "Beyond it is a narrow strip of forest and behind that are the farmhouses of Vuolaa."

When they had carefully skirted the field, Leppo halted and pointed toward the road, only thirty-five meters away. A large formation of Russians was moving slowly toward the Finnish line, trudging along clumsily on foot through the snow. Stromberg tapped Otto on the shoulder, pointing his Suomi toward the Russians, but Otto shook his head.

They remained silent until the Soviet troops had passed. Then Raimo skied up beside Otto.

"There's a very good chance that they are broadcasting right now from this vicinity, Corporal," he whispered. "That Finn who makes the propaganda broadcasts to the front may very well be set up around here."

Otto thought of what a joyous morale booster it would be to the men back at camp if they could quell that traitorous bastard's radio.

"Are there any buildings around here that the Russians might be using for a radio station?" Otto asked Leppo.

Leppo thought for a moment. "I imagine that most of the farmhouses have been burned." He was silent for a moment more, then said, "Old man Vuolaa had a large, dugout sauna on this side of his farmhouse. He used that sauna to cure meats, and I'll bet it stood up under the shelling unless there was a direct hit."

"Can you find it?"

"Sure. It's about half a kilometer to the east."

"Leppo and I are going to look around," Otto told the others. "Stay put and keep quiet. If you engage in any gunfire, do as much damage as you can and get out quick."

Otto and Leppo skied toward Vuolaa's farm. They advanced quietly under the cover of trees and emerged into an open field. Across the snow lay the gutted remains of the Vuolaa's farmhouse. Only one hay barn remained. A lone guard plodded through the snow fifty meters from them on the slope. "That's it over there. That guard is covering the sauna entrance," Leppo whispered.

"Look at the barn," Otto said, pointing to where smoke curled up from a vent under the rafters. "How far is the main road from here?"

"There's a slope just past the barn and the road is at the bottom of it. Less than a kilometer."

"That's where the tanks should be. Let's get back," Otto said, already formulating a plan while heading to meet the members of his squad.

"We'll go and find the tanks first," he told his men. "But no guns! Use your knives quietly on the guards so that we'll have plenty of time to plant the explosives. Remember that we can set a timer for the detonators on these satchels. We'll go after the men and burn the barn. He explained the procedure in detail. Then, the seven men moved through the woods and toward the road where they hoped to find the Russian tanks.

They came to the end of the field where the land sloped gently downward, and stopped to survey the area below them. There were eighty or more tanks and at least twenty supply trucks! Otto whistled almost audibly and stared at the awesome sight.

"Where the hell are all their guards?" he whispered to Stromberg warily.

Then he saw smoke, or steam, escaping from the back of a canvas covered truck. He nudged Stromberg and pointed in that direction. The guards had a small heating stove burning. Far down the line two guards tramped doggedly through the snow. Otto motioned to Stromberg and Hietala that they should crawl down and dispose of them. He pointed his knife at Stromberg, who nodded and crawled off with Hietala.

223

The two men overpowered the guards from behind and without a sound drew their knives across the throats of the Russians, who fell dead on the snow.

They moved closer to the convoy, still dragging their toboggans. After he had removed half of the satchel charges and Molotov Cocktails, Otto told Raimo, "Be careful, and watch Hietala. He'll show you what to do. Tuoppi, Leppo, Aalto—let's go! I'll start at this end, Tuoppi. You start ten up from me, and Leppo, you take ten up from Tuoppi. Aalto, stay on the ridge and keep your eyes open. Set the timers for the maximum, about twenty minutes," he said, and the men began to move slowly down to their assigned positions.

The truck with the guards in it was fourth from the end. Otto carefully wedged the satchel underneath a rear tire and covered it up with snow. He then crawled on to the next truck and then to the first five tanks. The timers were crude and inaccurate, and setting them for the intended twenty minutes could mean fifteen or twenty-five minutes; there was no way to tell. They would have to hurry wanted to destroy the barn and check the sauna before the first satchel detonated.

This time Tuoppi finished before the others. He was waiting with Aalto when Leppo and Otto crawled up the slope. The four of them moved down the line to meet Raimo, Hietala, and Stromberg.

"So far, so good," Otto said, satisfied with their work. "Hietala, you and Raimo take the sauna. Leppo, show them where it is—we'll meet you there. Let's go!"

Two Russians sentries were huddled together outside the entrance to the old barn, their faces covered by the fur collars on their heavy, quilted overcoats. "Stromberg, you take the one on the right. I'll take the other one. Aalto and Tuoppi, open up four Cocktails, splash them on the side of the barn, and get going!"

As the barn began to blaze, the satchel charges which they had planted began to erupt—not in unison but sporadically, one after another. A tremendously powerful explosion shook the snow-covered ground beneath them. Otto knew it must have been the ammunition truck. The whole camp was instantly in panic. Russians came out screaming from inside the burning barn and the Finns cut them down from the hillside with their Suomis. In two minutes flames covered every wall. Otto motioned his men to follow him to the sauna, leaving the blazing barn, filled with the bodies of hundreds of Russians, to burn to the ground.

They reached the sauna in ten minutes. Raimo was standing alone by the door. The body of the Russian guard lay at his feet. Raimo was nervous and anxious to see Otto and the others.

"Where's Hietala?" Otto asked sharply.

"Still down in the Sauna."

Otto jumped through the door, shouting "Hurry it . . . ," but stopped in mid-sentence. Standing there, his hands on top of his head, was the gangly figure of Kalle Kaira. His face wore the terrified look of a man who expected to be shot at any moment.

Hietala was jubilant. "Look what we found, Arola! The voice of the comrade workingman in person. Shall we kill him now or later?"

Otto could neither move nor speak for a minute. It was too perfect—and so ironic that Kalle's own radio should lead the Finns to him.

"Get your coat, you bastard. You're coming back with us!" Otto said through clenched teeth.

"Corporal—hey, Arola, there's a tank on the slope. It's stopped there," Raimo shouted, peering into the sauna.

"Get Kalle outside fast," Otto snapped. He stooped down to get out the low door of the sauna and saw a lone tank rumbling slowly along the road only fifty meters away. It stopped parallel with the blazing barn. Otto didn't know if the tank was trying to escape or pursue.

"Raimo, put on that Russian overcoat and hat," Otto ordered, pointing to the dead guard at their feet. "We're going to take a tank back with us! Everybody else get back into the sauna. Now look, Raimo. You must go there and flag it down, get them to open the hatch. Can you speak Russian well enough to do that?"

"I can try, Corporal," he said, buttoning the large Russian overcoat.

"When you see me coming from behind, don't look at me or it'll give me away! As soon as I shoot him I want you right behind me in that tank.''

"I've got it, I've got it," Raimo said nervously.

Otto opened the door down into the sauna and told the others to wait. "Kaira will go back with us," he said, "but first let's take care of the tank."

He crawled down toward the tank with Raimo, under the protective bushes. He began to move slowly around behind the vehicle, while Raimo headed for the road. The tank was moving forward again, and Raimo trudged up the road toward it.

Raimo was flagging the tank down. The tank stopped but the hatch didn't open. Raimo was shouting and standing directly in front of the tank, so that the crew could make sure he was one of them. Otto moved fast toward the rear of the tank. As he did so, the hatch opened and a man appeared from the waist up, speaking to Raimo.

Otto hopped up on the tank and ripped the man's back open with a burst of fire. He pulled the Russian out and flung him into the snow. Then Otto dropped into the tank expecting to face more men, but there was only one other Russian. The frightened driver was groping frantically for his gun, but Otto slammed the barrel of his pistol into the man's stomach, doubling him over. Raimo followed Otto into the tank.

"Raimo, tell him to move this thing over to the sauna right now, or I'll blow his head off," Otto growled.

Raimo told him, and the terrified man spoke in short, frightened gasps. "What did he say?" demanded Otto.

"He says he's not the driver. He says that he's a gunner."

"Tell him he's got five seconds to become a driver or he's dead," Otto said, putting his pistol to the man's temple. The man needed no further coaxing and set the tank jerkily in motion.

"Get Kalle up here fast," Otto yelled at Stromberg, who had Kaira by the collar. He started dragging him up on the tank. Kaira's hands were tied behind his back, and he fell through the hatch, banging his head and crying out in pain and fear.

"Stromberg, load all the stuff from the toboggan in here. Hurry it up!" Otto shouted over the roar of the tank's engine.

As soon as the tank was loaded, Otto told his men, "All right, now, get out of here. And for God's sake let our men know we're coming back in a tank. Don't let them fire on us or throw any cocktails."

The five men skied off across the field as a squad of Russians was advancing, curious as to what their tank was doing so far away from the rest. They opened fire on the Finns, but Otto didn't return their fire. "Get this thing going," he screamed at Raimo, who translated for the driver.

The squad of infantrymen continued to fire, but the tank lumbered out along the road into the safety of the woods. Stromberg and the others had already disappeared into the forest. They would be sure to arrive at camp before the tank. Now Otto faced the problem of making it back, not only through enemy lines, but also through the Finnish mines which had been so liberally sprinkled in no-man's land.

# Chapter 37

The thirty-ton Russian attack tank didn't bounce around much on the deep snow; it ate its way forward on the narrow road. Both shoulders of the road were edged by tall timbers thick enough to stop any vehicle—even one six meters long—dead in its tracks. Otto and Raimo felt safe inside the thick, steel plate shelter. They had already heard bullets bouncing off its rounded sides like pebbles thrown at a windowpane.

Although the tank had room for a four- or five-man operating unit, Arola had been lucky to find only the driver and loader inside. It would have been much tougher to take the tank if there had been a five-man crew. Otto kept his pistol pointed straight at the driver's head as the steel tracks rolled over the ten huge wheels, moving the tank steadily forward.

It was night, and most of the Russians were sleeping. There was some irony in Otto's feeling of relief that the Finns didn't have any tanks. If they had, the Russians would surely have learned to use Molotov Cocktails against them, and he and Raimo would never have had a chance to reach no-man's land. Rifles don't faze a tank, and he knew they wouldn't dare shell the tank while it was still within their own territory, but there were heavy armored cannons they could point in the tank's direction. Their salvation would be to get through the Russian territory before the men in the camps along the way had a chance to wake up.

"Check the fuel," Otto told Raimo. "Tell the driver to let us know how much diesel fuel is in the tank."

Raimo talked to the driver and learned that the gas tank was half-full. He also learned that the tank had a gigantic twelve-cylinder motor in the rear which could generate a speed of fifty kilometers per hour.

"Get him to speed it up if this dinosaur can really go fifty kilometers an hour!" Otto shouted over the roar of the engine.

After another short conversation, Raimo shook his head and informed Otto that the snow was too deep to make it go faster than twenty-five kilometers per hour.

"How do we operate this howitzer? And doesn't this tank have any machine guns?" Otto demanded, his voice becoming hoarse. Raimo had headphones on his ears, which further complicated their discussion.

Raimo removed his headphones and shook his head again. "Only the one twenty-two millimeter howitzer," he said.

Otto looked around the interior of the tank in which he was now confined, and saw a good supply of ammunition. After examining everything, he realized from what he had learned in gunsmith school that this was a TR 34 assault tank. Its gun had over two-and-a-half meters of barrel and could pierce heavy steel, but it had a short range. He needed a machine gun.

"Where is the vent?" he asked next.

The driver quickly pointed to a heavy steel cover that opened into a fist-sized hole on the back of the turret.

"Raimo, hand me your clip of Suomi rounds. I have only one full clip myself."

Otto took his Suomi, opened the vent trap, and was satisfied that there was enough hole space to give him a clear view out to the rear. He wanted, however, to be able to shoot toward the front, where he expected the Russians to be. He examined the driver's lookout opening, but he found it too hard to fit the Suomi barrel into it, so he had to settle for the vent opening.

He remembered hearing about a soldier who had done something that really took a lot of guts on a mission. He had watched a tank approach him, having only two hand grenades to stop the monster. He knew throwing them would do no good. The soldier had known that nothing could be heard from outside, and had jumped daringly onto the rear of the two-meter-tall tank. He crawled over its steel surface to the turret then used his grenade to knock on the lid, and shouted, "Ivan, open up—it's Death knocking here for you!" Nothing happened the first time. He didn't know the Russian language, so he repeated the same sentence in Finnish again and waited. Suddenly the turret opened. In a split second Einar had dropped the two hand grenades into the tank and dashed away on the snow to safety just before the tank blew up.

As they rolled past the long piles of Russian shells, the road seemed endless. "My God, how long is this going to take!" he shouted, but no one heard him. Kalle was stopped over in the corner, his head still bleeding from a big gash in his forehead. The heavy steel wheels crunched on the snow under them. The camps were filled with tent after tent of Russian soldiers. Here and there a Russian who had died lay frozen on the snow—no one had bothered to remove the bodies.

"They have just radioed to the front that their own tank seems to be defecting to the enemy," Raimo said when he took off his earphones.

"My God, we're in trouble."

He saw pile after pile of weapons, ammunition, and tents to house and supply more men than he had ever thought the Russians could actually muster. He was glad there were no skis lined up by the tents.

They passed a field where hay was left in high stacks, now covered with snow. Only a short while ago, this had been active farm-country. Now, all that remained of the Karelian homes they passed, were a blackened chimney rising from rude rock foundations.

Smoke curled up from the tents. It rose piercingly toward the sky in the freezing weahter—thirty-four degrees below zero now. At least it was a little warmer in the tank. Otto's lips were white, but it was from tension more than from the cold. His cheeks were covered by his woolen mask, but the eyeholes revealed eyes wild with fear as he stared out at the driver, Kalle, and then Raimo.

Suddenly rifle fire rang out and began popping against the steel surface of the tank.

He set the Suomi on the vent opening and saw a swarm of Russians at the side of the road, rifles in their hands, firing.

A long swiping motion from his Suomi, as the tank rolled past, flattened the men on the snow, although he couldn't be sure if they were dead or just frightened.

Otto kept firing on every group they passed. He realized with horror that there could be a tank ahead of them, or maybe an antitank gun or howitzer.

"Goddamn it, this howitzer—how do I load it?" His gunsmith school had given him some elementary lessons with heavy weapons. He quickly pulled, fumbled, and jerked the gun. Yanking one of the mechanisms, he was happy to see the chamber open. He loaded a heavy twenty-two millimeter shell into it. He could see over the barrel fairly well. I'll blast any damn thing that comes in our way, he assured himself.

Tears were wetting the driver's cheeks. His lips were swollen and white from tightening over his teeth. The diesel kept roaring, though, and Raimo coolly threatened the driver and forced him to keep on going. Otto felt sorry for the man. He still might be lucky enough to survive the trip; if not, they would all probably share his tragic fate.

Otto could only guess, but he assumed, from the length of time they had been moving, that they would soon be out of the forest and heading straight into no-man's land, perhaps even into the Parkkila swamp. This worried him, for even if his men had warned the Finns of his imminent arrival in a tank, the swamp could engulf them as it had so many other Russian tanks during the three-day Christmas offensive. There were huge unfrozen holes in the swamp that were like quicksand, and they would be swallowed up helplessly if they blundered head-on into one of them.

The driver was pushing the tank at about the same speed, twenty-five kilometers per hour. Suddenly there were no more trees around them. The Russians were left behind as they moved into no-man's land. Otto feared rifle fire from the Finns, but none came. They weren't within range yet, he realized. If the Finns were going to attack, they would wait for the land mines to do their work and then attack with Molotov Cocktails.

He was more terrified of the Finns now than he had been of the Russians. Being caught inside a burning tank seemed to him the most horrible way to die. "I'll kill myself and Raimo before we burn to death," Otto muttered.

The first few meters of open swampland were solidly frozen and the tank rolled on, whining and clanking. Inside, Otto thought he was hearing more of the engine's whine and less noise from the treads. The whining grew louder and the tank began to swerve. The Russian driver said something to Raimo in an even voice, and Raimo told Otto, "The snow is too thick and soft for the treads to get good traction."

Otto nodded, looking out the slit. All he could see before them was whiteness and trees. He wasn't sure where they were. It was difficult for him to determine their position from inside the tank, but he hoped they were going in the right direction. He thought he had recognized Parkkila and soon they should be near Kyyrola.

The thought occurred to him that they might have made a gross miscalculation. They might be kilometers too wide of the Third Company sector of the defense line. If they ran into some other Finnish company, no one would know that the tank had been commandeered by two Finns! Yet there was no choice but to keep going. No direct gunfire greeted them, although shells fired from behind the Russian line kept bursting around them.

Suddenly they were lifted up and slammed down again, and the tank jerked and shuddered to a stop. All four of the men crashed forward in the metal interior. For a second the explosion took the breath out of Otto, but he quickly recovered. Land mine! he thought. Got to get out of here before they set us on fire.

He tried to stand up, but his left elbow collapsed as he put his weight on it to push himself up. He looked up at the Russian, who seemed to be unconscious, slumped forward over the controls. The diesel engine was dead. Kaira writhed on the steel floor and groaned softly. Blood was oozing from his hair.

"C'mon, Raimo. We've got to get out of here. Raimo? Are you all right?" Otto asked, but there was no answer.

Otto saw with relief that Raimo, dazed, was shaking his head. There was a large bloody bump on his forehead. The Russian was moaning now, and Otto shook him violently. "Raimo! We've got to get out of here!"

The Russian staggered to his feet and opened the steel hatch. The lid was hinged back, to give them added protection. "Move!" Otto growled, prodding the man with his Suomi. Shots from the Russian side were zipping all around them and striking the steel surface, only to ricochet off.

"Come on, Raimo. Follow me," Otto said, sliding down behind the driver. Raimo was right behind, pulling Kaira by the shoulders of his overcoat. They all tumbled down into the snow at the front of the tank, which provided them protection from the Russian rifle fire.

"We'd better head toward the Finnish line," Otto said, grabbing Kaira by the coat sleeve and crawling through the hip-deep snow with him. The tank behind them tilted crazily.

Otto could see the vague shape of the barbed wire fortifications ahead of him. Only a hundred meters more to go and they would be safe at last. He remembered glumly how Talvi had died, and then he made Kalle crawl ahead of him as insurance.

The Russian firing increased. "Let's lie in the snow, hopefully the Russians will think we're dead," he told Raimo.

Time passed slowly. Meter by meter they advanced, never elevating their heads above the level of the snowbank or the small snow-covered bushes that afforded them some protection.

Now only ten meters more to go and they would reach a large boulder . . .

"Kalle, keep crawling ahead of us, damn it—get a taste of a land mine yourself," Otto poked him with the tip of his Suomi barrel. Raimo followed Otto, and the Russian was behind him, docile and giving no problem.

"Don't shoot, don't shoot! It's Arola, Corporal Otto Arola! Do you hear me?"

There was no reply.

"It's Arola . . ."

"What's the password?" a husky, low voice twenty meters away asked. The voice came from behind a boulder to their right.

Otto glanced at Raimo. Raimo shook his head. They couldn't think of the password. "Say something," Raimo begged.

"Yskjarvi," Arola said, thinking that perhaps just saying the name of the lake adjacent to the camp would identify them.

"Who the devil has changed the password again?" the voice grumbled. It was Tuoppi. He had recognized Otto's voice but thought Arola was telling him a new password. "Don't raise your head," Tuoppi whispered loudly.

Several more minutes passed before they reached safety behind the boulder. Finally Stromberg and Tuoppi helped them stagger to the tunnel beneath the barbed wire, and soon they were back in the dugout.

# Chapter 38

After a fretful four hours of sleep, full of disturbing night-mares, Otto sat on the bed staring into space with glassy eyes. It took him a full minute to realize he was safely in the dugout.

"Ekstrom wants to see you," a private told him from the doorway.

Otto shook his head to clear his thoughts and looked around at Tuoppi, Hietala, and Stromberg. They were still sleeping.

"He wants to speak with me when I'm not even awake." He managed to put on his coat, but couldn't bring himself to go out and wash in the snow.

"Where is that Kalle," he mumbled to himself as he staggered through the snow to Ekstrom's dugout.

"Congratulations are in order, Arola," Ekstrom said.

Suddenly the curtain on the doorway was pulled to the side, and Lieutenant Klami stepped inside. It occurred to Otto that he hadn't seen the man for over a week.

"From what Ekstrom has told me about the success of your night raid and bringing Kaira back, I presume it was an act of revenge. I want everyone to know that the interrogation will be handled by the Battalion Commander."

This was more than Otto could stand. He leaped to his feet, vehemently protesting the lieutenant's decision. He couldn't control his feelings about what Kaira had done to

Talvi. "You can't do that, Lieutenant," he pleaded. "That bastard was back at his . . . he was the one who . . ." But despite his efforts, Otto couldn't get the words out, and the lieutenant politely excused himself and left.

Otto made an effort at self-control. "Look, Sergeant Ekstrom, I risked my life to capture that bastard, and if anyone has a right to make him pay for his deceit and treachery, I do! Kaira killed Talvi by mistake—it was really me he wanted to kill! I demand that I be allowed to . . ."

"Listen, Corporal," Ekstrom cut in, "you don't stand in here and *demand* anything! Understand? I don't know why all of a sudden you think you can tell a company commander what he can and cannot do."

Otto was shocked into silence, hearing Ekstrom defend the lieutenant.

"Klami is just now coming around to where he can be of some use to us. He made the right decision, Arola, and you're going to obey his orders. Now get back to the crater and get to work."

Otto walked to the entrance of the dugout, preoccupied, thinking about how he was going to handle Klami. Finally he made up his mind, and walked directly to the lieutenant's dugout. He politely asked permission to enter and stood before the young officer who sat hunched over a map.

"Corporal Arola," he said, "what can I do for you?"

Otto knew that he could verbally annihilate the man for his past cowardice and foolhardy waste of ammunition—in short, for his poor leadership but he also knew that that would accomplish nothing.

"Well, Lieutenant, I feel very deeply about this thing, and I think maybe if I explained to you about Kaira and why it . . ."

"Sergeant Ekstrom has already briefed me thoroughly, Arola. I know about Kuuritsansuo and the death of the company clerk. After my initial interrogation, he 'll be sent back to Battalion Command, and they'll know what to do."

"Lieutenant, let me speak frankly to you. Kaira is terrified of me because he knows how much I hate him. If you let me have him for an hour—no, just for fifteen minutes—I'm sure I can soften him up and get him to tell you everything he knows. That's why I brought him back. I

236

could just as easily have shot him when we found him. The whole squad wanted to kill him on the spot. I stopped them because I knew he would be valuable to us.''

"Corporal Arola," he said in an official voice, "regulations state that a commanding officer is to interrogate prisoners and that's how it must be. You see, Corporal, if anything happened physically to Kaira here, I would be held responsible. You might lose control of your temper and kill the man. So I hope you understand that the decision has been made, and that's final."

Otto looked at the man intently while the Lieutenant stared back eye-to-eye. There was no way he could argue any more.

"Yes, sir," he finally said, but the words came from lips trembling with the anguish of defeat. It was the first time Otto had ever seen any true dignity in the officer's demeanor or had even thought of saluting him. He pulled his feet together, pressed his hands to his sides slightly, but enough to indicate a sloppy salute. He walked out of the dugout and slowly made his way over the soft snow back to the crater. He felt as if he had lost all of his strength.

Even Ekstrom sided with the lieutenant, he thought sourly, shaking his head.

The crater was empty. His squad was still asleep, he guessed. Only the lamb was there, munching a few pieces of hay in her dainty way.

"You are the best lamb in the world, my friend," Arola said, his gloved hand stroking her thick wool. "Don't ever escape from here—stay with me, I need you." Otto spoke quietly, as if to his own child whom he loved and cherished.

No matter how Arola wanted to change his train of thought, he kept coming back to Kalle. "If I have to go to jail myself, I'll catch that man one way or another; somewhere, sometime."

# Chapter 39

Otto kept his plans for revenge on Kaira to himself. He helped the new reserves who had arrived to replace the men who had been killed or wounded. The size of the company had dwindled down to seventy-five percent of its original size. One shortage was constant and pressing: ammunition arrived only in small dispatches. Otto pleaded with the men to fire only at live targets. "When you see the whites of their eyes, fire between them," he would say as he supplied rounds to the men who were on their way to the front.

One day, Otto was delighted to find a fat envelope, addressed to him by Sirkka. When he opened it, he found a letter from Anna was enclosed.

"You are always on my mind—my first thought in the morning, and my last thought I have as my head is on the pillow, is of you. No matter what we go through, my thoughts are still constantly of you, dearest.

"But when I don't know what you are thinking, how you feel about me—it's a dreadful feeling. I love you and only you. The consequences of what happened are behind us, over without a trace. I found a woman who helped me—I wouldn't have the baby, Otto, when day after day I remembered the look on your face as you left.

"Please write soon. I am trying my best to endure the waiting . . . please, please write and tell me you still love me."

The letter filled Otto with guilt. He still didn't understand why he was unable to make the decision to write to her. Could it be because Johanna had been in his dreams lately?

He turned to Sirkka's letter with relief. He'd had enough confusion in his mind for one day, and her letters were always full of intersting news. He was glad to see that she had changed the tone of her advice to him about writing to Anna. Insted of repeating it and arguing in favor of reconciliation, she merely mentioned it once.

"Hannes continues in the job protecting Vaino Tanner," she said as before. "I wish I could write to you about what happens in the government circles at the Foreign Minister's office. Hannes hears so much and learns, day to day, more than any other civilian. He has gained the confidence of Tanner, and as they drive out to meeting places Tanner tells Hannes of confidential matters. I wish I could tell you all about it . . ."

Sirkka wanted to tell him that Foreign Minister Tanner had had a meeting at which he played his last diplomatic card, If this card didn't win him the hand, he would make an all-out appeal for aid to the Allied countries. He was convinced that such a demand, regardless of the immediate Allied reaction, would lead to disastrous consequences. It was, however, a last resort.

This important meeting was with the Godmother, Siiri Vahalampi. Siiri knew the Finnish working people and was a known Communist.

Vaino Tanner knew her not as a friend, of course, but because of her political background. They had met at various times before, during, and after the Civil War. Now Tanner had learned through the Finnish Intelligence service that Ivanich had met with Vahalampi while he was in Helsinki.

She could be of use to us, Tanner had thought, and so he arranged the meeting between them that day. Tanner was a man prepared to use any means to secure aide for Finland.

After the initial courtesies, Tanner began almost abruptly.

"Siiri, let's get right to the point. There is not time to waste. I'll tell you quite frankly that the fate of Europe may hinge on what we say here. I'm inclined to believe that you are no fonder of Kuusinen's government, or the Russian

239

devastation of our country, than I am. Is that correct?'' The Foreign Minister was watching her closely, eager to hear her response.

"I would do almost anything to restore peace to my beloved country,'' she assured Tanner, "before I would accept Kuusinen to govern this land.''

"I believe you are acquainted with Alexei Ivanich?'' Tanner asked.

"Why, of course. I met him last year when he was working in Helsinki with the Russian Embassy,'' she replied. "I believe he is now in Stockholm. What about him?''

"He was a dedicated worker for Moscow, and I believe he was instrumental in helping to bring about this war. He is also a man who might very well be able to reach Molotov. Since it has proven impossible for me to communicate our ideas to Molotov via diplomatic channels, I must try another way. I would like to make a direct approach through Ivanich, whom I have also met. The difficulty in doing that arises from my official position in the government. I can't leave the country without being trailed by a dozen news correspondents, who would instantly start rumors concerning peace negotiations. This would do us no good at all. Therefore, I want you to travel to Stockholm as my personal emissary.'' His words were clear and concise, and his eyes rested on hers expectantly.

"I shall gladly go,'' she said, with only a faint hint of surprise in her tone, "and I hope I shall not disappoint you. Although I can't understand your logic, I shall accept your assignment with gratitude that I may be of some service.''

"Good. I want you to tell Ivanich that Finland is prepared to fight until the last bullet has been used. In the meantime, we shall certainly have to ask the Allied nations for help. This means that the Soviets will be drawn into a fight against the Allies side by side with the Nazis! Imagine, Bolsheviks and Nazis!

"Furthermore, that will result in French Air Force troops stationed in the Near East destroying the Soviet oil wells at Baku and Maikop, and this would bring Russian industry to a screeching halt. It would severely hamper any military effort required to withstand any future Nazi aggression—which is, in my mind, an inevitability as soon as Hitler was subdued Europe. It won't be long, either, at the rate he's going. Do I make myself clear?''

Her eyes fastened on his with blazing intensity. He had succeeded in rekindling the fire of her hatred for the Fascists and redirecting it toward the Nazis.

"Vaino, you know I'm a born revolutionary. In this, we see eye to eye. And we can't afford the catastrophic effects of a prolonged war. Brief me for my mission.''

It was only two days after his letters came, while Otto and his squad were waiting for a new supply of ammunition to arrive at the crater, that the men faced another totally unexpected surprise.

During a fierce period of shelling, Kalle Kaira came tumbling through the entrance flap into the Molotov Crater followed closely at the heels by Corporal Viiro, the company medic. Viiro was a tall, muscular man, but usually was gentle and mild-mannered despite—or perhaps because of—his brawny strength. He had been a close friend of Kauko Talvi and hated Kaira just as much as, if not even more than, any of the others.

Kaira's face was badly bruised from the tank ride, and there was a bandage around his head. His hands were tied behind him, so he was unable to break his fall as Viiro pushed him inside the crater. Fresh blood trickled from his nose and he moaned softly.

Otto looked at Viiro in astonishment. He had never seen him do anything violent.

"Here, I brought you a present, Arola," Viiro said, kicking Kaira sharply, but without real force, in the stomach. "The supply sleigh is on its way here with ammunition, and they're going to take him back.''

Otto stood up and walked over to where Kaira lay cowering before the men he had betrayed.

"Good to see you again, Kalle," Otto said, smiling malevolently. He could scarcely believe his good fortune. To have Kaira under his thumb even for a short while seemed almost too good to be true.

"I'm not supposed to leave him here alone with you and your squad, but I've got a lot of wounded men to take care of and I don't have the time to babysit with this bastard. Just don't kill him, Arola—unless, of course, he tries to

241

escape,'' Viiro said, winking and backing out of the crater.

Otto looked at Kaira and laughed loudly. "I think he's about to piss in his pants if we don't let him outside to go. What do you think?"

"He can't take a piss with his hands tied," Stromberg noted.

"You're right, Stromberg," Otto said as he pulled his knife and cut the rope which bound the man's hands.

"C'mon, Kalle, let's go for a walk."

Kaira didn't move, afraid the men would leap on him at the slightest movement, but Otto jerked him roughly to his feet. Kaira panicked and bolted for the entrance, but Hietala grabbed him and pulled him back inside.

"I think that would qualify as an attempted escape," Otto said. He picked Kaira up by his jacket collar and drove his fist into the man's stomach. When he doubled over from the blow, Otto lifted a knee into his face, and Kaira crumpled back to the ground.

"Stromberg, would you like to say anything to our friend?"

Stromberg smiled and walked over to Kaira, who had managed to prop himself up against a wall of the crater. Without any warning, Stromberg delivered a brutal kick between the man's legs, sending him upward and then crumpling him to the floor groaning and retching in agony. Every man in the room shuddered at the sight and Stromberg continued to kick him viciously about the body. Finally he backed off, smiling, pulled out his knife, and reached for a stone. He began sharpening his blade on the stone and knelt in front of the whimpering figure.

Otto had desperately wanted to kill Kaira only a moment before, but now suddenly he was repulsed by the idea. He looked at the miserable creature, who was totally alone, and at the mercy of a group of men who were anxious to take his life. Stromberg was taking great delight in Kaira's agony, as Otto had known he would.

Otto's mind flashed back, for a moment, to a childhood vision of his father dying violently at the hands of three soldiers. Suddenly, he realized with indisputable clarity, that they had all been pathetically brutalized by this war, just as every other soldier had been, in every other war. It was as if he had become another person during the last few months and he wondered how such feelings had ever gained control of his life. He had fallen victim to the desire for revenge, to murder a man, to slaughter him as a butcher would . . . like the White Guard butchers.

He looked at Kaira. Stromberg was brandishing his knife, describing in a gutteral tone which parts of the prisoner's anatomy would be the first to be removed. Kaira was crying pathetically as Stromberg described how he would slice off the testicles first, then the fingernails, and then go on to the ears.

He's just like a frightened animal Otto thought. Nothing more than a terrified beast about to be slaughtered—only worse off, because he knows it's going to happen. His life is over whether we take it or not. He's got no chance to overcome the shame he's brought on himself and his family. And here we stand, ready to cut him up like meat. God in Heaven, we're as bad as he is! I'll kill a lot of men before this war is over, but I won't let this pathetic bastard he butchered. What good would it do, except to turn me into a butcher?

"Put that knife away, Stromberg!" Otto commanded, his voice quiet and firm.

Stromberg continued waving the knife about menacingly in front of Kaira's face, not listening to Otto.

"Get away from him, I said," Otto warned, reaching for a loaded Suomi.

"What's the matter with you, Corporal?" Stromberg snarled back at him, enraged that Otto would threaten him with a gun. "You were the one who wanted to blow his head off!"

"Let him be. We've done enough. He'll get what he deserves when he goes to trial."

"Don't tell me you're going 'military' on us!"

"Just the opposite, Stromberg. You couldn't be more wrong. Now get out of here, all of you."

He waited while the others straggled out of the crater. Stromberg was flushed and muttering as he left.

The prisoner was still whimpering, weeping and gasping for breath. He had seen what a man sees when he stands alone on the gallows with the rope around his neck. He tried to get up, but his legs buckled beneath him and he bent at the waist. He stumbled grotesquely around the crater, unable to gain his balance, and finally collapsed in a heap.

Otto sat down on a wooden box and waited in silence for the supply sleigh to arrive. He hoped it would bring orders for them to fall back to the Mannerheim Line. Maybe it would cure the men's nerves, to fight in more secure surroundings. Meanwhile, he would have to wait.

# Chapter 40

As Otto stood watching that evening, a small delivery of ammunition arrived at the Molotov Crater. Tuoppi and Hietala quietly slipped in to help unload the boxes from the sleigh. Then the men lifted the wounded on, and the sleigh headed to the first-aid center, two kilometers back. It was a heart-rending task for the surviving soldiers to watch their comrades be taken away. Many had such mutilated bodies that they would never be able to return to normal life, and words of sympathy did little good. What counted was to get the wounded safely to the rear for medical treatment.

The traitorous Kaira had to be loaded onto the sleigh like an unwieldy sack of potatoes. He couldn't walk after the blow he had received between his legs from Stromberg. The men still cursed him, despite the obvious pain and suffering he was experiencing. They hated him for both what he had done to his country and what he had done to them.

After the ammunition was in the crater, Otto returned to his dugout. Inside his men were pursuing a very unpleasant, tedious chore: the killing of lice. Almost two months of fighting at the front without a sauna and only rare changes of underwear had fostered the growth of these unwelcome guests. Only two of the men were courageous enough to go out to wash themselves in the icy snow at thirty degrees below zero; the others decided it was better to hunt and scratch than to freeze in the snow.

Tuoppi sat naked on the elevated platform which was his bed, cracking the uninvited enemies with his fingernails.

"These damn vermin," he told Otto, "make another louse each time I kill one. At home I could finish them off in one trip to the smoke sauna." His fingers vanished into his black pubic hair, his head bent over as he squinted into his hunting grounds.

Stromberg had withdrawn into a sullen rage after his confrontation with Otto. He kept his hands in his pants pockets, scratching to relieve his itching, but he said nothing.

Otto watched the men for a few minutes, then he laid down on his bunk. He thought how the company manpower was being rapidly exhausted. Some of the more optimistic rumors explained that it was the result of having the regular troops gather at the Mannerheim Line, but Otto was skeptical. He had heard too many wild tales, too often, concerning the Mannerheim Line.

Later in January, the regular fighting thinned out to night raids. The Russians however, became more alert. Two four-man squads had been ambushed as they raided Russian camps. That kind of activity becoming more and more risky. The Russians had increased their guards and had even begun stationing men on the outskirts of the forest at night. Yet the Finns had become so stealthy, so accomplished in the arts of guerilla warfare, that they were able to continue harassing the Russian division. The Finns found that the Russians were continuously building up their forces in the area, tripling the number of men and machines. It was obvious that another offensive was in the making.

The Ordnance Squad had been passed by when their turn came fro another night raid. Otto knew the reason, and was glad. A widening gap existed between Otto and Stromberg which also affected the others, creating awkward situations for all of them. It was true that they would no longer make a good team. Otto and Stromberg seldom spoke to each other at all, and when it was unavoidable, they kept their tones official and their conversation limited to the matter at hand.

Otto was becoming more withdrawn from his relationships with the others, too, and they sensed his desire to be left alone. He spent most of his time in the crater, with no company except the lamb that had adopted him. Even Tuoppi was finding it difficult to feel at ease with Otto, who made no effort to reassure any members of his squad that their friendship hadn't been permanently altered in some strange way. He didn't seem to care. When parts for satchel charges were needed, he skied into Kyyrola alone, but he seldom came back with anything to show for his efforts. The village had been sacked completely, and everyone knew it. But they also realized that Otto needed to get away from camp and be alone with his thoughts.

He felt that the only thing he had in common with any of the other men in Third Company was his desire to fall back to the Mannerheim Line.

Otto and Tuoppi were in the Molotov Crater when six replacements reported for ammunition. Otto handed one of them an ammo belt and was reaching to grab another. He leaned toward Tuoppi, in confidence, and asked, "Why don't they leave these old guys back there to work on the Mannerheim Line? We don't have time to be training them."

"I heard that . . . ah, what are you, a corporal?"

"Yeah, that's right. Corporal Arola."

"What you just said, Corporal. About us working on the Mannerheim Line."

"I didn't mean it as an insult, soldier. It's just that we've been here such a long time and we can't see waiting much longer before we withdraw to the real defense position."

"You're talking about the Mannerheim Line?" queried the old man as if he were highly amused by some secret joke.

"That's right," Otto said, growing slightly irritated. "The Man-ner-heim-Line," he said, enunciating the syllables with exaggerated clarity.

"Well, maybe I'm a little mixed up here," the old fellow said, "but I could swear they told us that *this* was the Mannerheim Line."

Otto stared at the newcomer and then shifted his gaze to the man's companions.

"This is Third Company," Otto said, trying to control

his irritation. "I think you have made a terrible mistake, or else whoever dispatched you didn't know what he was talking about," he said, not wanting to hear what he knew was coming.

"No, no, the Third Company is the right outfit," the big-bellied spokesman for the group said. "The Third Company is where we're supposed to be, all right. But they told us that this is part of the Mannerheim Line."

"Look, Beerbelly," Otto said angrily, ignoring Tuoppi's attempts to mollify his anger, "this is just a temporary line of defense, you understand? Temporary. You should be back at the Line building cement bunkers or something. You're no good to us here."

"Cement bunkers!" the fat spokesman cried, laughing incredulously. "Corporal, it's fifty below outside. You can't even piss without leaving a frozen arc, let alone pour cement! How on earth do you suppose they could build the kind of bunkers you're talking about?"

Otto stared at the man, his face white with anger. Then he turned to Tuoppi, who seemed to be accepting the news in his usual placid way. Otto's silent fury wasn't an attempt at self-control; he just couldn't vent his rage. After all, this man wasn't responsible for the big deception. "Who is responsible?" Otto mumbled to himself. "Mannerheim himself and the whole damned General Staff, sitting on their fat asses manipulating us like so many chessmen!"

Otto's composure returned. "Tuoppi, take care of the rest of them." He nodded to the pot-bellied spokesman of the new recruits. "You, come with me. The rest of you wait here until I get back."

Otto and the elderly replacement went directly to Sergeant Ekstrom's dugout and found him nibbling on hardtack with the men from his platoon.

"Corporal Arola," he said as Otto led the new soldier into the shelter, "to what do we owe . . ."

"Sergeant, could I speak to you alone?" Otto asked. "Or better yet, could we go to the Lieutenant's dugout?"

"Can you give me a few minutes to finish my feast?"

"Sergeant, if you don't mind terribly, this is important."

Ekstrom was slightly irked, but knowing Otto, he said, "Well, if you think it's that important, Arola, I guess I'd

248

better take care of it now. Who's this new man?" he asked as an afterthought, getting up from his bunker.

"Reserve soldier Osmo Hautala," the fat man said. "Just got here today."

"We can use new soldiers," Ekstrom said, "We're glad to have you here. Now, Otto, what seems to be the problem?" he asked, leaving the dugout with Otto and Hautala. "You seem to be upset."

"You'll be upset too when you hear what this guy's got to say," Otto snapped. "I want the lieutenant to hear it too."

"What are you talking about?"

"The Mannerheim Line, that's what!" Otto exclaimed. "The Mannerheim Line. It doesn't exist—I mean, we're it!"

"Take it easy, Arola. Take it easy. You've been crazy ever since the Kaira episode." Ekstrom hadn't meant to say that, it just slipped out. He feared the Arola would become more withdrawn now, but to his surprise Oto didn't appear to take offense.

"Well, maybe I have. Who hasn't? The point is that our army has been pulling the wool over our eyes. This guy says there aren't any cement bunkers behind us. No tank traps, no cannons, none of that stuff they've led us to believe was there!"

"Damn it!" Ekstrom cursed.

They approached the lieutenant's dugout, where Ekstrom paused and requested permission to enter. It was a formality that was disposed of between the petty officers in the company, but Klami liked it.

"Come in, come in, gentlemen," the lieutenant said.

"Lieutenant Klami," Otto blurted out, "this man here has just arrived from the rear and he says that he has been told that *we* are the Mannerheim Line! If that is true, Lieutenant, it means that we are stuck here, and it also means that every soldier in the company has been betrayed. What do you know about this?"

The lieutenant stared at him stoney-eyed. "I don't like your tone of voice, Corporal Arola, nor your attempt to implicate me in this conspiracy. Sit down, gentlemen," he ordered, and they sat at the edge of the platform.

"What about it, Lieutenant?" Ekstrom asked. "Do we have a right to know if we've been duped?"

Klami looked at Ekstrom quizzically, as though he'd said something strange. "Duped? Yes, I guess we have been duped in a way. I don't exactly know who created the idea of a Mannerheim Line," he began. "I imagine the Russians or the General Staff, never been made clear to me. My orders, aside from commanding the company, include stressing the importance of our stand here, to enable the completion of the so-called Mannerheim Line. But to be honest with you, I've never seen any physical evidence of its existence. There are six or seven cement bunkers north of here, but nothing much else I'm afraid."

He stopped to light a cigarette and seemed to be considering what to say. Otto, Ekstrom, and Hautala remained silent, waiting. The lieutenant's hand lifted in a sudden gesture.

"Whether or not the Mannerheim Line was intended to become the foundation of our morale I can't say, but it has become exactly that. The foundation. Even the Russians are blaming their heavy losses on the Mannerheim Line. To the civilians it is a symbol of strength and hope. To us soldiers it is, or has been up to now, a reason to hold on for a little longer."

He paused, looking at Arola.

"I won't say that you haven't any right to be angry with me for allowing you to be 'duped,' as Sergeant Ekstrom calls it. But I know that without their faith in the Mannerheim Line, the Finnish soldiers would have been walked over."

"But we have nothing to fall back on," Otto interrupted. "Tell me what we are fighting for! We're already using old men as replacements. We're constantly low on ammunition. How can we withhold this information from our men if we have no hope?"

"We're holding out for foreign aid—at least that's my belief," Klami continued. "And the Mannerheim Line idea means a lot to the people back home, and to the fighting men too. The worst thing you could possibly do would be to tell your men that no such line of defense exists. After what they've been through, it would crush their spirits. I'm afraid to think of the desertion rate if that got out. I can't order you to keep silent because it wouldn't do any good, but I hope you can see it as I do."

"He's right, Arola," Ekstrom said finally in a dismal tone, but with conviction. "I don't like it any more than you do, but he *is* right. The way it stands now, at least we're holding our own until we get some kind of relief. We've taken everything they have to throw against us. I don't see why we can't keep right on doing it . . ." But this time his words trailed off without conviction. He knew that the Russians were mobilizing a large-scale offensive.

Otto, nevertheless, realized that they were right.

"Any idea when some of their foreign aid might start coming through?" he asked lamely, trying to let them know that he would go along with their judgment.

"No, I'm afraid not, Corporal," the lieutenant said. "I really can't tell you what to expect."

"And you, soldier," Klami turned to the fat recruit, "you can just forget that this meeting ever took place. Do I make myself clear?"

"Yes, sir. Very clear, sir."

"I should have thought you would have more sense than to go around shooting your mouth off like this, but obviously you didn't. I'm grateful to you, Corporal Arola, for bringing this to my attention. You may go, gentlemen, if you have nothing more to add."

Otto walked back to the crater, still puzzled about how forcefully Lieutenant Klami had handled the meeting. "Klami is in just as much danger as we are," he mused, "yet he seems to accept this farce. He's either a changed man or the world's best actor. Either way, I imagine I'll have to go along with him on this."

He climbed back into the crater and was relieved that no one else had been there while he was away. "Tuoppi, take Hautala and these other men and report to Sergeant Hakli," he said. "If there's any loose talk about this, Hautala, I'll hold you responsible."

Hautala nodded gravely and followed Tuoppi to Sergeant Hakli's dugout.

# Chapter 41

The first week of February marked a turning point for the war at the Karelian front. Until that time, the increased level of shelling had continued throughout the region. Then, on a clear February morning, the most devastating artillery attack the Finns had seen was launched against them. The snow-covered no-man's land was bombarded with shells weighing up to five-hundred kilos. The ground turned black from them.

Supply traffic between the rear and the front lines had all but ceased. Russian reconnaissance planes buzzed constantly overhead, directing the artillery and calling Soviet fighter planes to strafe any visible ground activity. These fighters had been flying over Karelia since the war began but never with such consistently destructive force and accuracy. They hit supply trains, they damaged the few existing Finnish artillery installations; they blew up sleighs of hot food, medicine, weapons, and even wounded soldiers, in direct violation of the commitment to honor first-aid vehicles. Only at night could ammunition or replacement troops sometimes be transported to the front line, when cloud cover lessened the danger of detection.

A big offensive was clearly imminent. Every soldier in the Third Company knew that soon they would face the most overwhelming land attack that the Russians could muster.

Otto's sense of duty forced him to make a greater effort to overcome his depression, and he became much less withdrawn. He realized that he had better make a serious attempt to restore the squad's confidence in him and in each other, and establish a degree of discipline.

The continuous heavy shelling made the men edgy and nervous, yet they continued to maintain a positive attitude. They were still confident that they would survive this attack just as they had resisted previous Russian attempts to break through their lines. Stromberg became more belligerent than ever, even toward his friends, and Otto had to act as mediator to prevent fights. Tuoppi's sweet temperament helped them all endure the tension. He patiently allowed himself to be made the butt of many jokes and occasional tongue lashings.

Otto and Stromberg still addressed each other with curt politeness when they had to communicate, despite the damage each knew it was doing to the squad's morale.

Night raids had been impeded by the tremendous shelling. Crossing no-man's land now was nothing but suicide. The perimeter of this open area increased steadily as the shells blew the surrounding trees into splinters. Only one two-man patrol from Ekstrom's platoon had succeeded in penetrating into Russian territory. They brought back disturbing news.

"They've equipped their men with skis!" Ekstrom announced to Klami at a meeting of the platoon leaders, in which Otto, as ordnance officer, was included. "They spotted our men before they even got close to the tanks, and then the bastards chased them halfway back here on skis! I think some changes have been made in their general staff. It makes sense that they would put someone new in command after what's been happening to them."

"How did these Russians appear to be superior to those we've encountered in the past? That is, other than the fact that they were on skis?" Klami wanted to know.

"Well," Ekstrom said, "they were ready and they could really shoot. They weren't the least bit afraid to come into the woods after our men, either. There's no doubt in my mind that they've put somebody more capable in command and whoever he is he's going to make the big move to break

253

through right here." He pointed to a section of the defense line on the map which ran across the northern park of Lake Yskjarvi. "There were more troops and tanks on the east side of the lake than ever before. The men told me that there seemed to be thousands of tents and a huge number of tanks. A massive buildup!" he added emphatically.

Ekstrom didn't stop talking long enough to give anyone else a chance. Although he was not normally a talkative man, he was excited and agitated. He stressed the urgency of the situation, and speculated about what would happen and where the offensive would most likely be centered. Yskjarvi had been frozen solid for over a month now, but the Russians hadn't attempted to bring their tanks across it yet for fear they it still might not support their heavy tanks. It now appeared that they were no longer afraid and that the ice was thick enough to withstand the weight of their tanks and machinery.

Ekstrom continued. "They will attack the defense line on the lake, I'm sure, if for no other reason than to surprise us with their daring. A new commander certainly isn't going to continue attacking in the same place where his predecessor met with such stinging defeats."

"I agree with you, Sergeant," Klami said. "Your estimates have generally proven to be accurate and I defer to your expertise. I'm prepared to listen further."

The men in the dugout knew that Ekstrom was once again their commanding officer.

"We've got to dynamite the lake," he said forcefully, "and do it fast! Arola, do you have enough wire and detonators to rig up an efficient system?"

"I think my squad and a couple of extra men would be able to do it. We could take a horse and sleigh to get the dynamite to the lake shore, and from there we could use toboggans to haul it out."

"It's going to be quite a job to get a horse and sleigh through this shelling," Sergeant Hakli muttered. "I think you would be better off taking more men, and packing the explosives in their rucksacks. A sleigh and a horse, or even a toboggan, is too easy a target for a plane."

"How many men do we have out there now?" Otto asked.

"Two squads," Ekstrom replied, "and the Russians are being very careful not to shell that area."

"Why don't we relieve the two squads? My men and another squad can pack in the dynamite and stay there until we're relieved or until the Russians make their move onto the lake."

"That's good, Arola. That's good," Ekstrom nodded. "We'll do it that way. You'll go tonight if you can be ready."

"We'll be ready. Send the other squad over to the crater as soon as you can," Otto said. "We've got a lot of preparations to make."

"One of my squads will go," Ekstrom added out of consideration.

In the Molotov Crater the men worked as fast as they could, packing the dynamite into their rucksacks. There was a feeling of anxiety and fear in the air, but it was mingled with some degree of relief, too, at being on the move again.

Ekstrom finished packing his rucksack first, and he hefted it both to get the feel of it and to balance the weight for easier carrying. Each man would carry thirty-two sticks of dynamite and eleven grenades.

Perhaps the most essential factor in reaching the lake safely was the spacing of the men. They had to travel far enough apart to avoid a chain reaction of the explosives in the event that one of them was struck by a shell. This would mean that the first and last men would be unable to see each other. Ekstrom had experienced a similar situation in the Civil War in 1918 and it had ended disastrously, with his squad being separated behind enemy lines. Only he and one other man had returned from the patrol, and he wanted to avoid a repetition of that scenario.

When all of the men had finished loading, Ekstrom explained the travel plans. The forest was still the best route to take, although it had been badly damaged by artillery fire. The lake was two kilometers from camp—at least half an hour's trip.

They left the Molotov Crater at seven in the evening with Ekstrom in the lead and Otto the last man in line. When he rolled into the trench behind Yskjarvi, Otto felt as though he would never be warm again. It was thirty-five below zero. The penetrating cold had completely occupied his mind during the exhausting trip to the lake, but the two squads arrived without any casualties, and that in itself was a triumph. They had encountered heavy shelling until they came within half a kilometer of the shore.

Ekstrom hustled the men into a dugout behind the trenches for half an hour's rest before going out to set up the charges on the lake. They had eight hours of night left in which to spread the dynamite in a horse-shoe pattern on the ice, the configuration that they had decided would be most effective.

Otto took his squad out to the left side of the lake and Ekstrom took his men out to the right. Once again, they used their skis as small sleighs, under their bellies. The two groups of men moved cautiously toward each other, laying the dynamite out from opposite ends of the horseshoe line, and connecting the two half-lines in the center. Ekstrom and Otto ran the detonating wire all the way back to the trenches overlooking the lake. The ice was now more than half a meter thick. Otto hoped that the tanks' weight would help to break through it.

While the men lay waiting in the dugouts, Otto and Ekstrom sat haggard and bleary-eyed in the trench watching the sun rise. They chewed hardtack and looked out at the bright icy lake. They could hear the tanks beyond the lake but they saw nothing alien to the pastoral scene before them. It remained this way during their first day at Yskjarvi.

Otto slept through the following night and when he awoke he saw that Stromberg, Hietala, Tuoppi, and Aalto were still sleeping. He crawled out and made his way to the trench, where Ekstrom and his squad sat waiting for any signs of enemy movement.

"Anything happening yet?" he asked Ekstrom.

"Nothing," Ekstrom replied gruffly. "I'm beginning to think they may have seen us planting the dynamite. Maybe this is all a bluff to catch us off guard at Kyyrola."

Otto looked at Ekstrom in surprise.

Ekstrom pulled a map from inside his coat and unfolded it. "If I can make it out there," he said, indicating the center of the lake with his finger, "I'll be able to see what

256

they're up to. I'm just not sure what they're going to do once they get out on the lake.''

"You think they might go straight across to Kyyrola?" Otto asked.

"Maybe. They might go both west *and* north. I don't know, but I'll find out tonight.''

"You want anyone from my squad to go with you?''

"No! If they come this way while I'm gone, I want you to blow out this lake and then get back to Kyyrola. If you break up the lake you won't be needed here. If you don't, two squads won't matter against those odds. I'll take one of my own men.''

The ordnance squad relieved Ekstrom's men at ten in the morning. At six that evening, Ekstrom and a small soldier named Ahila set out across the lake, moving south toward the whirring, clanking sound of Russian tanks far off in the distance. For the first time in weeks, a very thin cloud layer hung suspended in front of the moon, giving the Finns a slight advantage. After four hours of sliding through the snow on their belly-sleighs, the two white-cloaked men suddenly came upon the terrifying sight they had been expecting. At least a hundred tanks were lined up in formation facing them. Others rumbled through the snow and were angling into position to join the already menacing force. They were pointed north. Much relieved by their discovery, Ekstrom motioned Ahila to turn back.

Otto waited up until Ekstrom returned and learned that it was exactly as Ekstrom had predicted. The Russians would attempt to break through at the northern tip of the lake to encircle the Finnish troops around Kyyrola.

"Arola! Ekstrom!" Tuoppi screamed the alarm as he dropped into the dugout. "They're coming. I can see them coming!"

Otto jerked his head up and looked around frantically for a moment before he realized what Tuoppi was talking about. Ekstrom had jumped up immediately and began to bark orders at his sleeping men, pulling one after another to his feet.

"Let's go," he growled. "Hurry it up!"

It took only seconds for the weary men to grasp what was happening. Their common anxiety over this moment

257

was too intense for them to think of anything else, and Tuoppi's excitement, along with Ekstrom's growl, warned them that the time had arrived. The tanks were still nothing more than a thin, dark line stretched across a flat, white background, but their sound was unmistakable to every man in the trench, and no one was deceived by their seeming remoteness. Behind each tank a mass of soldiers followed in the tracks made by the luumbering treads.

Otto pulled his battery from his pack and checked the detonation wire to make sure the ends were in good shape. His hands shook violently and panicky thoughts raced through his mind. Had they spread the dynamite properly? How could they be sure that one or more connections in the line hadn't frayed? or separated? Get hold of yourse,f he chastised, but his hands continued to shake, and not just from the cold.

"Relax, Arola," Ekstrom said. "You've got at least forty-five minutes before they get close enough. Just let 'em roll up into the horseshoe and let about a third of the troops follow them. The weight of the tanks will help to crack the ice. Don't worry, it'll work out all right," Ekstrom said as he started crawling off along the trench, whispering encouragement to each man and going over what each one was to do after the explosions.

Otto stared down at the lake and then looked over to Stromberg who was on his left kneeling and watching the Russians. He seemed oblivious to Otto, to the tension and hostility that had developed between them. He looked scared, too, Otto noticed, and he wished there were something he could say to encourage him and to let him know that he wanted to resume their friendship. But he could think of nothing and returned his attention to the lake.

From the eastern shore, more Russian troops moved out of the forest and fell in behind the tanks. They were still too far off to see clearly. Otto's stomach knotted and began to ache disconcertingly. He wondered how many times he would have to go through these situations before he stopped experiencing this terrible tightened feeling in his midsection.

"Do you want me to do it?" Ekstrom was asking.

"No, I'll do it. Just tell me *when*."

"It won't be long now. Just hold on until I tell you."

It was probably the longest three-quarters of an hour of Otto's life. He bit his lip under his woolen mask.

The tanks plowed forward until they seemed unbearably close to the two markings on the lake. Sergeant Ekstrom leaned toward Otto. "Now." he said quietly.

Otto reacted instantly to the order, ripping his mittens off, and holding the battery with one hand while touching one of the wires to the negative terminal. Almost simultaneously, he took the other wire in his hand and touched it to the positive terminal. He held them there as tightly as if his life depended on it.

Ekstrom grabbed him by the arm and forced him to look down at the lake. None of the men spoke. No one could utter a sound. The first of four lines of tanks had reached the dynamite line with the troops following close behind. And then the dynamite exploded!

What they saw was so spectacular that it left them speechless. Many of the Russian soldiers simply disappeared before the ice even opened up—blown apart by the explosion. Those who survived the blast found themselves suddenly without anything to stand on, as the tanks ahead of them sank into the icy water, taking the ice sheet down with them.

The cracking of the ice sent up a tremendous roar which echoed long after the explosions had ceased to rend the air. A few tanks tried to turn around, and ran into each other and over some of their own terrified men.

"My God, look at that," Ekstrom said, squinting through his binoculars and pointing to the gruesome sight of men being crushed into the snow under the tank treads.

The Finns began to relax as they watched the steel dinosaurs being slain by the elements, but a Russian plane suddenly appeared off to the east and Ekstrom ordered all of them except Otto to take cover in the dugout.

"He'll be looking for movement but we're not going to give him any," said Ekstrom as he looked up at the approaching plane.

"What do we do now?" Otto asked, suddenly taut and tense as ever, reacting to the new threat.

"We'll wait until the plane is gone and then head back

to camp. No sense waiting around here. They're not going to get behind us from the lake. I'd say that they'll either regroup around the southern tip and hit us again at Kyyrola, or go on the eastern shore and strike at Muolaa. Maybe even both! But either way, it'll give us some time to get ready for them.''

# Chapter 42

The two squads returned to camp, but there were few of their own men there. Everyone was in the trenches. Rifle and machine-gun fire rattled through the evening air, and it was obvious that it had not been quiet during their expedition to following their departure for Yskjarvi.

Ekstrom had badly misjudged the Russians' intent. He had been sure that they would attack across the lake but he had neglected the possibility of a simultaneous push toward Kyyrola. The air was tense with excitement. Otto and Ekstrom entered the Molotov Crater and found a soldier named Virta shuffling through the stacks of ammunition.

"What's going on here, soldier?" Ekstrom asked him. "Sir?"

"When did they attack?" Ekstrom questioned the man crossly. "The Russians, man, the Russians!"

"Oh, this morning, Sergeant," Virta answered nervously. He was fat and bulbously muscular, like a wrestler, and was most likely a new replacement.

"You can go back to you squad; soldier. Corporal Arola will take over here." The man limped to the entrance and clumsily crawled out into snow.

"Damn," Ekstrom mumbled. "He must be over fifty years old."

"Sergeant, do you want us to go out to the trenches?"

"No, no. Stay here. Get something to eat from the cooks

and be ready with full ammo toboggans. They'll probably make the big push at daybreak. I'm going to find Hakli, as soon as I report to Klami."

Finally back at the trenches, Ekstrom could hear the men methodically cocking their rifles, inserting brass cartridges into the chambers. He listened as the block moved snugly back into position. He was imagining a sight he knew all too well: the cold finger covered by its woolen mitten curving around the trigger almost caressingly, the barrel aiming at some enemy's head or body, the finger pressing the trigger—and wham!

To the veterans it was a ritual, but the newcomers were bewildered with fear and the knowledge that they were all at the mercy of whoever was standing next to them. They would learn that the trick to surviving was to stay calm and to fire to kill.

The soldiers who wore leather boots couldn't stand for very long on one spot without freezing their toes, but those who were lucky enough to have some confiscated Russian felt boots fared better. Ekstrom swore at the unrelenting coldness of the night as he approached Hakli.

"How's it going here?" Ekstrom asked He noticed absent-mindedly that Hakli's Hittleresque mustache had grown still more and now stuck out lumpily under the woolen mask. His hips were white and thinly drawn together, displaying his fear of the inevitable Russian break through the Finnish line.

"We're in trouble, Ekstrom," Hakli whispered succinctly. He motioned Ekstrom to crawl out of earshot of the others and continued, "Those new reserves are useless. We lost sixteen of them just yesterday."

"What happened?" Ekstrom asked, looking aghast.

"They got one glimpse of the tanks, stood up, and tried to run off through the snow. Machine guns cut 'em down. But with the help of the Fourth Company platoon we took twenty-eight prisoners."

"How many others did we lose?"

"Only four wounded, but I think they were just feeling us out on the first day. They only sent ten tanks out, and from the sound of it there are at least forty or fifty more behind the trees. How did it go at the lake?" Hakli asked eagerly, hoping for some better news from that mission. He cast his weary eyes toward no–man's land, as if to see for himself what was across it on the other side.

Ekstrom told him all that had happened and the two talked about Klami, who still spent most of his time safely tucked away in his dugout. Neither one could comprehend how he could have been made company commander.

"We're better off with him just staying out of the way."

They were silent for a few minutes and each man knew that the other was trying to think of some constructive suggestion for a plan of defense. Nothing came. They could only do as they had done in the past, except with fewer men and less ammunition.

"You're right, old friend," Ekstrom said finally. "We are in trouble. Hakli, should we pull back? We can't hold out more than a few days here, anyway."

Hakli was stunned by the suggestion of retreat. He had never heard Ekstrom sound so dispirited.

"Are you crazy? Where would we go? There's nothing behind us, Ekstrom. You know that. At least we've got trenches here and a few new mines in front of us."

That's what Ekstrom had needed to hear.

Hakli continued. "We've got no choice now. Besides, since the shelling has let up a little, there's a good chance that more supplies can get through to us. More men, too." He suddenly checked himself, realizing that he was sounding overly optimistic now, when only a moment before he had been pointing out the gravity of their situation. "Well, anything's possible . . . ."

"I'm going back to camp to get some food. Hold tight," Ekstrom said.

"Right."

The Ordnance Squad had set to work in the crater as soon as they had eaten, and by the time Ekstrom returned, four toboggans of ammunition were ready to be taken to the front line. They had expected a hero's welcome when they returned from Yskjarvi and were disappointed to have been deprived of it. Otto was preoccupied with taking an inventory of their remaining supplies. He was no pleased with the results. Very little dynamite remained and there was only enough ammunition to last through four or five days of fighting.

At seven o'clock the next morning, Otto heard the a land mine exploding. It was the first sound of the assault. Following closely, was another explosion, and then another. Then the turret cannons opened fire and the battle was underway. He knew the pattern very well: light weapon fire until the tanks rolled close of the trenches. When the Russian troops who followed behind the tanks got close enough, the Finns would open fire, but not before. Another land mine exploded but Otto could only guess whether they were doing the job on the tanks. If a mine exploded directly under the tread it would break it and stop the tank.

Only Tuoppi remained in the crater with Otto. Ekstrom led the rest of the squad back with him to the trenches. Experienced soldiers were scarce and Otto and Tuoppi were able to handle the distribution of what little ammunition they had left.

Otto was standing outside the crater when a shell dropped from a Russian plane. It burst behind him in the forest and the sound deafened him momentarily. He jumped back into the crater as many other shells came screaming down. He held his hands over both ears.

"Those bombers scare me," he yelled at Tuoppi. "They're not taking any chances on letting supplies reach us. If the cannon shells don't stop our transport people, those bombers will." He shook his head and in a few minutes regained his hearing.

"They're really mad at us, all right," Tuoppi replied, looking sympathetically at Otto, who was still shaking his head occasionally.

Otto had worked through the night fixing frozen guns. He was exhausted but felt that he had to be there with Tuoppi. They were waiting for someone to come back from the front with an empty tobaggan so that they could reload it and send it back to the trenches with weapons.

Otto and Tuoppi turned their attention to the distinctive chatter of the Suomis stuttering and barking irregularly, accompanied by rifle and heavy machine-gun fire. Something sounded different. This attack didn't erupt as in the previous battle when the Russians stormed blindly toward the Finnish trenches. Otto guessed that the enemy was seeking out weak spots in the defense line, making the Finns waste their precious ammunition without really getting a chance at the "meat" of the Russian division.

The first man to come back for more ammunition was Hietala. He pulled an empty toboggan behind him as he skied up to the Molotov Crater. Otto and Tuoppi were anxious to hear about the battle.

"How's it going out there?" Otto asked as the weary man slid into the crater.

"They're coming in a slow but steady stream," gasped Hietala, breathing heavily. "Ekstrom was right—these guys are real soldiers."

"What do you mean?" asked Tuoppi.

Hietala took several deep breaths before answering. "Just what I said. They don't panic and they stay hidden behind the tanks like they're supposed to. We've lost three men trying to get at the tanks with Cocktails."

Otto had already stripped him of his ammunition belt and was refilling it with cartridges, Cocktails, satchel charges, and grenades.

"I can't sit here gabbing all day," Hietala said. "You got another toboggan ready?"

They hoisted the heavy toboggan outside, Hietala slung the pullstrap over his broad shoulder, and fastened it to his belt buckle.

"See you later," he mumbled, as he laboriously pulled out.

Another man appeared with another empty toboggan. Otto and Tuoppi jumped back down into the crater and began to sort ammunition to reload it.

The fighting didn't cease at night. Fresh troops continued to harass the Finns, who returned the fire only when a clear shot was possible. Ekstrom sent no guerilla patrols behind the lines; the nights were too clear and the Russians too alert. Russian ski troops were now prowling through the woods, waiting for an opportunity to take revenge on the marauding Finns who had been so bold in their past commando raids.

For two days and nights Otto and Tuoppi remained at the

crater without any sleep and with little food. They loaded and reloaded ammunition toboggans, and helped carry the wounded to the dugouts were they received first-aid treatment. Most of the casualties were the more recent replacements—the older, untrained men who had no business being sent to the trenches in the first place.

Otto recognized the pot-bellied man who had told him that there was no Mannerheim Line to fall back on. His hand had been severed and half of his lower jaw had been blown away. What was left of his face was contorted in terrible agony. There were at least twenty casualties in two dugouts, all badly wounded and in severe pain. Still no help came from the rear. Otto wondered if any of them would ever make it to a field hospital.

Each day the battle seemed to double in intensity, and Otto and Tuoppi, although they couldn't see it, were very much aware of what was happening to their comrades.

The Russian tanks pounded the Third Company with a tremendous barrage of cannon fire before they started rolling forward. In the long nights preceding the battle, several daring Finns had crawled out to plant additional mines in no-man's land. The mines slowed the Russian panzers enough to make them easier marks for accurately thrown Molotov Cocktails.

Heavy shelling zeroed in on the Finnish trenches before noon of the sixth day. They dug in and waited it out. When the artillery fire ceased and the tank howitzers began, Otto looked at his watch. It was two o'clock in the afternoon. Otto realized that without some drastic intervention in the way things were going, the Finns faced a disaster.

Perhaps this will be the final disaster for all of us, he thought, and wondered if it was his turn to die.

# Chapter 43

For the wounded soldiers in the Molotov Crater, waiting to be transported to the rear, the final disaster had already struck. Their white cloaks and coats were drenched with their own blood or that of a comrade, and their faces reflected the pain and suffering they were enduring. The fat one who looked like a wrestler held a piece of dirty torn undershirt to the side of his head. "Corporal Arola?"

"Yes, I'm Arola."

"Sergeant Ekstrom says that you are to load all of the ammunition onto one sleigh and pull it near the trenches with a horse. He can't spare any more men to come back with toboggans." The man staggered and fell clumsily to his knees.

"Are you all right?" Tuoppi asked compassionately.

The soldier said nothing but motioned to Tuoppi that he would be able to manage without help.

"Tuoppi, give me a hand, Quick! Move!" Otto said.

"Want me to hitch up the horse?" Tuoppi asked.

"Yes," he said nervously. "And hurry!"

After Tuoppi returned with the horse, they went to the edge of the woods, twenty meters away, and tossed the snow-covered fir boughs off one of the sleighs. With Tuoppi pushing from behind and Otto pulling, they moved the sleigh slowly across the crusty snow to the entrance of the crater. The wounded wrestler had vanished. Otto stood by the entrance and Tuoppi handed him the few explosives that were left.

Tuoppi was naturally good with horses and apparently liked all animals. Otto noticed that he had become quite attached to the lamb which still slept near them in the crater. The animal had tried to follow them to Lake Yskjarvi but someone had been there to restrain her. He petted the frail little animal and whispered a few words to her as if she would understand, before he climbed out of the crater.

"All right," he told Tuoppi, "I'll see you up at the front later on. Be careful!"

He tugged at the horse's reins and the animal stepped forward grudgingly, not at all eager to pull such a heavy burden through the knee-deep snow. Otto coaxed the animal persuasively and the sleigh moved forward toward the sounds of the heavy battle.

The forest provided some cover for Otto, and he felt somewhat relieved, but his feeling of security vanished when a pistol shot rang out behind him. He dropped to his belly from the sleigh to take cover behind a tree. "Snipers, the bastards," he muttered to himself, terrified at the thought of being surrounded and not being able to see the enemy. Another sharp crack sounded to his left. He rolled onto his right side and raised his Suomi to fire back at the would-be assailant.

Nothing moved. He lay still, looking around for movement of some kind, something to shoot at. Then, another report and a piece of frozen wood flew from the trunk of the tree directly in front of him. He realized that the pistol shots were actually explosive bullets, dum-dums being fired by the Russians from no-man's land.

He breathed a little easier simply because he understood the nature of the danger confronting him.

He jumped up and tugged at the horse's reins. He had three or four-hundred meters to go before leaving the horse and sleigh somewhere in the woods.

Otto came to a boulder big enough to protect a horse and decided that it was close enough. The dum-dum bullets were popping around him with distrubing frequency. He could almost see the open space of no-man's land through the broken trees. He led the horse behind the boulder, tethered the animal's reins to a tree, and took the toboggan off the sleigh. He loaded it hastily and advanced slowly toward the trenches.

After pulling it about three hundred meters through dense underbrush, he stopped behind a tree to survey briefly what lay ahead. As he turned toward his right he saw a line of Finnish soldiers advancing toward him. He didn't recognize any of them, but he was relieved just the same. He watched them file by, then stepped out and hailed the last man in the line.

"Who are you guys?" he asked.

"Machine-Gun Company," the soldier said. He was dressed in a fresh white cloak and looked younger than Otto. "You from the Third?" he asked.

"That's right. "It's good to see you guys! Where did you come from?"

"Muolaa. Your lieutenant sounded pretty desperate, so we were ordered to come and give you a hand."

Otto felt a surge of confidence and optimism. The young soldier's assurance inspired him immediately. "I'd better get this ammo to my outfit," Otto said. "Good luck to you."

"Same to you," the soldier said.

Otto tugged at the rope of the toboggan and walked a hundred meters. As he yanked on the rope again, he felt a needle-sharp sting in his right hand and the rope fell to the snow. Strangely, he hadn't heard a shot.

When he looked down at his hand he saw blood spurting out of his wrist, through the heavy leather glove. He stared, unbelievingly, at his own hand hanging from his arm by nothing but shreds of tendon and skin. A sharp pain shot suddenly through his right arm and he dropped to the snow, still staring at the mangled wrist. It was spurting blood in a pulsating shower.

For some unknown reason he plunged his arm into the snow. His wrist was covered by the soft whiteness but his hand remained exposed, stretching grotesquely away from the wrist. The sight shocked him thoroughly, and he tried desperately to push the hand through the snow, hoping it would relieve the pressure of the stretching skin and stop the bleeding—but he discovered to his horror that he couldn't make the hand disappear!

With his left hand he pulled the arm out. He could tell that an artery had been severed by the way the blood kept pumping in regular spurts. He looked around and began to whisper out for help, afraid that a loud cry might bring another shot. His second effort at attracting attention was answered by a moan. Not fifteen meters away lay the soldier with whom he had been speaking only moments before. There was blood oozing through his heavy pants in three places on his right leg, but he wasn't bleeding nearly so profusely as Otto. The cold helped to minimize the loss of blood but no amount of cold could prevent a severed artery from pouring out blood as regularly as the heart beat.

"Help me, quick," Otto begged. "Please! Do you have any string . . . anything I can use to cut off this bleeding?" He crawled over to the man.

The soldier with the leg wounds was amazingly calm. He looked at Otto's wrist and immediately took a satchel charge from his belt. The sticks of dynamite were wrapped together with a thin piece of wire. Without a word, he wrapped the wire around Otto's arm, but unfortunately just at the edge of the wound. As he twisted it tight, the wire cut deep into Otto's flesh.

Otto's lips turned snow white, and he cried out in anguish. Never had he imagined such an incredible degree of pain. He nearly collapsed as the soldier secured the wire. He felt as if his wrist were being bathed in hot coals and at the same time pumped full of scalding air like a balloon. But the bleeding had nearly stopped.

Machine-gun fire sputtered nearby and Otto looked up to see a Russian tank behind some bushes, only fifty meters away. He had been so preoccupied with his wound that he had failed to notice a tank pulling out from behind a small group of trees and opening fire on them. How it had managed to break through the defense line he didn't know.

The tank's success, however, was short-lived. The Machine-Gun Company had encircled it by this time, and as Otto watched, two of them managed to get close enough to throw Molotov Cocktails at it. It burst into flames. The Russian crewmen were suffocating inside. One frightened man tried to escape, but a string of bullets from a Suomi dropped him back into the burning tomb.

Otto let himself fall back into the snow. He was faint from the loss of blood. He watched a man from the Machine-Gun Company ski over to his fallen comrade. The huge man gently slung the soldier over his shoulder and swiftly skied away.

Otto waited until his double vision focused again and he felt strong enough to start toward the horse. He didn't dare elevate his head much above the snow. He heard the steady machine-gun, Suomi, and rifle chatter, and the sound of dum-dum bullets striking the trees around him. With the help of his left elbow he inched forward, crawling, with his right arm dragging uselessly at his side.

Once he was about three-hundred meters into the woods he rolled over painfully onto his stomach and drew his knees up under him, pushing himself up with his left arm. He was breathing heavily and felt exhausted from the effort, but his head and his vision had cleared. He stood up, stooped over, and leaned against a tree. Several bullets smashed into the trees around him and he fell forward again into the snow, screaming as his right arm was pinned beneath his body. He rolled off it and began to pull himself forward with his left hand, kicking with his feet in an attempt to push himself.

He reached the footpath which led back to his horse. He couldn't remember how far he had crawled nor how long it had taken him, but after what seemed to be hours he saw the familiar boulder some seventy meters in front of him. The popping of the dum-dum bullets against the trees made him more nervous than ever, but he had already been wounded, and he felt sure that the odds were against his being shot again. It just wouldn't be fair.

He lay at the base of the huge boulder and rested. He was safe now from the front-line bullets. He was bleeding, but not so profusely as before.

If only the pain would ease off, he hoped silently. If only I had some morphine . . . if only . . .

"Arola, what happened? Otto? Otto?" It was Tuoppi, coming from the crater, dragging a toboggan.

"Help me get the horse and sleigh," Otto pleaded. "Just help me get out of here."

"Take it easy, Otto. Jesus, your wrist!"

271

"Tuoppi . . ." he urged desperately.

"Just stay still, Otto. Stay still. I'm going to unload the sleigh and put you on it."

"Hurry!" His voice was weak and anguished.

Tuoppi scrambled around to the sleigh and started to unload it quickly but carefully. One couldn't afford to throw explosives around, even in the snow. He remembered what Otto had taught him.

Arola writhed in agony, groaning and begging Tuoppi to hurry. He felt something nudge at his feet. The little lamb had followed Tuoppi from the crater and she snuggled against Otto's legs. "Goddamn lamb," he muttered. "You must be crazy." He was glad to see her just the same. He looked at her pink nose, her big sad eyes that were watching him intently as if she knew his pain. He felt better just looking into the animal's innocent adoring eyes. Tuoppi helped him into the sleigh and put the lamb in beside him. Otto would have to find his own way back while Tuoppi delivered ammunition to the desperate men in the trenches.

Tuoppi handed the reins to him in his left hand, but Otto did little coaching, since the horse knew its way back to the crater.

Otto heard the steady sound of hooves moving over the snow in an even rhythm, each step taking him farther and farther away from the front. Clear sky above and bright sunshine through the forest—he would have been an easy target for an airplane, but he was lucky. There were no planes in sight.

The sleigh jerked along violently. Otto's severed hand dropped to the floor of the sleigh. He put the reins in his teeth. With his left hand he repositioned his wounded hand on his lap.

After what seemed to be an eternity, the horse and sleigh pulled up to the entrance of the Molotov Crater. He lifted his head and raised himself weakly on his elbow. He crawled down off the sleigh, and staggered throw the snow to the dugout where the wounded were awaiting transportation to the medical-aid station.

Otto stuck his head down into the dugout. "I've got a horse and a sleigh waiting outside. Anybody who can make it can come with me. I'm leaving now, so hurry up."

Otto and seven other men arrived at the medical aid tent at Kangaspelto over an hour later. A soldier with a flesh wound in his leg had driven the sleigh this time. Otto, followed by the lamb, staggered into the large medical tent, which was well camouflaged from aerial view under trees and bushes. The place was packed with at least fifty wounded soldiers waiting for one of the two medics to tend them.

"Get that sheep out of here," yelled an officer whose leg had been severed above the knee. "We've got enough problems without more damned lice!"

Otto nudged the animal outside. He hurt too badly to argue over the lamb.

Soon a young medic spoke to him. "You'll have to wait your turn, Corporal. I'll get to you as soon as I can."

"Can't you do something? Please! It hurts!"

"Here, I'll give you an injection. This'll ease the pain. Now just wait here and I'll be back to patch you up as soon as I can," the medic repeated.

Otto obeyed. The lamb slipped back inside unnoticed, and he covered it with the hem of his cloak, leaned back, and closed his eyes. The pain was an angry wall against sleep and the medication gave no relief.

# Chapter 44

A short, fat, round-faced medic was on duty. He had been trained at the army's medical school to perform first aid, but was now mostly limited to giving morphine shots to lessen pain. The tent had no medical equipment to do much more than that, nor was he qualified to administer more complicated treatment.

The first shot of morphine hadn't helped Otto, nor had the towels that were wrapped around his arm. The wire kept cutting deeply into the flesh along the edge of the wound like some mad wolf's teeth that were gnawing their way to the bone.

"Medic! Medic! Where are you with my shot?" Otto yelled loudly enough to be heard in every corner of the tent. His face was contorted into a mask of pain. He looked frantically around for the fat medic to run to him, but he wasn't rushing toward him as expected. Otto looked at the dull, twisted, painful expression on each wounded man's face. They were sitting helplessly around the edges of the tent on the cold frozen floor. He moved his right hand to a better position on his lap, but the balloon-like swollen hand inside the tight sleeve and towel continued burning like hot coals.

Finally the other medic, a scar-faced man, stood in front of Otto looking down at the misery drawn on his face. The medic was about Otto's age, perhaps having gone into the service at about the same time Otto had gone to Terijoki, but his past history didn't interest Otto now. All he wanted was to get some relief from his pain.

"What is this lamb doing here?" was the medic's first comment. The long scar across his cheek made him look as if he were mad at everybody.

"Just give me a shot and leave the lamb alone, damn it! I can't take the pain any more. Can't you see . . . here . . . this damn thing is sticking through the skin. It can't stretch any more!" Arola summoned all his strength for this plea, but his entreaties and his facial contortions apparently meant nothing to the scar-faced medic. His hoarse voice fell on deaf ears and he was about to black out from the strain. The medic silently looked and listened, totally impassive.

"Please, why can't you take this wire out and retie something softer, above the elbow? It's cutting through me like a knife. I can feel it in the bone!"

The scar-faced individual softened a little and said in a more compassionate voice, "We can't do any more for you than we've already done. If we were to reopen that artery now you would bleed to death. Your arm has swollen all the way to your shoulder, and to put a tourniquet around that bloated arm would do nothing to cut down the bleeding. Do you understand, Corporal? You'll get another shot in two hours," he added patiently.

"In two hours! I'll be dead by then!"

"We're freezing to death in here," shouted the man crouched next to Otto. The pain had changed their resignation to irritating nastiness, but every complaint was in vain and the men knew it.

In the rear of the tent stood a cold, wooden stove. It had not seen a fire for days or nights. Burning wood would have given out smoke, and the Russian planes would have swarmed over them and bombed the place into the ground in a matter of minutes.

Otto looked toward the entrance. A man was being brought in. He had a heavy, black beard, and long icicles hung from it. His face was white, almost icy blue. He breathed slowly and slobber had dribbled down from his lips. His head rested upon his left shoulder. His nose was white and frozen.

The ceiling of the tent was covered with hoarfrost from the steam of breaths that rose up to the cold canvas. The leather boots worn by several of the men were frozen, as if they had been made of sheet metal.

Outside the temperature was thirty-two degrees below zero. The sun shone but did nothing to warm the place—instead it allowed Russian planes easy visibility of the Finnish positions. The noise of planes and shelling was constant. Shells flew over the tent and exploded all around the area of Kangaspelto. Otto thought that it would take a miracle to save the tent from a direct hit.

On the second day there was no sign of a change in the clear weather. No clouds meant no transportation for the wounded. At night the February moon shone just as plainly as the sun did during the day.

Otto had eaten nothing. The morphine induced vomiting and nausea. His only concern was to get to a hospital, but they told him over and over again that no one was to be moved.

"The sky is too clear and there are too many enemy planes around. It would be suicide to try. You're better off here."

Otto didn't care about the planes, and when the announcement was made on the second night that three sleighs were available to try to transport the more seriously wounded back to a field hospital, he was eager to take the chance. The medic gave him his morphine an hour early. He knew that it would take the sleighs at least three hours to reach the hospital even if they were unmolested by planes.

"That corporal with the shot-up wrist has lost a lot of blood. Even if he survives the trip," the scar-faced medic told his colleague, "he's going to be in bad shape and severe pain by the time he gets to Heinjoki."

The fat medic nodded his agreement and looked around at the other men. "They're all going to be hurting pretty bad."

"Why don't you give them all an extra shot?" the scar-faced medic suggested.

"I already have," the fat man replied, and went on with his work.

276

At three o'clock on a bright February morning, the Karelian countryside sparkled and glowed under a full moon. The air was still. The temperature hovered around thirty-three below zero. The drivers of the sleighs cursed and wished that they hadn't been ordered to transport these wounded soldiers to the hospital.

The sleighs were painted white for camouflage. The horses had been covered with white blankets, too, but everyone knew that a low flying plane could still spot the shadow thrown by an object as large as a sleigh or horse. The men were hoisted up on the flatbed sleighs, cushioned with hay, and the first one pulled out a little after three o'clock. Otto was on it. As it jerked forward he felt the weight of the lamb, who wouldn't leave him, across his ankles. Somehow she was like an insurance of safety to Otto. He was glad she was there.

Otto belched painfully several times before he could settle back into the foggy daze created by the drug. Still the pain burned through his arm, it throbbing and pulsating with his heartbeat. Otto glanced down at the lamb across his feet. "So you want to get out of here, too," he whispered to her. "I hope we both make it!"

It was a lonely journey. Trees flanked the road, which was just wide enough for the sleigh to fit through. If another horse had come along it would have had to pass by going into the woods. Otto kept his eyes straight ahead, staring into the distance. He kept hoping that Heinjoki would be around the next bend, but it never was. Time passed painfully.

Suddenly, the entire roadside was littered with piles and piles of frosty, bloody, grotesquely frozen bodies—hundreds of dead soldiers still dressed in the white cloaks that identified them as Finns. They included young, old faceless, armless, and legless men. How horrible a sight it would be for their fathers or mothers, Otto thought. Otto was overwhelmed by the carnage, and remembered that at least one of his brothers-in-law had been killed. Was his body among those lying in the freezing snow, piled up like cordwood for delivery to their respective homes?

The horse's hooves made an even rhythm on the snow. The driver was careful not to trot the horse since speed would shake the sleigh and cause more pain to the men in his care. Soon they would reach the village of Heikurila on the western tip of Lake Ayrapaa. It was still hours before they would reach Heinjoki, twenty kilometers away.

Otto steadied his wounded arm, his face twisted with suffering. His mask was freezing around his mouth and nose because of the moisture of his exhaled breath.

Through its misty halo, the moon stared back impersonally at Otto as he lifted his face upward. Russian shells from their long-range cannons flew over the sleigh or fell short, exploding here and there at odd intervals. He prayed that the horse would travel faster, faster—away from the range of howitzers and cannons.

His ears detected the low-pitched sound of a heavy motor—but not a tank. There couldn't be one here. He looked up into the sky and to his horror saw an airplane above him. In his mind's eye he saw again those grotesque bodies by the roadside. One plane dived down toward them, then another, and they strafed the sleigh. A third plane approached with deadly speed above the trees on the right and they received their third strafing. Fortunately, none of the string of bullets made direct hits.

The driver cracked the whip against the horse's flesh, but it did no good.

"Driver, go into the woods, damn it! Can't you see? Go into the woods for cover!"

Otto was shouting as loudly as he could, but his voice was so hoarse from the morphine that the driver could scarcely hear it. And his eyes were so hazy from the morphine, that he couldn't see the high, impassable snowbanks on both sides of the road.

Otto looked once more, terrified, at the planes above, saw first three, and then four planes diving down at them, strafing them again with thousands of bullets.

Damn it, Otto thought, this is worse than being at the front!

Just as suddenly as they had come, the planes fell back. Otto guessed they had moved on to strafe the other two sleighs that followed behind.

Suddenly shells started falling near the road ahead of them. Otto's arm ached and pained him with every explo-

278

sion that shook the ground beneath them.

Once more there was the sound of a bomber. He had heard and seen them flying over the front lines many times. It must be on its way to bomb our cities, he thought sadly, just when the plane was almost directly overhead, the lamb suddenly got restless. She jerked and twisted and moved closer to Otto's body, nestling in his lap. There was a tremendous explosion nearby. Whistling sounds indicated that other bombs were falling from the plane. Otto heard one more huge crash and then felt himself and the lamb being hurled up into the air. He never felt the impact of landing, because he had lost consciousness before he hit the ground. He didn't see the little lamb's body, either, tumbling through the air, nor did he realize that a hot piece of shrapnel had entered through her thick fur and killed her instantly. But once more she had saved his life.

# Chapter 45

Otto's consciousness returned slowly, days later. At first he felt and heard himself screaming. In a nightmare he seemed to be lying on a roadside, waiting for a Russian tank to roll off his hand. He tried to reach for a Molotov Cocktail with his free hand, but he could not. He couldn't find or strike a match, either. The tank rolled heavily, slowly over him, mashing his right arm beneath the treads. The Russians were forcefully pulling his crushed hand, and his fingers seemed stuck between the crushing irons.

They were speaking words he couldn't understand and he wanted to scream at them to stop, but he couldn't. The pain stopped every sound. Then he heard his own scream echoing back from the tank as if he were in a long tunnel. The buzzing sound in his ears felt like one of them had taken a drill and was drilling a hole in his fingernails to force them out, only with the power of the tank.

Oh, God—I've been captured!'' he wanted to scream to the figure nearby, but he couldn't make out who or what it was. ''They're tearing my ⸱ . . . they have torn my . . .'' His words stopped short after each beginning.

The shadow of men's figures—Russians, he was sure—stood out against the sky. He could tell already that his right arm had been extended along his side. He couldn't pull it back; it was being held tightly and forcefully by a man who had captured him. He heard a drill, an electric drill—then felt its sharp bit going through the tip of one of his fingers. He shrieked with all his strength, but nothing came from his lips—they were as dry as cork. His tongue stiffened inside his mouth. "Give me snow, water—something to moisten my mouth!" he wanted to say.

He finally forced himself to sit up and tried to strike out at his capturers, his torturers, but he found himself on a bench tight in a vise. There was that dreadful sound of a drill again, then another excruciating pain.

"My pistol . . . where is my pistol . . ." His cork-dry tongue couldn't move in his mouth. His eyes saw only silhouettes of figures—one, two, three, four. "My God, there's a whole squad of Russians!" He felt the men dipping his right hand into hot, boiling oil and inserting heated metal under his fingernails.

When Otto woke up, much later, he was lying on his back in a soft bed. He stared at an empty gray ceiling and tried to reconstruct what had happened to him. He slowly turned his head to look, and he saw that his right arm was propped in a standing metal brace beside his bed. His arm was bent at the elbow, with his forearm stretched upward by wires that were piercing his fingernails and his hand was surrounded with a metal cage. He closed his eyes and fell asleep, frightened by the horrible bloody sight.

When he awoke again, he saw the blurry outline of a man standing by his bed, wearing a white coat. He must be one of my captors, Otto thought. His eyes began to focus and he was astounded to realize that the man was a doctor—and a friend, not an enemy.

"Aku Harma!" he cried, as the tears rolled down his cheeks.

"How are you doing, Otto? You've been through a hell of a mess, old friend."

Otto was too elated to speak. He gazed joyfully at his Terijoki friend and tears streamed down to his pillow—tears of happiness, as he realized that he was in a Finnish hospital. He reached for Aku's hand with his one good one, and pressed it with the little strength he had left. Then the reality of the pain cut through his mind like a knife.

"What are you trying to do to me? I thought you were

a Russian. What is this contraption? Please, Aku, I can't stand this pain. It will kill me!'' He wanted to say much more, but the morphine thickened his tongue and clouded his mind.

"You'll be all right, Otto," Harma comforted him. He had a hypodermic needle in his hand and a bottle of alcohol. He inserted the needle in Otto's good arm before he spoke again.

"You and another soldier were brought to the hospital by a driver who survived the airplane attack. You three, and one horse, were the only survivors."

Otto thought for a moment of the lamb and mourned for it, then felt the pain again. "You've got to take those damned wires out! Please, Aku, you've got to relieve the pain somehow."

"Now Otto, take it easy. You've suffered enough, that's for sure. Don't make it any harder on yourself. This device will set the bones in your wrist, we hope."

"Who were those foreigners? I know I heard a Russian talking."

"They weren't Russians, that's for sure," Aku laughed. "Probably what fooled you was the language the doctor was speaking—Danish. That's Melvin Jergensen, the surgeon in charge of your operation. He's a Dane and a volunteer—and one of the best. If it hadn't been for him, you would have lost your whole hand. None of the other doctors thought it could be saved, but the Dane refused to let them amputate."

"I wish they *had* taken it off," Otto moaned. "I can't stand this pain," he pleaded. The shot was slow to take effect.

Aku grimaced, then his face hardened. Sympathy was stupid; Otto had had a chance to save his hand.

"You could be a lot worse off, man, Your hand . . ."

"Don't lecture me," Otto yelled. "It feels like there's a ton of weight pulling on those fingernails. You have no idea!"

Aku didn't resent Otto's bitterness. It was true that the young Danish volunteer was highly respected by the chief surgeon, but everyone knew that his operation on Otto and the post-operative traction device were purely experimental.

Otto might still lose his hand; her certainly would lose his fingernails before the Dane was through. Aku could do nothing but try to comfort him.

"I'll see you soon, Otto," he promised as he left.

During the days that followed, Otto fought the intense pain. The frequent injections of morphine didn't totally relieve it, but they kept him in a twilight, semi-comatose condition. The shots nauseated him to the point where he could keep nothing down except, surprisingly, sugared lingonberries.

At least once a day the bombers came and he was taken out of traction, placed on a stretcher, and rushed to the shelter despite his protests. The move jarred the broken bones in his wrist and multiplied his agony.

The air raids went on. Shells, large and small, rained down on the city. Only five meters from the outside wall of the hospital lay a five-hundred-kilo bomb that hadn't gone off on impact. No one knew if it was a dud or had been set to go off on a timer. It stood there, half-buried in the frozen ground, while sirens continued to pierce the air, and the days and nights crept slowly by.

At the city of Lahti, the girls-college dormitory had been converted into an army hospital. Otto's bed occupied a room on the fourth floor. Drawn and thin-faced, he stared at the ceiling, unable to move while his hand was held tightly in the experimental binding contraption. The morphine shots given to relieve the excruciating pain were blurring his vision and interfering with his thoughts processes. He listlessly watched the legless man who occupied the bed next to him. He moaned in pain for toes that were now somewhere at the Karelian front, still attached to his severed legs, because the nerves remaining were sending messages of painful sensations. His muscled hands were still strong, but his face, like Otto's, was thin and pale as the sheet on which he lay. Every night he tried to push his bed from one side of the room to get in front of the window.

"I'm going to jump out—I can't stand it any more!" the muscular man repeated in his deep voice. He never made it before the orderly walked in and pushed the bed back, never even wondering why his patient kept trying to get to the window.

Early one morning, a white-uniformed nurse, her blonde hair combed neatly under her cap, and her lips carefully outlined in red lipstick, leaned over Otto's bed as he woke up. Her blue eyes were soft and friendly as she raised his head and plumped his pillow, then let his head fall back gently.

"Feel better now?"

"Thank you," he mumbled in a sleepy tone. He had slept only half an hour that night, and the old nightmare had returned as soon as he had dozed off. The tank was constantly rolling over his hand, crushing it into the frozen earth, then the electrifying sirens and the drone of the Russian planes would follow. Hours later he saw a flame reaching through the window, high up into the sky, burning the city that lay there smoldering after the raid was over.

Aku Harma took care to see that he got enough morphine to ease his pain. The burning sensation in his fingertips made his mind half crazy and he became irritated with the slightest movement that jerked his bed.

Before the day was over two men lifted Otto onto the stretcher once more. The hospital needed space for new wounded men who were being wheeled in every hour. Otto was rushed through the entrance out to the bitter cold and carried into a train. As the train lunged on its tracks Otto heard another siren, then the sound of planes above him. They dived down in a thundering roar and strafed the train, once directly overhead, then a second time. Bullets were continuously piercing the thin walls of the passenger coach.

At midnight, after a ten-hour train trip, Otto's stretcher was wheeled through a large entrance into the big gymnasium at Vierumaki's athletic training center, which had been taken over by the Dutch Red Cross. It was staffed by volunteer nurses who, unfortunately, couldn't speak Finnish.

A brunette, with a round face, and deep, dark eyes, beamed at Otto as she wiped the sweat from his pale brow. She covered him with a warm blanket, plumped the pillow, and then smoothed the covers for him. She stared curiously at the contraption where Otto's hand was confined by his bedside. The bloody fingers remained holding the weight of the hand. The sympathetic nurse could feel the tension and pain through touching of his skin. She shook her head sympathetically and said something in Dutch, but Otto didn't understand a word.

"I am Tony—understand?" she said, speaking the only Finnish words she knew.

"Otto," he replied, his eyes listless but watching the pretty nurse who seemed so anxious to ease his pain.

"Hungry?" Tony pointed to her mouth, indicating the motion of eating.

"Lingonberries—please."

She shook her head and lifted her shapely shoulders. She took a glass of water and gave some to Otto, but as soon as he swallowed it he vomited it back up, much to her dismay.

Otto wished that Aku Harma had followed along with the wounded to Vierumaki. The friendly Dutch nurses were supremely helpful, but his rapidly weakening body was continually in agony.

Otto couldn't believe that this preposterous situation could last for very long. He remembered the time he was so vigorously active, before the war, and even at the front . . . He felt that he would go crazy if they didn't remove the contraption that held him and relieve his fingers of the terrible stress it put on them. He would have been nicer if there was freedom from pain. He wished he had a stronger voice to speak out, to shout, to yell—to complain—but he scarcely seemed able to manage a weak smile and could hardly open his hazy eyes.

One day a windy storm came, short but welcome. It blackened the sky for a while—maybe hours, maybe half a day, but enough to bring Otto some joy. By his bedside stood Sirkka. When he opened his eyes, she was holding his left hand. Otto's eyes brightened, and tears fell downward onto his white pillow.

"You have a beautiful hat," was all Otto could think of to say to her. Teardrops moistened her rosy cheeks, her eyes were bright, and she was fighting to hold back more tears, but failed.

"After I learned about you, I came as soon as they would allow me to travel by train." She spoke softly, sitting by his bed.

Otto's weak hand tightening on hers felt a warm, tingling stream going up his arm to his heart.

"How is Anna?"

"She is fine. She wanted to come, but she was afraid you didn't . . ." Then she paused and rephrased what she wanted to say. "You never wrote to her."

"I don't know why, I don't know . . ."

Sirkka said nothing more about Anna.

You've lost weight, your hair is almost gone, and you look so pale and weak, she thought to herself. But all she said was, "I brought you pancakes and lingonberries. You must be hungry."

"Lingonberries—yes," Otto answered softly.

Tony brought Otto another shot of morphine. A few minutes after the shot he was sleepily looking at Sirkka, her dark shoulder-length hair in curls. He enjoyed looking at her but was too weak to talk.

"Hannes sends you his greetings."

"Thank you-u-u," he replied slowly. "Are you going . . . to marry . . . that policeman of yours?"

"Yes, we've decided to get married. Aren't you glad?"

Sirkka soon had to leave Otto and return to Helsinki. Train travel was restricted and she had to take the first opportunity presented to return to work.

"Will you help me write a letter to Anna before you go—so you can take it with you to her?" Otto asked Sirkka as she sat by his bed.

Sirkka took out a pen and a piece of paper from her purse. Otto dictated his letter to her:

"I am sorry I hurt you, dear Anna. I didn't know what I was doing that night in Helsinki when I left you. I was wrong to leave you that way. If you can forgive me, I would like to be your friend."

He broke off, too weak to continue and not sure of what he wanted to say. Slow tears of weakness slid from his eyes while Sirkka held his hand and stroked his forehead.

"Otto, Otto, it's all right," Sirkka soothed him. "I'll give her your letter."

"Tell Mother that I'll be all right soon," he said more strongly. "Tell her that when I get home I'll have a sauna every day and eat all her pancakes whenever she wants to fry some for me. Tell her I'll be home soon.''

"I'll write to you often," Sirkka said, her eyes glistening with tears again.

Sirkka waved her hand at Otto from the entrance as she left the large gymnasium. Seventy wounded soldiers there, were being attended by the Dutch doctors and nurses.

# Chapter 46

Less than a week after Otto had arrived at Vierumaki there was a meeting at his bedside. Several doctors were in attendance, all speaking at machine-gun speed in Dutch. They had examined him very carefully. The sight of Otto's contraption where his hand hung down made them all shake their heads. Although Otto understood nothing that was said, he knew from the doctors' expressions that his hand would be taken down, to rest by his side on a firm pillow. For weeks it had hung up there so painfully, and all his fingernails had been torn out.

The nurses did their best to comfort him, but he continued to grow weaker day by day because the food wouldn't stay in him long enough to provide any nourishment.

News from the radio broke the silence several times during the day. "The Russian army has broken through the Mannerheim Line in the Karelian Isthmus," reported the well-modulated tones of the newscaster. That didn't surprise Otto. What did surprise him was that they had been able to hold out that long.

It wasn't long until a new patient came to fill the bed next to Otto—a soldier who had been wounded in the leg. When Otto looked at the man's taut face he immediately recognized his old friend Eino Leppo from the Third Company, who soon brought him up to date on all the news from Kyyrola.

"On our first withdrawal, Lieutenant Klami panicked and would have completely lost his nerve if it hadn't been for Ekstrom and Hakli. They took over the command and we made a safe retreat. First we established a temporary line of defense at Hotokka," Leppo related, in a voice tinged with sadness. "The only thing we could do then was to retreat all the way back to Repola. Tuoppi, Stromberg, and Hietala were still fighting when I was wounded at Hotokka on the last day before the retreat to Repola. Just before I left I saw Aalto catch a bullet right between the eyes. He never knew what hit him. I think he was dead before he hit the ground. I was lucky. It's just a flesh wound in my calf," Leppo sighed, his hands resting on top of his warm blanket.

"We were sure lucky to have Ekstrom and Hakli," Otto reflected, trying vainly to keep his eyes focused on Leppo sitting on his bed. His last morphine shot was taking effect but he was anxious for news of the Third Company, so he struggled to fix his attention on Leppo's words.

"By the time I left, the company was whittled down to twenty-six men out of the hundred. Most of them were the real veterans, the ones who had been there from the beginning and really knew how to take care of themselves. I heard that all the companies had just about the same number of men left, and that there were no more reserves available," Leppo said.

Otto's eyes closed. He was asleep.

Every day passed painfully in the large ward. The only diversion was radio music, broadcast continually from Helsinki over the state broadcasting system. Every half hour a short newscast brought the latest word from the front lines.

The men in the ward heard the newscaster saying, "The city of Viipuri may be surrendered at any time. Enemy planes dot the blue skies like swarms of bees, attacking even the smallest moving targets. No help is in sight for the tiny number of volunteers who are without any fighting experience or military training."

The news depressed the men. Those able to walk tried to entertain the others, but nothing cheered the suffering men. They knew that the war was about to be lost.

Otto finally felt a change in his health—a strange, vaguely elevated burst of energy. He was suddenly able to eat the lingonberries that Sirkka had sent him. The sugar in them gave him an energy boost, and the berries provided both moisture and nourishment. He ate them with good appetite.

Outside, the sun shone brightly throughout the country. "Another day for bombing," everyone said as they looked at the blue sky above.

It was March 13, 1940, and it marked a surprising feat of fighting against overwhelming odds: the hundred-and-fifth day of resistance against the Russian aggressors with their mighty, monstrous panzers of thirty-, forty-, fifty-, and even sixty-ton tanks rolling over every hillside and road in the Karelian Isthmus.

The radio poured music into the gym, inspiring those men with less serious wounds to join in humming along with the music. In one corner of the gym a husky, short-necked, barrel-chested man who had lost a leg on the first day of the war tried to amuse his friends by getting on his one foot, playing his harmonica in tune with the radio music, and dancing on the soft mattress of his bed.

Suddenly the large gym went silent. The music stopped, too. The broadcaster interrupted the silence with his voice cracking.

"The war is over. At eleven this morning the fighting stopped. The government has signed an armistice with the Russians," he said, his voice quivering as he continued to brief his fellow countrymen about the drastic terms of the armistice.

"After 24,000 men were killed, and 45,000 wounded, and 450,000 people left homeless, we have had to surrender more land than the Russian army conquered in the war, and more than they had originally asked for. We had no choice. We could have gotten from friendly Allied nations, but it wouldn't have arrived here in time. All of our cities would have been destroyed and the enemy would have marched to the Gulf to Pohjanlahti on the Swedish border."

They had heard enough. Most of the wounded men cried. For a moment it seemed as if a dark curtain had covered the sun. The flag outside the hospital was drawn to half mast, as were others throughout the country.

Otto's eyes were wet with tears. Had all this been for nothing?

Such news affected all of the men, wounded or not. As the day wore on, they talked about the armistice but no one smiled. No one knew what it would mean for Finland or for them. Many had reached a point beyond caring any more, and for many, it wouldn't make much difference anyway; first their capacity for life had been severely limited by the pain of bullets, and now the words had wounded their souls. They began to feel numb.

They were still feeling the shock the next morning, but there was a gratifying surprise for these men who had shown fortitude in their crises. When Otto opened his eyes after dozing awhile, he saw a tall, lean figure standing at the foot of his bed. The man, in a tight-fitting dress uniform, saluted him.

Otto's hands quivered in answer to the salute. What would such a man be doing by his bedside? He had never seen so many decorations and fancy ribbons on one uniform. The man's dark eyes seemed to pierce right through him, not painfully, but with sympathy, friendliness, and firmness.

If Otto could have stood next to him, the man would have been more than a head taller. He was a true military person—a man who loved his soldiers. It showed through every move the man made and every word he spoke.

"Corporal Arola!" the man said with a voice that made Otto shiver all over. Now he knew who the man was. He was Commander of all Defense Forces of Finland, Field Marshal Gustav Mannerheim.

"We have just experienced the saddest day in our history. I am thankful for the soldiers who fought with me in this war, so that it hasn't been a totally disastrous day. Your tenacity made it possible to end this war in armistice instead of in surrender. We will be eternally grateful to every man, whatever his rank role or in the war."

He stepped in between the beds.

"I want to present to you this Medal of Honor and a Medal of Bravery." He pinned the two medals onto Otto's hospital gown and placed two certificates on top of the blanket. He saluted with military dignity. The spurs on the field marshal's boots jingled as he turned and repeated his actions until each man had received either one or two medals. Otto left his medals on his nightshirt until late that night. He went to sleep amidst a mixture of feelings: happiness that it was all over, gratitude for the unexpected honor, and a deep sense of regret and loss for those friends he would never see again and for all those Finns who were homeless and starving.

The following morning Otto's bed was wheeled onto the warm sun porch at the south end of the building. Here he had a good view of the yard and a chance to enjoy the spring sunshine as it came through the large window panes. Because of the relaxed atmosphere and the warm sunshine he fell asleep, listening to music from the radio. When he woke up from his nap, his heart jumped at the sight of a blurred figure standing at the entrance to the sun porch. He saw the hazy outline of a small woman with long blond hair, dressed in a fur-collared coat. She rushed toward his bed.

"Anna," he mumbled, his left hand stretching out to her.

"Otto, I had to come after Sirkka brought me your letter. I love you so much, and I've thought of nothing else but finding you again and begging you to forget the past. Please, dear Otto . . ."

"Anna, it is you who must forgive me for my stubborness in not writing to you. I have nothing to do here but think . . . and I've come to realize—how wrong I was—to condemn you while I myself . . . was being unfaithful to you, too, in Terijoki and Viipuri. No," he said as she raised her hand to stop his words. "I must tell you this now, while I am strong. I didn't really think I would ever see you again . . . I hope we can forgive each other for our past weaknesses and . . . be friends. I didn't want to hurt you, Anna—you have been too dear to me . . ."

Anna wanted to overwhelm him with her love, but he was so weak, so thin. He was not the passionate Otto with whom she had shared so much. She took his hand and smiled for him.

"I have rented an apartment. I want you to come home

292

soon. Sirkka will live with me until you get home—then the apartment will be ours, just the two of us, dear, the two of us . . .'' Anna could not prevent herself from saying that much.

The nurse had given Otto another shot of morphine. He looked at Anna, puzzled, and wondered how long it would be until he could return to Helsinki. His mind was growing hazy, and he tried to think of what he must tell her, that things had changed. But his eyes closed and he was asleep.

Late that afternoon, when Otto awoke, Anna was gone. He was sorry he had not been able to talk with her. But perhaps she had seen that he was not the same boy she had made love with in Helsinki.

# Chapter 47

Otto wound his way out, among the bushes, on a narrow path to a wooden platform at the lake shore. In the near distance the sport center was without a sign of athletics. He had been brought out this far the first time by a pretty Dutch nurse who held him by the arm, steadying him in his efforts at learning to walk again. The distance at first seemed totally beyond the realm of possibility, but he had gained some strength and now he was fumbling along by himself.

Otto sat on a bench made years ago of hand-hewn, round, wooden rungs, for the athletes who trained there to sit on, after swimming or running around the lake. He tried to think of the sports events held here, but his mind kept turning to the future. He would never be able to play the violin again, or use his training from gunsmith school. He wondered just what he would be able to do.

With the help of a cane, Otto returned to the building. He turned to the right at the entrance, and after a moment he was in the sunroom where it was warmer.

There were a few men there already, some in beds, others in wheelchairs, and a few who carried their arms in a sling on the side like Otto. He avoided the others and stood alone in front of the window, his nostrils inhaling the heavy smell of ether. He hated the smell; he had been put to sleep over dozens of times already, in the doctors' efforts to improve his hand, but his hand seemed to him a hopeless mess.

Would his fingernails ever grow back, and would his finger... ever work, he wondered.

Otto forced himself to quit thinking about it. Instead, a vision of a woman he hadn't been able to forget since the last time he saw her in Viipuri entered his mind. He could only think of her and their times together. Johanna's face kept reappearing in his dreams had been so real, and so natural. He could almost feel his hands slipping over her smooth skin, holding her close to him in the darkness.

Otto went back to bed, but every day he walked again and again in the sunroom. His only wish was to be alone. A few weeks later during his daily stroll, his eyes met a figure seated alone, drying her eyes with a handkerchief.

Though in agony, Otto walked nearer to her. It was as if a sliver of pain had entered his fingers with each step, but it seemed to him that the woman must have suffered, too. He could not resist trying to comfort her, to talk to her in her trouble.

Standing in front of her, he coughed politely and saw the lady raise her head as if it caused her excruciating pain. She slowly turned her eyes toward him.

Otto's pale face was haggard from his ordeal; his dark-rimmed eyes, dull and listless, appeared to stare out from under the thin remnant of his once-thick, curly black hair. The drug, too, had left its mark.

Gazing at her sad blue eyes and her red cheeks under the fur-trimmed hat, he saw in them someone so familiar it almost took his breath away. "Why are your eyes so sad and expressionless?" he longed to ask.

Here was the woman he had dreamed of for so long and prayed so hopelessly to meet again some day. His voice failed him. He could not even whisper. In the sunshine he saw Johanna's face glistening wet with tears. With sudden sadness, he realized she did not recognize him in his emaciated state. It was as if he had changed into someone else since leaving Viipuri.

Finally, Otto asked, "May I sit next to you?" Sitting beside her, turning so that his right arm in the airplane contraption was sideways in front of the chair, he faced her halfway.

The woman looked at him for an instant. Their eyes met

once more. Then with hands trembling, she covered her eyes as she dried the moisture from them. "I came to see a wounded officer who was in command of the company my husband was serving . . ." Her hands dropped and she quietly began sobbing. "He said my husband was a brave man but he was lost . . . killed . . . in action . . ." She mumbled so quietly that Otto could hardly hear her. He remembered the man who had opened the door for him at her apartment in Viipuri. So tall and handsome—now dead!

"Would you like to walk outside a little, out by the waterfront?" Otto asked, his voice quivering in sympathy. His face remained immobile as he struggled along, steadying himself now and then as he walked beside Johanna. He stumbled over a little branch that was sticking out into the pathway. Johanna grabbed his left arm. The touch of her fingers warmed him through the hospital shirt and gray, morning robe. He wanted to shout to her that he was Otto, but he felt this was not the right moment to tell her. Then he thought, perhaps it would be better if she never knew who the sad-looking soldier was, in such a miserable condition.

Johanna, Johanna, he wanted to say, his heart pounding as his brain screamed the words inside his head. But still he could not bring himself to speak to her.

"Let's sit down on this bench," Otto said, trying to collect his energy and reach the platform by the lake.

"Your voice . . ." she said as he sat next to her. Otto remained very still, not daring even to look at her. She smoothed her blue coat. Your voice has a familiar sound."

Otto did not know what he should do. He wanted to hug her, to embrace her tightly in his arms—but still he could not reveal his identity. Carrying his arm in that awkward contraption on his side, with every movement causing a fresh streak of pain, distracted him. Finally he turned to Johanna and looked into her eyes with this plea forming on his lips: Don't you see my face—my nose, my lips that have touched yours, my eyes that have gazed so fondly at you through the darkness . . . ? They are now filled with sadness for you, but, darling, I have thought of you so much . . . Still he remained silent.

She sat patiently next to him. Her face was motionless,

her mind buried in thoughts of her husband.

Otto's memory of her beauty was confirmed. Her skin was as silky smooth as before. He saw a ring on her finger—two gold rings. Her husband had given them to her, but now the war had taken away their meaning. Otto turned his face away.

Once or twice as he looked at her, she returned a glance that was so warm, yet so sad, that Otto could see it was hard for her to forget what she had just heard about her husband and to give her thoughts to the wounded soldier at her side.

Thus they sat for a while, not speaking except to make small talk about how glad they were that this tragic war was over.

"Would you like a piece of an apple?" she asked, reaching for her purse.

Otto shook his head.

"It won't stay down," he said in a low voice. "You eat it yourself."

She nibbled, holding the red apple in her gloved hand.

As they were walking along the narrow path toward the hospital, she again gazed questioningly at him. Otto had decided not to tell her who he was though he wanted desperately for her to recognize him. He assumed that his ghastly appearance had changed him into a total stranger—weak, trembling, and frail, with an emaciated body, little resembling what he had once been. He wondered if he would ever return to a normal condition, remembering with a grimace that Sirkka had once said the army might make a man of him.

He stood at the doorway to the large hall to catch a last glimpse of Johanna as she walked away.

"Goodbye," he whispered, "I'll find you when I'm well . . ." He stood motionless, grasping the door for support.

# HITLER'S LAST GAMBLE
## Jacques Nobecourt

PRICE: $2.25   T51474
CATEGORY: War

Here, in full detail, is the true account of the most dangerous and dramatic battle of World War II—the Battle of the Bulge.

In December 1944—when she seemed on the verge of complete collapse, her armies driven from Normandy almost to the Rhine—Germany launched a sudden counter attack. The Battle of the Bulge was the last gasp of the Third Reich's great war machine and it proved to be the ultimate challenge to the strength and bravery of the U.S. Army.

# DISPOSABLE PEOPLE
# By Marshall Goldberg, M.D.
# (Author of Critial List)
# and Kenneth Kay

PRICE: $2.25 BT51574
CATEGORY: Novel (Original)

The ultimate thriller, in which today's medical and
political morality determines for millions—who
shall live and who shall die!

A disease more horrifying than the Black Plague
rages out of control. In a mighty effort to contain it,
Dr. Noah Blanchard is assigned by the President to
head the Epidemic Task Force. When the hard
choices have to be made, doctors and politicians
are forced into a sinister plot to choose the "Dis-
posable People."

# A CORPSE FOR A CANDIDATE
## Michael Geller
## (#2 in Bud Dugan Series)

PRICE: $1.75—BT51478
CATEGORY: Mystery (Original)

When the incumbent mayor of New York decides
not to run for re-election, the field is wide open for
Amanda Mellis, beautiful and intelligent Cultural
Affairs Commissioner, and her opponent Fullerton
Mack, charismatic leader of the black com-
munity. It's a "go-for-the-jugular" campaign, and
the outcome is anybody's guess. Then Amanda is
found shot to death. Lieutenant Bud Dugan goes
into action to find the murderer before the lid
blows off the racially divided city.

OTHER TITLES IN THE "BUD DUGAN" SERIES:
<u>MAYHEM ON THE CONEY BEAT</u>—BT51353
ALSO BY MICHAEL GELLER:
<u>THE MAN WHO NEEDED ACTION</u>—BT51436

# THE CLAIRVOYANT
## By Hans Holzer

PRICE: $2.25 T51573
CATEGORY: Novel (Hardcover publisher:
Mason/Charter 1976)

The story of a beautiful young Viennese girl whose
gift of prophecy took her from the mountains of
Austria to the glittering drawing rooms of Beverly
Hills. She began to exhibit psychic powers at the
age of four. Terrified of their daughter's "gift," her
parents sent her to a remote school. As she moved
from school to school and then from man to man,
she used her psychic abilities to climb to perilous
heights of fame and success!

# Author of the best-selling
# Murder In Amityville

# THE KESSLER ALLIANCE
## By Thomas Horstman

PRICE: $2.25  BT51463
CATEGORY: Novel (original)

A devastatingly prophetic novel of what could happen to the world, if Nazi extremists remained unchecked and their forces overthrew the world. Munich, Germany is the focal point of events and the birthplace of Wilhelm Kessler, a youth who becomes fascinated with Adolph Hitler. Another youth, Leo Maeder, becomes a Catholic priest. The lives of these two men become entwined as a bizarre series of events shake the world, and nations convulse under tremendous economic, political and social pressures. Only one man knew of the diabolical plot, but no one would believe him!

# DEATH OF A SCAVENGER
## By Keith Spore

PRICE: $2.25   BT51465
CATEGORY: Mystery (Original)

Dr. Hugo Enclave takes on only the most clever
and cunning crimes, and is intrigued by those
considered unsolvable by the police. Enclave set
out to unravel the tangled threads surrounding the
death of Harland Rockmore, an investigator for a
law firm, whose body was found near his boss's
home after a scavenger hunt. Enclave moves
through a torturous labyrinth of murder, mayhem
and mystery to uncover a conspiracy aimed at
the White House itself!

SEND TO:  **TOWER PUBLICATIONS**
**P.O. BOX 270**
**NORWALK, CONN. 06852**

## PLEASE SEND ME THE FOLLOWING TITLES:

| Quantity | Book Number | Price |
|----------|-------------|-------|
|          |             |       |
|          |             |       |
|          |             |       |
|          |             |       |
|          |             |       |

**IN THE EVENT THAT WE ARE OUT OF STOCK ON ANY OF YOUR SELECTIONS, PLEASE LIST ALTERNATE TITLES BELOW:**

|  |  |  |
|--|--|--|
|  |  |  |
|  |  |  |
|  |  |  |

Postage/Handling

I enclose...

**FOR U.S. ORDERS,** add 50c for the first book and 10c for each additional book to cover cost of postage and handling. Buy five or more copies and we will pay for shipping. Sorry, no C.O.D.'s.

**FOR ORDERS SENT OUTSIDE THE U.S.A.,** add $1.00 for the first book and 25c for each additional book. PAY BY foreign draft or money order drawn on a U.S. bank, payable in U.S. ($) dollars.

☐ **PLEASE SEND ME A FREE CATALOG.**

**NAME**_____

(Please print)

**ADDRESS**_____

**CITY**_____**STATE**_____**ZIP**_____

Allow Four Weeks for Delivery